THE STEWARDESS'S JOURNEY

Part 3
of
The Windsor Street Family Saga

By

VL McBeath

The Stewardess's Journey
By VL McBeath

Editing services provided by Susan Cunningham at Perfect Prose Services
Cover design by Books Covered

ISBNs: 978-1-913838-18-8 (Ebook Edition)
978-1-913838-19-5 (Paperback)

Main category - FICTION / Historical
Other category - FICTION / Sagas

Legal Notices

This story was inspired by real-life events but as it took place over one hundred years ago, parts of the storyline and all characterisation are fictitious. Names have been changed and any resemblance to real persons, living or dead, is purely coincidental.

Explanatory Notes

Meal Times

In the United Kingdom, meal times are referred to by a variety of names. Based on traditional working-class practices in northern England in the nineteenth century, the following terms have been used:

Dinner: The meal eaten around midday. This may be a hot or cold meal depending on the day of the week and a person's occupation.

Tea: Not to be confused with the high tea of the aristocracy or the beverage of the same name, tea was the meal eaten at the end of the working day, typically around five or six o'clock. This could either be a hot or cold meal.

Money

In the nineteenth century, the currency in the United Kingdom was Pounds, Shillings and Pence.

- There were twenty shillings to each pound and twelve pence to a shilling.
- A crown and half crown were five shillings and two shillings and sixpence, respectively.

For further information on Victorian-era England visit:
https://vlmcbeath.com/victorian-era

Previously in
The Windsor Street Family Saga

Part 1: *The Sailor's Promise*
Part 2: *The Wife's Dilemma*

Set in Liverpool (UK), *The Windsor Street Family Saga* was inspired by a true story and it is **recommended that the books are read in order.**

For further information visit my website at:

https://valmcbeath.com/windsor-street/

Please note: This series is written in UK English

CHAPTER ONE

Liverpool, January 1882

Nell tightened her grip on James' arm as they made their way through the crowds walking along the banks of the River Mersey. The sun hadn't risen over the buildings opposite the landing stage, and the hull and exposed masts of the SS *Wisconsin* rose like a shadow from the still dark sky.

"Is this it?" Her heart pounded as she spoke to her newfound companion.

"It is." Mrs Swift studied the ship. "Our home for the rest of the year."

"I hadn't thought of it like that."

"Don't look so worried." Her nephew James patted her hand. "You're not seeing it at its best at the moment. Wait until you're on the open ocean and the sails are fully rigged. Then you'll appreciate it."

Nell watched a steady stream of black smoke billowing from the chimney. "I hope so."

"Come on. Let's get you settled. You'll feel better, then." Mrs Swift made her way onto the gangplank and Nell watched as she climbed towards the opening at the top.

"She makes it look easy."

"That's because it is. You go straight up and I'll follow with this." James indicated to her bag as Nell took a deep breath. A moment later, she stepped onto the wooden incline and grabbed the handrails on either side.

"There's no need to worry, it's quite safe."

"That's easy for you to say." The swell of the waves buffeted the ship, and Nell's knuckles were white as she clung on.

"That's it, Aunty Nell. Keep going."

She wished she could turn around and hold his arm, but she daren't let go until she had both feet firmly on a solid platform.

"You'll get used to it."

She looked up as she approached the top and smiled as Mrs Swift waited for her by the entrance, an arm outstretched. "That's it, you're here now."

After a moment's hesitation, Nell stepped onto the metal flooring, landing with a clang.

"I'm not sure I'll be so keen to get off again, if we need to go through that every time." She waited for James to join her.

"There you are." He placed her bag by her feet and peered into the body of the ship. "This is where I leave you." He leaned forward to kiss her cheek, but Nell stopped him.

"Can't you come aboard?"

"I'm afraid not, but I'm sure this gentleman will look after you." He indicated to a steward of similar age to himself, who was waiting for them.

"Mr Price at your service, ladies. You must be Mrs Swift and Mrs Riley."

"Yes." Nell's mouth fell open as she looked first to James, then to Mrs Swift. "How do you know?"

"There are only three female crew members on board and I saw Matron upstairs before I came to meet you."

"Oh, I see."

"That's one more than we had last year." Mrs Swift's dark brown eyes sparkled. "I was on my own for most of the time, so having you here will be a pleasant change."

James nodded. "We typically only have one stewardess on our ships, too." He took out his pocket watch. "Right, I'd better be going. You have a wonderful trip and I'll see you soon."

He gave her shoulders a final hug and turned to walk back down the gangplank, turning to wave once he reached the footpath.

"I'll see you soon." Nell's voice was weak, and she fumbled for a handkerchief.

"Come on, Mr Price will show us to our cabin." Mrs Swift reached for her arm. "We've a lot to do before the passengers board in the morning."

Nell glanced at her. "You mean we don't sail today?"

"No. Didn't your nephew tell you? We need to get everything ready first. Trust me, you'll be glad of it. You'll have some training to do, too."

"You will indeed." Mr Price picked up their suitcases.

"If you'd like to follow me, we'll get you settled in. Am I right in thinking you've been on board before, Mrs Swift?"

"I was here last year. Will we be in the cabins at the back of the ship again?"

"You will. This way, please."

Nell followed the elegant young man along a cold, grey corridor that echoed to the sound of their footsteps.

"It's the unglamorous entrance for us, I'm afraid," Mrs Swift whispered as they reached a flight of steps. "Hopefully, they'll let me show you around the guest areas later. Then you'll see how the other half live."

"That would be nice, although I'm not sure how I'll find my way without getting lost." Nell placed a foot on the bottom step, but paused to stare along a corridor that disappeared into darkness. "Does that go all the way to the front of the ship?"

"It does." Mr Price continued up the stairs. "Not that you need to worry yourself about it. This section houses the boilers and engines, and the mail room and coal store are at the far end. There'll be no need for you to come down here."

"That's a relief." Nell counted the steps as they walked. Twenty. "So we only come down here to get on and off the ship?"

"Correct. You'll spend most of your time on the top two decks, but before I take you upstairs, let me show you your quarters."

Nell followed Mr Price as he took a corridor leading to the back of the ship.

"As you can imagine, when the ship was built, we didn't expect to employ women, and so we've had to take a couple of the steerage cabins that were intended for married couples." He stopped outside two doors that were as far as you could walk without doubling back on yourself. He pushed open the one on the right. "Mrs Riley, you'll be in this one with Mrs Swift. The other is Matron's. She has a spare bunk should the captain decide to take on another woman."

Nell stepped into the small, neat room with bunk beds along the far wall and a settee opposite the door.

"This is nice enough."

Mrs Swift bustled in beside her. "It'll be rather cosy, but don't worry, we won't spend much time in here other than sleeping, and there's a small sitting room opposite, where we eat and rest our feet."

Nell nodded as she appraised the red flocked wallpaper. "Is there anywhere for washing?"

"Over here. Let me show you." Mrs Swift waited for Mr Price to step backwards and led Nell into the corridor and opened a door. "Here's the lavatory but look in here." She pushed open a second door with a flourish. "A basin, and we're allowed a bath whenever we need one."

Nell's heart skipped a beat as she stared at the long white tub that ran the length of the room. "It certainly beats our tin one at home."

Mrs Swift laughed. "We might be short of space down here, but it has its benefits."

Mr Price joined them as they returned to the corridor. "I've put your suitcases in your room, but rather than unpack, I'll take you upstairs to meet Matron. She'll be expecting you, and you need to pick up your uniforms."

A uniform! James was right. Nell reached for the clasp of her cloak. "Shall I leave this here?"

"No, Keep it with you." Mrs Swift shuddered. "We won't be indoors all the time."

"Oh, right." Nell's cheeks coloured as she fell into step with the steward as he marched down the corridor. Eventually, he disappeared around a corner, and Nell followed him into an open area with a central staircase.

"We need to go up two flights of stairs and then walk towards the front of the ship. There are twenty first-class staterooms, ten on each side of the ship. You'll be working on the port side, while Mrs Swift services those on the starboard side. The bridge and officer accommodation are at the very front, also on this level."

Nell nodded. "Where are the other staff quarters?"

"You've no need to worry." Mrs Swift walked in step beside her. "The stewards are on the same deck as us, but at the front of the ship. You can't walk directly through on that level, so they don't trouble us."

"The junior officers and engineers are on the deck above." Mr Price set off up the next flight of stairs. "Again, there's no direct access between the front and back of the ship on this level."

"So, the only way to get from the front to the back is past the boilers or on the top deck?" Nell's brow creased.

"Precisely." Mr Price studied her, his pale blue eyes holding her gaze. "We don't want the steerage passengers accidentally stumbling into the first-class areas."

"Nor the male staff troubling us," Mrs Swift added. "You'll find everything's above board."

Nell put a hand to her chest. "I'm sure it will delight my sister to hear that."

Mr Price didn't stop as he reached the top of the second flight of stairs, and Nell followed him as he left the stairwell and headed to a door on the port side of the ship.

"It's not far now." He held it open, but a bitter wind caused Nell to take a step backwards.

"We have to go outside?"

He extended an arm to usher her through the door. "I'm afraid it's the only way to the first-class area from the back of the ship. Hold onto your hat."

Nell stepped onto the deck, but stopped when she saw the view. She'd lived in Liverpool all her life, but had never seen it from the sea. Or from this high up.

"If you'd like to keep walking…" Mr Price waited as Mrs Swift hurried on ahead.

"Yes, I'm sorry." The wind caught her unawares, and she grabbed the handrail to stop herself from being blown along. "I'll have to get used to this." She put her head down and hurried after Mrs Swift.

Once they were indoors, Nell released her grip on her cloak and paused to study her new surroundings. The dull grey metal corridors had transformed into luxurious walkways with red-and-gold embossed wallpaper and carpet running down the centre.

"Gracious, I didn't expect this."

"It gets better." Mrs Swift grinned at her. "The only downside is that at the end of each day, we have to go back to our own sparse surroundings."

"That's a shame." She continued to follow Mr Price as he led them to an office at the front of the ship.

"Mrs Riley, Mrs Swift, this is Dr Clarke and Mrs Granger. Otherwise known as Matron."

"Ah, you're here." A short, stocky woman with tightly curled greying hair pulled herself up to her full height and stared at Nell. "Welcome aboard. I'm sure you'll be very happy as long as you put in an honest day's work."

"Thank you, Matron, I'm sure I will."

"Mrs Swift, it's good to have you back."

"Indeed, it is." The doctor was a tall man with greying hair and he nodded at each of them. "It's nice to meet you, Mrs Riley, but I must get on. I need to do a full inspection of the ship before the passengers embark. I'll leave you with Matron."

Mr Price clicked his heels together and turned to follow the doctor. "If you'll wait here, I'll tell the captain you've arrived. He likes to meet new crew members."

"The captain." Nell grimaced at Mrs Swift, but Matron tutted.

"We'll have none of that, Mrs Riley. Captain Robertson is very amenable. Now, while we wait, you can tell me if you've done work like this before."

"A little. I was a ladies' maid last year."

"And what did that involve?"

"Nothing special. Helping the lady dress, fetching and carrying after her, acting as a companion when she needed it."

"So why did you leave?"

"Well..." Nell stuttered. "I ... erm, I heard about the role of a stewardess ... from my nephew, he's a steward ... and thought it sounded more interesting."

"You're not here to be interested, Mrs Riley. You're here to make the lives of our passengers as pleasant as possible for the duration of the voyage. If you have time to stop and think, you're not working hard enough."

"No. I'm sorry."

"Now, you'll need to go and fetch your uniforms..." Matron stopped as two smartly dressed men approached. "Good morning, Captain Robertson."

"Good morning, ladies." His face was stern. "Mrs Swift, I know. You must be Mrs Riley."

Nell's cheeks flushed as she curtsied. "Yes, Captain."

"It's very nice to meet you. This is Mr Driver, our head steward."

"Pleased to meet you, Mr Driver."

"Likewise." He gave a slight bow. "I'll let you get your uniforms and then I'll run through your duties with you. We like to run a tidy and efficient ship, and everyone needs to play their part."

"Yes, sir. I'll try my best."

"Splendid." The captain rubbed his hands together. "My wife sends her apologies. She was hoping to be here to welcome you, but she's feeling a bit under the weather. Nothing serious, I'm pleased to say."

Matron scowled. "She said nothing to me."

"It's only an upset stomach. I'm sure she'll be fine by tomorrow."

"Well, she must let me know if she isn't."

"Yes, Matron." The captain winked at Nell as a smile flicked across his lips. "Don't do anything to upset Matron or you'll be in trouble."

Nell's eyes darted between them. "I'll try not to, sir."

"Enough of that." Matron huffed as she stood behind Nell and Mrs Swift and ushered them into the corridor. "Mrs Swift, take Mrs Riley to the store and find yourselves some uniforms. Once you're changed, come straight back here. We need the rooms shipshape by this time tomorrow.

CHAPTER TWO

Nell followed Mrs Swift as she hurried towards a central staircase and down the steps.

"Is she always like that?"

Mrs Swift laughed. "You'll get used to her. She's quite nice once you get to know her, but likes you to know who's in charge."

Nell shuddered. "She's done that. I'm beginning to wonder what I've let myself in for."

They reached the bottom of the stairs, and Mrs Swift stopped and glanced over both shoulders. "Let me show you around while I can; once she gets us started on the staterooms, we won't have a minute to ourselves." She pushed on one of two polished oak doors. "This is the dining room. It's rather dark at the moment; they mustn't have got around to lighting the lamps yet."

"Even in this light it looks splendid. What are the various sections for?" Nell studied the rows of tables with pristine white tablecloths separated by flower arrangements.

"We're in the men's section here and the smaller space at the far side is for unaccompanied ladies."

"They sit separately?"

"Oh, yes, and that's where we'll spend most of our time. The rules are getting stricter, and one of our main jobs is to make sure we protect the ladies from the men."

"What if they're married?"

"That's the middle section. It's for married couples, but we may serve there if the ladies require it. The first-class passengers are privileged to have this section. Husband and wives in steerage aren't able to see each other at all."

"That's harsh."

"It's all to do with the best use of the space. The company's determined to maintain order and ensure the honour of the female passengers."

"I'd no idea. I thought I'd be serving food or fetching drinks."

"Oh, you'll be doing that too, but if you notice any men approaching the ladies' tables, you must report it to Mr Driver immediately."

Nell grimaced. "Does it happen very often?"

"More than you'd imagine, but don't worry. They're usually on their best behaviour for the first couple of nights, so you'll pick it up as you go along." Mrs Swift clapped her hands together. "Now, enough of this, we'd better collect our uniforms."

The ship's third mate was outside another door as they rounded the corner near the bridge.

"Here we are." Mrs Swift held out a hand to slow her

down. "Good morning, officer. My companion and I are here to collect our uniforms."

"Which uniforms would they be, ladies?" He stood in a wide stance with his arms folded across his broad chest.

"The stewardess outfits." Mrs Swift raised an eyebrow at Nell. "Besides Matron, we're the only two women on the ship."

The officer bristled. "I suggest you watch yourselves, walking around on your own, especially if you answer back like that."

Mrs Swift took a step backwards as he towered over her. "I wasn't aware we needed chaperoning."

"Well, think on in future." He ran his eyes over her.

"Yes, sir, I'm sorry." Mrs Swift reached for Nell's arm. "May we go in? Matron will be waiting for us to get back."

The officer's gaze lingered on Nell. "You'd better be quick then."

Nell's mouth was dry as she chased after her colleague. "Are they all like that?"

"Not all of them." Mrs Swift continued walking to a counter, where a steward greeted them.

"Good morning, ladies, Mr Cooper at your service. Are you here for the stewardess uniforms?"

Nell smiled at the short, dark-haired man, but left the talking to her colleague.

"Yes, please. I'm Mrs Swift, this is Mrs Riley. I expect we'll be working together."

Mr Cooper's face darkened. "Probably not. I'm in steerage for the time being, although I'll see you from time to time. Now, your uniforms." He studied each of them. "Let me see what I've got."

Once his back was turned, Mrs Swift glanced over to the door. "Watch the likes of him."

"Who? Mr Cooper or the officer?"

"Both, but especially him." She nodded at the officer. "You mark my words, he'll have just passed his exams and the authority's gone to his head. I'd suggest you stay out of his way if possible."

Nell shuddered. "I had hoped they'd all be gentlemen..." She stopped as Mr Cooper appeared with two dark-coloured dresses with matching hats.

Black! That's all I need.

"These should be about the right size."

Nell lowered her eyes as he looked her up and down again.

"You can bring them back if they're not."

"What about the aprons?"

Mr Cooper sighed. "For goodness' sake."

Nell watched him disappear once more into the dimly lit recesses of the room, but flinched at a noise behind her.

"I thought you were in a hurry."

Mrs Swift turned on her heel as the third mate strode towards her.

"We're waiting for Mr Cooper. He forgot the aprons."

"A likely tale. I hope you weren't doing anything to *distract* him."

"No, we weren't. We're here to pick up our uniforms like everyone else."

Nell took a step backwards but bumped into the counter, diverting the officer's attention.

"What are you doing?"

"Nothing." Nell's heart raced, and she breathed a sigh of relief as Mr Cooper returned.

"Here we are, ladies. Two aprons each so you've always got a spare. Will that be all?"

Nell pulled on Mrs Swift's arm as she continued to glare at the third mate. "Do we need anything else?"

She straightened her shoulders and collected her dress. "No. Not today. We'll come back if we do."

"Well, don't leave it too late; we won't be here all day." The officer stood across the door for a little longer than was necessary before stepping to one side, letting them into the foyer.

Nell grabbed Mrs Swift's arm and dragged her to the stairwell. "I wasn't expecting that."

"You'd better get used to it and learn how to stand up for yourself." Mrs Swift didn't pause as she hurried up the stairs. "We need an empty cabin to get changed. At least these will make us look more official."

Nell stepped out of her dress and lay it on the bottom bunk in a room of identical design to the one she'd be sharing with Mrs Swift.

"Let's see what this looks like." She stepped into her new uniform and put her arms into the sleeves.

"At least it's navy; I thought I was going to be back in my mourning clothes."

Mrs Swift buttoned up the front of her own dress. "Is that's why you're here?"

Nell gazed through the porthole at the familiar sight of the dock road. "It's not even a year since I lost him, but it

15

feels like a lifetime ago. I was due to go to sea with him as the captain's wife..."

"Oh, I'm sorry. This is going to be quite a comedown."

"I hope not. We often spoke of travelling together, and of visiting America. This was the least I could do." Nell fastened her last button and studied herself in the mirror. "It's not exactly flattering, is it?"

"You'll be thankful for it. Put the apron on and it will pull in the waist. It could be worse."

Nell hooked the neck of the apron over her head and fastened a bow behind her back. "That will have to do. What about the hat?" She rested the small navy rim on the top of her bun and secured it with the hatpin. "That should hold it; I don't want to lose it."

Mrs Swift nodded. "It does get rather windy. You look quite the part now."

Nell stared at her feet. "I'll have to take the hem up tonight. I'll be falling over it if I'm not careful. It's all right for you being that bit taller."

"I'm not so sure. I could do with it being an inch or two longer. Not that anyone will notice." Mrs Swift straightened the dresses on the bunk. "We can leave these here for now and come back for them later. It's only a maid's room and I want to show you the first-class saloon before we start on the staterooms. Did Mr Driver give you a set of keys?"

"Yes, I nearly forgot them." She foraged in the pocket of her dress. "Here they are. Do you keep them in your apron, or do we hang them somewhere?"

"I always keep them with me; that way I don't lose them. Right, off we go." Mrs Swift held open the cabin door and led the way out of the cabin and into the corridor. "Here we are. These people don't have far to walk."

They walked through a grand foyer and into the saloon.

"Goodness." The smell of flowers struck Nell as she studied the elaborate arrangements that divided the low-level tables and chairs into more intimate groupings. After a moment she glanced up at the numerous light fittings, each with five oil lamps. "It must take hours to light all those."

"It's not that bad. A couple of stewards arrive at dusk and take care of them."

"And look at this." Nell walked into the centre of the room and gazed up through a rectangular skylight. "You can see the sky."

"You can, although you're not seeing it at its best in this weather, but it makes the room lovely and bright in the summer."

"I'm sure it does, but..." Nell stopped as Matron appeared at the door.

"What have you been doing?" There was no smile on Matron's face. "I was expecting you back half an hour ago. We've thirty cabins to service between now and the end of the day and the stewards have already made a start. Now get a move on."

The light outside had long since disappeared by the time Nell and Mrs Swift trudged back along the promenade to their quarters. Nell pulled up her hood and wrapped her cloak tightly around her.

"What a horrible evening."

The rain lashed against the side of the ship, drenching

the dress she had collected from the bunk on their way past the cabin. "You'd think they'd put some protection up against the weather."

"That's not likely to happen." Mrs Swift dashed through the door towards the back of the ship and held it open for Nell. "It doesn't affect anyone but us. All the stewards and officers are at the front and the steerage passengers don't move far from their bunks."

Nell shook her cloak as she went inside. "I hadn't thought of that. Maybe one day they'll realise."

"I'll probably be dead and buried by then. Come along. If we walk back past the galley next to the steerage cabins, we can ask for a pot of tea."

"Ooh, that would be nice. I'm used to at least a dozen cups a day." Nell hurried to keep up. "Do we get much food while we're working?"

"We usually have an hour or so to ourselves in the afternoon once we've straightened all the staterooms and the guests are settled after luncheon. The chef will make something for us."

Nell's feet were throbbing as they knocked on the door to the galley, and she leaned against the wall as Mrs Swift popped her head around inside.

"Is anyone here?"

"Who is it?" A tall, thin man with jet-black hair appeared from a storeroom. "Mrs Swift?"

"Ah, Mr Potter, am I glad to see you again." Mrs Swift indicated to Nell. "I have a companion this year. Mrs Riley, this is our chef, Mr Potter. Mr Potter, Mrs Riley."

"Charmed, I'm sure." He nodded to Nell before turning back to Mrs Swift. "I wasn't sure you'd be back."

"I didn't have a choice, but I don't believe he's on board. But less of that. May we trouble you for some tea?"

"Your timing's excellent. The water's just boiled, and I was helping myself to a slice of cake. Would you care for some?"

"Oh, yes, please." Nell pushed a hand into her stomach as it rumbled. "We've not stopped this afternoon."

Mr Potter chuckled. "You'll get used to it. Either that, or you won't be back for the next voyage."

CHAPTER THREE

N ell woke with a start and sat bolt upright.

"What was that?" She stared into the blackness punctured only by the night light fixed to the wall, as the ship banged against the dock.

When she got no reply, she peered towards the clock on the opposite side of the room, but the glow from the flame failed to reach it. *How are you supposed to know what time it is, with no windows?*

She leaned over the top bunk to see the shape of Mrs Swift huddled beneath the covers. *It can't be morning yet.*

The ship swayed as she lay back down and closed her eyes. *If it's as rough as this now, what will it be like when we're at sea?* A cold shiver tingled down her back, and she pulled the blankets more tightly around her. *Stop worrying.* She rolled onto her side and reached out an arm. There was no Elenor. Unbidden, tears ran onto the pillow. *This is her first night without me.* She let out a low sob. *Was it really only this morning when I saw her? I hope she's all right.* She wiped her cheeks with the back of a hand and turned to face the wall. *Stop being silly. If you don't like it, you needn't come back.*

Thoughts of the family sitting around the dinner table flashed through her mind, pushing any notion of sleep further away. She grew accustomed to the ship rolling and the occasional crashes as it hit the wall, until she finally drifted off, images of Jack on the bridge at the forefront of her mind. *I should be at the front of the ship, not down here...*

The sound of a bell jolted her upright again. "What on earth was that?"

Mrs Swift's voice croaked from beneath her. "Time to get up." She climbed from the bunk and lit a taper from the night light before transferring the flame to the oil light in the centre of the wall.

"I wondered how we'd know it was morning. What time is it?"

Mrs Swift glanced at the clock. "Half past five. A couple of stewards walk around the ship to wake us up."

"Gracious. I hope we don't have to do that."

"No, thankfully we're spared. Did you sleep well?"

"Not really. The ship was being blown by the wind; it didn't seem to trouble you, though."

"You'll get used to it soon enough. Is this your first time on a ship?"

"It is."

"So you won't know whether you'll suffer from seasickness then."

"No."

"It's to be hoped you don't, for your sake. There are a lot of ladies who struggle and we need to tend to them."

"Ugh. James didn't mention that to me, either."

Mrs Swift laughed as she fastened the buttons on her dress. "He probably didn't want to put you off. Don't worry, once they're over the first bout of sickness, I find a brandy with a spot of ginger ale works wonders. Or a ginger biscuit if they prefer."

Nell climbed down from her bunk and reached for her uniform as Mrs Swift took a seat on the settee. "Where do we get them from?"

"Oh, you'll be in and out of the galley for the first few days. Didn't Mr Driver show you where everything was yesterday when he was going through your training?"

"He did but there's so much to remember. Do I just ask for it?"

"Yes, there's always someone in there. They're a pleasant enough bunch."

Nell fastened her last button and picked up her hairbrush. "That's good. I hope we don't come across that third mate again. He wasn't so nice."

"Try not to be on your own. Keep close to the passengers if you can. The men won't trouble you in public."

Nell took a deep breath as she pushed the last hairgrip into her bun. "Right you are."

"Oh, and we always need to walk back together, especially when it's dark."

Nell fixed her hat. "Isn't it safe?"

"Let's say, it's better not to tempt fate."

. . .

Matron was waiting for them when they arrived in the sitting room across the corridor, a large pot of tea on the table.

"Good morning, Mrs Riley. Did you sleep well?"

Nell twisted her fingers together. "Once I got used to the ship rocking."

"Well, let's get you something to eat. When we get upstairs, you won't have a minute. The passengers will start arriving at ten o'clock and we need to be ready to greet them."

Nell helped herself to a slice of bread and one of the boiled eggs in a bowl beside it. "This is a treat, having eggs for breakfast. Is it usually like this?"

Matron reached for the jam. "They feed us well enough, but make the most of it, you're unlikely to get anything else until this afternoon."

"Do we collect the food ourselves?"

"Not usually." Mrs Swift picked up the teapot. "Someone from the steerage galley brings us breakfast at a quarter to six, and then dinner when we come back of an evening. We can eat luncheon in the first-class dining room once the passengers have left."

Nell caught her breath. "I didn't think men were allowed down here."

"Generally, they're not, but if we want to eat, it helps if our trays are delivered."

"I see." Nell bit down on her lip.

"Don't worry. The chefs are all respectable. You just have to hope you get a good set of passengers for your first voyage."

. . .

Nell followed Mrs Swift to the foyer outside the first-class saloon and stood to attention with her back pressed against the boiler casing, as the captain and first mate waited to greet the guests. They looked smart in their navy suits with gold stripes around the sleeves, their dark beards neatly trimmed. *Not as smart as Jack would have been.* She wiped away a tear as the first guests arrived.

"Good morning, sir. Captain Robertson at your service." He bowed to an elderly man with an impressive handlebar moustache before indicating to his colleague. "This is my first mate, Officer Jones."

"Good morning, Captain." The gentleman shook the captain's hand. "The weather's choppy today; too much wind."

The captain's smile didn't falter. "We'll do what we can to minimise any disturbance, sir. Mr Scott, isn't it?"

"Indeed." He turned to the petite, grey-haired woman to his left. "This is my good lady wife. Is there someone to help her unpack?"

"Yes, of course. If you'd like to step into the saloon for refreshments, we'll see to it for you."

The head steward, Mr Driver, ran a hand over his greased-back black hair and ushered the couple inside while the captain welcomed the next arrivals.

"What do we do?" Nell whispered to Mrs Swift. "Do we start unpacking now?"

"Not yet. The stewards should be here with their luggage shortly. Let's hope she hasn't brought a huge trunk."

"I doubt it given the size of her."

The captain interrupted them as he bowed to the latest

arrivals. "Lord Faulkner, how lovely to meet you. I trust you had a pleasant journey."

"As good as it could be with two women in tow."

"You should be jolly grateful we were, the fuss you made at the hotel last night." A tall, slim woman with platinum blond hair under an elegant grey hat tapped his arm before extending a hand to the captain. "Good morning, Captain. Is the room ready for my maid? I'd like her to get settled before my luggage arrives."

"Yes, of course, my lady." The captain indicated to Mrs Swift. "Could you show Lady Annabel's maid to her room?"

Mrs Swift caught the attention of the rather young girl who stood several paces behind the Faulkners, and after a few words of introduction, they disappeared towards the maid's quarters near the front of the ship. Nell held her breath as they left. *I hope nobody else arrives while Mrs Swift's away.*

She watched as a couple of young men arrived and were directed to the saloon by one of the many stewards. *The poor steward, he can't understand them. It must be his first trip, too. I hadn't imagined any of them wouldn't speak English.*

"Don't look so scared." Mrs Swift crept back to the side of her. "All you need to do is show the maids to their rooms. Their names are on the doors; it's quite easy."

"I know; it's the first time that's the worst... And what if I can't understand them?"

"Stop worrying. Did you see the age of the young girl I've just dealt with? No more than sixteen if she's a day. They're probably more scared of you than the other way around."

"I suppose so."

Mrs Swift nudged her. "There's another one coming. You can deal with her."

"Now?" Nell's mouth was dry as she studied the girl. She was older than the first, but still no age.

"Mrs Riley," the captain called to her, "will you show Mrs Barker's maid to her cabin?"

"Yes, Captain." Nell curtsied to the guests before beckoning over the maid. "Come this way."

"I hope I've been given a room of my own."

Nell stopped. "I'm sorry, I believe the maids' rooms have two occupants."

"Typical." The girl stamped her foot. "I told them I was only coming if I had my own room."

"You speak to them like that?"

The girl looked down at her. "Not her, but he'll do whatever I want, if I ask nicely." She wrapped a piece of hair around her finger, but her eyes narrowed. "I bet *she* saw the paperwork... Not to worry. Show me where I need to go and I'll sort it out later. Are all the rooms taken, do you know?"

"We only have first-class staterooms up here but there may be some smaller cabins free on the deck below..."

The girl pursed her lips. "That could work out better. Leave it with me."

"Y-yes, of course. May I take your name?"

"Lilly. Lilly Atherton. And you are?"

Nell hesitated. "Mrs Riley. Nell Riley." She walked along the corridor and opened the door to the last of the maids' rooms. "You're in here with Lady Annabel's maid."

"For now, perhaps. I'll see you later, Mrs Riley."

"Yes, indeed."

Mrs Swift was busy by the time Nell returned to the foyer and she spent the next hour assisting the ladies and their maids to the saloon before she set about unpacking for Mrs Scott. Nell stared down at the size of the trunk. *Thank goodness we're only travelling for two weeks.*

The work was more enjoyable than Nell expected as she lifted exquisite dresses from the trunk and hung them on the padded hangers that accompanied them. *Would Jack have bought me anything as glamorous as this?* She doubted it. *We wouldn't have been able to afford it.* She looked down at the turquoise blue dress in her hand; it was about her size. She stepped to the mirror and held it up in front of her. *It doesn't really match my hat, but...* She swished the skirt around her legs but jumped as the door opened.

"What on earth are you doing?"

Nell's heart skipped as she spun to see Mrs Swift behind her. "Oh my goodness. Thank heavens it's you." Her pulse was racing as she wandered to the wardrobe to hang the dress.

"What were you doing?"

Nell shrugged. "Seeing if it would suit me. It didn't go with the hat though." A grin formed on her lips, but it dropped at the look on Mrs Swift's face. "What's the matter?"

"You really need to be careful. The ladies could come back at any time. I called to warn you that Mrs..."

Mrs Swift stopped as a key sounded in the lock. A moment later, Mrs Scott joined them.

"Are you nearly finished?"

Nell curtsied. "Yes, madam. I've just hung the last dress. I'll arrange to have the trunk removed for you."

Mrs Scott put the back of a hand to her forehead. "Would you move it outside before you leave? It's been a rather tiring morning, and I'd like a lie-down before luncheon."

"Yes, of course. Can I get you anything before I go?"

"No, that will be all."

"Very good, madam." She indicated for Mrs Swift to pick up the handle on the other side of the trunk. "Will you help me out with it?"

Nell paused for breath as they placed the trunk outside the room. "Will anyone know to collect this, or do I have to ask someone?"

"I'd ask anyone who doesn't look too busy, to be on the safe side."

Nell walked back along the corridor. "I don't know what was up with her. All she's done is get on the ship and sit down for morning coffee. It's hardly taxing."

Mrs Swift nodded. "Don't let it upset you. You have to remember that under normal circumstances, these women have nothing better to do than arrange social events. Boarding a ship is quite outside their usual sphere."

"It's hardly part of mine! There's another thing, too. That first maid I directed to her room wasn't content being on the ship; she insisted on having a cabin of her own."

Mrs Swift's brow creased. "She can't have a stateroom."

"I told her that, but she said she'd speak to Mr Barker to ask if she could be moved. She was convinced she'd be able to persuade him."

"What did you tell her?"

Nell shrank back at Mrs Swift's tone. "Nothing. Only that she'd have to move to a room on the deck below."

"What's her name?"

"Lilly Atherton. Very sure of herself, she was."

"Very attractive, too, if I remember rightly. If I'm not mistaken, she's up to no good, and it will be your job to keep an eye on her."

"Mine?" Nell put a hand to her chest. "Why?"

"Because she's on your side of the ship. We need to have a word with Mr Driver about her, too. I don't want you getting into trouble on your first voyage for not stopping any indecorum."

"She wouldn't..."

Mrs Swift put a hand on Nell's arm. "I can see you've got a lot to learn. Come along. We'll see if we can find a steward."

CHAPTER FOUR

T he sound of the ship's bell marking four o'clock signified afternoon tea for the first-class passengers, but as the ship pulled away from its moorings, the cakes sat untouched. Nell clung to the railings of the promenade as the guests gathered to wave farewell to those on the landing stage.

Is this their last view of Liverpool or have they booked a return journey? She glanced at the faces leaning over the side of the ship. *I expect I'll find out soon enough.*

As the ship moved further from the landing stage, the red-brick warehouses on the dock road merged into one another, but Nell fixed her gaze on the white stone of the customs house that stood distinctively amongst them. *Dear Lord, please let me see that again.*

"Come along." Mrs Swift pulled on her arm. "We need to be in the dining room in case we're needed."

Nell's shoulders slumped. "It's all right for you. I bet you've seen the view plenty of times before."

"And you will too, but believe me, it looks even more

impressive on the way back. Most of the passengers aren't out of bed at that hour, so you get a better vantage point."

Nell's smile returned. "I imagine I'll be up early that day. So, what do we do now?"

"We stand in the background until we're summoned. Once the passengers realise we're available, they'll ask for all sorts of petty things; some of them will even want help to get ready for dinner. Now's the time to study them." A twinkle appeared in Mrs Swift's eyes. "It's usually great fun."

Several passengers were already in their seats by the time they arrived in the dining room and Nell nodded towards the maids, who stood as close to their employers' tables as possible.

"What was the name of that young girl you showed to her cabin?"

"Grace. She's terribly shy. I can't imagine how she came to be working for Lady Annabel."

"She's different to Lilly." Nell spotted the tall, dark-haired girl. "I can't believe she got moved to a cabin of her own. Without us being told, too."

"She's up to no good. Have you seen the way she keeps fluttering her eyelashes at Mr Barker?" Mrs Swift pulled back her head and shoulders and peered down her nose as she glared at Lilly.

"He encourages her. I'm not surprised he sat Mrs Barker with her back to her."

"It wouldn't surprise me if she latches onto Lady Annabel. Poor Grace won't stand a chance if Lilly has ambitions to work for the aristocracy."

"You're right." Nell studied the rest of the room. "I

wonder what they all do to earn enough money to travel like this."

"Now that's the question for the next couple of days. The guest list is in alphabetical order, and so they'll all be trying to work out the pecking order, and who they should fawn over. Ah, there we are. First point to Lady Annabel."

Nell stared at her friend. "Why, what did she say?"

"Didn't you hear her? She asked the steward for a clean teaspoon for Lord Faulkner. Anyone who aspires to anything will have heard her. You watch."

"Ah! I've got a lot to learn."

"You'll pick it up as you go along. Oh, one moment. I'm being called."

Nell stood with her hands behind her back as Mrs Swift bent forward to speak to one of the female guests she hadn't seen board. *What else could they possibly want with all this food laid on?* Her mind raced until a minute later, when a passenger beckoned her. She kept her smile polite.

"How may I help?"

Mr Scott dabbed his mouth with a napkin. "My wife here would like assistance changing for dinner. I'll be out of the cabin by half past five."

"Very good, sir."

"She'd also like breakfast in bed at eight o'clock every morning. See to it, will you?"

"Yes, sir. Will it just be for the lady?"

"Yes, yes. I'll be down here."

"Certainly." Nell straightened up and wandered back to her place by the wall. *I really need to memorise the guest list if I don't want to end up in the wrong cabin.* She glanced around the room again. *What are they doing in the corner?*

The young men she had seen arrive had taken seats at the far end of the table away from the rest of the passengers, their backs to the room and their heads close together. *How strange that they don't want to even face the rest of the guests.*

Mrs Swift reappeared beside her. "Are you studying the spies?"

"Spies?" Nell's eyes widened, and she put a hand to her mouth. "How do you know that?"

Mrs Swift grinned. "I don't, but look at the way they're behaving. They look very shifty to me. We'll have to find out which steward is cleaning their stateroom and ask if he knows what they're up to. It's usually an entertaining topic of conversation."

Nell nodded at the pair. "They're leaving already."

Mrs Swift raised an eyebrow. "You mark my words, they're up to something. Let me clear their table and see if they left anything of interest."

"Righty-ho. I'll start clearing some tables while you do."

Nell had no sooner wiped down the last of the tables and set it up for dinner than the half-hour bell sounded.

Gracious. Mrs Scott. She'll be waiting for me. Where's that room list?

"What are you doing now?" Mrs Swift sidled up beside her.

"I need to help Mrs Scott get ready for dinner. What about you?"

"I'm the same with a couple of my ladies."

"Two? How do you do two at once?"

"Quickly, so I'd better be going. I'll meet you in the saloon shortly after six." Mrs Swift made to leave, but Nell stopped her.

"Is the food served up there?"

"No, it's drinks before dinner. Cocktails if you listen to the Americans talking. It's quite handy, actually. A lot are brandy- or whisky-based, so they help settle the passengers' stomachs. We don't want any cases of seasickness this close to home."

"Do the ladies have spirits, too?"

"If we can persuade them. There's a cocktail that combines whisky with sweet vermouth. The Manhattan. It makes it more palatable."

Nell screwed up her face. "I'll take your word for it."

Mr Scott was leaving his stateroom as Nell approached, and she waited for him to disappear down the stairs before knocking on the door.

"May I come in?"

"Oh, please do." Mrs Scott smiled as Nell entered. "I've chosen a particularly fussy dress for tonight, with far too many buttons. Would you help me on with it?"

Nell eyed Mrs Scott's neatly styled hair, which she wore parted down the centre, looped around the sides and secured into an updo. "I'll try, but I don't want to disturb your hair."

"Oh, don't worry about it. It has so many hairgrips, it won't move."

"Very well then." Nell held up the turquoise dress she'd

admired earlier. "This really is a lovely colour. It's almost the same shade as your eyes."

Mrs Scott beamed. "That's what Mr Scott said when he bought it for me. He can be rather charming when the mood takes him."

Nell held the dress over Mrs Scott's head, helping her as she searched for the armholes.

"There we are. That should do it." Nell let the material fall to the floor and pulled the shoulders straight. "What does Mr Scott do for a living? It must be lovely having him buy you dresses like this."

"He's a bank manager, been with the same branch since he was a boy."

"In Liverpool?" She began buttoning down the back.

"No, Manchester. That's why I needed a lie-down earlier. He wouldn't pay for a hotel overnight and so we were up in the early hours of the morning."

"That's a shame."

"You'll need to come back after dinner to get me out of this as well."

"Very good. I don't expect you'll be late, with having such a long day."

"Not at all, but my nap earlier did me the world of good. I should be able to stay in the saloon after dinner."

Oh good. "So this isn't your first trip, then?"

"Oh, no. We do the same journey most years. My husband has a brother in New York. He's a banker too."

"How nice. Will you stay long?"

"A month. I expect we'll see you on the return journey. I hope so, anyway; you'll have got used to my ways by then. I toyed with the idea of bringing my maid, but it didn't seem necessary given I'll be well provided for in New York."

"I'll be sure to look out for you then." Nell straightened out the material at the back of the dress. "There we are. That looks lovely. What a way to make an entrance on your first evening."

"That's what I thought." She handed Nell a long, thin box. "Will you put this on for me? I do struggle with the fiddly catches."

Nell laid the box on the nearby table and opened it to reveal a triple-stranded pearl necklace. "These are beautiful."

"Aren't they? They were a present for our twenty-fifth wedding anniversary." Mrs Scott put a hand to her chest as Nell struggled with the catch. "Mr Scott does spoil me occasionally."

"And quite right too. Now, there we are." Nell stepped back to admire Mrs Scott's transformation. "Is that it?"

Mrs Scott studied herself in the mirror over a console table. "Not quite. I have some pearls to put in my hair." She passed Nell a square box. "Would you mind fixing them into the top for me?"

Nell lifted the lid and ran her fingers over a row of seven pearls of a similar hue to the necklace that was attached to a comb. "If you'd take a seat for me." Nell pushed the comb into the hair and straightened the pearls. "That should do it. Are you ready to leave?"

Mrs Scott looked around the room. "I think I have everything. Would you mind walking me to the saloon? It feels so strange going by myself."

. . .

Mrs Swift was already serving drinks when they arrived, and she smiled at Nell as she walked past with a Y-shaped glass on a tray alongside an unstemmed tumbler, both containing amber-coloured drinks. Nell continued to the table occupied by Mr Scott and held out a chair for his wife.

"May I order you a drink, madam?"

"A sweet sherry, please." Mrs Scott adjusted her seat as she gazed around the room, but as Nell was about to leave, she beckoned her back. "Which one's the captain's wife?"

Nell studied the passengers. "If I'm honest, I don't know. She's not been well and so we've not been introduced yet."

Mrs Scott's face dropped. "That's a pity. Would you be able to find out for me?"

"I'm sure my colleague will know. Leave it with me."

Mrs Swift was in her position by the wall when Nell found her. "What kept you?"

"Mrs Scott. It took me ages to get her into that dress."

Mrs Swift followed her gaze. "She's sending out a strong signal, though. She wants to be seen as having money. Did she tell you what Mr Scott does?"

"He's a bank manager."

"Ah, not quite so wealthy as she'd like to make out then. Did she mention she was going to bring her maid but decided not to?"

"How did you know?"

Mrs Swift smirked. "You'll soon learn. She'll want you to spread the word that she has her own maid, but for whatever reason couldn't bring her."

"She told me they're going to stay with family so they'll provide a maid while they're there."

"Of course they will." Mrs Swift rolled her eyes.

"Don't be like that, she's very nice. She asked me if Captain Robertson's wife was in the saloon tonight. Can you see her?"

Mrs Swift scanned the room. "She's not here yet, although she does tend to make an entrance. You won't miss her. She's quite tall, with auburn hair that she wears in some very elaborate updos. She always wears lovely dresses, too."

Nell sighed. "It should be me in the nice dresses, not this ugly uniform."

Mrs Swift huffed. "That's as maybe, but you may find you're grateful for the uniform. You've not got a husband here to protect you."

CHAPTER FIVE

The rumble of the engines was the only thing to disturb the silence of the corridor as Nell left Mrs Scott's stateroom and headed the short distance to the cloakroom.

"Here you are." Mrs Swift pushed herself away from the wall as Nell hurried towards her.

"I'm sorry, she wanted to talk. Shall we go?" Nell fastened her cloak and pulled up her hood as Mrs Swift held open the door.

The night was dark as they stepped outside, and the few oil lamps on the deck did little to illuminate it. Nell glanced up at the thick grey clouds.

"We could do with the moon being out."

"Or more lights. At least I've got you with me this year. It makes it slightly less uncomfortable."

"I can imagine. I wouldn't like to be out here on my own, especially if the weather turns."

"Which it will." Mrs Swift hurried to open the door at the other end of the promenade, and they walked down a flight of stairs to the galley. With the promise of a tray of food to follow them, they headed downstairs to their sitting room.

"It's a lot noisier down here than it was this morning."

"We're only one deck above the engines. That's why they put us down here, and the steerage passengers. They can't charge so much for the rooms. Not that the stewards have it as bad. From what I hear, their quarters are above the mail storage, not the engines."

"That must be better."

"I imagine so. It's the same reason the first-class rooms are quieter, too." Mrs Swift led the way to the sitting room where Nell sank onto the settee. "I'm ready for something to eat. I hadn't realised we'd be around so much food but not be able to have any of it."

"The food in first class is a lot nicer than we'll get down here, so I'll need to play the poor woman tomorrow and see if they'll take pity and feed us once they've finished serving."

"That would be nice. I imagine it will be easier now all the guests are on board, too."

Mrs Swift shook her head. "Have you forgotten that by the time we wake up tomorrow, we'll have stopped in Queenstown to pick up the Irish passengers?"

"Gracious, yes, I had. Will we have any more in first class?"

"I think they'll be down in steerage. At least, I hope so. It will make our lives easier."

"That's good." Nell looked up as a young man arrived with a tray.

"Here you are, ladies. An Irish stew in honour of tomorrow's port of call."

"And a pot of tea, too. Lovely." Nell smiled up at him. "Thank you."

Neither of them spoke as they ate, but with a clean plate in front of her, Nell sat back.

"That was nice enough. I don't know what you're complaining about."

"It wasn't lobster, or chicken, or a roast dinner though, was it?"

"I don't know whether I like lobster. I've never tried it."

"I hadn't until last year, but it's one of my favourites now. Especially when it's covered with butter."

"I'll have to try it then." Nell reached for her tea. "The trouble is, if the food's too nice I won't want to go home."

Mrs Swift gave her a sideways glance. "Do you have much of a home to go to?"

"Oh yes. My daughters for one. My niece is looking after them, but we live together anyway, with my sister and her family. I've another sister who lives over the road and my brother and his family are around the corner. Oh, and another sister who's recently moved back from Ireland."

"That must be nice."

Nell creased the side of her mouth. "It's not always as cosy as it sounds. In fact, the arguments from last year are one of the reasons I'm here, but they all mean well. What about you? Do you have any family?"

"Of sorts. My mother and sister are at home. Mam isn't well, so my sister takes care of her, while I earn the money."

"Are you widowed, too?"

"I never married."

"But *Mrs* Swift..."

Mrs Swift stared through the door into the corridor. "It's just easier to let people think I've a husband at home."

"I suppose so." Nell fidgeted in her chair before collecting up the plates and stacking them on the tray. "Will Matron join us of an evening?"

"Probably not. The steerage passengers usually keep her busy with their poor health and seasickness, so she eats as soon as she's able, then turns in for the night. Not that I blame the passengers, being shut away down here for two weeks."

"Aren't they allowed out?"

"They can go up to the back of the top deck, but there are more of them than there is space, so they can't all go at once. It's not the best weather for it either."

"I don't suppose it is."

Mrs Swift pushed herself up. "Leave the tray, someone will collect it. We really shouldn't walk around by ourselves at night. Come on, we need to get some sleep. We don't know what awaits us tomorrow."

The ship had already docked by the time Nell and Mrs Swift stepped out onto the deck the next morning. The sky was grey and the wind bitter, but Nell stopped to stare at the small stone cottages dotted on a hillside beside a magnificent cathedral.

"Why does such a small village need such a big church?"

"Goodness knows. Come along. Can we go back inside?"

Nell continued to survey the hills surrounding the harbour. "I've never seen so much green."

"It's green because it rains all the time. Now, will you get a move on?"

"Wait. Look down there." Nell pointed to a figure walking away from the ship.

Mrs Swift followed her gaze. "It's only someone disembarking. It's not uncommon."

"But look who it is. Isn't it one of the spies?"

Mrs Swift leaned further over the railings. "So it is. Only one of them, though. I wonder why the other man didn't leave."

"Maybe they argued."

"That's annoying." Mrs Swift's forehead creased. "I've only just found out it's Mr Ramsbottom's servicing their room, and I've not had a chance to ask him about them."

"Perhaps they're not really spies, just passengers who don't like to mix with the others."

"I hope not, my idea's much more interesting." Mrs Swift carried on walking. "Now, hurry up, we can think about it later."

Nell followed Mrs Swift to the first-class facilities and took off her cloak as she went inside. "Right, what do we do now?"

"Breakfasts. There'll be a list in the dining room of the ladies who want it in their room."

"Ah, yes. I already know Mrs Scott does. Do we deliver it and come straight back to the dining room?"

Mrs Swift nodded as she led the way to the stairs. "If you can. Sometimes they want to talk, and so you can't

43

leave, but try your best. There will be others in the dining room who want attention."

Mrs Scott was sitting up in one of the single beds when Nell arrived, her husband nowhere to be seen.

"Good morning, Mrs Scott. Did you sleep well?"

"Surprisingly so, thank you. Until we docked, that is. The thump against the wall woke me."

Nell placed the tray on her lap. "I missed that. I was so tired after yesterday, I'd have slept through anything."

"I'm sure it's tiring being on your feet all day. Why don't you take a seat and keep me company?"

"Thank you, although I mustn't stay long. They'll need me in the dining room." Nell perched on the edge of the settee as Mrs Scott sliced the top off a boiled egg.

"Is this your first time on a ship?"

"Yes, it is."

"I thought you looked rather nervous yesterday. Are you settling in?"

"I'm learning as I go. Once we get out to sea and have a more familiar routine, I'm sure I'll be fine."

"You've not encountered any seasickness yet?"

"No, thankfully not, although we haven't entered the open ocean yet."

"We should do that sometime this afternoon. If we leave here at midday, I expect we'll pass Mizen Head at around two or three o'clock. It's the last time we'll see land until we approach Newfoundland."

The smile fell from Nell's face. "Mizen Head?"

"Is there a problem?"

Tears welled in Nell's eyes as she put a hand to her mouth. "Will you excuse me?"

The door slammed harder than she expected as she left the stateroom, but without a care for who may be around, she put her head down and dashed to the outside terrace. *Why hadn't I even thought we'd sail past Mizen Head? Why didn't James warn me?*

She leaned over the side of the ship, willing her breakfast to stay in her stomach as she retched. *Deep breaths.* Her shoulders heaved up and down as she gulped down the cool air, but within a minute, the wind was biting at her fingers. She wrapped her arms around herself. One more minute.

"Mrs Riley. Are you all right?" Nell jumped at the sound of a man's voice behind her and turned to see Mr Price holding onto his hat, his mousy brown hair fluttering in the breeze.

"Oh, yes, sir. I'm fine. I just came over a little queasy."

"It's a strange time to get your first bout of seasickness, while we're in port."

"Yes, I'm sorry. I'm fine now. I was about to go back inside." She rubbed her hands together. "The cold air works wonders."

He extended an arm to usher her back through the door. "We don't want you catching pneumonia. Get yourself a ginger biscuit. They usually help."

"I will. Thank you." She headed back down the stairs, but bumped into Mrs Swift in the foyer.

"Where've you been? I know I said you should talk to the passengers, but..."

"I'm sorry, I came over all peculiar and needed some air. I'll be all right. What do you want me to do?"

"There's a lady over there, feeling unwell. Will you take

her back to her room and get her settled? Find a steward to bring her a brandy if she doesn't feel better once she's lying down."

Nell took another deep breath. "Will someone collect Mrs Scott's tray? I left rather abruptly."

"I'll take care of that. Now, off you go."

Nell gulped. "Thank you."

Nell was so busy over luncheon she hadn't noticed the ship pull away from the dock until several of the ladies complained of seasickness. *If they're like this now, heaven help us once we're in the middle of the ocean.* She struggled to get them all to their rooms, but once they were settled, she found her cloak and made her way to the first-class promenade. *It should be quieter here than on the main deck.* Finding a sheltered corner, she leaned against the wall and watched the rugged coastline as it passed by in the distance. *It would be beautiful if it wasn't so deadly.*

She straightened her posture as a lighthouse came into view. *Is that it?* She stepped to the rails and checked both ways. *It's a strange place to have one, set back on the headland, and there's still land to come. This mustn't be it.* A tightening gripped her chest as she stayed by the rail, gazing out to her left. *Here it is.* Tears fell down her cheeks as the last of the rocks sank into the sea.

She reached beneath her cloak and pulled out the single rose she'd taken from the display in the dining room. Resting her lips on the bright red petals, she closed her eyes before tossing it over the side of the ship. "Goodbye, Jack. I love you."

She didn't know how long she'd stood watching the waves sweep by, but the sound of footsteps jolted her from her trance. She looked up to see that the land had gone and there was nothing but grey sea merging into a grey sky on the horizon.

"Here you are. I've been looking everywhere for you."

She wiped her eyes as Mrs Swift came up behind her. "I'm sorry, I needed a minute."

"A minute? I'd say it was more like an hour. I ordered you something to eat, but you didn't turn up. Are you still feeling off colour?"

"Not exactly." She bit her lip as she gazed over the side of the ship in the direction they'd just travelled. "My husband died in a shipwreck off Mizen Head. I needed to be alone."

Mrs Swift placed a hand on hers. "I'm sorry. You should have told me."

"There wasn't much to say." She sniffed and rubbed her hands over her face. "I'll be all right now; it's done. Shall we go and find a pot of tea?"

CHAPTER SIX

T he first of the guests had already arrived for cocktails by the time Nell and Mrs Swift walked into the saloon.

"Oh goodness." Nell put a hand to her mouth. "I've just remembered, Mrs Scott will be expecting me to help her dress for dinner. I'd completely forgotten."

"You'd better go then. Mr Scott's here already. Tell her you weren't feeling so well."

"I will. I'll be as quick as I can." She hurried from the saloon but hadn't reached Mrs Scott's stateroom when she bumped into Lilly.

"Oh, I'm sorry." Nell flushed as the girl stared at her.

"You should watch where you're going."

"I'm sorry, I'm in a hurry. Please, after you." Nell stepped to one side to usher the maid past.

"No, it doesn't matter now." Without another word, Lilly disappeared down the stairs.

How strange. Nell shrugged as she took the last few

steps to the stateroom and knocked on the door. "Mrs Scott, are you expecting me?"

"Yes, come in." Mrs Scott was lying on the bed, a towel over her head.

"Oh dear. Do you have seasickness?"

Mrs Scott removed the covering from her face. "Only a touch. I'm sure it would help if I had something to eat. I'd like to wear my navy dress tonight if you wouldn't mind lifting it out."

Nell stepped to the wardrobe and flicked through the dresses. "Ah, yes. Very nice." She laid the dress over the back of the settee, but Mrs Scott stayed where she was. "Shall I come back?"

"No, I'll be fine in a minute. How did you manage your seasickness this morning?"

Nell's mouth fell open. "I ... erm, yes. I stepped out onto the promenade and after a few breaths of fresh air, I was as right as rain. Would you care to try it?"

"Oh, no. I don't think so. Not in the dark with the wind blowing as it is."

"That's probably wise, especially as you've already done your hair. Shall we get you to the saloon? A brandy or a Manhattan may do the trick."

Mrs Scott's face perked up. "That sounds like a better idea."

Mr Scott stood up and offered his wife a seat as Nell escorted her to the table.

"You're looking better, my dear. What will you have?"

Mrs Scott beamed at Nell. "Mrs Riley's been telling me about the cocktails. She suggested I try a Manhattan."

"Good grief, steady on, old girl."

Nell saw the disappointment on Mrs Scott's face. "I thought it may settle your wife's stomach, sir. And it's sweeter with the vermouth in it."

Mr Scott studied his wife. "Just the one then."

Nell nodded and backed away from the table. "I'll ask a steward to bring it over."

After passing on the instruction, Nell picked up some empty glasses and carried them to the galley. Mrs Swift was by the counter.

"Are you any better?"

"I'll be fine. I was wondering..." Nell squealed as someone pressed up behind her.

"Good evening, ladies." A steward, with light brown curly hair that refused to be greased down, rested his hands on her hips. "I've been watching you work. It should be fun having you around."

"It won't be fun if you don't get your hands off Mrs Riley."

Nell moved away as Mrs Swift pulled on the steward's arm.

"All right, keep your hair on. I was only being friendly."

"Maybe you were, but Mrs Riley's not used to your humour. Aren't you going to introduce yourself properly?"

Nell studied the man she guessed was of a similar age to her.

"Mrs Riley, it's nice to make your acquaintance. I'm Mr Ramsbottom." He offered her his hand, but Nell stepped towards the door.

"Pleased to meet you, too. Will you excuse me, Mrs Scott's beckoning." She left Mr Ramsbottom with his hand outstretched and hurried to Mrs Scott's side. "How may I help?"

Mrs Scott's eyes sparkled. "I thought you could do with some assistance."

Nell's cheeks flushed. "You saw?"

"I could see you were uncomfortable. Was he troubling you?"

"A little, but I was probably overreacting. I'm sure he was only being friendly."

Mrs Scott took her hand. "You shouldn't be so quick to blame yourself. You're an attractive woman and the men are on this ship for a long time. You need to watch out for yourself."

Nell's cheeks suddenly burned. "I-I'm sure I will."

"Don't look so worried." Mrs Scott tittered, causing Nell to sigh.

"Can I assume you're feeling better?"

"I am, thanks to this." She held up her half-empty glass. "I could get quite used to drinking these."

"Would you like another one?"

"Oh, gracious no. Mr Scott wouldn't approve." She glanced to her husband, who was in deep conversation with a fellow passenger, and leaned closer to Nell. "Not yet, anyway. Perhaps after dinner."

Nell grinned at her. "As you wish. How about some lemonade for when you finish that?"

"Yes, that would be lovely. Thank you."

Mrs Swift was close behind her as Nell put her order to the barman.

"Are you all right?"

"I'm fine, just shocked. I suppose I need to get used to it."

"You will. They're not all like Mr Ramsbottom. He just likes to be friendly."

"A bit overfriendly, if you ask me." Nell scanned the nearby table. "Where are Lord and Lady Faulkner? They're late tonight."

"They're on the captain's table. Have you seen the elaborate room behind the ladies' section of the dining room? It wouldn't surprise me if they're downstairs already."

"I took a peek inside yesterday when Mr Driver was setting the table. It's very grand."

"Oh, it is, and sitting with the captain is the highlight of the voyage for any up-and-coming society lady, although someone like Lady Annabel probably takes it all for granted."

"So, do all the guests get an invite?"

"Most of them, although it varies as to whether they're invited to an intimate table with the captain and his wife, or if they sit with a group. I would imagine it will just be the Faulkners with Captain and Mrs Robertson."

"Do you know if Mrs Robertson's feeling any better?"

"I don't know, although I've not seen her in the saloon so far on this trip. She spent a lot of time in there last year when she was with us."

"She's so fortunate to be able to travel with him like that." Nell's shoulders sagged.

"Why look so down about it then? You can't blame her."

"Oh, no, I don't, but if Jack had become captain, it

would have been me entertaining. Now look at me, waiting on everyone else."

"Well, if it's any consolation, the head steward always serves the table, and he says it's not as glamorous as it sounds. Not for the captain, at any rate. Can you imagine listening to a group of people telling you how important they are?"

"Not really. It would have been nice to be given the chance though."

The wind rocked the ship as the last of the guests left the dining room and retired to the saloon or their staterooms, and Nell helped with the clearing of the tables.

"Lady Annabel was in her element tonight, with everyone's eyes on her."

"I get the impression she likes to flaunt herself. Did you see the dress she was wearing? It was quite indecent."

"She looked very nice, I thought." Nell grabbed hold of a chair as the ship rolled. "Not many women in our area have blond hair. Perhaps that's what makes the difference."

Mrs Swift snorted. "Whatever it is, she likes the attention."

"You can't blame her. The captain's wife isn't at all how I imagined her to be."

"What were you expecting?"

Nell cocked her head to one side. "I don't know, but I didn't expect her to be so young. She must be ten years younger than him."

"And the rest. Rumour has it the first Mrs Robertson

died, and he met this new one on a voyage. They were married three months later."

Nell shuddered. "So she didn't have to go through all the years while he was training. Perhaps that's what I should do next time."

"Will there be a next time?"

Nell shrugged. "Who knows? Not at the moment, but if the right man came along…" A flash of lightning lit up the room and Nell clung to the chair as the thunder followed seconds later. "I hope Mrs Scott doesn't want a late night tonight. I won't settle until I'm back in our sitting room."

Mrs Swift glanced up at the skylight as the rain pounded the glass. "I must admit it's not very nice out there." She paused and stepped closer to Nell. "I don't often do this, but I suggest we go back to the other side of the ship via the engine room. It's the only route that's all indoors."

Nell's forehead creased. "I thought we were told not to go that way."

"We shouldn't, and believe me, if we had a choice I wouldn't, but if they won't give us a covered walkway, they leave us little option. It should be fine with two of us, anyway." She nodded to the stewards, who were clearing the tables in the men's section. "It's all right for them, they don't need to go outside."

"All right, but you will wait for me, won't you?"

"Of course I will. I don't want to go down there on my own." Mrs Swift shuddered.

"Right, well, we're nearly finished here. Let me find out what Mrs Scott's up to and encourage her to have an early night."

"I'll see you up there."

Nell clasped the handrails as she headed up the stairs, the roll of the ship making it difficult to stand upright. *If Mrs Scott isn't suffering from seasickness, I'll be amazed.* The saloon was half empty when she arrived, most of the ladies having disappeared. She immediately spotted Mr Scott.

"Excuse me, sir." Nell waited for him to look up from his card game. "Has Mrs Scott gone to her room?"

"Yes, she wasn't feeling well, so I escorted her myself. There's no need for you to disturb her."

A wave of relief washed over her. "Very good, sir. Have a nice evening."

A smile flitted across Nell's lips as she left the saloon and headed back down the stairs. She wasn't halfway down when she bumped into Mrs Swift coming the other way.

"Good news. We've been given permission to go back to our rooms."

Nell's brow creased. "Who by?"

"Mr Driver. He was serving at the captain's table, but once the guests left, he joined us. You must have missed him."

"That's good of him. Shall we go? Mrs Scott doesn't need me tonight."

Mrs Swift led the way down the central staircase, past the dining room and down the next flight of stairs. As they approached the lower deck, she hesitated. "I can't hear anything."

"I'm not surprised over the noise of the engines. What's the matter?"

"Nothing. I'm just getting my bearings."

"It's quite gloomy down here." Nell held onto the handrail as her pace slowed.

"Steerage passengers don't get so many lights and there are even fewer in the engine rooms."

"Have you been down there before?"

"Once or twice, when the weather's been too bad to go outside." Mrs Swift's voice faltered and she coughed. "I wouldn't do it if I didn't have to. It's rather dark at the front of the ship, because that's where they carry the mail and coal, but you get extra light as you go towards the back if the boiler doors are open. We need to pull our cloaks tightly around us to hide our aprons so we're less likely to be seen."

"Do the men work through the night?"

"They do; they work shifts. Eight on at a time so we need to hope they're busy." Mrs Swift put a finger to her lips. "Quiet now."

She opened a heavy metal door and Nell stepped back as a barrage of heat and noise hit her. "Good grief."

Mrs Swift tilted her head. "Come on, but be careful. You can see where the doors are open by the patches of light."

They moved quickly along the narrow corridor, stopping whenever they reached an open door to check they wouldn't be seen. With the sound of engines drowning out their footsteps on the metal walkway they made good speed, but as they approached halfway, Mrs Swift stopped, her hand held out to push Nell against the wall. They both stayed silent as the silhouettes of two men appeared ahead of them.

Nell's mouth was dry as her heart pounded. *Please don't*

let them see us. One of the men staggered as the ship rolled, and moments later, they both disappeared through a door to the left. Mrs Swift grabbed her arm, creeping forward until she stopped to peer into the room. A second later, she yanked Nell across the doorway, upping her pace as she went. They were almost at the far end when a voice rang out after them.

"Is anyone there?"

They sank into a darkened area of the corridor, holding their breath, and after a moment, the man disappeared.

"That was close." Mrs Swift pushed on the door at the other end and waited for Nell to join her.

"What would have happened if he'd seen us?"

Mrs Swift gasped. "Who knows? Probably nothing, but I didn't want to risk it."

"Well, let's thank the Lord the engines are so noisy."

CHAPTER SEVEN

Matron was waiting for them in the sitting room the next morning, three cups of tea already poured.

"That was well timed. How are you getting on, Mrs Riley? I'm sorry I've not seen much of you since you started. The seasickness kept me extremely busy yesterday."

"I'm sure it did. The storm last night was terrible." Nell helped herself to a slice of bread.

"I was so late, it was easing before I headed back. Did you get very wet?"

Nell choked on a piece of toast, but Mrs Swift didn't look up.

"We were all right. We made a dash for it."

"Oh good. I have asked them to put a door in on one of the lower levels, but the captain said it's too big an expense when there are only three of us."

Mrs Swift let her spoon drop on the side of the bowl. "They'd arrange for one soon enough if the male stewards were at this end of the ship. Still, if it means they're less likely to bother with us, we shouldn't complain too much."

"I'm sure they won't trouble us whatever the weather, as long as we keep to ourselves." Matron stood up. "You'd better eat up. The guests will be waiting."

The winds buffeted the sails that had been hoisted overnight, but with the rain bouncing from the deck, Nell had no time to admire them as she dashed to the first-class area.

"January's always the worst." Matron hung up her cloak and straightened her hat.

"I'm surprised there are any passengers. You'd think they'd want to walk along the promenade rather than being stuck indoors for two weeks." Nell adjusted her hat as she waited for Mrs Swift.

"It's the money. It's much cheaper at this time of year."

"I suppose so, although you wouldn't expect Lord Faulkner to worry about that."

Matron held the door open as they left for the stairs. "You never know with the likes of His Lordship. He may have business that can't wait. I doubt he's travelling for pleasure. Now, I must leave you. Hopefully, I'll see you later."

Nell followed Mrs Swift to the dining room. "It's quiet in here this morning. Might the passengers still be suffering from seasickness?"

"Possibly. We'll have to visit the staterooms of anyone who doesn't come down to check they're all right."

Nell nodded to a table in the far corner of the room. "Look who's over there."

"Well, well." Mrs Swift took a few steps forward. "The remaining spy has a new friend."

"They're deep in conversation."

Mrs Swift glanced around. "Most of the stewards must be delivering breakfasts. Let me see if I can help."

"What about our trays?"

"You start with yours; I'll take mine in a minute."

Mrs Scott was sitting up in bed when Nell arrived, but her face was a similar colour to the starched white sheets.

"Good morning." Nell walked in with a smile. "How are you feeling today?"

Mrs Scott put the back of a hand to her forehead. "I'm better than last night, but I'm hoping you've some ginger biscuits on the tray, or at least some dry toast. I can't face much to eat."

"I have some toast, but no biscuits. Would you like me to get you some?"

"Oh, no, don't worry yourself." She straightened out the bedcovers as Nell placed the tray on her knee. "I'll have some in the saloon later if I'm no better." She unwrapped the triangles of toast from the cotton napkin and broke off a corner.

"As long as you're sure. I need to go back to the dining room, but I'll call later to collect the tray and tidy up in here."

"Thank you, dear. I don't know what I'd do without you."

Nell took a deep breath as she left the stateroom. *At least she appreciates me.*

She was about to head to the stairs, but stopped as the captain appeared on the landing with Dr Clarke. She curtsied as they approached.

"Good morning, Captain, Dr Clarke."

"Mrs Riley, isn't it?"

Her heart raced as the captain studied her. "Yes, Captain. I've been delivering breakfasts."

"Splendid. You avoided the seasickness, did you?"

"Yes, sir." She tried to keep a smile in her voice. "Hopefully, the weather will be calmer today."

"I can't promise that, but hopefully Officer Jones will keep her steady while the doctor and I do our inspection."

"I hope so." She fixed a grin on her face. *What else do I say?*

"Right, well, don't let us keep you."

"Thank you, Captain." She disappeared down the stairs, and with her heart pounding, she stopped to take a breath before sauntering into the dining room. *Still quiet, good. But the spies have gone.*

"Good morning, Mrs Riley." The frown that had settled on Nell's face froze as she felt an arm around her waist. "Don't look so scared, I won't bite."

She stepped away. "No, of course not. You startled me, that's all."

"There's no need to worry about me. I'm only watching out for you."

"That's very kind. I'm on my way to check if there are any more trays to be delivered."

"So am I, as it happens. Let me escort you." He put an arm around her shoulders as he ushered her towards the galley. "There aren't many down here this morning, I imagine the trays are stacking up."

"Yes." Nell stopped and stepped away from him. "Why don't you go first? You'll probably have more to take than me, and these tables need tidying."

"As you like." He winked at her. "I'll catch up with you later."

Nell waited for Mr Ramsbottom to disappear upstairs before she walked into the galley.

"Are there any more ladies' trays?"

The head chef, Mr Ross, pushed one forward. "Only this for Lady Annabel."

"Lady Annabel?" Nell cocked her head to one side. "I thought her maid always collected her tray."

"She's not been down for it. I don't imagine Her Ladyship will be best pleased."

"No, although I hope she's all right. She may have gone down with seasickness."

He shrugged. "Maybe she has."

Nell picked up the tray. "I'll ask Lady Annabel when I go up and hope she doesn't bite my head off."

The chef grinned at her as she headed for the stairs. "Best of luck."

The tray grew heavy as Nell stood outside the large corner suite, before knocking on the door, but she didn't need to wait long before Lady Annabel called her in. She was reclining on the settee as Nell entered.

"Good morning, madam. I hope you don't mind me

intruding, but your maid hasn't been to collect your tray, so I've brought it for you."

Lady Annabel sat up straight. "What's the matter with her?"

"I'm afraid I don't know. Seasickness, I shouldn't wonder. Shall I put the tray on the table?"

"Oh, would you? And pour the tea while you're here. I've a tremendous headache."

Nell studied the pale, lifeless features of the usually attractive face. "Would you like me to fetch the doctor for you?"

"That would probably be sensible, although I've only got myself to blame. The captain was too hospitable last night."

Nell pursed her lips. "I couldn't help noticing you were enjoying yourself."

"Oh, I was. He's such a charming man. Not that I'd want him to see me like this." She pulled her elegant pink dressing gown more tightly around her as Nell handed her a cup of tea. "I'm sure it will be good enough for the doctor, though."

"I'm sure it will. It's lovely. Should I ask the doctor or Matron to call on Grace, as well?"

Lady Annabel sipped her tea. "Matron will be enough, but only if she's not too busy. I don't want to burden her if half the ship is ill."

"It's no trouble, but I'll call in and ask how Grace is first. I'm sure you'd like her to be back on her feet."

"I would. I only hadn't missed her because of this headache. Why don't you go now? I can manage here until the doctor arrives."

Nell surveyed the corridor as she stepped from the stateroom. *Nobody. Let me check on Grace first, then I'll know if I need Matron, too.* She headed to the front of the ship where the first-class staterooms ended and small cabins resembling the one she shared with Mrs Swift took over.

Nell paused and put an ear to the door before she knocked. When she got no reply, she tried again. "Grace, are you in there?" She pushed on the door and peered into the darkness. "Grace?"

"Who is it?"

"Mrs Riley. One of the stewardesses. Lady Annabel is wondering how you are. She told me you were suffering from seasickness."

"Keep the door shut."

Nell took the wick from the night light and lit the oil lamp attached to the wall before closing the door.

"How are you feeling?"

The girl's eyes were red as she glanced at Nell from under her bedcovers. "I can't go out there."

"I'm sure there's no need if you're ill. I'll see to Lady Annabel for the time being." Nell crouched by the side of the bunk as the girl rolled over to face the wall. "Would you like me to bring you some ginger biscuits? They often help."

The girl remained silent as her shoulders heaved up and down.

"I'll tell you what. I'll go and fetch some and then you can eat them when you're ready. I'll ask Matron to call, too." Nell ran a hand over Grace's head as she sobbed into the pillow.

"Will you lock the door on your way out?"

Nell's brow creased as she stood up. "If you like, although I'm sure it's not necessary."

Grace wiped her tears. "I don't want anyone seeing me like this."

"Very well. Now, try to relax."

Nell fumbled with the keys as she searched for the right one, but once she'd locked the door, she headed for the doctor's quarters, which were at the front of the ship on the corner of the bridge. *It's as good a place as any to start.*

The medical room was empty when she arrived, and with a quick glance around the small office, fitted with a curtained bed at one end and a large table at the other, she left. *Goodness knows where they'll be.*

She headed along the corridor adjacent to the bridge, but froze at the sound of a voice behind her.

"What are you doing up here?"

She turned to see the third mate she'd encountered on the first day. "I'm looking for the doctor or Matron. You wouldn't know where they are, would you?"

The officer stepped towards her. "Aren't you supposed to look after the guests? That's what they pay you for, isn't it?"

Nell stepped backwards. "I ... I am, and Lady Annabel Faulkner would like the doctor to visit."

The sneer dropped from his face. "Well, you'd better be quick, then before he does his inspection."

"I will. Thank you."

Nell hurried to the opposite side of the ship and took a deep breath as she rounded the corner. *Why is he so disagreeable?*

After walking the length of the upper deck without

success, Nell headed down to the dining room level, but paused as she studied the remaining flight of stairs. *They'll probably be in steerage. Do I follow them? What choice do I have?*

She crept down the stairs, but when she reached the lower level, she stopped to glance around. *I can't go into the male section.*

"Well I never, what do we have here?" A middle-aged man with straw-coloured hair and a twinkle in his eye walked to her side. "I've never seen a woman doing work like this before."

"It's a new role. The thing is, I'm looking for the doctor or Matron, but I'm not allowed into the men's dormitory. Would you mind checking inside to see if either of them is there?"

"It would be an honour for a nice lady like you." He smirked as she took a step backwards. "Give me a minute." He disappeared through the door, and Nell stepped to the other side of the corridor. Perhaps Maria had been right after all. This wasn't a place for a woman. She waited for a couple of minutes and was wondering if he'd come back when he reappeared. "No. No sign of either of them."

"Never mind, thank you for looking." Her shoulders slumped as she glanced around. "They must be on the other side of the ship. You can't get to it from here."

"I'll escort you there if you like." The man stretched out an arm to lean against the wall.

"No ... thank you, but I need to ask one of the stewards to find them. I shouldn't be down here on my own."

"Don't be worrying about that; you've brightened my day."

Nell's cheeks burned. "If you'll excuse me, I must go." She hurried to the foyer, not pausing for breath as she raced up the stairs. Once on the top deck, she ran straight into Mrs Swift.

"There you are. I've been looking everywhere for you."

"I'm sorry. I needed to find Matron or the doctor, but they're nowhere to be found."

"They were here, not five minutes ago. What do you want them for?"

Nell peered into the saloon. "Do you know where they went? Lady Annabel's feeling under the weather and wanted the doctor to call. I also said I'd ask Matron to call on her maid. She's struggling with seasickness."

Mrs Swift paused. "I suspect they're already with Lady Annabel. They were heading in that direction with his Lordship, anyway. You shouldn't go wandering off like that without telling anyone."

Nell followed Mrs Swift into the dining room. "Believe me, I won't. I didn't expect it would be so hard to find them."

"Very well; we'll say no more about it. Now, we need to start tidying the staterooms while they're all in the saloon. They'll all be wanting to change for luncheon soon."

Matron was in the sitting room when Nell and Mrs Swift arrived downstairs that evening.

"Good evening. It's not often we find you still here." Mrs Swift smiled as she took a seat next to the older woman.

"It's been another busy day. Hopefully, the wind will drop some more tomorrow."

Nell took the seat opposite Matron. "Did you call on young Grace, Lady Annabel's maid?"

Matron's brow creased. "No, I didn't know I needed to."

"Oh, dear." Nell gave a deep sigh. "I came looking for you and Dr Clarke earlier, but when Mrs Swift saw you visiting Lady Annabel's stateroom, I presumed she'd pass on the message to visit Grace. The poor girl was suffering dreadfully."

"Lady Annabel was too concerned with her own headache to worry about anyone else." Matron tutted. "Still, it couldn't have been serious or the maid sharing her cabin would have come to find me."

"She's on her own. She should have been in with that other maid, Lilly, but she moved to her own cabin, if you remember."

Matron's eyes flicked between them. "She's in there on her own?"

Nell nodded. "She asked me to lock the door when I left, so I doubt anyone else will have called."

Matron stood up. "This really isn't good enough. I'll speak to Dr Clarke tomorrow about how we can avoid such a mix-up. I'd better go and see her. In fact–" she picked up some bread and cheese and wrapped it in a napkin "–I'll take her something to eat. She'll be famished if she's not eaten all day."

Matron had no sooner left than the chef from upstairs carried in a tray. "Here you are, ladies. Fish and chips."

"Ooh, lovely." Nell licked her lips as he put the plates down. "I'm suddenly rather hungry."

"Well, enjoy it. I'll call back for the dishes later."

Nell was halfway through her food when she spoke

again. "I can't believe Lady Annabel didn't tell Matron about Grace."

"Sadly, people like that tend to only think of themselves. I wish I hadn't stopped you going after them now."

"You weren't to know. I hope Matron means it about making it easier to leave her messages, though. I don't want to go down to steerage again."

Mrs Swift stopped and stared at her. "Is that where you'd come back from when you nearly ran into me?"

Nell nodded.

"I'm not surprised you were in such a hurry. That was the men's side you came out of."

"I know that now."

Mrs Swift laid down her knife and fork. "Did you see anyone?"

"There was one man who stopped to talk, but he was quite helpful in the end. He went into the dormitory for me to see if they were there."

"You were very fortunate. You don't know who you could have met." Mrs Swift retrieved her cutlery.

"Some of the stewards in the first-class area are bad enough. I'm not sure the steerage passengers could be much worse. Or that third mate. I bumped into him when I was near the doctor's office." Nell shuddered. "He's the worst."

"Yes, he is. I'll have a word with Matron about him. She may be able to get one of the other officers to speak to him."

Nell took a mouthful of fish. "I've not had a chance to ask you about the spies. Did you speak to them earlier?"

Mrs Swift snorted. "I tried to, but they don't speak English."

"That's unfortunate." Nell stabbed several pieces of carrot. "What about Mr Ramsbottom? Did you ask him about them?"

Mrs Swift rolled her eyes. "I did but he thought I was crazy."

"He won't think that if we're right about them."

Mrs Swift chuckled. "We'll have to hope we are then."

CHAPTER EIGHT

The following morning the sky was still grey, and Nell clutched her cloak around her as she gazed up at the clouds.

"We'll need to be quick; it will be raining in a minute." She scurried across the deck, with Mrs Swift close behind.

"I hope it doesn't turn nasty again. I'd rather not go through the engine room tonight."

"It wasn't that bad and I'd rather get hot and dusty down there than catch our death of cold out here."

"We'll see." Mrs Swift took the door from Nell as she unfastened her cloak. "At least it's done for another morning. Let's see how many have made it to breakfast today."

A handful of stewards were already in the dining room when they arrived, and Nell saw one of them nudge his colleague and nod towards them. Within seconds, several others were staring at them.

"What's up with them?"

Mrs Swift didn't look up. "I spoke to Matron yesterday

afternoon about that third mate, Officer Hughes. Word must have got around."

"But why would it? We only want him to be polite to us."

"I know, but he's probably said something to get us in trouble."

"Good morning, ladies." Mr Driver, the head steward, appeared beside them, his neatly trimmed moustache twitching as he stared down at them. "How are you today?"

"We're very well, thank you." Nell hesitated as Mrs Swift studied the tray roster. "We're about to take the trays."

"Before you do, may I suggest we walk to my office?"

Nell looked to Mrs Swift, who shrugged. "If you must, but wouldn't it be better to do this first?"

Mr Driver cleared his throat. "This won't take long."

They followed him around the outside of the dining room and into a small room next to the galley. He offered them both a seat.

"I understand you put in a complaint about one of our colleagues." His eyes bored into Nell.

"It wasn't a complaint..."

"Yes, it was." Mrs Swift cut across her. "The man hasn't had a civil word to say to us since we boarded. We're here to do a job. All we ask is that we can do it without being insulted."

"I see." Mr Driver clamped his hands together and rested his chin on his index fingers. "In future, if you have cause for complaint about any member of staff, I want you to raise it with the gentleman concerned, rather than his superiors. I'm sure nobody has any intention of upsetting you."

Nell studied her lap as Mrs Swift replied. "Maybe not, but I doubt stewards have to put up with the same behaviour. All we're requesting is some civility."

"And there are ways of doing that." He stood up and paced around them. "I'd ask that you refrain from taking such trivial complaints to the officers. They have no reason to be involved."

"Yes, sir," Nell mumbled into her chest.

But Mrs Swift got to her feet, planting her hands on her hips. "I assure you that if his behaviour improves, there'll be no need. If he doesn't..."

Mr Driver raised one of his thick, dark eyebrows. "I'm sorry. I mustn't have made myself clear. If you wish to continue working on this ship, you won't speak to the officers again."

Mrs Swift's eyes widened. "We didn't go to them this time, we only told Matron. As we're entitled to."

Mr Driver pursed his lips. "As head steward, it's me you should come to with any complaints. Not her. Is that clear?"

"Yes, sir." Mrs Swift spat out her words before storming from the room. Nell gave Mr Driver a weak smile and followed her out, chasing her along the top deck until she pushed through the outside door and stepped onto the promenade.

"Are you all right?" Nell joined her at the railings.

"No, I'm not. It all makes me so mad. Why do *we* get into trouble for *his* behaviour?"

Nell shuddered as she looked out to sea. "I suppose he feels humiliated."

"What about him humiliating us?"

"That doesn't matter to the likes of him. I suggest we

keep out of his way, if we can. It shouldn't be difficult given he doesn't come to the dining room very often."

"You're right. I should know better." Mrs Swift took a deep breath but immediately shivered. "Come on, we need to get inside. We'll freeze out here."

Only the chef, Mr Ross, was waiting for them when they returned to the galley.

"Where've you been? These eggs will be hard."

"You can blame Mr Driver." Mrs Swift reached for the tray roster. "He wanted a word with us."

"Ah, about the complaint, I imagine."

Mrs Swift shook her head. "Does everyone know about it?"

The chef shrugged. "I can't speak for the passengers, but the staff aren't too pleased with you."

"I don't know why we even got the blame. I only spoke to Matron about an officer being rude to us. We didn't mention it to anyone else."

Mr Ross brought a couple of fresh eggs for one of the trays. "That's not what I heard."

"What did you hear then?"

"You can take that tray before those eggs go hard. Lady Annabel won't be pleased; you're late as it is."

Nell's head jerked up. "Lady Annabel. Why's she taking breakfast in her room again?"

"To heck with Lady Annabel." Mrs Swift glared at the chef. "What have people been saying about us?"

He leaned forward and lowered his voice. "Listen, I

shouldn't be telling you this, but we were told you reported one of the crew for *improper* behaviour."

"That's what we've just said. Being rude is improper behaviour for an officer." Nell picked up the tray as the chef straightened up.

"Ah, yes, that must be it." Mr Ross rubbed his neck. "They've obviously blown it out of all proportion."

A frown settled on Nell's face as she climbed the stairs to Lady Annabel's stateroom. *What a strange start to the day.*

Lady Annabel was on the settee when she let herself in. "Ah, you're here. Good. I thought you may have been in trouble."

"In trouble? Why?"

"Over poor Grace."

"Grace?" Nell put the tray on the table. "Oh, you mean because Matron only called on her last night? I'm sorry about that, but after I left you yesterday morning, I couldn't find her until I saw her with Dr Clarke heading in here. I assumed you'd ask her to call; it was only later we realised our mistake. Matron came straight back to see her when we realised. Is she all right?"

"No, actually, she's not. That's why I had to speak to the captain."

Nell raised an eyebrow. "You spoke to the captain about Grace?"

"What else could I do? I was in the saloon after dinner when Matron came to tell me the girl was distraught. Couldn't you see that when you visited her?"

"Well ... yes, but it was because of the seasickness."

"Did she tell you that?"

"I-I think so. She asked me to lock the door after me because she didn't want anyone seeing her as she was. She was very pale."

"I'm not surprised, given she was in there on her own. What were you thinking, letting that happen?"

"Me? I'm sorry. It was the other maid, Lilly, who wanted a cabin of her own."

"Someone should have stopped her. Have you spoken to Matron about this?"

"No, she wasn't at breakfast this morning..."

"Well, I suggest you do, and I expect you to undertake some of Grace's duties until we get to New York. The poor girl can't face the idea of leaving her room after what happened."

What did happen? "Very well, madam. Do Matron or the captain know of the new arrangements?"

"Not yet. You'll have to tell them."

Nell nodded. "How would you like me to help?"

"You can come back to help me dress for a walk on the promenade. I need some air after all this."

"It's very blustery outside, madam."

"Then I'll need my thick cloak. Be back here in half an hour."

Lady Annabel dismissed Nell with a flick of her hand, but as she reached the corridor, Nell paused and leaned against the wall. *Why are we in trouble because a maid moved cabins?*

Mrs Swift was nowhere to be seen when Nell returned to the galley, so she picked up the tray for Mrs Scott and headed back upstairs. She was sitting on the settee when she arrived.

"Ah, here you are, dear. I thought you'd forgotten about me."

Nell sighed. "No, I'm sorry. There's been a lot going on this morning and I didn't realise the time."

"I hope they're not overworking you."

"Nothing for you to worry about, although I may have to help Lady Annabel more than usual. Her maid's been struck down with seasickness."

"Oh, what a shame." Mrs Scott smiled up at her. "I can't be doing too badly though, if I'm sharing a maid with Lady Annabel."

"I don't suppose you can." Nell forced a smile. "Will you excuse me? I need to get back downstairs."

Lady Annabel was waiting for her when she returned, but with neither in the mood to talk, she was ready for her walk by the time Lord Faulkner arrived to collect her. Nell led them to the deck and held open the door, but as soon as they were outside, she hurried back down the stairs, jumping over the last step. She was about to dart into the dining room when she bumped straight into the captain.

"Good grief, Mrs Riley."

Nell's cheeks burned. "I do apologise, Captain. I didn't expect to see you."

"Clearly." He looked at her more closely. "Is everything all right?"

"I'm sure it will be, sir."

He glanced over both shoulders. "Will you walk

with me?"

"Me?" Nell's voice squeaked.

"You seem troubled, and I'd like to know why." He indicated towards the stairs.

"If I'm being honest, I don't know. As far as I can tell, something happened yesterday and Mrs Swift and I are getting the blame for it."

"The blame? From who?"

Nell's heart pounded. "I really can't say. I've been told not to..."

"Mrs Riley, I'm the captain of this ship. If I want to know what's going on, I expect you to tell me."

"I ... we ... yes, we were told that if we wanted to carry on working on the ship, we weren't to speak to any of the officers."

"By that I presume you mean yourself and Mrs Swift?" He ushered her in the direction of the bridge.

"Yes, Captain. We didn't mean to get Officer Hughes into trouble, we only wanted him to be more polite."

"And that's what you think all this is about?"

"Yes, sir." She studied his inscrutable profile. "Isn't it?"

"I agree Officer Hughes could improve how he handles himself. Has word of your *complaint* become common knowledge amongst the staff?"

"Yes, sir. We're being blamed for it."

Captain Robertson stopped as they reached the door to the bridge. "Leave it with me, Mrs Riley. And please don't worry. If you need to speak to anyone, you can ask for me. I'm here every afternoon between two and four o'clock."

"Thank you, Captain." Nell hesitated as she stared at her fingers.

"Is there something else?"

"Lady Annabel asked if I can take over from her maid, who's feeling unwell."

"Lady Annabel." He sighed and put a hand on Nell's shoulder. "If you must, but don't let her take all your time. I'll remind her we have other passengers."

"Thank you, Captain." Nell finally smiled. "That would be a great help."

Hoping Lady Annabel could hang up her own cloak, Nell hurried back to the dining room. The tables wouldn't clear themselves, and with morning coffee about to be served, she needed to be upstairs to tidy the staterooms.

She was tidying the last one when Mrs Swift popped her head around the door.

"Are you nearly finished?"

"Another five minutes. Why?"

"Matron wants to see us in the dining room." Mrs Swift picked up the brush and swept the floor.

"Oh, my. What have we done now? I've just had to explain myself to the captain."

"You've not!" Mrs Swift's mouth dropped. "Why?"

"I bumped into him and he thought I looked out of sorts."

"Because of Mr Driver?"

"Partly, but there's more to it. I spoke to Lady Annabel this morning. I've not had a chance to tell you, but..."

Mrs Swift studied the clock. "It will have to wait. We don't have time now." She collected the dirty linen off the floor. "Let's see what Matron has to say first."

CHAPTER NINE

Matron sat in the dimly lit corner of the dining room at the end of the table often used by the spies. Nell's stomach churned at the sight of her sour face.

"Good morning, Matron."

"Good morning, Mrs Riley. I'm sorry to drag you both away from your work, but we need to talk, and it couldn't wait until this evening."

"Is it to do with my complaint about Officer Hughes?" Mrs Swift took the seat opposite Matron while Nell sat between them.

"Not exactly. I wanted to report back on my visit to the young maid, Grace."

Nell nodded. "Lady Annabel said you'd spoken to her in the saloon after you'd seen Grace."

"I'm afraid I had no choice." Matron fidgeted with the tablecloth. "She told me that one of the male members of staff had forced himself into her room earlier in the day."

"No!" Nell and Mrs Swift stared at each other.

"Unfortunately, not many believe her. When

challenged, the man in question said it had all been her idea and she had only blamed him when she realised her reputation would be in tatters."

"That doesn't sound like Grace." Nell's eyes narrowed. "It wasn't Officer Hughes, was it? Or Mr Ramsbottom?"

"It's best that we keep the identity of the gentleman private. The reason I'm telling you is because it was necessary to involve you." Matron gazed at them.

"Us?" Nell gasped. "Why? How?"

"Naturally, I had to tell Lady Annabel what had happened, and she went straight to Captain Robertson. Unfortunately, it was shortly before I spoke to him about Officer Hughes and for reasons of his own, the captain merged the two complaints together."

"But you were the one who spoke to him, not us."

"Yes." Matron's gaze didn't move from the tablecloth. "The thing is, if the men need nursing they have to trust me ... so they couldn't know I was the source of the complaint."

"So you agreed we should take the blame ... and on another charge."

"I'm sorry, but it was the only way."

Mrs Swift shook her head. "Have you any idea how difficult it's been this morning? The stewards are all whispering behind our backs and Mr Driver reprimanded us earlier."

"And Lady Annabel seems to hold me responsible for Grace being on her own in the first place." Nell gasped, causing Matron to look up.

"I was going to ask you about that. Why was she alone?"

Nell's shoulders slumped. "It was Lilly's fault; Mrs

Barker's maid. She wanted a cabin to herself and so Mr Barker arranged it for her."

"Who agreed to it?"

Nell and Mrs Swift both shrugged.

"You don't know?" Matron's voice was raised. "Whoever it was should have known not to leave such a young girl on her own. This is exactly the reason for putting maids together; for their own protection. I need to speak to that madam."

"And in the meantime, we've got to put up with all the snide comments from the crew?" Mrs Swift's face was stern. "We've already been told not to talk to any of the officers again if we want to carry on working."

"Who told you that?"

"Mr Driver."

"Right, I'll have a word with him, too."

"No." Mrs Swift banged a hand on the table. "Can't you see it will only make it worse? Word will be all round the stewards by the time we reach the other side of the ship."

Nell pursed her lips together. "Could you somehow let it be known it wasn't us who made the complaint? Perhaps say it was Lord Faulkner, given it was Lady Annabel's maid. They'd be much less likely to intimidate him."

"We can't possibly do that while he's still on board, although maybe once we reach New York..." Matron nodded to herself. "You'll have to take extra care of yourselves between now and then. Don't go anywhere alone outside of the first-class area and don't dawdle. I'll see if I can arrange for a chaperone."

"No, don't. It would raise suspicions and we don't know

who to trust." Mrs Swift studied Nell. "Perhaps we should find something heavy to carry, just in case."

Nell nodded. "What about each of us carrying a flat iron? Nobody will miss them overnight."

"That's a good idea; I'll see to it later."

Nell and Mrs Swift bade Matron farewell and headed back to the stairs.

"I need to check Lady Annabel doesn't want anything."

"Will you say anything to her?"

Nell studied her friend. "I don't know. What do you think?"

"I'm not sure. Would it do any good?"

"Probably not. It might make her angrier." Nell glanced at the clock as they reached the foyer. "If she asks why I'm late, I'll tell her I was talking to Matron. At least it should hint to the fact that I know."

Mrs Swift nodded. "I'm going to find out who agreed to Lilly moving rooms."

"How will you do that? You can hardly question the captain, and if it was one of the stewards, they're not likely to tell you."

"Somebody might, or if not, I'll ask Mrs Barker if I ever catch her in her room. She's usually too busy talking to other passengers in the saloon."

"Would Mr Barker tell you?"

Mrs Swift sighed. "I doubt it; he only deals with the stewards. Besides, if he really is besotted with Lilly, he's not likely to get her into trouble."

They stopped when they reached Lady Annabel's room.

"Whatever you do, take care. I'll see you later."

～

It was almost ten o'clock when Nell joined Mrs Swift by the cloakroom that evening.

"Is Her Ladyship in bed already?"

"No, but she can sort herself out. I've turned down the sheets but I'm not waiting for her, the trouble she's caused."

Mrs Swift waited for Nell to fasten her cloak before handing her an iron. "How's this afternoon been?"

"Marginally better than this morning, but the stewards haven't missed a chance to make a comment. What about you?" She pushed open the door and stepped onto the deck.

"Pretty much the same. I didn't get very far with Mr Barker..."

"Are you going somewhere, ladies?"

An icy shiver ran down Nell's spine as Mrs Swift took her arm and kept walking.

"Ignore them."

Them?

"I said, are you going somewhere?" Mr Ramsbottom and two of his colleagues came from behind and stepped in front of them.

"I'm sure you're aware we're heading back to our quarters."

Nell couldn't miss the squeak in Mrs Swift's voice.

"It's a shame you need to make this journey every evening." He stepped to Nell's side and ran a finger down her cheek. "We don't like snitches."

"We're nothing of the sort." Nell's mouth was dry.

"That's not what we heard, is it, lads? We heard you like to get your colleagues into trouble."

His two companions took a step closer.

"We don't. We haven't got anyone into trouble." Nell clutched the handle of the iron, but her arm refused to move as Mr Ramsbottom leaned forward until his face was almost touching hers.

"Well, see that you don't. And not a word to anyone about our little chat." He stepped back to let them pass. "Have a nice evening."

Nell thought her chest would explode as they raced to the door at the other end of the deck. It wasn't until they were inside and within shouting distance of the galley that they stopped.

"I didn't sign up for this." Tears appeared on her cheeks.

"Neither did I, but what can we do? We're halfway to America with no way out." Mrs Swift reached for her own handkerchief.

"We can't even tell Matron. She's bound to say something."

Nell sighed. "What I don't understand is why Mr Ramsbottom's involved."

Mrs Swift shrugged. "He's probably worried we'll report him."

"But why would we?"

Mrs Swift raised an eyebrow. "Because he's up to no good himself? I tell you, we should find out what, so that if he comes after us again..."

Nell shuddered. "You can if you like; I don't want to speak to him again. And that goes for finding out about the spies too. I don't care what they're up to if it means asking him." She paused as Mr Potter appeared at the galley door.

"I thought that was you. Would you like me to bring the tray down?"

Mrs Swift nodded. "Yes, please. You don't have any brandy in there too, do you? We've had rather a shock and need to calm our nerves."

His brow creased. "I'm sorry to hear that. Are you all right?"

"We will be if we can have a tot of brandy."

A smile lit up his face. "Leave it to me. You get yourselves downstairs and I'll be right behind you."

Mrs Swift clinked Nell's glass as she poured them both a second glass of brandy.

"It was good of him to leave the bottle."

Nell chuckled. "I didn't even know I liked the stuff, but I must admit, it's working."

Mrs Swift took a sip. "We can't let them bully us. We need to stand up for ourselves."

"But how do we do that? Even the irons were no use against three of them. They'd have grabbed them off us before we'd lifted our arms."

"We'll have to find something else to carry."

"Should we consider Matron's idea of a chaperone? Mr Potter's nice enough, and he didn't even ask what the problem was."

Mrs Swift shook her head. "I worry we'd get him into trouble. So far, the problem's confined to the other half of the ship, and I'd like to keep it that way."

"That means we need to wait until Lord Faulkner gets off and then hope the captain tells everyone it was him who made the complaint." Nell cradled her drink in her hands, but as the tension left her shoulders, a noise caused her to sit up straight. "Did you hear that?"

"I did." Mrs Swift put down her glass and crept to the door. "Nothing."

"Do you think someone was listening?"

Mrs Swift disappeared into the corridor but was back within seconds. "Possibly. I imagine we'll find out tomorrow."

"What do you mean?"

"You've just mentioned it was Lord Faulkner who reported the officer. If someone was listening, it will be all over the ship by the morning."

Nell took a gulp from her glass. "Let's hope so."

CHAPTER TEN

The following morning, Nell's stomach fluttered at the sight of the captain talking to Mr Driver in the corner of the dining room.

"Have you seen them?" She nudged Mrs Swift.

"Oh, gracious, that's all we need. If Mr Driver thinks we've been telling tales again, we could be out of a job."

Nell straightened her back and walked to the galley. "You know what, I don't care any more. The company said I could use this first voyage as a test and if I didn't like it, I needn't stay. Well, the way I feel at the moment, I'd rather not do another trip."

Mrs Swift's eyes widened. "You're serious, aren't you?"

"I am. I lay in bed worrying about it last night, and if anyone says another word to me, I'll be telling the captain, and to heck with the consequences."

"You won't blame me, will you? I need this job."

"So do I, but is it worth being bullied for?"

Mrs Swift sighed. "You know as well as I do, it happens everywhere. If you want to work, you'd better get used to it."

"We'll see." Nell paused as the captain walked towards them.

"Good morning, ladies."

"Good morning, Captain." Nell braced herself for another rebuke, but he smiled.

"I hope you don't mind me joining you for breakfast. I like to get out and talk to the staff."

"Not at all." Nell gestured around the room. "Is there anywhere in particular you'd like to sit?"

"Somewhere close to the middle, I'd say, so I can see the comings and goings."

Mrs Swift wandered to the galley as Nell showed him to his table. "May I get you a pot of tea while you're waiting? I'll ask a steward to take your breakfast order."

"Tea for two, please. I'm expecting Officer Hughes any time now."

Nell's stomach sank as she turned from the captain. *What's he playing at bringing the third mate here?* "Yes, Captain."

Nell hurried back to the galley and picked up the tray for Lady Annabel. "I'm going. Officer Hughes is joining the captain and I don't want to be around when he arrives."

"Blimey, neither do I. Wait for me."

The two of them made their way upstairs, and when Nell reached Lady Annabel's stateroom, she knocked on the door and walked in.

"Good morning, madam."

Lady Annabel was still in bed as Nell put the tray on the table.

"Is everything all right?"

Her Ladyship pushed herself up while Nell arranged her pillows. "I heard what happened to you last night."

Nell's forehead creased. "What did you hear?"

"That a group of stewards accosted you."

Nell took a step back. "How did you know about that?"

"It's all right, don't look so worried. A few of us were playing cards in the saloon long after everyone else had gone to bed. My husband overheard them boasting that they'd taught you a lesson."

Nell gulped. "I'm sorry, madam. We didn't say anything."

"No. I'm aware of that. If it's any consolation, Lord Faulkner spoke to them."

"He did?" Nell's voice brightened.

"Yes. He told them that a group of men frightening two defenceless women was hardly something to boast about and they should be ashamed of themselves."

"That was good of him." *I hope.*

"Precisely. They should think twice in the future. Now, will you pass the tray? I'll take breakfast here."

The captain and third mate were deep in conversation when Nell returned to the dining room, and she kept her head down as she hurried past. Mr Ross was waiting for her in the galley.

"Is this ready to go?"

"It is. You'd better be quick if your lady likes her eggs soft."

Nell cocked her head to one side. "I don't know whether

she does or not, but she's never complained." She picked up the tray. "I won't be long."

Nell didn't look at the captain's table as she hurried past, but in her haste, she almost bumped into Mrs Swift on the stairs.

"What's the hurry?"

"I'm sorry. I wanted to get away from the captain and third mate..."

"Lucky for you. I'll have to go in there on my own."

"You can hold the doors for me, if you like."

"What a splendid idea. After you."

Nell paused outside Mrs Scott's stateroom while Mrs Swift knocked on the door.

"Shall I open it for you?"

"Please..."

"Going round in twos now, are you?"

Nell stopped as Lilly eyed them both up.

"I imagine you're the reason I've had to go back to the shared room."

Nell ignored the open door. "What's that supposed to mean?"

"It's all over the ship that you reported one of the crew for being in Grace's room. Didn't it occur to you it was all her doing? Are you pleased with yourselves for getting a fellow worker into so much trouble?"

"We did no such thing." The tray was heavy and Nell sidestepped into Mrs Scott's room while her eyes remained fixed on Lilly. "Forgive me, Mrs Scott. I won't be long."

"Take your time, dearie. And leave the door open."

Nell followed Lilly, who had begun the walk to her room. "Who told you that?"

The girl shrugged. "Everyone knows about it."

"The passengers don't. Who've you been talking to?"

"What does it matter? Thanks to you, I've had to give up my cabin and move up here with that little flirt Grace."

"She's no such thing." Nell fought the urge to knock the sneer from Lilly's lips.

"Why else would anyone be interested in her? I'd seen her smiling at the crew before all this happened. What are they supposed to think?"

Nell gasped as Mrs Swift joined her. "Didn't it cross anyone's mind she was being friendly?"

Lilly snorted. "As if they'd do that. If you want nothing to do with them, you keep your head down. Otherwise, you've no one but yourself to blame."

Nell's mouth dropped open as Lilly disappeared down the corridor. "How could she say such a thing?"

Mrs Swift glared after her. "I've no idea, but I'd say she's the flirt around here, not Grace."

"Why?"

"Well, we've seen how she is with Mr Barker and she's obviously been talking to one of the stewards. Besides, why else would she be so keen to have her own cabin if it wasn't to do a spot of *entertaining*."

"You don't mean...?" Nell put a hand to her mouth.

Mrs Swift nodded. "It makes sense to me."

"And me." Mrs Scott stepped out from the doorway.

"Oh, I'm so sorry, madam." Nell ushered her back into the room. "Please come in and I'll pour your tea."

"Oh, don't worry about me. It makes a change." There was a twinkle in Mrs Scott's eyes. "I don't know what's going on, but I saw that maid talking to Mr Barker last night.

Well, I say talking, it was a rather heated argument, actually."

Mrs Swift raised an eyebrow. "We thought they got along rather well."

Nell shrugged. "They could have fallen out when he told her she had to move rooms."

"It may have been that, but somehow I don't think so." Mrs Scott took a seat on her settee. "He looked more like a spurned lover."

"Mrs Scott!" Nell put a hand over her mouth, but sniggered at the expression on the older woman's face.

"Just because I'm past my first flush of youth, doesn't mean I wasn't young once. I'll keep an eye on her for you, if you'd like."

"Can you do that from here?"

"I can stroll the corridors. You'd be surprised what you see when you're not expecting it."

"If you don't mind."

Mrs Scott grinned. "I'd be delighted."

The dining room was filling up by the time Nell and Mrs Swift returned, and as Nell strode to the galley, the captain beckoned her over.

Nell hesitated as she approached the table. "May I help?"

"I'm sorry to disturb you when you're busy, but Officer Hughes and I were wondering if there's a reason so few women come downstairs for breakfast."

Nell glanced at the rows of gentlemen sitting on either side of a long trestle table. "I'm afraid I can't say. There are usually more than this. Maybe they had a late night, last night."

"Yes, perhaps. Thank you, Mrs Riley."

Nell left the table and went to the galley, her forehead creased.

"What was that about?" Mrs Swift looked up from the list of those still requiring breakfast.

"I don't really know. He was interested in the lack of women having breakfast."

"It's probably because they all saw Officer Hughes in the dining room, and went straight back to their rooms."

Nell laughed. "He was very sheepish when I was at the table. Maybe the captain had a word with him."

"Let's hope so." Mrs Swift picked up a tray. "Mrs Barker asked for a tray this morning, too. I wondered if you'd like to take it."

"Oh, yes, please. With any luck, Lilly will be in there. Let's see what she's got to say for herself in front of Mrs Barker."

Lilly was brushing Mrs Barker's hair in front of the dressing table when Nell let herself into the stateroom.

"Good morning, Mrs Barker. It's not like you to take breakfast in your room."

"I've a bad head and thought having something here would help."

"I'm sorry. Shall I ask Matron to call?"

"Not at the moment. I'll send Lilly for her later if need be."

"Very well. Would you like me to pour?" Nell indicated to the teapot.

"Yes, please. Lilly's rather preoccupied this morning."

"Changing cabins partway through the voyage must have taken its toll." Nell smirked at Lilly as she handed Mrs Barker her tea.

"I'm not entirely sure why she changed rooms in the first place." Mrs Barker tutted as Lilly yanked on a knot in her hair.

"Be careful, girl. You'll have this tea all over me."

Lilly's pout worsened. "Begging your pardon, madam."

Nell bit on her lip. "At least you still have a maid. Lady Annabel's having to muddle through without hers."

"Seasickness, isn't it?" Mrs Barker took a sip of her tea.

"So I believe, the poor girl." Nell raised an eyebrow at Lilly. "Perhaps having company will help her."

"I doubt..." Lilly scowled at Nell. "I don't know that it will. She wants to be on her own and I can't say I blame her. I would too, if I looked as wretched as she does."

"At least you can try to make her feel better." Nell flashed her a smile. "I'll see you both later."

As the evening ended, a sudden roll of the ship caused the crockery to rattle in the galley. Nell reached out to grab the back of a chair and looked up to the skylight as large droplets of rain pelted the glass.

"It looks like we'll get wet tonight."

"Again. At least it may keep Mr Ramsbottom inside."

"You're right. He won't go out in this. Perhaps we should hope for rain every evening."

Mrs Swift gave Nell a wry smile. "There's a good chance of that. Have you got much to do?"

"No, I've spoken to Lady Annabel and persuaded her she can put herself to bed. Once we've set these tables for breakfast, we should be able to go."

"Splendid...."

"Good evening, ladies." Captain Robertson smiled down at her.

They both stopped what they were doing.

"Good evening, Captain." Nell wiped her hands on her apron. "Did you have a pleasant dinner?"

"I did, thank you, and I heard a lot about you from Mrs Scott. She's very taken with you."

Nell's cheeks coloured. "That's very nice of her to say."

"I didn't realise your husband had been a master mariner. What was his name?"

Nell lowered her gaze. "Jack. Jack Riley."

The captain put a finger to his chin. "I used to know a Jack Riley. Not that he was a master mariner. I sailed to China with him, taught him all he needed to know to be a first mate."

Nell lifted her head. "When was that?"

"Now you're asking. It must be at least ten years ago. Yes, it was, because we were stranded in Hong Kong by the typhoon of 1881."

"That was him." Nell's voice was low. "We were married when he came home from that voyage."

"That's right." Captain Robertson rubbed his hand across

his beard. "He told us he was giving up the sea, but the captain and I always thought he'd be back. He was a true seaman. So, he made master mariner, did he? Which ship was he on?"

"He didn't actually get to be a captain. He was on his way home to take over a ship, but he was first mate on the *Flechero* when it ran aground off Mizen Head."

"Mizen Head? That wasn't long ago, was it?" The captain put a hand to his head.

"Last February." Nell wiped a tear that had spilled onto her cheek.

"I'm sorry, I'd no idea."

Nell reached for her handkerchief. "You had no reason to."

"Come on, don't upset yourself." Mrs Swift put a hand on Nell's arm. "We're almost done here. Would you excuse us, Captain?"

"Actually, no. Let me walk you back to your quarters. I wanted to talk to you about what happened last night..."

"You heard?" Nell's eyes were wide.

"You can't keep things quiet on a ship like this, but I'm afraid I only found out about an hour ago. Are you both all right?"

Nell glanced at Mrs Swift. "We are now, thank you."

"Well, I want you to know I'll be speaking to the stewards involved. I don't want it happening again."

"Will you make sure they know it wasn't us who reported them?" Nell's voice tremored. "We don't want them blaming us."

"I shall tell them I was informed by one of the passengers, which I was."

"Oh, thank you, Captain." Nell let out a loud sigh as he rested a hand on her shoulder.

"I've dealt with issues like this before. Now, let's get you safely over to the other side." He led them up the stairs and offered them their cloaks. "It's a shocking night, tonight. You really shouldn't have to go out in such weather."

"There's no other way, unless we go through the engine room." Mrs Swift pulled on her hood.

"No, I'm sorry about that. I must look into it." The captain opened the door, and the three of them raced across the deck. "There we are. At least it's done for another night."

He closed the door behind them as Mrs Swift led them down the stairs.

"It's not far now. We call into the galley to tell Mr Potter we're back and he sorts us out with something to eat."

"Splendid. Perhaps I'll stop and have a word with him before I head back."

Nell stacked the empty plates and bowls in the middle of the table and relaxed into her chair, her hands on her lap.

"That was one of the strangest days."

"You're telling me." Mrs Swift topped up their cups. "I've never known the captain to dine with us so often, certainly not talking to the staff. Normally, once he's said farewell to the guests who've joined him in the evening, he disappears to the bridge."

"Could it be because of what happened yesterday?"

"I would say so. I don't believe it's a coincidence that Mr

and Mrs Scott were on the captain's table tonight either. He'll have known you've been seeing to her."

Nell's forehead creased. "I wonder why he didn't say anything."

"It's not the sort of thing you talk about, is it?"

"Not usually, but yesterday wasn't usual. He'd obviously heard about the incident last night, too. And why have breakfast with the third mate?"

Mrs Swift picked up her cup. "I've a feeling there was a reason for it, even though we don't know what it is. How strange that he sailed with your late husband, too."

Nell shuddered. "I probably should be mad at him. If he was the one who encouraged Jack to take his first-mate exams, although none of us could have known what would happen... What was that?" She froze at the sound of a door closing outside.

"Not again." Mrs Swift stared at her, but a second later, Matron appeared through the door.

"Oh, Matron, you gave us quite a turn." Nell put a hand to her chest. "You're out late tonight."

Matron took a seat opposite her. "I had to speak to the captain. He's been very concerned about all the goings-on this last couple of days."

Mrs Swift nodded. "We've just been talking about that. He was in the dining room for breakfast, luncheon and dinner."

"I think he's satisfied it's been sorted out."

"Oh good." Nell relaxed back into the seat. "Will anything happen to Officer Hughes?"

"Officer Hughes?" Lines creased Matron's forehead and Nell glanced at Mrs Swift.

"Wasn't he the one who caused the trouble with Grace?"

"No ... not at all, but rest assured, he won't be rude to you again."

Mrs Swift raised her eyebrows. "At least that's something."

"May I ask how Grace is?"

"She'll be right as rain as soon as she gets off the ship." Matron stood up and peered out of the door. "Sorry, I'm waiting for Mr Potter to bring me a tray. He should be here in a minute. Ah, are those footsteps?" She stepped out of the door. "Yes, here we are. Thank you, Mr Potter."

Nell waited for him to leave. "Does that mean she isn't all right at the moment?"

"She's feeling a little sheepish, but she's learned her lesson about being a tease. Now, let me eat this and then it's time for bed. It's been a busy day."

CHAPTER ELEVEN

N ell hurried to deliver the last of the dirty breakfast dishes to the galley before stopping to collect Mrs Swift.

"Are you coming? You'll miss it if you're not quick."

"I won't miss anything. Once we see land, it will be with us until we arrive in New York. Besides, I've seen it plenty of times."

"But it's America."

Mrs Swift chuckled. "It isn't actually, it's Newfoundland, but you go. I'll finish here."

Nell raced up the stairs, grabbed her cloak and hurried out onto the top deck. When she arrived, most of the passengers were already gathered, staring at a barely visible grey outline in the distance as one of the deckhands pointed to the land.

"It will be another couple of hours before we can see it properly, but by the time we all go to bed tonight, we'll be in touching distance of the United States of America."

The passengers gasped, and Nell watched their smiling faces. *If only Jack were here, or even James.*

"Don't look so nervous." Mrs Scott squeezed in beside her while Mr Scott stayed close behind.

"I didn't mean to. I was thinking how nice it would be to have someone to share the moment with."

"Then you must share it with us." Mrs Scott linked her arm. "I never tire of this view. You can't see it yet, but seeing the snowy hills and rocks for the first time is special."

Nell shuddered. "I'm sure it is, although I can't stand here waiting for it to arrive. Perhaps I'll come back after morning coffee."

Mrs Scott patted her hand. "It's such a shame you need to work, but we should be close enough to land by midday. I'm going to do the same as you. It's too cold to stay out here."

Once Nell had escorted the Scotts to the saloon and offered them a hot drink, she hurried back to the dining room. *At least it gives the impression I've been working.* Mrs Swift looked up when she arrived.

"Are we nearly there?"

"Not yet; you were right not to hurry. I had to squint to get a glimpse of anything."

Mrs Swift laughed. "I remember doing that on my first voyage. I'll walk out with you after luncheon."

"Oh." Nell put a hand to her mouth. "I offered to go back outside with Mr and Mrs Scott."

"You can go twice then." Mrs Swift smiled. "They really seem to have taken to you."

"I know. They're like the parents I never had. I'm

hoping to ask her if she's seen anything of Lilly, too. It's all gone rather quiet."

"I thought about her earlier. Maybe she's been told to stay in her room."

"She'd still have to call on Mrs Barker, though." Nell glanced around the room, happy the stewards were paying them no attention. "Are you nearly ready to tidy upstairs? We can have a snoop around before we start."

"Yes, why not. Nobody will miss us."

Lady Annabel was in her room when Nell let herself in.

"Oh, excuse me, Your Ladyship. I didn't expect you to be here."

"I'm running late. Let me get out of your way."

"I can come back if you'd prefer…"

"No, not at all. The truth is, I sent a note asking Grace to call, but she hasn't."

"If you don't mind me asking, who did you send the note with? I could have taken it for you."

"I saw the Barkers' maid leaving their room earlier and asked her to take it."

"Hmm."

"Did I do the wrong thing?"

"I'm sure it's not for me to say, but well … I wouldn't be surprised if your note didn't get delivered."

Lady Annabel shot Nell a glance. "Why wouldn't it be?"

"Lilly's annoyed about moving back in with Grace. She may not feel like doing her any favours."

Lady Annabel's brow creased. "She's in with Grace? She didn't say. She even asked me which room she was in."

"That's strange." Nell wandered to the bed and began straightening the sheets. "Might I make a suggestion? If you write Grace another note, I'll deliver it for you."

Lady Annabel nodded. "Very well. I don't have time now, but it will be ready for luncheon."

Nell held the door as Lady Annabel swept out, but stopped when a shape appeared from the other end of the corridor.

"Grace?"

The young girl's frame appeared more fragile than ever. "Is Lady Annabel in there?"

Nell stepped out to meet her and ushered her into the stateroom. "You've just missed her. She thought you weren't coming. If you'd like to wait here, I'll get her for you."

Grace looked down at her hands as she twisted her fingers. "Do you know why she asked to see me?"

"Not exactly, but I imagine she wants to know how you are." Nell offered her a chair. "Are you feeling better?"

Grace shrugged. "What do you think when everyone's talking about me? I won't be able to face anyone again."

"Nobody's talking about you."

"But Lilly said…"

Nell took a deep breath. "Take no notice of Lilly. She doesn't know what people are talking about."

"She said Mrs Barker told her."

"Listen, I've spoken to Mrs Barker and I don't believe she's any idea what's going on, other than her maid is sulking because she couldn't stay in her single room. If you want my opinion, I'd say Lilly's become rather friendly with one or more of the stewards, and that's where she's getting her information."

"So they all know?" Grace's eyes widened.

"I doubt they know any details. Earlier in the week Mrs Swift and I were in trouble when they thought we'd reported the officer responsible."

"The officer?" A frown settled on Grace's face.

"The one who ... you know..."

"It wasn't an officer, it was a steward."

Nell's mouth fell open. "Really? Then I've no idea what happened. Mrs Swift had told Matron that one of the officers was being rude, and we were led to believe that he was the one who overpowered you."

"No! It was nothing like that." Grace's head shot up. "The man in question came looking for Lilly, and when I told him she'd moved to another cabin, he pushed his way in and shut the door. He didn't do anything though. You have to believe me. I wouldn't..."

"I'm sure you wouldn't, not deliberately anyway, but how did you get rid of him?"

"He kept coming closer and I backed away, but as he pinned me against the frame of the bunk, Lilly walked in on us. She was so angry. I can still hear her shouting, but when she fled, he chased after her."

Nell studied the maid. "So the steward was looking for her, but when he couldn't find her, he turned his attention to you? She won't have liked that."

"She didn't. The next time I saw her she called me all manner of horrible names and then said that the whole ship thought I was a flirt." Tears welled in her eyes. "I didn't know what to do..."

Nell took a seat beside her on the settee. "So she was the one who started the rumours? Unfortunately for us, Mrs Swift reported Officer Hughes for being rude at the same time, which is how we were dragged into it."

"Did you get into trouble?"

"It wasn't pleasant, but the worst is over." Nell studied Grace. "Have you told any of this to Lady Annabel?"

"I've not seen her, but the note said she wanted to speak to me."

"It did. You wait here and I'll go and fetch her."

Once Lady Annabel was back in her stateroom, Nell hurried to service the remaining rooms, deliberately leaving the Scotts' room until last. *At least I'll know when they come back for their coats.* She was positioning some clean towels by the washstand when the door opened and Mrs Scott joined her.

"Have you nearly finished?"

"I have." Nell smiled. "Are you ready to go out on deck?"

"We are. I love this part of the journey." Mrs Scott watched as Nell tidied away her cleaning cloths and hurried to get her cloak from the cupboard. Mr Scott held open the outside door, letting in a gust of icy air.

"I won't be staying out for too long in this cold." Mrs Scott shuddered as she moved towards the front of the ship. "Look at that view, though."

There was a swirl of fog hanging over the rocky, snow-covered landscape, but with the sun shining, the sea dazzled despite the freezing temperatures. It was like nothing Nell had ever seen, and even Liverpool hadn't prepared her for the noise of gulls and other birds circling overhead.

"What are they doing? It's as if they're looking for something."

Mr Scott pointed to the sea. "Look down there. Dolphins."

Nell's mouth dropped open. "Really? They're so elegant."

"They must be after some fish, which is why the birds are above."

Nell put her hands to her head. "It's beyond anything I could have imagined. Jack never told me about this."

"If most of his travels were to China, it would have been different." She pointed to a large white mass in the distance. "There'd be no icebergs for one thing."

Nell stared at it. "What is it?"

"Nothing more than ice that's broken away from the land."

"But it's enormous."

"That's only part of it. Most is under the sea. As it floats south, it will warm up and break into smaller pieces. They can be dangerous if you're not careful. If a ship hits one, it can cause a lot of damage."

"I can imagine. Thank goodness it's a long way away." Nell pulled her cloak more tightly around her and wrapped her hands in the material to keep them warm.

"Would you like to go back indoors? It is rather cold."

"May I have another few minutes? I'd like to take it all in while I have the chance."

As the layer of fog over the hills thickened again, the

passengers made their way inside. Nell was about to follow Mr and Mrs Scott when a voice called her back.

"I didn't realise you were now a passenger, Mrs Riley." Mr Driver stood behind her, his hands thrust into the deep pockets of his woollen coat.

"No, I-I'm not..." She glanced at a group of three stewards standing on the far side of the deck. "I, erm..."

"She escorted us up here." Mr Scott stepped forward and put himself between Nell and the head steward. "My wife needed some help."

"Y-yes. I was about to take them to the dining room."

Mr Driver glared at her. "See that you're quick, then. Luncheon has started."

"Yes, sir." She ushered Mr and Mrs Scott to the door, conscious of Mr Driver's eyes boring into the back of her. She walked them to their table, checking Mr Driver hadn't followed them. "Thank you, Mr Scott. I'm not his favourite person at the moment."

"Well, if you have any trouble with him, tell me."

"Yes, sir, I will. I'll see you later."

CHAPTER TWELVE

S tepping out onto the deck each morning had taken on a fresh excitement. The land continued to glide by as the ship followed the coast, but it was changing. Gone were the hills and rocks of Newfoundland, along with much of the snow; instead, the landscape had flattened, and fields appeared. Each day brought them closer to New York, and Nell struggled to keep the smile from her face as she stood by the railings, marvelling at the houses dotted near the shore.

"Will we really be there by this time tomorrow?"

"Not quite, but nearly." Mrs Swift grinned. "I told you, we'll be there when most of the passengers wake, but not at this hour."

"Do you think they'll let us off the ship?"

"I doubt it, especially after what happened last week. They'll keep us here as a punishment."

"It's so unfair..."

"I wouldn't worry about it. I'd rather get off in the

summer; it's too cold now." Mrs Swift pointed to the shore. "There are still signs of snow."

"I suppose so, but I wasn't planning on coming again."

"You're serious, then? The captain won't be pleased."

"He may not be, but once we're back to Liverpool, I'll tell him why. We shouldn't have to put up with being treated like we were last week."

"I can't argue with you, but you're fortunate you don't need the money."

"Oh, I do, but I'll have to get a job in Liverpool instead, and hope my brother-in-law and nephew have found themselves jobs by the time I get home."

"That would help." Mrs Swift linked her arm. "Come on, let's go in."

"Wait a moment." Nell stopped and nodded to the other side of the deck where the men they'd decided were spies stood by the railings. "What are they doing out so early?"

"They'll be up to no good, I shouldn't wonder."

"Is that a telescope they're looking through?"

Mrs Swift stared at them. "I'm not sure; it looks more like two telescopes stuck together."

Nell followed the direction of their attention. "They seem to be studying the houses. Could they be planning a robbery? That may explain why they've huddled together so much. Should we tell someone?"

"What would we say? We can't be sure that's what they're doing, and besides, what could anyone do? We're still a day away from New York; those houses could be anywhere."

"I hadn't thought of that."

"Oh, look, they're coming. We'd better go." Mrs Swift led the way to the galley, where Mr Ross was waiting for them.

"Good morning, ladies. Welcome to the last day of normal service."

"Is it?" Nell raised her eyebrows.

Mrs Swift nodded. "We have to get everyone off the ship by ten o'clock tomorrow morning. The first-class passengers can leave from eight, so they don't have time for a full breakfast. There are no trays either."

"That will make a change. Do they already know or do we need to tell them?"

"They should know, but there's no harm mentioning it."

"Very good. Shall we get started?"

Lady Annabel was waiting on the settee when Nell arrived with her tray.

"Good morning, my lady."

"Mrs Riley."

"Will you need any help packing today or will Grace be assisting you?"

"I've persuaded Grace to join me. She's feeling a little better, and I told her this is the last day. After tomorrow, she won't see any of this crew again."

"That's very true, although what about the return journey? Are you on a different schedule?"

"We're changing shipping line. We only came on the *Wisconsin* as a favour to Mr Guion. He wanted to advertise that lords and ladies travel with the Guion Line, but we'll travel back with Cunard. If I'm being honest, they are better."

"That's a shame, although I can't say I blame you."

"No, it's all been very unfortunate, for you as well, I imagine."

"It's not been the best of experiences, but I'll put it behind me. At least I'll get to see New York from the ship, and then after that, I don't know. I may stay in Liverpool."

"For what it's worth, it's been very helpful having you with us, particularly after what happened to Grace. I'm sure I'll see you before we leave."

Nell smiled. "You will indeed. Don't forget, there are no breakfast trays in the morning. You'll start disembarking from eight o'clock."

"Yes, of course. We already have breakfast booked in the Fifth Avenue Hotel. It's rather a drive, but well worth it."

"That sounds wonderful. Will you stay long?"

"Two months. Lord Faulkner has work to do and so he may as well get it all done while we're here. We need to take time to explore the city, too. Have you been to Central Park? It really is splendid."

"No, I'm afraid I've not. Maybe one day."

"Yes, of course. I wasn't thinking." Lady Annabel lifted the lid covering her kippers. "Right, well, I'd better eat these before they go cold. I'll be out of the room by ten o'clock if you'd like to come back then."

Nell pulled the door closed behind her, but stopped as she spotted Lilly walking towards her.

"Good morning, Lilly."

Lilly said nothing as a scowl grew on her face.

"I imagine you've a busy day ahead, packing for Mrs Barker."

"What does it matter to you?"

"I'm sure it doesn't; I'm just trying to be polite. You should try it sometime."

"Why would I be courteous to you?"

Nell crossed her arms over her chest. "May I ask what I've done to upset you? If anyone should be angry, it's me."

"You? You were the one who had me moved back to share with that little…"

"I did no such thing, and she's nothing of the sort. I got into a lot of trouble because of your tantrum. Why did you have to tell lies to the entire crew?"

"She asked for it."

"No, she didn't. If you hadn't encouraged Mr Ramsbottom, none of this would have happened."

"Mr Ramsbottom? You don't think I'd encourage a scoundrel like him."

Nell stared at her. "It wasn't him? Who was it, then?"

Lilly laughed and pushed her way past. "I'm hardly likely to tell you. Why don't you ask your little friend?"

Nell's mouth fell open as Lilly darted into the Barkers' stateroom. *If it wasn't Mr Ramsbottom, who was it?* She shook her head. *I've no idea.*

Breakfast was well under way when she returned to the dining room, and Mr Scott called her over.

"Good morning, my dear. Are you all ready to see New York tomorrow?"

"I am." Nell clapped her hands together. "It's the whole reason I came, although I doubt I'll be getting off the ship. I imagine you're looking forward to seeing your family."

"Indeed; although I'll be equally pleased to get home again. Don't you find it's lovely to see people, but it's nice to leave again."

Nell laughed. "I do. Whoever said that absence makes the heart grow fonder knew what they were talking about. Now, please excuse me, I need to deliver Mrs Scott's tray."

"Yes, of course. She'd like you to help with her packing, too, but before you go, here's a little something for looking after Mrs Scott so well. I may not get the chance to give it to you without her being with us."

Nell glanced down at the gold sovereign he thrust into her hand. "Mr Scott. What can I say? Thank you so much."

He patted her shoulder. "You're welcome. I hear you have two little girls at home, so I imagine you could do with it."

"Oh, yes, sir. I've promised them each a new dress, but I'll be able to do so much more, now." She tucked the money into the pocket of her apron. "Thank you, again. I'll see you later."

Mrs Scott was staring down at the trunk on the ottoman when Nell carried her tray in.

"I see you're ready for packing."

"Oh, Mrs Riley. I don't know where to start. My mind gets so confused about which dresses to put where."

"Not to worry. I bumped into Mr Scott and he mentioned you'd like some help. I need to be in the dining room until breakfast is over, but I'll be back as soon as I'm free."

Mrs Scott's watery blue eyes sparkled. "Oh, I am relieved. That means I can eat my breakfast in peace."

Nell was about to open the door when Mrs Scott called her back. "Before you go, I had a bit of gossip to tell you."

"Really? That sounds exciting."

"I'm not sure if it is or not, but it's to do with that young maid, Lilly."

Nell raised her eyebrows. "That's even better."

"Mr Scott and I were late walking back to our room last night, and we saw her sneaking outside with one of the stewards." Mrs Scott paused. "Mr Driver, if you like."

"No!" Nell put a hand to her mouth. "That explains so much. Oh, Mrs Scott, well done."

She chuckled. "I can't take all the credit for it. It was me who saw them leaving, but Mr Scott told me the man's name. I've had nothing to do with him."

"Well, you wouldn't, but he was the one who gave me and Mrs Swift a dressing- down for complaining to the captain. He must have been worried."

"Possibly." She sat down and lifted the lid from her porridge. "A word of advice, though, if you don't mind. Store the information away and keep it to yourself for the time being. You never know when you might need it."

"Oh." Nell's shoulders dropped. "Would it be all right if I tell Mrs Swift?"

"Yes, of course. I mean, you shouldn't confront him about it without reason. It will be more useful to you that way."

Nell pursed her lips as she opened the door. "What a marvellous idea. I'll be back in about an hour. Enjoy your breakfast."

.   .   .

Mrs Swift was clearing the tables when Nell rejoined her.

"What are you looking so pleased about?"

"Where to begin?" Nell grinned. "It's been a good start to the day, as it happens, although I'd better not tell you about it here." She stopped and glanced over her shoulders. "Too many ears listening."

"Go and do those tables over there, and we can go out on deck before we start on the staterooms. I need some cheering up."

Mrs Swift was standing by the railings, gazing out at the ever-flattening landscape, when Nell joined her.

"We seem to be getting further away from the land here."

"We are, but there are a couple of islands coming up that we need to avoid. We'll have to hope we can sneak out later to get a better view of Long Island."

"I'm sure we'll be able to, if we plan it right, but even if we don't, we needn't worry about Mr Driver mistreating us any more."

"Why?"

Nell leaned forward and kept her voice low. "Because he's Lilly's mystery man."

"No!"

Nell nodded. "Mrs Scott saw them going onto the deck last night when most of the guests were in bed."

"Well, I never. Does that mean he's Grace's attacker too?"

"I haven't asked her but it would make sense. And..." Nell felt a tingle down her spine. "...who was Mr Barker most likely to speak to when he wanted a single cabin for Lilly?"

"Mr Driver."

"Exactly. He'd have known all along that the two of them were in separate rooms."

"Good grief, you're right. It would explain why he was so determined to stop us speaking to the officers."

"Mrs Scott suggested we say nothing for now, but if he causes us any more trouble, we can let him know we're aware of what he's been up to."

Mrs Swift's eyes narrowed. "I would say it's better to confront him while Lilly's on the ship. Once she leaves, he can deny everything."

Nell stared out to sea as waves broke against a nearby coastline. "I hadn't thought of that, although what if he makes a habit of it? We could keep an eye on him on the way back in case he attaches himself to someone else."

"I'd rather not leave it to chance. We need to work this to our advantage. Let me think about it."

Nell breathed a sigh of relief as the last of the guests left the saloon following afternoon tea.

"Nice and early, today."

Mrs Swift smiled. "If they've not gone onto the deck, they'll be doing their last bits of packing and getting ready for an early dinner tonight. For many of them, it's an early start in the morning, so they won't want to be late to bed."

"I'm not sure it would matter. If it were me, I'd be awake for half the night knowing I was going into New York tomorrow." Nell sighed. "Some people don't know how fortunate they are."

"There's no point moaning about it. The closest we're likely to get is seeing it from the ship, so if we're quick tidying up here, we can go outside and catch a glimpse of Long Island before dark."

"I'm going as fast as I can." Nell glanced around her. "Where have all the stewards disappeared to? There are a couple of tablecloths need changing and they've not done them."

Mrs Swift shook her head. "They're probably on the deck already. Why don't we change them quickly?"

"Imagine the fuss if we'd done that." Nell pulled a cloth from the table but stopped as a slip of paper fell to the floor. "What's this?"

Mrs Swift arrived and peered over her shoulder. "That could be what we've been wondering about. The spies were sitting here and one of them pushed something under the cloth when a steward called to serve them. They must have forgotten it."

Nell turned the paper over in her hands. "It doesn't say much. New York in one column and Chicago in another. There's writing underneath but I don't understand it."

Mrs Swift took it from her. "Let me have a look." She shook her head and handed it back to Nell. "I've heard that a lot of immigrants go to Chicago. Perhaps that's what they've been doing all this time. Working out where to live when they arrive."

Nell groaned. "Do you really think so, after all our guessing?"

Mrs Swift chuckled. "It looks like we got the wrong end of the stick. Never mind, it was fun while it lasted."

"It was. It helped to pass the time..." Nell's sentence was cut short when Mr Driver appeared from the galley. "What are you two doing, still here? A little less talking and you'd be finished quicker."

"Yes, sir."

"The guests will be in the dining room shortly." He didn't stop as he swept past them.

"Miserable thing." Mrs Swift pulled a face after him. "Perhaps he should help out himself."

"To be honest, I'd rather he didn't. It's better when he's not around."

"That's true." Mrs Swift wiped her hands on a cloth. "That's us done. Shall we nip outside before anyone notices?"

The late afternoon sun was setting over the starboard side of the ship as they stepped onto the deck, and shafts of light broke through the heavy grey clouds, dazzling them as they walked to the railings.

"What a lovely evening. And the land is back." Nell studied the fields of crops. "I wonder what they're growing."

Mrs Swift shrugged, but paused as they both heard a noise. "What was that?"

"I don't know. Is it someone talking?"

"It may be some steerage passengers not yet gone for dinner. Not that I can see anyone."

They both scanned the deck as the voices grew louder.

"I thought you wanted me."

A man's voice.

"Well, you thought wrong. You said you needed to talk to me ... not this."

Mrs Swift gave Nell a sideways glance. "Shall we carry on walking?"

They headed along the promenade towards the back of the ship, but slowed as they approached the last lifeboat.

"Get off me."

"No, Lilly, please. I wanted to say I'm sorry... It wasn't my fault you were moved back into the maids' cabin."

"Yes, it was. If you hadn't visited Grace... You knew she'd be on her own..."

"I wouldn't have done it if you hadn't been flirting with every other man on the ship..."

"What's that supposed to mean?"

"It means you used me to get your own way. Just like you use Mr Barker."

"I do no such thing. If he can't take his eyes off me, I might as well make the most of it. Now leave me alone." A second later Lilly appeared from behind the boiler casing, her hair dishevelled and several buttons on her dress unfastened. She stopped and stared at them, but fled as Mr Driver appeared behind her.

"Mr Driver!" Mrs Swift's voice carried over the deck.

His cheeks coloured as he straightened his jacket. "It's not what it looks like." He hurried after Lilly, but Mrs Swift called after him.

"I'd say it's exactly what it looks like. We'll see you tomorrow, *sir*."

CHAPTER THIRTEEN

The sky was still dark as Nell and Mrs Swift stepped out onto the deck the following morning. Away to their right, shafts of light were inching over the horizon, but Nell knew she'd have to wait to get her first glance of the city.

"Come on, no dawdling." Mrs Swift continued along the promenade. "The eager guests will be waiting for us."

"It's funny, but I'll be sorry to see some of them go. You get used to them over the two weeks."

"Some of them will be back, although sadly it's usually those you'd rather not see again."

Nell grimaced. "I'm still not sure that's of any concern to me, but never mind. What do we do this morning?"

"Hopefully, there'll be some teapots waiting for us. Take them around the tables and check if anyone needs anything else."

The room filled up more quickly than Nell expected and she headed to the table where Mr and Mrs Scott were seated. "Are you all ready to go?"

"We are." Mrs Scott dabbed her lips with her napkin. "The trunks have been taken, and we'll be following them soon. I hope you have a better journey home."

"I've a feeling we will." Nell glanced over both shoulders and bent closer to Mrs Scott. "I can't go into detail, but your gossip about Lilly and a certain steward was right. We caught them red-handed, and red-faced, last night."

Mrs Scott clapped her hands as she laughed. "Oh, I am pleased. That should give you an easier time. You'll have to tell me all about it when we come back."

Nell's stomach churned as she bit her lip. "Actually, I may not do another trip."

The smile disappeared from Mrs Scott's lips. "Why not?"

Nell shrugged. "If I'm going to be threatened for doing my job..."

"Listen, my dear." Mr Scott shuffled his chair closer to his wife. "Don't let them bully you. You must tell the captain if anything else happens. He's the one who hires and fires people, not the likes of Mr Driver, and I happen to know he's keeping an eye out for you."

Nell grimaced. "I'll see how things are on the way home."

"I'm sure you'll be fine." He looked up, but stopped at the sight of Lady Annabel waving in their direction. "It looks like you need to go; we'll see you before we leave."

"I hope so." Nell straightened up and crossed the room. "Good morning, madam. Shall I pour you some tea?"

"Yes, please, and for Lord Faulkner. We'd like to thank you for all you've done. It wasn't easy for you."

"You're welcome. At least we know it was Lilly who caused most of the trouble. I'm sure none of us will be sorry to see the back of her."

"No, indeed." Lady Annabel signalled to her husband.

"Oh, yes, righto." He reached into his inside pocket and produced an envelope. "A little something for you. We hope it makes up for the goings-on of this trip."

Nell's smiled broadened as she put it in her apron pocket. "Thank you. Both of you. That's very kind. I hope you have an enjoyable stay in New York. I'm sorry you won't be travelling home with us."

"It's set me back a bob or two changing lines, I can tell you, but not to worry." He leaned towards her. "If you ever want a job with Cunard, mention my name. I'll be happy to vouch for you."

"Thank you, sir. Maybe one day I will."

Mrs Swift was in the galley as Nell went to refill her teapot.

"We need to start clearing the tables and encourage them to leave. The steerage passengers can't disembark until all those in first-class have left."

"No more tea, then?"

"Perhaps one, but warn them before you pour it..."

"Come along, ladies, you've no time to stand around talking." Mr Ramsbottom pushed past Nell.

"Excuse me, but we were here first." Nell glared at him. "You can join the queue."

His mouth dropped as he stared at her. "You can't talk to me like that."

"Why not? You shouldn't come barging in." Nell

squeezed back past him and slid the teapot Mr Ross had placed on the counter to Mrs Swift. "You were here first."

"Thank you, it's nice to see someone has manners. I won't be long."

"You're asking for trouble." Mr Ramsbottom sneered at her.

"Why? Are you going to tell Mr Driver?" She picked up the next teapot and turned to leave. "Try it if you like."

With a feeling of déjà vu, Nell stood in the foyer with Mrs Swift and several stewards as the captain greeted the guests for the final time. It was all she could do to keep her eyes forward, rather than peering through the door to the landscape beyond, but they'd be here for a couple of days. Plenty of time to take in the sights.

"Thank you for travelling with the Guion Line." Captain Robertson spoke with sincerity to each guest, but to some he added that he was looking forward to seeing them on the return journey. Nell noted those who didn't get the second sentence, and wasn't surprised when he gave Lord Faulkner a firm farewell. She guessed he already knew they wouldn't be travelling back.

Lilly scowled as she walked past Nell.

"Goodbye, Lilly. Will you be returning with Mrs Barker?" Nell found her sweetest smile.

"What's it to you?"

"I'm wondering if we'll be able to enjoy your company again."

Lilly scowled, but said nothing as Mrs Barker beckoned her forward to make room for the Scotts.

"Ah, Captain. Thank you for such an enjoyable trip."
Mr Scott shook his hand and gestured to Nell and Mrs
Swift. "You will take care of the ladies for me, won't you?"

The captain nodded. "You have my word."

Mr Scott winked at Nell as he left. "We'll see you in a
month."

With the last of the passengers trudging down the
gangplank, Nell stepped outside and rested her arms on the
rails on the side of the ship.

"I wish I was going with them."

Mrs Swift grinned. "Perhaps you should become a
ladies' maid and travel with them. Lilly certainly enjoyed
herself."

"Are you sure? Lilly always seemed miserable to me.
Besides, I doubt she gets her wages topped up with tips. Did
you get any?"

"I did, and judging by the look on your face, you did,
too. How much did you get?"

Nell reached for the envelope Lord Faulkner had given
her. "I've not counted it all up yet, but the Scotts and
Faulkners both gave me a gold sovereign." She peered into
the envelope. "Goodness, I've a few crown coins, too. There
must be about three pounds here." Her smile almost split
her face. "I've never had so much before. Not all to myself,
anyway."

"You did well. I got closer to two. I'll have to look after
the aristocracy on the next trip."

Nell laughed. "It makes a difference earning some real
money. I've finally remembered why I'm here."

"So you've changed your mind about doing another voyage?"

"I'm not sure about that." She gazed back over the low-level buildings near the harbour entrance. "It would still be nice to see New York."

"You mean, you're not content with the docks."

"James warned me it wasn't very exciting, but said it's much nicer when you go further inland. I wish we could get off the ship."

"Who would we walk with?"

Nell cocked her head to one side. "I hadn't thought of that. I'm used to walking by myself at home."

"Exactly, but we couldn't do that here, and I doubt any of the stewards would want to chaperone us."

"You're right. Even if we asked them to." Nell sighed. "There's always an obstacle to everything."

The staterooms needed cleaning from top to bottom, but with no guests on board, Nell took the time to admire the fine decor.

The two single beds filled most of one end of the stateroom, while an ottoman stood at the foot of the bed. On the opposite side of the room was a dark green settee with a highly polished walnut writing desk with a matching chair beside it. A washstand was placed discreetly beside a console table.

Nell sat down and pulled on the small key in the front of the desk. *Writing paper and postcards.* She picked up a blank postcard. *Should I write one to send home?* Reaching for the elegant fountain pen that sat on a ridge within the desk, she positioned it in her fingers. She'd never written with anything so fancy. *What if I damage it?* She put the pen and postcard down again. *There's no point, anyway. It would only arrive at the same time as me. This is probably the next mail ship back to Liverpool.*

She'd no sooner closed the door on the desk when footsteps in the corridor made her jump to her feet with her duster in hand.

"Are you still in there?"

Nell looked up as Mrs Swift joined her. "I was admiring the writing desk. Imagine having the money to stay in one of these."

"You wouldn't like it." Mrs Swift scowled. "The likes of us don't sit round all day doing nothing."

"You're right, but I'd still like to try." Nell polished her fingermarks from the wood. "Did you want me for anything?"

"Yes, it's time for a break. They put tea and biscuits on for us in the dining room when there are no passengers."

"Oh, very nice. I've nearly finished in here. I can sweep the floor later."

One of the long tables to the left of the door was occupied by the stewards, and Nell hesitated as they walked in.

"Where shall we sit? Should we go into the ladies' section?"

"No, that will all be clean. We may as well start a new table here. I'll fetch a pot of tea."

"Wait for me." Nell scurried after her as a dozen pairs of eyes watched them. "I'll get the biscuits."

Mr Ross was nowhere to be seen when they reached the galley and Mrs Swift picked up the kettle.

"They've used all the water. I'll have to boil it again."

"I can't say I'm sorry. I thought it would be nice to sit in here, but with no passengers, it suddenly feels frightening."

"You noticed it? I thought it was just me."

"No." Nell peered around the corner of the door, back into the dining room. "Mr Driver isn't with them. Do you think that's why they're behaving like that?"

"Possibly, although I doubt he'd do anything to stop them."

"You're probably right." Nell jumped as a door closed behind them.

"Good morning, ladies." Mr Ross appeared from around a corner, the front of his dark brown hair falling over one eye. "I'd forgotten you'd be joining us. I'm sorry about that."

"Not to worry." Mrs Swift gave a weak smile. "We were obviously a few minutes after the stewards. The kettle's nearly boiled now."

He handed Nell a plate of biscuits. "You take them and I'll bring the tea as soon as it's ready. Help yourselves to a cup and saucer on your way out."

The room fell silent as the two of them walked from the galley back to the empty table.

"Aren't you joining us, ladies?" Mr Ramsbottom smirked as the rest of the stewards laughed.

"Thank you for asking, but we wouldn't want to spoil your fun." There was steel in Mrs Swift's voice.

"We could always make room. You could squeeze in here by me. One of you on each side."

The men around the table laughed again, but fell quiet as Mr Ross appeared.

"Leave them alone, lads. This is supposed to be a respectable ship."

"We are respectable." Mr Ramsbottom's mouth dropped open as he feigned his innocence.

"Well, see you keep it that way." Mr Ross put the teapot on the table in front of Mrs Swift. "Do you mind if I join you? It might help."

"Please do. I don't know what's got into them."

Nell watched her friend pour the milk into the cups. "What did you do last year when you were on your own? It must have been awful."

Mrs Swift shrugged. "I ignored most of it. There wasn't much else to do. I spent as much time as I could with Matron, although she's always busy."

"I don't know how you do it." Mr Ross poured out the tea. "It's not right that you have to work on a ship."

"It's not the working that's the problem. We both enjoy meeting the passengers..."

Nell nodded. "Or most of them, at least."

"And we need the money. Like everyone else, I imagine."

Mr Ross looked up as the dining room door opened and Mr Driver strode in with Mr Price.

"Good morning, gentlemen." Mr Ross jumped to his feet. "There's a fresh pot of tea here if you'd like to join us. I'll fetch some cups and saucers."

Mr Driver hesitated. "I ... erm..." He glanced to the table beyond them and then to the empty tables in the middle of the room. "Mr Price and I need to talk. Please excuse us."

"As you like."

Mrs Swift watched them leave. "He can't even bring himself to talk to us."

Nell raised an eyebrow. "Are you surprised?"

"Not exactly, but an apology would be nice."

She snorted. "It will take something very serious before we get one of them."

CHAPTER FOURTEEN

N ell stood by the white enamel bathtub set in the middle of the tiled bathroom, mesmerised by the steam rising from it. She'd never had a fresh bath to herself before. She was usually way down the list when it came to bath night, and it was nothing but a time to get clean. This was different. She placed the new bar of soap on the side and stepped in, sinking into the water. *Oh, that's nice.*

She lay against the backrest and slid down, but the water splashed over her face and onto the floor as the ship rolled with the waves. *Perhaps not so much next time.* She inched further up the bath, but the warmth of the water and the swaying motion caused her to close her eyes. I could get used to this. Her mind drifted to the old tin bath at home. She had to sit up in that; there was no lying down. A smile flitted to her lips. *Maybe I'm being hasty about not coming on another trip.*

I wonder what the girls are doing now. She had no idea. They'd changed the clocks so many times since leaving

Liverpool, she couldn't even guess what time it was at home. *I wonder if they're missing me. I hope so, but I'll be on my way back tomorrow. Only two weeks to go.* The water lapped around her neck as she adjusted her position, but she paused at the familiar sinking feeling in her stomach. *Have I missed them?* She ran a hand across her face. *Not as much as I should ... but I've not had time. There's been too much to do.*

A knock on the door caused her to jump.

"Are you nearly done in there? Dinner's in half an hour." Mrs Swift sounded impatient.

"I'm sorry, give me five minutes."

Pushing the girls from her mind, she raced to get washed and dressed. Mrs Swift was waiting with her towel as she stepped into the corridor.

"I'm sorry. I've never had such a nice bath. I didn't realise the time."

Mrs Swift scowled. "I'll be in first next time, then. I need to be quick now."

The sun had disappeared and the moon was full when Nell and Mrs Swift headed back across the promenade.

"What a beautiful evening. No clouds." Nell gazed up at the sky. "Look at the moon, and all those stars. I'm sure there are more here than at home."

Mrs Swift followed her gaze. "I've never noticed before. I usually put my head down and make a dash for the other end when I'm on my own. Besides, it's freezing."

Nell touched the frost that had settled on the railings.

"You're right. Come along, we don't want to catch our death." Once inside, she hung her cloak in the cupboard. "What can we expect tonight?"

"We usually get a nice meal, which is why it's worth getting smartened up. Not that we can do much about these uniforms." She pulled on her dress.

"It still feels special having had a bath. If I'd known how nice it would be, I'd have had one sooner."

Mrs Swift laughed. "When? We never get a minute when we have passengers."

"That's true."

They made their way down the main staircase, where the captain and his wife were on the door to greet them.

"Good evening, ladies. I was hoping you'd join us." He gestured to his wife. "This is Mrs Robertson. She'll be joining you and Matron this evening."

Mrs Swift smiled at the captain's wife, who wore a handsome green dress, flecked with gold. "It's nice to meet you again. I'm glad to see you're feeling better."

Mrs Robertson put a hand to her chest. "I am for now, but it comes and goes. It's most annoying."

"I'm sure it is." Mrs Swift indicated to Nell. "This is my new colleague, Mrs Riley."

"Good evening, Mrs Riley."

Nell couldn't stop herself curtsying. "Pleased to meet you."

Mrs Robertson gazed over their shoulders. "Is Matron not with you?"

Nell glanced at Mrs Swift. "We didn't see her, did we?"

"No. I thought she'd be here already."

"I've not seen her." The captain scanned the room. "I'm sure she'll be here soon. She told me she was coming."

Mrs Swift's frown lifted. "She must be getting herself ready."

"I imagine so." The captain ushered the ladies to the door. "Would you care to take a seat? I've asked the barman to prepare some cocktails. It's not often we all get to spend the evening together, without passengers."

"How lovely." Nell grinned at Mrs Swift, but her smile dropped as they entered the room. The long tables usually reserved for male guests were full of the ship's officers, stewards and a number of men she didn't recognise. Beside them, no longer separated by the flower arrangements, stood a solitary circular table, set out for four. "Gracious. I hadn't realised so many of the crew would join us. Who are they all?"

Mrs Robertson ran her eyes over them. "I can't say for sure, but most of the officers and the bosun are here. Some of the tradesmen and senior engineers are, too. My husband likes to encourage camaraderie between the crew members and this is one of the few opportunities."

Butterflies danced in Nell's stomach as she chose the seat with her back to the men. "Will the captain join us?"

Mrs Robertson stared at the table. "Assuming Matron joins us, he'll sit elsewhere. Someone only set four places."

Nell's cheeks flushed. "Of course." She waited for Mrs Robertson to take her seat before taking her own seat.

"You're a regular traveller, I believe."

"I am." Mrs Robertson gazed over at her husband. "If you have a handsome husband, it's as well to keep an eye on him."

Nell studied the captain. *I suppose he is rather nice.*

"Did you know Mrs Riley was a master mariner's wife?" Mrs Swift looked at Mrs Robertson.

"Really. I'd no idea..."

"She could have been sitting where you are had it not been for an act of God."

The smile fell from Mrs Robertson's face. "I'm sorry. It must be very hard."

"It's not been easy. Now I get to serve people I should have been hobnobbing with. Not that I mind. Do you have any children, Mrs Robertson?"

She rearranged her cutlery. "No, actually we don't."

"That's unfortunate."

"Yes..."

Mr Brennan, the barman, interrupted them. "Good evening, ladies. The captain's asked that I get you all a drink. Would you care for a Manhattan?"

"Ooh." Nell put a hand to her lips. "I don't know whether I should."

"Well, I'm having one. I'll have yours as well, if you don't want it." Mrs Swift smiled at the steward. "Two, please. Plus whatever Mrs Robertson wants."

"I'll have one as well, thank you."

Mr Brennan bowed, and Nell watched him leave the table.

"What's he done to be waiting tables tonight when everyone else is having fun?"

"He won't be at it for long. There'll be a few of them, and once the food's brought out, they'll sit down." Mrs Swift glanced around. "I wonder if Matron decided to have an early night. She was tired this morning when we saw her."

"It seems strange for her to miss such a nice meal, though." Nell stopped as the noise increased from the men's table. "What on earth...?"

Mrs Robertson tutted. "Nothing to be worried about, it's just young men being young men. They don't often get a chance to relax."

Neither do we. Nell swivelled in her chair. "I don't see Mr Driver with them. That could explain it, too."

Mrs Robertson picked up her drink. "I believe he had to sort something out. He won't be long."

Nell coughed as she took a first sip of her cocktail. "Oh, that's different."

"You get used to it." Mrs Swift took a gulp. "It settles the nerves, too."

Nell took another sip, but put down her glass as Matron joined them. From the corner of her eye, she saw Mr Driver walking towards the other tables.

"Sorry I'm late. I needed a word with Mr Driver."

"Did it go all right?" Mrs Robertson waved over to the barman.

"Yes, he'll be fine."

A puzzled expression crossed Mrs Swift's face. "Have we missed something?"

Matron clasped her hands on the table. "I wasn't going to say anything tonight, but I may as well tell you. The captain asked me to talk to Mr Driver about your welfare."

Mrs Swift raised an eyebrow. "Why? Because of what happened last week?"

"Indirectly. There's been some debate about whether you should report to me, as the senior female member of staff, or Mr Driver as head steward. After what happened, he thought it would be more appropriate for you to report to me."

"But we already did." Nell played with the stem of her glass.

"Exactly. It was Mr Driver who overstepped the mark."

Matron waited as a drink was placed in front of her. "Which is why I spoke to him. The events of last week shouldn't happen again."

"That's good..." Nell stopped as a bell rang and the captain stood up at the far end of the room.

"Good evening, gentleman ... and ladies." He smiled at their table. "I'd like to welcome you all here tonight, as well as give thanks to those of our colleagues who are continuing to keep the ship ticking over." The smile on his face dropped. "I know that many of you are aware of the issue we had last week between certain members of the team and the ladies who now join us on our voyages. May I remind you, that it's Guion Shipping Company policy to employ ladies like Mrs Swift and Mrs Riley to assist our female passengers. They're here to do a job the same as the rest of us, and deserve our support." His gaze lingered on each table. "I know you mean no harm with your banter, but please remember, it's not always humorous to the ladies. So–" his smile returned as he raised his glass "–may I propose a toast to the ladies, as we welcome them to the team. Welcome, ladies."

Almost as one, the men stood and raised their glasses. "Welcome, ladies."

"Splendid." The captain remained on his feet. "May I also raise a toast to our voyage back to Liverpool?"

"To our voyage." The men clinked tankards and retook their seats.

"Excellent." The captain gazed around the room. "A last word from me. Enjoy yourselves tonight, but remember, we need to be ready to welcome our guests at ten o'clock tomorrow morning. No bad heads."

The men cheered as Captain Robertson sat down, and Nell turned back to her companions. "Did you notice Mr Driver didn't stand for the first toast?"

Matron sighed. "I'm afraid he may be a little put out after our conversation, but you have to see it from his point of view. He's been stewarding for nearly twenty years and things are changing. It will take him time to adjust."

"As long as he doesn't threaten us again."

"Did he really do that?" Mrs Robertson gaped at Nell.

"He said we'd lose our jobs if we raised any complaints with the officers."

"It might not have been so bad if we had complained, but it was Matron who spoke to the captain."

Mrs Robertson looked at Matron. "They won't do anything to upset you. They know they might need you."

"I can handle myself after all these years. I just need to toughen these ladies up."

Nell was glad of her loose-fitting uniform after a dinner of roast chicken, roast and mashed potatoes, and vegetables, followed by apple pie and custard. She was also feeling the effects of the second Manhattan and held onto the back of the chair as she stood up.

"That was all very nice."

"Did you enjoy that, ladies?" The captain strolled to his wife's side.

"Yes, thank you."

"And you were successful, Matron?"

"I think so, but we need to watch the situation. He's still not happy."

The captain stared over Mrs Swift's head at the rowdy crew members. "I'll have another word with him. I hope my talk to the stewards helps."

"I'm sure it won't do any harm, but it's time we said goodnight." Matron linked her arm through Mrs Swift's. "Thank you, Captain."

"Yes, thank you. It was lovely." Nell followed her companions to the door, but stopped as Mr Ramsbottom stepped in front of her.

"Did you enjoy your evening, Mrs Riley?"

"Yes, thank you." She edged backwards as Mr Ramsbottom came closer. "Did you?"

"I had a lovely view. It was just a shame you had your back to me." There was a twinkle in his eye as he put an arm around her waist. "Anyway, I wanted to give you a proper welcome to the ship ... like the captain said. No hard feelings, I hope."

"Mrs Riley, are you coming?" Matron reappeared in the dining room.

"Yes, I'll be right with you. Good evening, Mr Ramsbottom."

Nell raced from the room and caught hold of Matron's arm, directing her back to the stairs. "I know the captain wanted the stewards to be more welcoming, but Mr Ramsbottom's taken him too literally."

"You shouldn't encourage them, especially not tonight when they've had more to drink than usual. You need to keep to yourself. Now, come along. We've a busy day tomorrow."

CHAPTER FIFTEEN

A ll the passengers had boarded by the time luncheon
was ready, and Nell stood in her usual place by the
wall as two elderly ladies strolled into the dining room.
She'd noticed their deep purple dresses as soon as they met
the captain, and concluded that one or both must have been
widowed around the same time as her. She grimaced
inwardly. It seemed fanciful now that she should still have
been in mourning, but she couldn't consider the customs of
the wealthy.

At least she'd get the chance to speak to them later.
They were in one of the staterooms she managed, although
when she'd directed them there earlier, neither had spoken.
After waiting for them to take their seats, she approached
the table.

"Good afternoon, ladies. Have you settled into your
stateroom?"

The woman who looked to be the older of the two
stared up at her. "Not yet. Our trunks have only just
arrived. It's most inconvenient."

"I'm sorry about that. I don't know why there would be a delay. Would you like any help with your unpacking later?"

"I'm sure we're perfectly capable of doing it ourselves. Now, if we could have luncheon promptly, we'll set to it."

"Yes, of course. May I offer you a drink first?"

"A pot of tea for two, but don't bring it until the food's ready. We don't want to drink it all while we wait."

"Very good, ladies." Nell bowed as she backed away.

"You've got a right pair there."

Nell turned round as Mrs Swift arrived in the galley. "I know. I'm going to make it a challenge to find out something about them before we get home. I'm struggling to work out how they're both Mrs Foster."

"Perhaps they married brothers."

"That's a possibility, although the way they talk and act, it wouldn't surprise me if they never married at all. They're very independent for recently bereaved women."

"Ah, but aren't they American? They always come over as more confident than us English."

"Do you know, I can't place their accents, not that I've any idea what an American accent sounds like."

"Come along, ladies, don't stand gossiping." Mr Ramsbottom joined them with his order. "Several couples have arrived in the dining room. You may want to attend to them." He winked at Nell.

"That's enough, Mr Ramsbottom."

He smirked as he pushed past her. "Later, then."

Nell escorted Mrs Swift from the galley. "I don't know what to do about him."

"Keep ignoring him, he'll soon get bored." She nodded

towards the new couples. "Who do you want? The Andersons and Walkers look as if they've made acquaintance with each other, already."

"You take them, then. I'll serve the Curtises." Nell strode purposefully to the table. "Good afternoon, sir, madam. Welcome to the SS *Wisconsin*."

Mr Curtis smiled up at her. "Actually, it's not our first time. We sailed over to America before Christmas..." he gazed at the young lady by his side "...on our honeymoon."

"May I offer my congratulations, then? That must have been very special."

"It was indeed. In fact, how about two Manhattan cocktails to remind us of our hotel?"

"Oh, yes. Let's." The woman giggled. "Don't you think it's rather early, though?"

"It's a special occasion. And we've nothing better to do this afternoon than sleep it off. We can always ask the stewards not to disturb us."

Nell's cheeks flushed as Mrs Curtis tittered again. "Two Manhattans then?" Without waiting for a reply, she set off to find the bartender.

"Good afternoon, Mr Brennan. Two Manhattans for the cooing couple over there."

He laughed. "I spotted them. Are they newly-weds?"

"They're travelling back from their honeymoon."

"Lucky them. My missus wouldn't entertain coming to sea, not that I'd ask her."

Nell frowned while she deciphered his Irish accent. "I've a sister like that. Can't understand why I wanted to work on a ship."

"It's a good question, that." He took a bottle of whisky

from the shelf. "Why do women want to travel if they don't have to?"

"Why shouldn't we?"

"It's not very ladylike, is it? Ships have always been for men; having women here isn't right."

"But the world's changing. Isn't that a good thing?"

He replaced the bottle of whisky and reached for the vermouth. "I'm not one for change myself. Stick with what you know, that's what I say."

Nell said nothing as he shook the cocktail and poured it into prepared glasses, finishing with a cherry in each.

"There you are. Send them my compliments."

Luncheon was a subdued affair as the guests began polite conversation with their neighbours, and Nell wasn't sorry when the last of them disappeared upstairs.

Mrs Swift joined her as she cleared the tables. "You're quiet."

"I'm all right, but I'd rather have the old passengers back than start again with this lot. Mr and Mrs Curtis, the honeymooners, are too busy gazing into each other's eyes to do anything else, and the women in mourning do nothing but bark orders and complain about everything. I even had Mr Brennan telling me women shouldn't be on the ship at all."

"Mr Brennan the bartender?"

Nell nodded.

"What made him say that?"

"I told him about the newly-weds spending their honeymoon in New York and he said he didn't

144

understand it. He was friendly enough on the outbound journey. Maybe it's what Captain Robertson said last night."

Mrs Swift grimaced. "I've had comments from a couple of stewards, too, so it could be."

Nell sighed. "Let's get this lot tidied up and disappear for an hour. Have you unpacked all the trunks you need to?"

"Yes, I'm all done, but I've a treat for you." Mrs Swift beamed at her. "I've asked Mr Ross if he'll save us some of the lobster they had for luncheon. We can eat it in here."

"Really! It looked nice."

"That's what I thought. They serve it on the first day to make the guests feel special."

"It certainly went down well. Except for the old dears, nobody left anything."

Mrs Swift tutted. "They really are a strange couple. You've got your work cut out finding out about them."

"I'm already working on it. It should be interesting."

Nell set two places at a table in the far corner of the room while Mrs Swift went to collect the lobster.

"Here we are. What do you think of these?" She set down two plates with a chunk of white flesh resting over mashed potato.

"They look nice."

"They're more than nice. Mr Ross said he'd bring a pot of tea over, too."

Nell cut a piece of lobster from the tail and dipped it into a jug of melted butter before tentatively raising it to her lips. "I hope I like it."

Mrs Swift grinned. "There'll be more for me if you don't."

Nell bit down into the smooth, soft flesh and nodded.

"Do you like it?"

"Hmm, it's lovely. Nothing like the fish we get at home."

"It's not the price of fish we get at home, either. Make the most of it."

"I will." They ate in silence until Nell suddenly looked up. "What was that? Are we moving?"

"Gracious, yes, we will be. We're due to sail at two o'clock and it must be that now. Not that we need to hurry. The ship doesn't travel quickly leaving the harbour and the sail past Long Island takes hours. As soon as we've finished here, we can go upstairs."

Nell didn't like to rush such extravagant food, but the pull of spending an hour on the deck before they needed to serve afternoon tea was too much. Within five minutes, her plate was empty.

"That was delicious. And in time for the tea, too."

Mr Ross placed the teapot on the table. "There you are, ladies. Did you enjoy that?"

"Very much, thank you." Nell smiled as he collected their plates.

"We've got fillet of beef tomorrow. I'll save you some of that as well. The company like us to serve the best food to the Americans when they get on. They reckon they have more expensive tastes than the Europeans."

"They're probably right." Nell picked up the teapot. "Will you go on deck, Mr Ross?"

"I may, for five minutes or so. I've done this trip so many

times now, there's no need. Besides, I have to prepare tonight's dinner. Braised oxtail. It takes a bit of cooking."

The ship had gained speed by the time they walked upstairs.

"I suggest we go on the first-class promenade." Mrs Swift opened the outside door. "That way we can say we're working if Mr Driver sees us. Guests often like a drink while they watch New York fade away."

Nell gasped as they stepped outside. Both sides of the river were clear to see, and she marvelled as the low-level buildings sped past them.

"I thought you said we'd only move slowly."

"This is slow. Wait another hour and it will be much quicker."

They strolled to the end of the first-class promenade where they had a better view as New York faded into the distance.

"Perhaps one day we'll see it properly."

"I wouldn't hold your breath...."

"Do you have to stand in the way and block the view?"

Nell turned to see the two Mrs Fosters sitting on deckchairs, their backs against the wall.

"I'm sorry, ladies. We didn't see you there." Nell stood to one side.

"You should pay more attention. It's not every day we sail out of New York."

"No." Nell gazed back at the shoreline. "It's wonderful, isn't it? Did you stay in the city?"

"We've lived here for over ten years and frankly, we'll be glad to see the back of it. Isn't that right, Cissy?"

The younger of the women nodded. "Dreadful place."

"Oh." Nell's cheeks coloured. "You stayed a long time if you didn't like it."

"It wasn't out of choice; it was that brother of ours. He wouldn't listen to us."

Nell bit on her lip. "Have you left him in New York?"

The older woman glared at her. "We buried him. Why else would we be in mourning?"

"Oh, I'm sorry, I didn't mean... Please, will you excuse me?" Nell chased after Mrs Swift, who had walked away. "Why did you leave me?"

Mrs Swift rolled her eyes. "I don't want to spend my time off with a pair of miseries like that. Besides, you were managing well enough. Did you find out anything about them?"

Nell perked up. "I did as it happens. They came to New York with their brother and stayed for about ten years. They didn't like it, and so when he died, they decided to leave."

Mrs Swift raised an eyebrow. "They didn't like New York? I tell you, the older of the two looks as if she'd complain about anything."

"The younger one isn't much better." Nell grimaced. "Isn't it typical that I'm the one serving them?"

CHAPTER SIXTEEN

Nell stood on the deck, staring into the distance as the mass of land that had provided shelter for the ship faded from view. The waves were already choppier than they had been for days, and with the wind biting at her fingers, she pulled her cloak tightly around her. After a final pause, she turned to leave, but Mrs Swift appeared at her side.

"Here you are. I've come to tell you Mr Ross is making some luncheon for us. What are you doing?"

"Nothing much, just wondering if I'll ever be back."

"Why wouldn't you? The journey's been easy enough so far."

Nell scanned the horizon. "For you. Those old women are driving me mad. It doesn't matter what I do, they're never happy."

"Some people are like that, but in another week you'll be looking forward to wishing them farewell."

"I hope so. I can't help wondering if I'm cut out for this,

though." Nell gazed into the distance. "I'm not ready for Mr Ramsbottom's attention, either."

Mrs Swift sighed. "That's more difficult."

"I wouldn't mind, but I've done nothing to encourage him."

"Sometimes you don't have to. If you're fortunate, he'll change ships when we get back."

"Has anything similar happened to you?"

Mrs Swift studied her fingers. "There was a chap who was a pest last year, but thankfully he moved on."

"What did you do about it?"

She took several paces across the deck. "In the end, I reported him to the captain. The matron at the time said it was just men being men."

Nell gulped. "What did the captain say?"

Mrs Swift twisted her face. "He didn't give the impression of being very sympathetic, but once we got to Liverpool, the man in question left the ship, so perhaps he was..."

Nell searched for the outline of the land that had merged between the greyness of the sea and the sky. "Should I report Mr Ramsbottom?"

Mrs Swift shook her head. "I wouldn't. In my case, the captain had a word with the man in question, which made the rest of the voyage very awkward. If I was in your position, I'd keep out of his way as best you can, and if he continues to trouble you, tell him you're still in mourning or that you're looking forward to seeing your daughters when you get home. That may frighten him off."

Nell nodded. "I suppose the captain had enough to deal

with on the outward journey, and we are the ones who put ourselves in this position."

Mrs Swift linked Nell's arm and led her back indoors. "Exactly. Whether we like it or not, we need to realise it's part of the job."

"It can't be easy for them having us on board. Perhaps I shouldn't be too hard on Mr Ramsbottom. He probably only wants to be friendly."

"Possibly. Now come along, Mr Ross was cooking some nice cod for us. It will be cold at this rate."

Several of the stewards were already at one of the long tables when they arrived in the dining room, but Nell and Mrs Swift continued walking until they reached the far corner.

Mr Ross followed them to their seats and put down two plates of cod fillet in a butter sauce with sautéed potatoes. "Here you are, ladies. I thought you'd forgotten."

Nell smiled up at him. "I'm sorry, it was my fault. I was taking a last look at America."

"Ah, yes. It's always a momentous occasion, especially the first time we leave, but don't worry, we'll be back in a month."

"You're right." Nell fumbled for her knife and fork. "This looks very nice."

"Only the best for first class. Would you like some of the ice cream they had for dessert?"

"Oh, please." Mrs Swift's face lit up. "It's my favourite."

"You eat up and I'll bring it over in five minutes."

Nell took a mouthful of fish as he disappeared. "I'm wondering if I should tell the captain I plan on leaving after this voyage. I hate lying to people, but he should be the first to know."

"I thought you'd decided it wasn't so bad after all, especially after you got all those tips."

"I did, but I'm having second thoughts."

Mrs Swift didn't look up from her food. "Suit yourself, but you won't earn eight or nine pounds for four weeks' work anywhere else."

"Eight or nine? I only got three pounds' worth of tips."

Mrs Swift rolled her eyes. "Plus your wages and any other tips you get when we arrive back in Liverpool..."

Nell bit down on her lip. "I hadn't thought of that, although I doubt I'll get much on this trip, the way these passengers are. They all want to keep to themselves."

"You'll still get something. Perhaps you should talk to Matron, see what she has to say."

Nell nodded. "I could. What do you think she'll say?"

Mrs Swift shrugged. "I've no idea."

"No, me neither." Nell laid her knife and fork on her empty plate as Mr Ross joined them with two bowls of ice cream.

"Here you are."

"Thank you." Nell looked up, waiting for him to leave, but was surprised when he took the seat beside her.

"I take it you've heard about Mr Driver?"

"No. What about him?"

"Word has it he was caught canoodling with a passenger."

Nell gasped. "No!"

Mrs Swift stabbed her spoon into the ice cream. "Don't look at me."

"Well, I've not said anything."

Mr Ross glanced from one to the other. "You mean you saw him?"

"We ... no, well, we're not sure what we saw ... are we?" Nell stared at Mrs Swift, who'd momentarily forgotten about the ice cream.

"When was he seen?"

"Last night."

"Last night!" Nell and Mrs Swift spoke together, but Mrs Swift continued.

"In that case, it was nothing to do with us. We've not laid eyes on him for a couple of days." She studied her dessert. "How do you know?"

He tapped the side of his nose. "I can't tell you that, but I was told he'd been summoned to see the captain."

"Could he lose his job?" Nell's mouth dropped open.

"I doubt it. Men like him usually get away with it. He'll get a quick telling-off and that will be it." Mrs Swift turned to Mr Ross. "Did you find out who he was with?"

"No. I was hoping you could tell me. The lads have been running a sweepstake on who it was. A farthing each and you can have a guess."

"I don't think so." Mrs Swift scowled at him. "What about the poor woman in all this? We already saw how the young maid was traumatised by the events of the last voyage."

"She needn't know. It's only a bit of fun."

"Perhaps it is to you, but you should still have some consideration." Mrs Swift suddenly raised an eyebrow. "Who caught him?"

Mr Ross checked over both shoulders before he leaned forward. "We're not sure, but my money's on Mr Price."

"No!" Nell put a hand to her mouth. "That makes no sense. Why would he do such a thing?"

"Fancies Driver's job, doesn't he? He's been moaning since we left Liverpool about being stuck in steerage, and Mr Driver's the only one stopping him coming up to first class."

Mrs Swift's brow creased. "It's rather drastic, especially given that Mr Driver will be with us all the way back. It could get difficult."

"We know." There was a glint in Mr Ross's eyes as he rubbed his hands together. "It should liven up the journey a bit."

Nell dug her spoon into the ice cream and waited for Mr Ross to be well out of earshot. "What do you make of that, then?"

Mrs Swift raised an eyebrow. "Mr Driver obviously fancies himself as a ladies' man. He wasn't on this ship last year, so I couldn't say whether he makes a habit of it."

"Could that be why he's here, because he had to leave his previous ship?"

"It's possible." Mrs Swift sucked on her spoon. "I wonder if Matron knows what's going on. It might be worth a farthing on their sweepstake if she does."

Nell laughed when she noticed the grin on Mrs Swift's face. "I don't know about the sweepstake, but we need to find out who the woman is to keep Mr Driver away from her. In fact, we could use that as an excuse to get Matron to tell us what she knows."

"Brilliant!" Mrs Swift scraped her spoon around her

bowl. "We'll have to be back in our sitting room before she goes to bed tonight."

Nell stood up and collected the dishes. "We'd better go upstairs and make sure everyone's settled for the afternoon, then we can start on these tables."

The saloon was quiet when they arrived upstairs, and Nell checked the clock. "Where is everyone?" She wandered to the centre of the room and stared out through the skylight. "The weather isn't good enough for them to go outside."

"The sea's rather choppy; we may start seeing some seasickness."

Nell groaned. "After half of them were boasting about being accustomed to sailing after the first crossing."

"All bravado, I'm afraid. You'll get used to it." She nodded towards Mr and Mrs Curtis, who were in the back corner of the room. "Have you seen who's over there? They usually take any opportunity they can to stay in their stateroom."

"They do, although I wondered if they'd argued over luncheon." Nell tried not to stare. "I could have sworn she'd been crying."

Mrs Swift cupped a hand around her mouth. "What if it was her!"

"If what was...? Oh, you mean... No, surely not." Nell's eyes widened. "She's not been away from her husband for long enough."

"That's true." Mrs Swift's shoulders dropped. "It's worth keeping an eye on her though; you never know."

"You're right." Nell glanced around the room. "Shall we

check the ladies have everything they want? Then we can go."

She wandered to a group of ladies, sitting around a low-level table, listening to Mrs Anderson telling a rather animated tale. "Good afternoon, ladies. May I get you anything?"

"Oh, Mrs Riley, I'm glad you're here." A middle-aged woman with curled blond hair interrupted Mrs Anderson. "Have you seen the younger Mrs Foster? She was looking for you about a quarter of an hour ago."

"No, I haven't. Thank you for telling me, Mrs Walker. Do you know where she went?"

"She was going back to her stateroom. She didn't give many details, but I got the impression her sister was feeling under the weather. Probably a touch of seasickness, but you've seen how they are. They wouldn't like to admit it."

"I'm sure you're right. Now, if you're all settled, I'll go and see if she still needs me."

CHAPTER SEVENTEEN

Nell straightened her apron as she stood by the Fosters' stateroom. The older of the sisters had disciplined her for looking dishevelled on the first day, and she made sure her uniform was smart before she gave three knocks. She had no sooner taken a step back than the door opened and the younger sister opened it.

"Oh, it's you."

"Yes, madam. I was told you were looking for me."

"I was, as it happens." Mrs Foster peered both ways along the corridor. "You'd better come in."

Nell stepped over the threshold, but her eyes hadn't adjusted to the dim light when there was a groan from the left-hand bed. "Is everything all right?"

She stayed where she was as Mrs Foster hurried to her sister. "Stay still, it's only the stewardess."

"Is she suffering from seasickness?"

"Certainly not!" Mrs Foster's shoulders rose and fell as she huffed. "I fear it's much more serious than that. We need the doctor. Can you fetch him for us?"

"I'll try my best, although he can be difficult to find…"

"That won't do. My sister's in a great deal of pain."

Nell's heart raced. "Of course, I'll go straight away. Shall I get you anything while you wait?"

"You haven't time for that. Now be off with you." Mrs Foster marched to the door and opened it wide.

"I'll be as quick as I can."

Nell stood outside in the corridor as the door slammed behind her. *Dr Clarke's office. That's the obvious place to start … although Officer Hughes may be there.* Her pulse quickened at the thought, but she ignored it. *What choice do I have?*

The doctor's office was only a short walk from the staterooms, but as she expected, it was empty when she arrived. Her arms flapped by her side as she turned in a full circle.

"Is everything all right, Mrs Riley?" The captain's face was stern as he walked towards her.

"No, not really. One of the Mrs Fosters needs the doctor, but he isn't here."

"Ah, no. There are several ladies in steerage feeling rather queasy and so he's down there. Could Matron help? She was up here not five minutes ago."

"I doubt it. The Fosters are quite particular and asked for the doctor." Nell hesitated. "Do you know how long he might be?"

"I'm afraid I don't. I'll pass a message to him when he returns if that helps."

"Actually, the younger sister said it was urgent. Perhaps I can find a steward downstairs to help me look for him."

"No." The captain's voice was firm. "I won't have you going into steerage on your own. In fact, wait here, and I'll get someone to go with you."

Nell waited as the captain disappeared. *I hope he's not long.* She twisted her fingers together as she waited, but her breathing stopped when he returned with Officer Hughes. *Oh no!*

"Here we are, Mrs Riley. Officer Hughes will direct you to the steerage area. I'm afraid you'll need to go outside to reach the ladies' quarters."

"Yes, thank you, Captain." *Why did he pick him, of all people?*

"This way." Officer Hughes sounded as pleased with his task as she was. "Keep up, I've work to do."

"Yes, I'm sorry." Nell trotted down the corridor behind him, until they reached the outside door, which he held open for her. "Thank you." *Do I say anything else?* "At least it's not raining."

"It will be soon."

Nell followed him to the entrance on the other side and down the steps into the steerage area. "Do you know where he is, or will we have to look for him?"

"Captain Robertson said he was with the ladies, so that should help." He raced ahead of her, but he stopped at the dormitories. "It would be as well for you to go in, rather than me."

"Yes, of course." Nell ventured through the door he held open and studied the long narrow room with bunk beds flanking either side and a row of tables down the centre. "Dr Clarke?"

Several women roused themselves from their beds to stare at her, and she paused by one on her right. "Have you seen the doctor recently?"

The woman nodded. "He was here about ten minutes ago, but he left."

"Oh, right. You didn't happen to catch where he was going, did you?"

She shook her head. "Sorry."

"Never mind. Thank you anyway."

Nell returned to the still open door, where Officer Hughes was waiting for her. "He's been and gone. Are there any other dormitories down here?"

Officer Hughes huffed. "Follow me."

The second room was only a few steps away and Nell peered into the room as Officer Hughes pulled back the door. "Dr Clarke?" She took a step inside and flinched as Dr Clarke stood up from a bunk to her left.

"Did someone call?"

"Oh, Doctor, I'm glad I found you." Nell put on her best smile. "One of the first-class passengers is in some discomfort and asked for you to visit as soon as possible."

"Have you come down on your own to tell me that?"

"Oh, no." Nell gestured towards the door. "I spoke to Captain Robertson, and he arranged for Officer Hughes to escort me."

"The captain knows you're here?" He suddenly paid her more attention.

"Yes. It's the older of the two Foster sisters. She's in some discomfort, but her sister is adamant it isn't seasickness. Could you visit her?"

He glanced down at the sickly-looking woman beside

him and picked up his bag. "I can't do much more here. Lead the way."

Officer Hughes walked with the doctor. "I thought we'd find you here. Have you been busy?"

"Busy enough, considering we're only half a day off the coast. It's likely to get worse before it gets better."

Officer Hughes snarled. "They shouldn't let women sail. They don't have the stomach for it."

"We can't blame them entirely; there are a fair few men suffering too."

"It's easy with the men, though. A couple of glasses of brandy and they're as right as rain."

Dr Clarke chuckled. "We give the ladies brandy, too. For medicinal purposes, of course. Some of them actually like it."

"Well, that's wrong. Whoever heard of women drinking brandy?"

Nell took a deep breath. *Perish the thought.*

The rain had started by the time they went back onto the deck, and with the wind blowing hard against the sails, they had to hurry to avoid getting drenched.

Officer Hughes held open the door to the first-class area. "Will you be needing me any more, Doctor?"

"No, we can manage from here. Thank you, sir."

"Yes, thank you."

If Officer Hughes heard Nell, he didn't acknowledge her before he disappeared in the direction of the bridge.

"Right, Mrs Riley, where are we going?"

"Just down here." Nell made her way to the third door along before giving it a short, sharp rap. "Mrs Foster, are you in there?"

The door opened instantly, and a pale-looking Mrs Foster took hold of the doctor's arm.

"Oh, praise the Lord, you're here. Please come in."

Nell hovered by the entrance as Dr Clarke stepped inside. *Do I go in?* She leaned forward and peered towards the beds at the far end of the room. *I doubt they'll notice one way or the other.* Dr Clarke was bent over a prone shape lying under a pile of blankets, while Mrs Foster sat on a chair at the other side.

"Do you know what's wrong, Doctor?" The young Mrs Foster fidgeted with a handkerchief.

"Not yet." He gazed around the room. "Could we have a little more light?"

Nell stepped further inside. "Allow me." She reached for the taper and lit the two lamps on the wall nearest the bed. "I'll be waiting outside if you need anything else."

"Splendid." The doctor spoke to the other Mrs Foster as he resumed his examination. "Tell me what happened?"

Nell hurried from the room, breathing a sigh of relief as she reached the corridor. *Whatever's wrong, it doesn't look good. It's certainly not seasickness.* She stood to attention outside the door, although she wasn't sure why. *At least it will stop any stewards walking in; not that they would. It's one of my rooms. It's not getting those tables ready for dinner, though.*

A shriek from inside the room disturbed her thoughts. *Oh my goodness. What do I do?* The cries intensified as she rejoined them. "Is there anything I can help with?"

The doctor spoke without looking up. "Yes, bring some hot water and clean towels. Quickly."

Nell raced into the corridor, down the stairs, and into the dining room. She headed directly for the galley, but Mrs Swift saw her.

"Where've you been? I thought we were setting these tables together."

"And we will if I can get away, but there's an emergency upstairs and I need some hot water and towels. Would you get the towels for me?"

"Yes ... why? What's happened?"

Nell searched for a large jug. "I don't know for certain, but it's the older Mrs Foster. The doctor's with her and she's not very well, at all."

Mrs Swift snorted. "All that talk about not suffering from seasickness..."

"That's not what it is. It sounds more serious."

"Oh." Mrs Swift's face dropped. "Let me get those towels and I'll come upstairs with you."

Despite Nell willing the water to boil, it took an age. When they finally arrived at the stateroom, she hurried inside after only the briefest of knocks.

"Here we are." She put the water jug on the edge of the washstand. "The towels are outside." She turned back and took them from Mrs Swift. "Will you be needing anything else?"

"No, thank you." The doctor finally looked up at her. "I've given her some laudanum, which should ease the pain. For now, at least."

Nell stared down at the drenched face of Mrs Foster and gave her sister a towel to wipe it. "She doesn't look very well."

"That's because she isn't." The younger Mrs Foster strode to the washstand and poured in some of the fresh water.

"No." Nell glanced around the room. "Would you like me to bring your dinner up here tonight?"

"I can't eat with all this going on." She pointed to her sister.

"No, I'm sorry, I'm not thinking. Perhaps a pot of tea later, then."

"Yes. In fact, you can bring one now. We missed afternoon tea because of this."

Nell bowed her head as she backed out of the room. "Very good, madam."

Mrs Swift was still in the corridor when Nell rejoined her. "How is she?"

"In a bad way, by the looks of it. She'd have been better off with seasickness, if you ask me. Come on, I need to bring a pot of tea up before I can start on the tables."

The room was calmer by the time Nell returned. She poured the tea and set it down on a bedside cabinet.

"I've brought you a selection of cakes, too." When she got no response, she gazed down at the patient. "She looks more peaceful now."

"I'm not surprised, drugged up to the eyeballs."

"Oh." Nell hesitated. "Does the doctor know if she'll get better?"

"He has no idea."

"I'm sorry. Shall I come back later to check on you?"

Mrs Foster peered at the clock. "Yes, at five o'clock. I'll decide what I'm doing about dinner then."

"Very good." Nell opened the door. "Enjoy your tea."

CHAPTER EIGHTEEN

As the clock struck five, Nell put an ear to the door of the Fosters' stateroom. Nothing. *That's a promising sign.* She gave it a light tap and was surprised when it opened so quickly.

"Good afternoon, Mrs Foster." Nell gave a broad smile. "It's five o'clock; is there anything I can get for you?"

"Not exactly, but you can sit with my sister while I use the facilities. She seems to be settled. I've not had a peep out of her."

"That's something then. At least she's not in any pain."

"For now."

As soon as Mrs Foster left the room, Nell took the chair beside the bed. The woman's already wrinkled face resembled wax and her hands twitched constantly. *What happens if she dies?*

Nell's stomach fluttered as someone knocked on the door. *Who's this?* She crept across the room and opened it an inch before she gave a deep sigh and let Matron in. "Am I glad to see you."

"What are you doing in here?"

"I came to ask if the other Mrs Foster needed anything, and she wanted me to sit with her sister while she used the lavatory."

Matron nodded. "How is she?"

"A lot calmer than when I brought the doctor. He gave her some laudanum."

"Yes, he told me. That's why I'm here. He suspects it's her kidneys."

Nell gulped. "Is she likely to *pass*?"

"We don't think so, but you can never be too sure. Mrs Foster was right to ask you to stay with her. She shouldn't be alone."

Nell put a hand to her chest. "What do I do if she does? Pass, that is."

"You come and fetch me or the doctor immediately."

"Right." She fidgeted with her fingers. "It's not always easy to find you, though."

"I won't be going far tonight. I'll either be near the doctor's room or in our quarters."

Nell gave a weak smile. "That's good to know. Actually, while you're here, Mrs Swift and I had a question..."

Nell stopped as the cabin door opened and Mrs Foster returned.

"Ah, Matron. Thank you for looking in on us. Dr Clarke said you would."

"I'm only doing my job. I've told Mrs Riley where she can find me if you need me tonight."

"Isn't the doctor coming back?"

"Oh, yes. Your sister will need some more laudanum

before the evening's out; it's in case you want me in the meantime."

"I'd better order a dinner tray then." Mrs Foster stared at Nell. "I presume you'll arrange it."

"Yes, of course." Nell walked back to the door. "If that's all for now, I'll go and place your order." She closed the door behind her, but stopped rather than heading for the stairs. *Should I wait for Matron? Not here.* She wandered to the foyer outside the saloon and studied the clock. *I need to go down to the galley, but the guests will be arriving for pre-dinner drinks any minute.*

As if on cue, Mr and Mrs Curtis joined her.

"Good evening, Mrs Riley. Is everything all right. You look confused."

"Oh, good evening, Mr Curtis. I'm fine, thank you. I was debating whether to go into the saloon or down to the dining room."

"If you're heading into the saloon, may we order a couple of Manhattans from you?" He gazed at his wife. "We can't bear the thought of leaving the United States."

"Well, then, you've helped me decide. Come and take a seat." She ushered them to their usual table. "Perhaps you can go back to New York one day."

"I'm sure we will." He patted his wife's hand. "We're already talking about it."

"That's something to look forward to, then." She headed to the bar, where Mr Brennan was shaking a cocktail.

"Evening, Mrs Riley. Would you like another couple of Manhattans for your honeymoon couple?"

"Yes, please. I imagine you know what all the passengers drink by now."

He laughed. "All except those who like to try everything on the menu ... and those two old women."

"They don't drink alcoholic drinks."

"That's the problem. I'm not likely to get any tips from them if they only have tea."

"I doubt any of us will. They're never happy. The older of the two isn't well either, so we'll see less of them for the time being."

Mr Brennan's eyebrow shot up, but he waited for the steward to collect the newly poured cocktail. "What's up with her?"

Nell shrugged. "I don't know, but the doctor and Matron have been to see her."

"Interesting."

Nell watched as he added two measures of whisky to the shaker. "What's that supposed to mean?"

He gave her a knowing look. "I believe Mr Ross has told you about the latest incident."

Nell's forehead creased. "You mean with Mr Driver?"

"That's the one."

Nell put a hand to her mouth. "You don't think..."

"Who knows?" He put the lid on the shaker and picked it up. "I wouldn't have thought she's his type, but if you're desperate..."

"What a terrible thing to say; besides, I doubt she's been out of her sister's sight."

"You're probably right." Mr Brennan's shoulders dropped. "It's an interesting idea, though."

"No, it's not, it's terrible." Nell shuddered. "At the very least, I hope the woman involved knew what she was doing."

"Ah, now that's the question." The twinkle returned to Mr Brennan's green eyes. "We've not seen Mr Driver all day, which usually means she wasn't."

"Does he make a habit of this...?" Nell gasped as he poured the drinks.

"I'm saying no more. I don't want to get into trouble." He glanced over both shoulders. "All I will say is, keep an eye on him."

Nell's hands were trembling as she carried the tray over to Mr and Mrs Curtis.

"You're looking lost again, Mrs Riley." Mr Curtis smiled as she placed their glasses on the table.

"Oh, I'm sorry, it's been a busy day, that's all."

"I hope you're not going down with seasickness. These waves are getting quite choppy."

"It's nothing like that." She straightened up. "Will that be all?"

"For now. I'll call if we want anything else."

Satisfied the guests were all comfortable, Nell hurried down to the galley with her order, but as she arrived, a wave hit the ship particularly hard and she stopped to steady herself.

"Are you all right there, Mrs Riley." Mr Ramsbottom wrapped an arm around her waist.

"Yes, I'm fine." She shrugged herself away from him. "If you'll excuse me, I need to get back upstairs. It's busy at the moment."

Nell didn't wait for a reply, and as she returned to the saloon, she approached a group of women sitting by the far wall. "Good evening, ladies. May I get you a drink?"

"Yes, you may." A large woman wearing a choker of

pearls around her ample double chin sat up straight. "Four sherries, please."

"Certainly, Mrs Anderson." Nell peered over her shoulder to the other side of the room. "Are your husbands sitting together? I need to confirm the order with them."

"You'll do nothing but inform them, if you don't mind. We'll decide for ourselves whether we'd like a drink."

"Certainly, madam. Will Mrs Walker be joining you?" Nell nodded to the empty chair where their younger friend usually sat.

"I doubt it. We've not seen her today. A touch of seasickness her husband said."

"That's unfortunate, but I know there's been a lot of it about. Hopefully, she'll be back tomorrow." Nell headed towards the bar, but Mrs Swift saw her and met her halfway.

"Here you are. I was beginning to think you'd got lost."

"I'm sorry, it's been a busy day."

"It has." Mrs Swift leaned forward and lowered her voice. "Have you had any joy with working out who our mystery lady is?"

"None at all. Matron called at the Fosters' stateroom when I was there on my own, but before I could ask her, Mrs Foster rejoined us. There's a chance she'll be in our sitting room tonight, if we can get back early enough."

"I hope she is; I want to know, if nothing else, to shut these stewards up."

Nell gasped. "You can't tell them who it is."

"Why not? At the moment, they're tarnishing the reputations of nearly every woman on the ship. At least if we put them right, the rest of them will be spared from ridicule."

"But what about the woman? It's not fair to her. Especially if she didn't ask for Mr Driver's attention."

"Do you know that?"

Nell shrugged. "Not really, but Mr Brennan said they'd not seen Mr Driver today, which was usually the case when he'd been up to no good."

"Well, I never." Mrs Swift grinned. "I'm even more intrigued now."

"I'm afraid you'll have to wait. I need to order some drinks for the ladies and then we need to get the trays delivered."

As the guests began moving to the dining room, Nell took Mrs Foster's dinner tray to her stateroom. She knocked, but when there was no reply, she put an ear to the door and knocked again. They can't have gone out. A second later, a cry pierced the air.

"Mrs Foster." Nell dashed into the room and put the tray on the console table. "Do you need the doctor?"

"Mrs Riley! Did I ask you to come in?"

"No, I'm sorry, I heard the scream…"

"That's still no reason to barge in. I can manage perfectly well."

Nell stared at the shape of the older Mrs Foster as she crouched on the floor by the side of the bed.

"If you're sure I can't help."

"No, she's not sure." The older sister's voice was strained as she pulled herself onto the bed. "I'd like a drink."

"Certainly. A pot of tea?"

"Brandy."

"Brandy?"

"You've heard of it, haven't you?"

"Well ... yes, but you don't usually drink spirits."

"I don't usually have pain like this. Now, hurry up."

The dining room was filling up as Nell rushed past the tables to the bar. "A large brandy, please."

"Give me a minute." Mr Brennan dried his hands before he reached for the bottle. "What do you want this for in the middle of the day?"

"It's for Mrs Foster."

"Mrs Foster? The grumpy one...?"

"Yes, and be quick. She wants it now."

Mr Brennan selected a glass. "All right, calm down. I'm sure another minute won't hurt."

Nell wiped the back of a hand over her forehead. "You're not the one who has to take it to her. She's bad enough when she's well; she's even worse when she's ill."

Mr Brennan hadn't replaced the lid of the bottle when Nell grabbed the glass and raced back through the dining room to the stairs. She paused for breath and knocked deliberately on the door, waiting for it to be answered.

"Finally." The younger sister opened the door. "Come on in. Don't just stand there."

Mrs Foster was sitting up in bed when Nell handed her the drink.

"You've more colour in your cheeks. Are you feeling better?"

Mrs Foster took a sip of the amber liquid. "The sharp pain's eased, but I still feel as if I've been beaten with a broom." She put a hand to her lower back. "I've no idea what it was."

"I believe the doctor wasn't sure himself."

"He's no doctor. All he did was poke and prod me. He didn't know what he was doing any more than I did. He probably thought I was being hysterical."

Nell nodded. "It's an easy diagnosis if you're a woman."

"Exactly." Mrs Foster took a large gulp of her drink as her sister hovered by her side.

"Slow down with that."

"The day I've had, I'll go as quickly as I like." She rested back on the pillows. "Hopefully a good night's sleep will do the trick."

Nell smiled at her. "I hope so. Would you like anything else before I leave you?"

Mrs Foster emptied her glass and held it out. "Another one of these wouldn't go amiss..."

"But Bertha..."

The older woman waved a hand at her sister. "But Bertha nothing. If the chef has a nice piece of fish, I could probably manage that too. When you're ready."

"I'll see what I can do."

The door clicked into place as Nell pulled it shut behind her. *Perhaps she should drink brandy more often.*

Mrs Swift was looking out for her when she returned. "Here you are. Are you still running around after that woman?"

"I am, but I need to arrange a tray for her and then I'm all yours."

"Good. While you're waiting, you can collect the plates from the table by the wall. Their main course is ready."

Nell glanced over to the table Mrs Anderson and her

friends now occupied. "You've not served them more drinks, have you?"

Mrs Swift's eyes narrowed. "I'll say. I don't need to ask their husbands for permission any more. They got tired of me interrupting them. They said I could serve what they wanted."

"They seem to be taking full advantage. It's not like them though. Maybe they're having a celebration."

Mrs Swift gave a wry smile. "Or they're drowning their sorrows. I've a feeling they're not happy about something."

CHAPTER NINETEEN

Nell was dead on her feet when they finally returned to their sitting room.

"Let me sit down." She flopped onto the settee and stretched out her legs. "What a day."

"You're right. It may be that I've got used to you being here, but I don't remember being so busy when I was on my own last year."

Nell giggled. "Perhaps I've made you go soft."

"Well, if you have, you can stop wandering off to look after the passengers." Mrs Swift paused at the sound of footsteps outside, but relaxed as Mr Potter appeared with their tray.

"Here you are, ladies. I managed to get some lamb cutlets for you from the first-class galley."

"That's very kind of you, thank you." Nell's stomach rumbled at the sight of the food.

"You look dead beat. Matron wasn't much better when she was here earlier."

"She's already eaten?" Nell sat with her knife and fork poised.

"About an hour ago. I don't think these choppy seas have helped; the women can't deal with the ship swaying like this."

"There are quite a few men suffering, too."

Mr Potter laughed. "I'm sure they're only saying that so they can have some peace and quiet. Talking of which, I'll leave you to eat your dinner."

"Cheek." Mrs Swift scowled after him as he left.

"Ignore him. I'm sure he was only being friendly."

"It's a good job I like him, then."

They ate in silence until Mrs Swift pushed away her empty plate. "Did you speak to Matron?"

Nell scooped up the last forkful of peas. "No. I told you, Mrs Foster interrupted us, and I didn't see her again after that."

"We need to be in here early in the morning then, to catch her over breakfast. She's a terrible habit of sneaking off while we're still eating."

Nell sat back in the chair. "You've noticed, too? I thought it was me being paranoid."

"She likes her own company, but she can't talk about the passengers, so it's probably easier if she says nothing."

"If all else fails, we need to find her some brandy, then. It's amazing how it changes people."

Mrs Swift laughed. "Perhaps we'll save that until one evening. I couldn't manage a glass for breakfast. Not if I wanted to do any work, anyway."

◈

Matron and Mrs Swift were at the table the next morning when Nell arrived. She yawned as she took her seat.

"That looks like a nice, strong cup of tea. I need it this morning."

Matron patted the seat beside her. "Didn't you sleep well?"

"I did, but I was so tired last night I wasn't ready to wake up. Did Mrs Swift tell you about our day?"

"I'd started. I've not got to Mr Ross's news yet."

Matron finished her bowl of porridge. "What news is that?"

"He told us about Mr Driver…"

Matron flinched as she picked up her cup of tea, spilling some onto the saucer. "What did he say?"

Mrs Swift raised an eyebrow. "That he'd been caught in a compromising position with a female passenger."

"Nonsense."

"Really?" Nell put down her spoon. "We heard the captain wanted to speak to him."

Matron pushed herself from the table. "I'd better go; Dr Clarke will be waiting for me."

"You can't walk away." Mrs Swift's voice was sharp. "One of our roles on this ship is to protect the ladies from unwanted attention. We need to know who he was with so we can keep an eye on her."

"I can't talk about it…"

"Why not? All the stewards are…"

Matron sighed and retook her seat. "What are they saying?"

"Only what we've told you … and that he was probably with the woman against her will."

"I can't confirm that." Matron fidgeted with a teaspoon. "You're right, he was found with a passenger, but he claims she was well aware of what she was doing. The problem arose when her husband caught them together."

"Her husband!" The blood drained from Nell's cheeks. "I'm not surprised Mr Driver's been called to the captain's office. What was he thinking? Or her for that matter."

Matron shrugged. "That's for them to answer, but you needn't worry about it. I doubt you'll see her again."

"What do you mean?" Nell's brow creased.

"She's been confined to her cabin. One of the stewards will take her tray upstairs, but her husband will deliver it."

"What about cleaning the room?"

"Don't worry. It's a stateroom a steward manages. Not that it matters. According to her husband, she'll do it herself."

Nell pulled a face at Mrs Swift. "I wouldn't like to be in her shoes."

"If she knew what she was doing, I've no sympathy for her. She's no one to blame but herself." Matron stood up once more. "Right, I need to go. And not a word to anyone, do you hear? The captain wants this kept quiet."

Nell nodded. "Nobody will hear anything from me."

Matron disappeared as Mrs Swift grinned at Nell. "It was fortunate I had my mouth full and couldn't answer. You'll have to let me do the talking."

The corridor outside the Fosters' stateroom was empty as Nell took a deep breath and knocked on their door. Seconds later, the older Mrs Foster opened it.

"Good morning. I didn't expect you to be out of bed." Nell followed her into the room and put the tray on the table.

"Thankfully, the pain has disappeared. I never want to feel anything like that again."

"I'm sure you don't. Is the other Mrs Foster not with you?"

"She's availing herself of the facilities. She'll be back presently."

"Would you prefer to take breakfast in the dining room?"

"Good grief, no, not after you've gone to the trouble of bringing this up. We'll join everyone for morning coffee later."

"As you wish. I'll look out for you. Would you like me to pour your tea before I go?"

"Yes, please. That would be lovely." Mrs Foster took a seat as Nell put the milk into the cups. "Before my sister comes back, may I thank you for all you did yesterday. I'm afraid I scared Cissy somewhat, and she didn't cope with it terribly well."

"It can't have been easy for her, but at least you're feeling better."

Nell straightened up from the table as the door opened and the other Mrs Foster joined them.

"Ah, Mrs Riley. I hope you've not tired my sister by getting her out of bed."

"No, she hasn't. I told you earlier, I'm much better this morning. Now come and sit down."

Nell didn't wait to be dismissed, but bumped into Dr Clarke as she pulled the door closed. "I'm sorry, I didn't see you there. Are you here to check on the patient?"

"Yes, indeed. How is she this morning?"

"I'm pleased to say she's much better. She opened the door to me and is even taking some breakfast."

"Splendid." The doctor reached for his pocket watch. "I'll let them finish eating before I disturb them. I've another case of seasickness I can be dealing with."

Nell watched him leave and headed in the opposite direction, down the corridor. Mrs Swift was leaving the dining room as she entered.

"There's one tray left for you. Mrs Curtis." She raised an eyebrow as she scurried to the stairs.

A frown settled on Nell's face. *That's not like her. Or him.* She hurried into the dining room, scanning the tables for Mr Curtis, but there was no sign of him.

"Is this tray ready to go, Mr Ross?"

The chef turned round. "It will be in a minute. It still needs a boiled egg." He leaned over the counter towards her. "I believe it was the husband who found them."

"The husband?" She stared at him, her brow creased. "Oh, I see what you mean. You've been talking to Mrs Swift." She checked over both shoulders. "We don't know *whose* husband though."

"That's what Mrs Swift said, but you must."

"Why must we?"

"You spoke to Matron, didn't you?"

"She wouldn't tell us who it was. But..." A grin flitted across Nell's lips. "You might be able to help. How many women are having breakfast, luncheon and dinner in their rooms at the moment?"

A frown crossed his face. "None that I'm aware of. No one today at any rate."

"Are you sure?" She studied him. "Will you check while I take this tray? I won't be long."

The Curtises' room was at the far end of the corridor and Nell paused and put her ear to the door. *All quiet.* When she got no response to her first knock, she rapped on the door again but gave a start when Mrs Curtis came to the door, her eyes matching the red of her silk dressing gown.

"Mrs Riley, come in. You can put the tray on the table."

Nell did as instructed, glancing around as she straightened up. "Is Mr Curtis not with you?"

"I expect he'll be in the dining room."

"Ah. I must have missed him. Right well, if that's all, I'll let you get on with your breakfast."

Nell headed to the door, but Mrs Curtis called after her. "Actually, there is one thing. If you see Mr Curtis, would you tell him I'd like to talk to him? I didn't have a chance earlier."

"Yes, of course." Nell smiled. "Don't worry. I'm sure things will be all right."

"Oh, I hope so." She sat down and reached for a handkerchief. "We've never quarrelled like this."

"I'm afraid it happens to everyone sooner or later. You'll get over it. You must know he loves you."

"I thought I did, but now I'm not so sure." She stared up at Nell. "You're married, I presume, Mrs Riley."

"I'm a widow."

"Oh, I'm sorry. That must make me sound even more selfish. I shouldn't be so upset over something so silly."

"It mustn't be silly to you, but I've seen the way Mr Curtis looks at you. He won't want to see you sad."

"I hope you're right." She scrunched up the handkerchief and wiped her eyes. "Thank you, Mrs Riley."

The dining room was busy by the time Nell got back, and as she strode towards the galley, she noticed Mrs Anderson and her friends once more sitting apart from their husbands. After a quick glance around the rest of the tables, she wandered over to them.

"Good morning, ladies. May I get you anything?"

There were no smiles when they looked up at her.

"A fresh pot of tea, please." Mrs Anderson handed her the teapot. "I trust you don't have to ask our husbands' permission for that."

"No, madam. That's all part of the service."

"I should hope so." She turned back to the table where the four women sat with their heads together.

Mrs Swift was in the galley when Nell arrived and plonked the teapot on the counter.

"I don't know what's up with everyone this morning. I'm surprised there are any married couples still speaking to each other."

"I noticed that. Could it be because one or more of the ladies have been a little too friendly with Mr Driver?"

Nell shook her head. "Matron said the woman in question had been locked in her stateroom."

Mrs Swift's eyes twinkled. "Maybe she's been let out."

"It's possible." Nell winced and backed into the wall as Mr Ramsbottom squeezed past her.

"Is this a queue?"

"No, not at all." Mrs Swift picked up a couple of plates of scrambled eggs. "I'm going."

"And I've tables to clear." Nell kept her head down as she left the counter. "I'll see you later."

CHAPTER TWENTY

Once luncheon was over, Nell sat down with a sigh as Mr Ross put two plates of fish stew in front of them.

"There you are, ladies. Have you had a good morning?"

Nell picked up her knife and fork. "It's been better than most, given half the couples on the ship don't seem to be talking to each other."

"Really!" Mr Ross slid into the seat beside her. "Like who?"

"The honeymoon couple for one. They've had their first argument, and then the group of women who've been sitting over here. I've seen them glaring at their husbands several times while I've been walking around." Nell put a hand to her mouth. "I was meant to tell Mr Curtis that his wife wanted to speak to him, and I forgot. Not that I saw him, now I think about it."

"I imagine he'll have gone back to the stateroom by now." Mrs Swift didn't look up from her food.

"You're right. Did you check the tray situation, Mr Ross?"

"I did, but it was as I thought. No ladies are getting full tray service."

"How strange." She cocked her head to one side as she stabbed a piece of salmon. "What about the men?"

His face dropped. "I didn't look at them. You finish your luncheon and I'll tell you later."

"What's all that about?" Mrs Swift paused as she reached for a piece of bread.

"I had a thought that we could find out who our mystery lady is if we knew who was getting tray service."

"That's a good idea."

"It would have been if any of them were, but now I'm wondering if it's in the husband's name."

Mrs Swift studied her. "If you ask me, that makes more sense, especially if the husband wants to stop Mr Driver from delivering it."

"That's true. Not that I've seen him for days. Have you?"

Mrs Swift shook her head. "No, although I noticed Mr Price up here earlier. What if they've swapped places, and he's gone to steerage?"

Nell giggled. "He won't like that."

"It serves him right. Hopefully, they'll keep him at the front of the ship so he can't get close to any other unsuspecting woman."

"Keeping him downstairs will be bad enough for him." Nell looked up as Mr Ross returned, two bowls of peaches and cream in his hands.

"Mr Walker."

Nell bashed her head with a hand. "Of course. Why didn't I see it? That makes perfect sense."

"What does?" Mrs Swift stared at her.

"Mrs Walker's part of Mrs Anderson's group. When I commented on her absence the other day, they said she had a bout of seasickness, but it sounds like it wasn't. She could be the woman in question and her friends have fallen out with their husbands over it."

Mr Ross's forehead creased as he retook his seat. "Why would they fall out with their husbands?"

Nell shrugged. "If it was my friend, I wouldn't be happy if she'd been kept in her room. The husbands may support Mr Walker, while the women are concerned for his wife."

"It isn't anyone else's business how he treats her," Mr Ross said.

"The ladies obviously don't agree." She tapped her fingers on the table. "Now you mention it, I've noticed one or two of them sneaking out of the room. I wonder if they go to visit when Mr Walker's in here or the saloon."

"You could ask them."

"I can't do that. Besides, why would I, other than to satisfy our curiosity?"

"Isn't that enough?" Mr Ross grinned as he stood up. "Now we've got a name, we need all the details."

"No, we don't. It's none of our business."

"It could be, if it upset her friends. You've got keys to all the staterooms, haven't you? You could set her free."

"And lose our jobs? I don't think so." Nell rolled her eyes. "Besides, even if we did, she wouldn't get very far on a ship. Mr Walker would be bound to find her and be angrier than he is."

"You'd better do a bit of prying, then." He left them with a broad grin.

"And how are we going to do that?"

Mrs Swift sliced into a peach. "You'll think of something. Now, we'd better get a move on. We need to be up in the saloon in ten minutes."

Mr Price was by the saloon door when Nell and Mrs Swift arrived up the stairs.

"Good afternoon, ladies."

"Mr Price, what brings you here?" Mrs Swift kept her voice neutral.

"Mr Driver has other business, so the captain asked me to step in. You'll be seeing rather more of me over the next few days."

"That's nice. I hope you're happy up here. It will be a change to being downstairs."

"I'll be glad to see some daylight, if I'm honest with you. Now, don't let me keep you, our guests are waiting."

Nell surveyed the place as they walked in and gasped at the sight of Mr Curtis sitting at a table by himself.

"I'd forgotten about Mr Curtis again. I'd better check he's visited his wife."

"He doesn't seem happy."

"No, he doesn't." Nell headed to the left-hand corner of the room, but Mr Curtis didn't look up as she approached. "May I interrupt your thoughts, sir?"

His head jerked up. "Mrs Riley, yes, of course. What can I do for you?"

"Forgive me for not finding you earlier, but when I took your wife's tray this morning, she asked me to tell you she'd like to speak with you."

He stared down into his coffee. "I'll see her soon enough."

"I hope so. She was very upset."

"She's upset?" He glared up at her.

"Well, yes. She mentioned you'd quarrelled..."

"She had no right to tell you that."

Nell pursed her lips. "I'm sorry, I shouldn't have mentioned it." She turned to leave, but Mr Curtis called her back.

"Do you have any children, Mrs Riley?"

"Why, yes. Two daughters."

"Yet you still travel? Do you bring them with you?"

"Gracious, no." Nell sniggered, but stopped at his stern expression. "I'm sorry. I share a house with my sister and her family and they take care of them for me."

"And the children don't mind?"

"If I'm being honest, this is my first trip, so I won't find out until I go home."

He nodded, deep in thought, but suddenly looked up. "Do you miss them?"

"The children? I suppose ... but with being so busy..."

"So you don't?" His gaze was intense.

"I-I wouldn't say that. I think about them often, but I'm doing this to give them a better life." She suddenly smiled. "I'm taking them shopping for dresses when I get home."

"So you do miss them." His shoulders slumped. "It's not normal for a woman to not want children, is it?"

"Not want any?" Nell screwed up her face. "You mean by choice?" Her cheeks coloured. "I don't know if it's appropriate to say this, but ... well, only the Lord can make such decisions."

He banged his hand on the table. "By Jove, you're right. It's not our position to decide one way or the other. We need to leave it to God. He'll do what's right..." He stood up. "Thank you, Mrs Riley. I need to see my wife."

Nell strolled back to the ladies' section of the room where the two Mrs Fosters were waiting.

"Good afternoon, ladies. Welcome back. May I get you anything?"

The older sister spoke. "I'd like a refreshing elderflower cordial. The doctor told me I've not been drinking enough fluids. That's why I was in pain."

"From not drinking?" Nell's eyes widened.

"Yes, it's most bizarre. He gave it a fancy name, but basically I had a stone in my kidney that wanted to come out."

Nell's brow creased. "How do you get a stone in your kidney?"

"That's an excellent question, and one I asked him, but he couldn't answer. He's no more a doctor than the next man."

The other Mrs Foster put a hand on her sister's arm. "Don't upset yourself, Bertha. At least the laudanum helped you through it. Nobody else could have given you that."

"Maybe it did, but I'd rather not go through it again. And nor should you. I suggest you take a cordial with me."

The younger Mrs Foster rolled back her shoulders. "I'm sure I'm perfectly fine, but if it keeps you happy..."

Mr Brennan gazed across the dining room as Nell approached the bar. "Is nobody drinking this afternoon?"

"Not at the moment. They're a funny lot on this voyage."

He reached for his cocktail shaker. "What may I get for you?"

"Oh, nothing fancy. Two elderflower cordials, please, for the Fosters."

"Blimey. What's up with them?"

Nell shrugged. "I'd say the older sister had something of an epiphany when she was ill. She's become much friendlier and is taking the doctor's advice to drink more."

"Is she sure he didn't mean cocktails?"

"I'm certain, although you never know. She enjoyed the brandy the other night, so perhaps she'll have one later."

Once the drinks had been delivered, Nell stood with her back to the wall, surveying the ladies in her area. Several were playing cards, but Mrs Anderson's group were huddled at the end of a long table. *Are they talking about Mrs Walker?* She stepped to one side to check the glasses. *I'll be able to clear them shortly. What do I say?*

"A penny for your thoughts."

Nell jumped as Mrs Swift joined her.

"I'm studying Mrs Anderson's table and wondering what to say when I go to clear it."

"They seem rather angry. I served them earlier, but they were in no mood to talk."

"Have you noticed the way the gents are sitting on the other side of the room? They've positioned the table so they can see through the flowers."

Mrs Swift wandered along the edge of their section, her hands behind her back, before turning on her heel.

"You're right. They've not taken their eyes off them, either."

"I'm surprised the ladies haven't moved to the far corner. That's where they usually sit."

"I wonder if they've been told to stay close."

Nell grimaced. "It would explain why they're so cross. Oh, look, Mrs Anderson's got up. Where's she going?"

"Why don't you follow her?" Mrs Swift gave her a nudge. "Pretend you're checking up on Mrs Curtis or something, if anyone asks. The Walkers' stateroom is only a couple of doors away."

Nell straightened her apron. "Very well, I won't be long." She hadn't gone two paces when she stopped. "Oh no!" She gestured towards Mr Anderson as he followed his wife from the room. "We're not the only ones who want to know where she's going."

"Blimey, this is serious."

"The poor woman may only want to use the lavatory, too."

Mrs Swift sniggered. "It doesn't mean you can't follow her. You can use the facilities, too."

"Not the guest ones."

Mrs Swift raised an eyebrow. "What if I told you that one of them needed cleaning? You'd have to inspect them."

Nell bit down on her lip as she stared at her colleague. "All right then. I'll go after her."

CHAPTER TWENTY-ONE

The Curtises' room was at the end of the corridor, and Nell strode purposefully along the corridor, slowing only as she approached. She grimaced at raised voices coming through the door and turned to go back to the dining room, without knocking.

She was almost there, when Mrs Anderson appeared.

"Good afternoon." Nell tried to sound casual. "May I open your door for you?"

Mrs Anderson glanced behind her, but hesitated as her husband rounded the corner. "Yes, please. I'd like to take a nap before afternoon tea."

Nell led Mrs Anderson back to the stateroom, but as she stopped to open the door, the slight figure of Mr Anderson joined them. He nodded, showing a bald spot on the top of his head.

"Mrs Riley."

"Good afternoon, sir. Have you come for a lie-down, too?"

"Most certainly not, but I saw my wife and wanted to check she was all right."

"I'm fine. Can't a woman take a rest without being followed?" Mrs Anderson spat out her words.

"Forgive my wife, Mrs Riley. She's rather touchy at the moment. If you wouldn't mind bringing her a tray for afternoon tea, I'm sure she'd appreciate it."

Mrs Anderson spun away from the door. "No, I would not! I came here for a quiet half hour, but you've completely ruined it. I may as well go back to the saloon, because I won't get any rest if you're watching me."

Nell fidgeted with the key as her eyes flicked between Mr and Mrs Anderson.

"I'll go with her, sir, and make sure she's all right. A nice cup of tea may help."

"As long as it's no more of those damn cocktails. Forgive my language, but she's grown too accustomed to them."

"Yes, sir." Nell left Mr Anderson by the stateroom door and hurried after his wife. *Let's hope she's not ordered one by the time I get there.*

She rounded the corner into the foyer faster than usual and bumped straight into Mr Ramsbottom, who held out his hands to stop her.

"My, that's an unexpected pleasure." A crooked grin spread across his face. "You really shouldn't rush, Mrs Riley."

Nell's cheeks burned. "I'm sorry but I need a word with Mrs Anderson." She moved to sidestep him, but he moved with her.

"There's no need to be hasty."

"Actually, there is. I promised Mr Anderson I'd keep an eye on his wife."

"I'm sure she can look after herself for a few minutes. I've been wanting to have a word with you."

"No, really, please, Mr Ramsbottom. Another time."

She pushed past him and stumbled into the saloon, as Mrs Swift left the ladies' table. *Too late.* She sighed. *At least I tried.* She carried on to the bar.

"What did she order?"

Mrs Swift tutted. "A brandy, if you like. At this time of day."

The colour drained from Nell's face.

"What's the matter?"

"I told Mr Anderson I'd get her a cup of tea. He said she's drinking too much."

"I wouldn't argue with him there, but I don't blame her." Mrs Swift picked up the glass from the bar. "Do you want to take it?"

"No, I don't." Nell shuddered. "If Mr Anderson saw me giving her that... You shouldn't take it to her either."

"I can't not serve someone." Mrs Swift walked to the table and handed Mrs Anderson the glass before returning to her station. "She's not very happy."

"I'm not surprised." Nell nodded at Mr Anderson as he strode across the room. "What's he doing?"

"I don't know, but he shouldn't be on this side of the partition. It's strictly for ladies."

"Will you tell him?" Nell blew out her cheeks as Mr Anderson snatched the glass from his wife.

"That's enough." He glared at Nell as he stormed back to his own table.

"Thankfully, there's no need, but I'll leave her to calm down before I go over again." Nell wandered to the table the Fosters had vacated and collected up the cups, but stopped as Mrs Anderson and her friends left the saloon in the direction of the promenade. *They won't stay out there for long without their cloaks.* She shuddered as a gust of wind made its way through the room, and she turned to Mrs Swift at the next table.

"It's time we had something to eat. Shall we go downstairs?"

Mrs Swift straightened up. "Didn't you want to follow them?"

"No, I've had enough for one day. Besides, I'm not going outside in this weather. They'll be back in a minute."

"I notice Mr Walker's followed them this time."

"If he's not gone to check on his wife. Poor Mrs Walker."

"It's times like this I'm glad I never married."

Nell bobbed her head from side to side. "It can be nice if you marry the right person. My Jack wouldn't have behaved like that."

"Then you were fortunate. Seeing what happened to some childhood friends when they married was one of the reasons I decided to take care of myself." Mrs Swift led the way to the dining room and their usual table.

"I know what you mean. My sisters have put me off, if I'm being honest."

"Do you think you'll ever remarry?"

Nell shrugged. "I doubt it. Not at the moment, anyway. I had a bit of a run-in with Mr Ramsbottom earlier and he frightened the life out of me."

Mrs Swift groaned as they took their seats. "What did he do?"

"He didn't do anything really. It was all my fault. I walked into the foyer too quickly and bumped straight into him. He was keen to talk to me, but I was in a hurry to stop Mrs Anderson ordering any alcohol."

"Ah. That's why you looked so crestfallen when I saw you."

Nell snorted. "You noticed."

"I could hardly not. Your face gives too much away."

She grimaced. "So I've been told. I keep working on it, but never manage to look stern."

"Here we are, ladies." Mr Ross put down two plates of lamb chops with boiled potatoes and carrots. "Give me a moment while I get your tea and I'll be back. I have some news."

"That sounds exciting." Mrs Swift picked up her knife and fork.

"Oh, it is." He scooted off with a twinkle in his eye.

"You wonder how he finds out so much being stuck in the galley all day."

"He's got all of us calling in and giving him titbits of information. He's bright enough to piece it all together and ask the right questions."

Nell chuckled. "I suppose it makes the job exciting. I hadn't realised how interesting the passengers would be."

"Me neither, but it's usually the thing that keeps us all sane, and talking to each other."

"Here we are." Mr Ross plonked the tray on the table and took a seat.

"What do you know then?" Mrs Swift raised an eyebrow at him.

"Mr Driver's been told to leave the ship when we get to Liverpool."

"Really?" Nell put a hand to her mouth. "That's a hefty price to pay."

"It is." Mr Ross chuckled. "Half the lads wouldn't be here if it was standard practice."

Nell coughed as a piece of meat caught in her throat. "You're telling me they're all like that?"

He shrugged. "Maybe not quite so bad, but ... they're not saints either."

"So why has it happened this time?" Mrs Swift kept her eyes on him.

"It would appear poor Mr Driver picked on the wrong woman. Her husband's fairly senior in head office."

"In Liverpool?"

"Yes."

Nell put down her knife and gazed over Mr Ross's head. "Do you know, I thought he looked familiar, but I decided he was just another man of medium build with a pencil moustache."

"There are plenty of us about." Mr Ross smoothed down his own moustache. "Did you see him at the office?"

"I must have done, but I couldn't say when. If I could remember, it might give us an idea of what position he holds. Do you think he's watching us?"

Mr Ross shifted in his seat. "I hadn't thought of that. I'd better make sure he gets the best cuts of meat."

.   .   .

Once dinner had been served, Nell strolled around the room, stopping at the Fosters' table.

"Is everything to your liking?"

The older woman stabbed her piece of halibut. "It's remarkably pleasant, thank you. How's yours, Cissy?"

The younger Mrs Foster sliced into a boiled potato. "Nice enough, not that I was hungry. We've not long since finished afternoon tea."

"I'm sure it can feel like that, but enjoy it anyway." She continued walking but stopped to stare at the Curtises. *Do I disturb them?*

Her decision was made when Mr Curtis beckoned her over.

"Good evening, sir. Two Manhattans?"

"No, thank you." Mr Curtis held out a glass. "Some more wine for me, please. My wife isn't feeling herself." He patted Mrs Curtis's hand.

"Oh, I'm sorry. Is there anything I can get for her?"

Mrs Curtis didn't look up as she shook her head. "No. I'll be going to the room shortly."

"Very good, madam." Nell collected their plates and delivered them to the galley on her way to the bar.

"A glass of red wine for Mr Curtis, please."

Mr Brennan stared at her. "Is that it?"

"I'm afraid so. They're not over their tiff by the looks of it."

"I'll be down on tips at this rate. The ladies aren't drinking tonight either." He placed the wine on the bar.

"I noticed that. They're all sat with their husbands, and the Andersons aren't here at all."

"It's hardly worth me opening up."

Nell reached for the glass. "I would if I were you. That's what you get paid for."

The dining room emptied quickly, and Nell helped Mrs Swift clear their section of tables.

"Do you know who took the tray to the Andersons' room tonight?"

Mrs Swift shook her head. "I've no idea. Why?"

"To see if whoever it was knows why they didn't come to dinner."

"Mr Ross will know."

Nell picked up a stack of bowls. "You're right. Let me go and ask him."

Mr Ross sucked air through his teeth at Nell's question. "I don't remember. It was hectic earlier on, and I was keen to make sure Mr Walker got the best cut. I'll have a note of it, somewhere." He took the dishes from her and came back with a piece of paper. "Here we are. Mr Cooper."

"Mr Cooper? He's usually in steerage." Nell's brow creased.

"He is ... and now I think about it, I don't remember seeing him again."

"How strange." Nell wandered back to the table, where Mrs Swift looked up expectantly.

"Mr Cooper."

"Mr *Cooper?*"

"That's what the rota said. He didn't serve anyone else, though."

"Perhaps they preferred to be served by someone they didn't know."

Nell nodded. "That would make sense. I doubt he'll be around when we go back to our quarters."

"Probably not, but Mr Potter will be. I'll leave a note asking Mr Cooper to bring breakfast for us tomorrow."

"Can we do that?"

Mrs Swift shrugged. "We'll soon find out."

CHAPTER TWENTY-TWO

Nell was up and dressed early the following morning, and Mrs Swift held the door open as they headed across the corridor to the sitting room. Matron was there when they arrived, sitting bolt upright on the settee.

"You're here early. We thought we'd beat you..." Mrs Swift breezed into the room, but stopped abruptly, causing Nell to walk into the back of her. "Mr Driver...!"

"What time do you call this, you conniving pair of troublemakers?"

Both took a step backwards, but Mr Driver stepped closer.

"I expect you've heard I'll be leaving the ship when we reach Liverpool. All thanks to you."

"Us?" Mrs Swift stared at him. "We had nothing to do with it."

Matron squirmed in her seat. "I'm afraid, Mr Driver, you've no one to blame but yourself."

"Me! It was them." The tip of his index finger almost

touched Mrs Swift's face as he pointed at them. "Running off to the captain ... again."

"We did no such thing." Nell's voice squeaked.

"I don't believe you..." He took another step forward and grabbed Nell's arm. "You've been trouble ever since you got on the ship..."

"Mr Driver, that's enough." Matron banged her hand on the table. "I suggest you leave us immediately unless you want this incident relaying to the captain, as well."

He glared at Matron and then Nell. "You'll regret this."

Nell's heart pounded as he released her arm and pushed past her.

"Come here." Matron patted the empty seat beside her as Mr Driver's footsteps echoed along the corridor. "I'll put some extra sugar in your tea."

Tears threatened to roll down Nell's cheeks, and she brushed them away with the back of a hand. "We didn't do anything."

"I'm aware of that. Now, sit down."

Mrs Swift steadied her as she walked to the table. "What was he doing here?"

Matron carried on buttering a piece of toast. "That's a very good question. I'll be having words with Mr Potter on my way out. And with Captain Robertson."

"Please don't get us into any more trouble." A tear escaped down Nell's cheek.

"Of course I won't, but the captain needs to be told what's going on. I'd like to know why Mr Driver blames you for his predicament. Did you see him with the woman in question?"

"No ... not exactly, but, well, we saw him with Lilly, the

maid from the last trip. We didn't say anything, but maybe he thought…"

Matron scowled at Mrs Swift. "Why didn't you report him? You should know better than that."

"I do, but it was on the last night before we arrived in New York and by ten o'clock the next morning she'd gone. There didn't seem much point."

"You should still have reported it. How can we expect to keep a respectable ship when the likes of Mr Driver behave so disgracefully?"

Mrs Swift turned her attention to her porridge. "Because we didn't think it was entirely his fault. It wouldn't surprise us if Lilly encouraged him."

"Is that what happened with Mrs Walker?" Nell took a sip of tea.

Matron's head spun to face her. "Who told you it was Mrs Walker?"

"Erm, well, you said it was the wife of the finance manager…"

"And where did you get that information from? It wasn't mentioned on the passenger list."

Mrs Swift sighed. "If you must know, it was a steward."

Matron slumped in her chair. "And how on earth did *they* find out?"

"We have to have something to keep us occupied." Mrs Swift's toast crunched as she bit into it.

"Well, I've no idea who's been talking. Besides me, only the captain, first officer and Mr Price were aware of this."

Mrs Swift tutted. "Can't you hazard a guess, then? Why was Mr Price even told?"

"It's because he reported them, isn't it!" Nell banged a hand on the table. "That's how you can be sure it wasn't us."

"Is that true?" Mrs Swift glared at the elderly lady. "Why did Mr Driver suspect us, then?"

Matron put a hand to her forehead. "I'm sorry, but Mr Driver is Mr Price's superior, and if he finds out the truth, it could be awkward."

"But it doesn't matter if he turns on us?" Mrs Swift's cheeks were red.

"We had no way of knowing he'd accuse you, but I'll tell the captain what's happened. In the meantime, not a word of this to anyone else."

Mrs Swift snorted. "Half the staff know about Mr Driver. There's a sweepstake amongst the stewards to guess who the woman is."

"You've not told them, have you?" Fear appeared on Matron's face. "I had to pay her a visit after *the incident* and I promised that no one would find out."

"We won't say a word, will we, Mrs Riley?"

Nell grimaced. "Not now we know it's a secret."

"Splendid. Right, I must be going." Matron shuffled around the table to stand up. "I'll speak to you later."

Nell grimaced as she listened to Matron's footsteps disappearing along the corridor. "What happened to Mr Cooper bringing breakfast?"

"I suspect Mr Driver got rid of him so he could bring it himself. He obviously wanted to speak to us."

Nell paused as she took a bite of toast. "What can we do about Mrs Walker? It will be all round the stewards already, now Mr Ross knows."

"I don't doubt it, but as it was him who let the cat out of the bag, it should at least get us off the hook."

"Unless he placed a wager." Nell studied Mrs Swift. "If he did, he won't want anyone else knowing, so we may be able to stop him." She emptied her teacup as Mrs Swift stood up.

"You're right. Come along, we need to be quick."

The galley was unusually quiet when they arrived, and Mr Ross was nowhere to be seen.

"The stewards must be taking their trays." Mrs Swift peered behind the counter.

"Or they've not arrived yet. It is still early."

"It is, but Mr Ross should be here." She stepped around the counter and peered into the pantry. "Here you are. What's going on?"

Mr Ross walked towards her and ushered her back to the counter, his face stern. "There's trouble. Someone's been telling tales."

Mrs Swift glanced at Nell. "What about?"

"You." His eyes flicked to both of them.

"Us! What have they been saying?"

He held up his hands. "Look, I'm only telling you for your own good. It's not come from me, but word is you were the ones who reported Mr Driver."

Nell's head swivelled between the two of them. "But we didn't. We've already told you..."

"I know, I know, but I'm warning you that there may be some *hostility* this morning."

Mrs Swift clenched her fists. "Not again. We're only

just getting over the last incident ... which also wasn't our fault." Her raised voice brought several members of the galley into view, and Mr Ross clapped his hands.

"All right, that's enough. Back to work, lads. There's nothing going on here."

"Yes, there is." Mrs Swift addressed the men hovering behind Mr Ross. "Whatever's been going on with Mr Driver has nothing to do with us. We didn't see him, let alone report him." She lowered her voice. "You believe us, don't you?"

Nell couldn't hear what was said as the men huddled together, but Mr Ross shrugged.

"If you say so."

"Yes, we do." Mrs Swift rolled her shoulders and straightened her dress. "Are there any trays to take?"

A sous chef placed one on the counter. "This is ready, but it's not for you. Mr Cooper should be here for it in a minute."

"Who's it for?" Mrs Swift grabbed the piece of paper attached. "The Andersons."

Nell reached past her and picked it up. "I'll take it. Mr Cooper seems to be indisposed this morning."

"No, you can't..."

Nell ignored Mr Ross's objections and set off for the stairs. *If people are going to hurl accusations at me, I want to know what I'm supposed to have done.*

Nell stepped aside as the Fosters passed her in the corridor, but otherwise saw no one. She leaned her ear to the door. *All quiet. Is that a good sign?* Her stomach fluttered as she balanced the tray on one arm and knocked.

Moments later, Mrs Anderson threw back the door, her pink chiffon robe billowing in the draught.

"Oh, Mrs Riley, it's you. Do come in."

Nell crossed the threshold and placed the tray on the table.

"It's most fortunate that you're here while my husband is using the facilities. I've been hoping to have a word with you."

Nell kept her face straight. "You have?"

"My acquaintances and I are rather worried about Mrs Walker. She's an old friend of mine, you know, and we need to find a way to talk to her."

Nell gulped. "How can I help?"

"You must have a key to her room. Would you be a dear and let me in when her husband isn't around?"

"Well, I ... erm ... I don't know. I've been told not to go into her room."

"You wouldn't be going in, just opening the door. She's being held in there against her wishes and for no reason."

Nell bit down on her lip. "Forgive my impertinence, but I understand she was found with a steward.?"

"That's nonsense. The poor thing stopped to ask him a question, but the waves rolled the ship and she fell into the man's arms at precisely the moment that fool of a husband saw her. I tell you, if he hadn't been following her, it would never have happened."

"I heard it was a steward who made the complaint to the captain."

Mrs Anderson flicked her hand. "Oh, it was, but only because Mr Walker *encouraged* him to."

"But there wasn't anything to report?"

"No, not at all. The problem was that Mr Walker already had the steward in his sights. He said he was a cut above himself."

Nell sighed. "I can't argue with that, but it's a rather harsh punishment to have him removed from the ship."

Mrs Anderson gasped. "Is that what will happen to him?"

Nell nodded. "So I understand."

"That's most unfair." Mrs Anderson cocked her head to one side as she studied Nell. "How do you know all this?"

Nell wandered to the door. "Word travels amongst the staff, and when we heard that Mr Driver was the man in question, we took more interest. He blames me and Mrs Swift for reporting him over the incident, and now half the crew aren't speaking to us." She jumped as Mrs Anderson banged a hand on the table.

"This has gone far enough. People's jobs are at stake because a man's ego can't bear a steward smiling at his wife. That's what this is all about."

Nell turned to face Mrs Anderson. "Thank you for being so honest. At least I know what I've been accused of."

"And we mustn't let Mr Walker get away with it. I've known him for years, but he's getting worse."

"I presume there's no talking to him."

"No. He's adamant that he's in the right, and has gone so far as to turn my own husband against me." She feigned a sob. "If only I could speak to Mrs Walker…"

"Perhaps I could open the stateroom door, then." Nell lifted her keys from her pocket, but immediately pushed them back as the door opened.

"What are you doing?"

Nell took a step backwards as Mr Anderson's eyes shifted between the two of them.

"She's brought the tray. Why we can't go to the dining room like everyone else, I've no idea."

"Yes, you do. I don't want you gossiping with those women." He glared at Nell. "I specifically asked for a steward to deliver this tray at eight o'clock, so I'd be here."

"Apologies, but Mr Cooper isn't well this morning and I didn't want you waiting."

"So you should be thanking her." Mrs Anderson poked a finger at her husband, but when he remained silent, she did it again. "What do you say?"

With a heavy sigh, he nodded. "Thank you, Mrs Riley."

"You're welcome. Right, I'd better be going; I'll see you later."

She hadn't taken two steps into the dining room when Mr Cooper marched towards her. "What are you doing, taking my tray?"

"Yours? I thought you were in steerage."

"I've been promoted. I'll be working up here for the rest of the voyage, and I'd thank you to keep your hands off my clients. If there are any tips to be had, they're mine."

Nell shrugged. "As you like, but I doubt you'll get much off that pair." She walked past him, but he caught hold of her arm.

"What does that mean?"

She bit down on her lip as she held his gaze. "I don't think they're impressed with the behaviour of some of the stewards."

"That's not my fault."

"It's not mine, either, but it's not stopped people blaming me for everything that's happened."

"Because you're a snitch."

Nell gritted her teeth. "I'm nothing of the sort, but if I am, perhaps you should thank me. I doubt you'd have got your promotion otherwise."

"It was coming."

"Not on this voyage it wasn't. Now, if you'll excuse me, I need to get on."

CHAPTER TWENTY-THREE

Once breakfast was over, Nell collected her cleaning cloths and headed to the Fosters' stateroom. She was about to let herself in when Mr Price called to her from the far end of the corridor.

"I'm sorry to shout, but the captain would like a word with you in his office. Now."

"The captain? Why?"

"I can't say. Will you come with me?"

Nell looked down at her bucket and cloths. "What do I do with these?"

"Leave them there. The guests are all settled in the saloon, so you'll be back by the time anyone notices."

The walk to the bridge was short, and Mr Price knocked on the door and walked straight in.

"Mrs Riley for you, Captain." He ushered Nell into the office. "I'll be outside if you need me."

"Ah, Mrs Riley. Take a seat."

Nell's stomach churned as she noticed a steeliness in the captain's eyes for the first time.

"Yes, Captain. Is there a problem?"

"That's for you to tell me. I hear you've been behaving inappropriately with Mr Ramsbottom."

"Mr Ramsbottom! No, sir," Nell spluttered as the blood drained from her cheeks. "He's given me some unwanted attention, but I've never encouraged him."

"So tell me about the event yesterday when you were seen embracing in the foyer outside the saloon."

"Yesterday?" Nell gave a nervous laugh. "We bumped into each other when I was hurrying back to the saloon. It was nothing more than that."

"And yet you made no attempt to pull away from him."

"But that's not true." Her mouth opened and closed several times. "Who told you?"

"I can't disclose that, but if it's true, I'll need to give you an official reprimand."

"But, sir, I mentioned on the outward journey that it's less than a year since I lost my husband. I've no desire to become acquainted with anyone else. Certainly not Mr Ramsbottom."

Captain Robertson sighed. "The problem is, the company insists I take matters of this nature very seriously. I have my orders to report any female crew member who behaves in an unbecoming manner."

"But it was an accident ... I was hurrying to the saloon..." Nell lowered her head, but slowly raised it again. "Will Mr Ramsbottom be reprimanded, too."

"I'll speak to him..."

"Is that all?" Nell gazed at her lap as tears formed. *Don't cry now.* She rubbed her face and straightened her back.

"I've done nothing wrong, and yet this is the second time today I've been accused of wrongdoing."

"May I ask what the other incident was?"

"Mr Driver. First thing this morning, he blamed me and Mrs Swift for reporting him to you... Wait a minute." She paused, studying the captain's rugged features. "You know we weren't the ones who reported him, but it's the same as it was on the outbound voyage. When the person making the complaint is more important than either me or Mrs Swift, we're left to take the blame."

"It's unfortunate that you see it that way..."

"What other way is there? Mr Driver's parting shot this morning was that I'd be sorry for losing him his job. He's the cause of this, isn't he?"

Captain Robertson lowered his eyes and flicked his fingers through the papers on his desk.

"Are you suggesting Mr Driver reported you because he believes you filed the complaint about him?"

"It's a strange coincidence otherwise, wouldn't you say?"

The captain pinched the beard on his chin. "Leave it with me. Believe me, Mrs Riley, I have no wish to report you." He stood up and encouraged her to the door.

"What does that mean?"

"I need to speak to a few other people. I'll be in touch."

Mr Price was waiting as she stepped outside, a smile brightening his face as he turned to look at her.

"Is everything all right?"

"No, it's not, as it happens."

"Oh, I'm sorry to hear that."

"Are you really?" Nell stopped to study him.

"What's that supposed to mean?"

"It means that you're the cause of my problems."

"Nonsense. If you want to canoodle with Ramsbottom in public, that's not my fault."

"As far as I'm aware, there was no one else in the foyer when I bumped into him, so who told you about it? The same man you reported to the captain for embracing Mrs Walker, based on nothing more than her husband's jealousy?"

"It was nothing of the sort."

"You saw it with your own eyes, did you?"

"Not exactly, but the information was passed to me on good authority."

"And it suited your purposes, given you've wanted to get back into first class rather than be downstairs with the steerage passengers. I imagine you didn't ask too many questions."

Mr Price stepped towards her. "It's got nothing to do with you."

"It has when I'm being blamed for it." Nell stopped and put a hand over her mouth as the captain appeared from his office. "I'm sorry, Captain. I didn't mean to shout."

"Get back to your duties, Mrs Riley. Mr Price, might I have a word?"

Mr Price glowered at Nell. "Yes, Captain."

Mrs Swift was finishing her last stateroom when Nell poked her head through the door.

"Are you nearly finished here? I need you to help me with my rooms." She stormed down the corridor without waiting for a response, and by the time Mrs Swift joined her, she'd stripped the beds in the Fosters' room.

"What's the matter with you?"

"Mr Price and Mr Driver. That's what."

Mrs Swift stopped and folded her arms. "All right, tell me what's up."

Nell's chest heaved. "There's a chance I'll be reported for embracing Mr Ramsbottom."

"What?"

"You heard. Someone must have seen me bump into him yesterday, and told the captain. He said it's company policy to report any female crew who behave inappropriately."

"But you told me it was an accident."

"It was. Why on earth would I do it deliberately? I don't even like the man."

"So what happens now?"

Nell sat on the settee. "I don't know. When I asked Captain Robertson if it was Mr Driver who'd told him, he wouldn't say, but said he'd speak to a few more people before he filed a report. He called Mr Price in as I was leaving, because we had a bit of an argument and the captain overheard..."

Mrs Swift sat beside her. "Blimey. And there was me, thinking you were skiving."

Nell reached for her handkerchief. "I'm not cut out for this. I thought it would be easy enough, and James had said that if I didn't like any of the passengers, I'd only need to put up with them for two weeks; he didn't mention problems with the crew."

"Probably because he's no idea."

Nell looked at her friend. "What do you mean? He's worked on a ship with a stewardess."

"Does he know what she has to put up with each day? How she'll lock herself into her cabin as soon as she's finished each evening to get away from unwanted attention?"

"I don't suppose he does."

"No, he wouldn't. But I do, because that's exactly what I did every night last year. It was made worse by the third mate who took a shine to me. He could go anywhere on the ship, so it wasn't easy to be rid of him."

Nell shook her head. "I'd no idea."

"You had no reason to, but you need to be tough to work on a ship. By the sound of it, you stood up for yourself well enough."

"I tried, but I felt sick when the captain said he'd report me. What would I say to Maria?"

"You wouldn't have to say anything."

Nell's shoulders heaved. "You're right. I could tell her I didn't like it and that I'm not going back. She doesn't want me to come back, anyway."

Mrs Swift sighed and stood up. "It would be a great shame if you didn't. You're good at what you do, and besides, I'd like you to stay. I'd rather not be on my own any more."

"They'll find someone else if I leave."

Mrs Swift wandered to the porthole and peered out. "Not when we're only in Liverpool for three days. There won't be time."

A lump settled in Nell's stomach. "I hadn't thought of that."

"Mrs Scott's expecting you on the next voyage, too."

"But if I'm reported..."

"Then the captain will have me and half the passengers to deal with. I've seen how they are with you, and they like you. I'm sure they'd want to help if they knew what was going on."

Nell wiped her eyes as she stood up. "We'll see. Come on, we'd better get a move on. It will be time for luncheon soon."

The dining room was already filling up by the time Nell and Mrs Swift arrived, and Nell pretended not to notice the stewards whispering to each other as they nodded in her direction.

"If you don't mind, I'll take the ladies-only tables today. I've no desire to come into contact with the stewards any more than I need to."

"If you must, but Mrs Anderson's in the couples' area with her husband and their friends. They must have had a reconciliation."

Nell surveyed the faces at the table. "I doubt it. I'd say their husbands want to keep an eye on them. Would you mind seeing to them? I won't be able to talk to Mrs Anderson, anyway."

"As you like. You can take care of the Fosters."

Nell smiled as she walked over to them. "Good afternoon, ladies. How may I help?"

"My sister and I were commenting that you appeared rather distracted. Is everything all right?"

"Nothing for you to worry about." Nell feigned a laugh.

"There was a bit of a misunderstanding this morning, but it will all be fine."

The older Mrs Foster stared up at her. "You don't tell lies very well, Mrs Riley."

"I'll take that as a compliment, but please don't worry. It's only a bit of something amongst the crew."

Mrs Foster laid down her knife. "Cissy and I were talking yesterday, and we said that it can't be easy for you and Mrs Swift being amongst so many stewards."

"There's Matron as well. She keeps an eye out for us."

"With all due respect, Matron is not an attractive young woman. She also has a position of authority, which means she won't get the same attention as you."

The younger Mrs Foster nodded in agreement. "You may find this hard to believe, Mrs Riley, but my sister and I were once something of a catch. Not only were we pleasing to the eye, we had money and property of our own. Our brother never tired of telling us that marriage wasn't in our interests and we believed him. Not that it stopped men trying. We ended up with our own ways of deterring them. We're really not as grumpy as many would have you believe." She adjusted the collar of her blouse as Nell watched.

"So it's all an act?"

"You could say that, although it's become less necessary as the years have taken their toll."

"You forget, Cissy, we still have enough money and assets to cause a man to overlook our appearance, and now we don't have our brother to take care of us, we can't let our guard down."

Nell's brow furrowed. *Why are they telling me this?*

It was as if the older Mrs Foster read her mind. "I've noticed several stewards talking about you behind their hands. Are they causing trouble?"

Nell glanced over her shoulder to see most of them going about their business. "They're gossiping. I was in a hurry yesterday and bumped into one of them. We were in contact with each other for no more than a second or two, but the captain's been told it was a deliberate act on my part..."

"And you're the one who'll receive a reprimand, not him?"

Nell nodded. "Something like that."

The younger Mrs Foster leaned forward. "Which steward was it?"

"I'm not sure I should say, but ... well, they're not keeping things to themselves. It was Mr Ramsbottom."

The sisters looked at each other before the elder turned back to Nell. "You may not have a brother with you, Mrs Riley, but you have us. Now stop worrying and put a scowl on your face."

CHAPTER TWENTY-FOUR

Nell groaned at the sound of the morning bell in the corridor. She'd had a poor night's sleep, only partly caused by the choppiness of the sea.

"What's the matter with you?" Mrs Swift peered up to the top bunk.

"I can't believe it's time to get up already. I barely slept a wink last night."

"You've got to ignore everything that's going on."

Nell swung her legs over the side of the bed. "It's all right for you. You're not the one who's going to have a disciplinary record. Not to mention all the snide remarks ... again."

"I'm getting as many comments as you, but I don't take any notice of them. You need to speak to Mr Ramsbottom today and see if he'll put a stop to it."

Nell snorted. "He's suddenly made himself scarce. I only saw the back of him yesterday as he scurried in the opposite direction."

"That's a good thing, then. At least you won't have him all over you." She chuckled at Nell's scowl. "You should look on the bright side. Now, hurry up, we need to speak to Matron before she disappears."

"You go first, I'll follow you. I've no desire to see Mr Driver again."

Mrs Swift pulled on the doorknob. "I doubt we will. At least, I hope not."

There was a cup of tea and a bowl of porridge waiting for Nell when she arrived in the sitting room.

"Good morning, Matron."

"Good morning, Mrs Riley. I see what Mrs Swift means." She studied Nell's face. "There's no point moping; you should hold your shoulders straight and your head high."

"She's told you I could be reported?"

"She has, and the captain mentioned it to me last night. I told him that they can't hope to recruit more stewardesses if they don't protect you."

Nell took a seat. "I was led to believe there is no shortage of women who'd like the job."

"There may be, but if they all leave after the first voyage, we'll get through them rather quickly."

Nell looked at Mrs Swift. "You told her?"

Matron spread some marmalade on her toast. "Yes, she did, and I'm not very pleased about it. We can't be retraining a new stewardess every month."

"But the contract I signed said I could use the first trip as a test and if I either didn't like it or was unsuitable, then I wouldn't have to do another one. The way things are looking, I won't be able to come back, even if I want to."

Matron pushed herself from the table. "We'll see about that. Good day, ladies."

Nell waited for Matron's footsteps to disappear down the corridor. "Did you tell her everything?"

"Pretty well. There didn't seem any point keeping anything back."

"Was she angry with me?"

"No, she wasn't, actually. She was cross at the way you'd been singled out. She knows full well who reported Mr Driver and can see that you're being picked on."

Nell sighed. "I hope so. I'd rather not leave under a cloud."

"And I don't want you to leave at all, so between us, we'll have to do something about it."

As soon as they entered the dining room, Nell's eyes were drawn to the table at the far side, where Mrs Anderson sat with her friends, well away from the prying ears of their husbands. She nudged Mrs Swift.

"It looks like they've broken free again."

"Mr Anderson probably couldn't put up with his wife for more than twenty-four hours at a time."

"I doubt anyone could." Nell chuckled at her friend. "I'll go and see if they need anything."

"What about your trays?"

"They can wait." She hurried across to them. "Good morning, ladies. It's nice to have you back on this side of the room."

"It most certainly is." She beckoned for Nell to step a little closer. "Do you still have your keys with you?"

"I do." Nell tapped her pocket. "I can let you into Mrs Walker's stateroom, when you're ready."

"Splendid." Mrs Anderson peered around the side of Nell, but a petite woman seated beside her drew her attention back to the table.

"You can't visit her. The men will be furious."

"They needn't know, but even if they do find out, it will be worth it. Poor Sarah's been locked in that cabin for days now, and for what?"

"But what about Mrs Riley? We don't want to get her into trouble."

Nell grimaced. "I'm afraid I already am on another matter. In for a penny, in for a pound."

"Oh, my dear. It's nothing to do with us, I hope."

"No. Not at all." *Although maybe a little, if you hadn't been so keen on having another brandy...*

Mrs Anderson put a hand to her chest. "That's a relief. I have a plan I'd like to share with you." She lowered her voice, and Nell leaned towards her, collecting some dishes as she did.

"Mrs Riley, I believe you service our staterooms once breakfast is over. I suggest that would be the best time for our little operation."

"Will you be able to get away from Mr Anderson?"

Mrs Anderson glared in the direction of her husband. "Don't worry about that. Last evening, he and Mr Walker made arrangements to take a walk on the deck this morning."

"Won't they have arranged for one of the others to keep an eye on us?" There was fear in the petite lady's eyes.

"Stop worrying, dear. If I go to my room for a lie-down, they won't follow me the way my husband would, and I'll wait until they go again before I look for Mrs Riley."

"You don't want me to be cleaning your room when you arrive?"

"Gracious, no, but if you could do my room first, that would be a help. I can hide out in there and come and find you when the coast's clear."

"Very good, madam." Nell checked the nearby clock. "Breakfast won't be over for another hour, so give me at least an hour and a half so I can have your stateroom finished."

Mrs Anderson smiled up at her, the pearls of her necklace held in place by the excess skin around her neck. "You really are a marvel."

Nell hurried back to the galley and plonked the bowls on the counter, startling Mr Ross.

"You're late. There's a tray here waiting."

"I'm sorry. I was needed at one of the tables. Who's it for?"

"The Curtises."

"Both of them?" Nell raised her eyebrows. "Does that mean they're on speaking terms again?"

Mr Ross shrugged. "I couldn't tell you." He disappeared into the back of the galley as Nell picked up the tray.

What's up with him this morning? She hadn't reached the door to the foyer when a voice called out behind her, "Don't go *accidentally* bumping into anyone, will you? You'll have to get your thrills later."

It sounded like Mr Cooper, but Nell didn't give him the satisfaction of turning round, and with her back straight she held her head high. *I need to find Mr Ramsbottom and sort this out.*

The corridor was quiet as she made her way to the Curtises' stateroom. After a brief knock, Mr Curtis pulled back the door with a flourish.

"Mrs Riley, come on in."

Nell hesitated at the sight of him in a dark navy dressing gown. "Actually, sir, I'd rather not." She indicated to his bare legs protruding from the bottom, causing him to throw back his head in laughter.

"Don't worry, I won't bite. Mrs Curtis is right here with me. Aren't you, dear?"

"Yes, I'm here." Mrs Curtis appeared beside him, in a similar state of undress. "Forgive us for still being in our morning clothes. There wasn't much point getting dressed when we were going to sit in bed to eat."

"No, I don't suppose there was." Nell offered her the tray. "May I pass this to you?"

"Of course. We should have thought about how it would look, but we wanted to thank you."

Nell put her hands behind her back as Mrs Curtis took the tray. "Really? Why?"

"Because you talked some sense into both of us." Mr Curtis watched his wife as she set down the tray. "Having children isn't in our gift. If the Lord plans it, then who are we to argue?"

"That's what the argument was about?"

Mrs Curtis became rather sheepish. "I'm afraid it was my fault. I've enjoyed our honeymoon so much I wanted to be able to do it again, but as Neville pointed out, once we have a family I'll be tied to the house. It seemed so unfair that he would continue travelling to New York..."

"On business," he interrupted.

"Yes, on business, but without me. But then you said that you haven't brought your children with you..."

"I do miss them, though." Unbidden, tears suddenly pricked Nell's eyes.

"I'm sure you do, but even if I could travel once a year, I'd be happy. And as Neville said, it may never happen."

"No..." Nell wiped a finger across her cheeks. "...but don't wish them away, for a few trips. You'll have your children for a lot longer."

Mr Curtis shook his head. "Mrs Riley, you're a marvel."

"I try, sir."

Nell couldn't concentrate as she made the beds and swept the floor in the Fosters' stateroom. There were more people using the corridor than usual and as each one passed, the queasy feeling in her stomach worsened in anticipation of Mrs Anderson appearing.

She was plumping up the cushions on the settee when there was a gentle knock on the door, and she popped her head into the room.

"Ah, I thought this was you. Are you ready?"

"Almost. Just let me get the cleaning things out of here." Nell gave a final glance around and pulled the door closed behind her. "I've been thinking about it, and if I let you in to see Mrs Walker, I can leave the door unlocked so you'll be able to let yourself out without me waiting for you."

"You'll leave me?" A look of panic crossed Mrs Anderson's face.

"I-I thought that would be for the best. If you're going to be in there for a while, it would be as well if I'm not lurking outside."

"Yes, you're right." Mrs Anderson took several deep breaths. "Nobody will know I'm in the room. Do you know what the weather's like today?"

"The weather? Well, it's cold but not as windy as it was."

"Splendid. Hopefully, my husband and Mr Walker won't hurry back inside. Come along, we'd better go."

Nell led the way down the corridor, with a wheezing Mrs Anderson following. Nell knocked as they reached the stateroom. "Mrs Walker, it's a stewardess here. May I come in?"

"You need to unlock it." Mrs Anderson's whisper was louder than necessary.

"I'm sorry, I wanted to warn her you're coming in." Nell fumbled for her keys and pushed open the door. "I'll be back later."

Mrs Anderson stumbled into the room, her voice quivering as she did. "Sarah, my dear."

Right. Let me get away from here.

Nell wiped her hands on her skirt, but froze as Mr Anderson and Mr Walker appeared in the corridor ahead. *What do I do?*

As they approached, she forced a smile to her lips. "Good morning, gentlemen. Have you been braving the weather?"

"The wind's too brisk to stay out for long. Once we're rid of our coats, we'll be back in the saloon."

"May I take them for you?"

Mr Walker sneered at her. "I'm sure there's no need for that. If you'll excuse me." He moved to one side, but Nell blocked his path.

"It's no trouble, sir."

"If you don't mind, I'd like to speak to my wife. She's still feeling unwell." He used an arm to move her out of the way and reached into his pocket for the key. He inserted it into the lock, wiggling it as he did. "What's going on here? It's already open."

He pushed on the door and went inside as Mr Anderson brushed past Nell and followed him.

"Beryl! What are you doing here?" Mr Anderson reappeared moments later, pulling Mrs Anderson by the arm. "How did you get in there?"

Nell took a step backwards as Mr Anderson glared at her. "Mrs Riley, might this have anything to do with you?"

Mrs Anderson pulled her arm away. "Leave her alone. I asked her to unlock the door for me and she did."

"Weren't you told that visitors weren't allowed in this room?"

Nell shuddered as his icy blue eyes glared at her.

"I-I'm sorry, sir. I was only trying to help." She winced as a woman's shriek came from the stateroom.

"What are you doing to her, you monster?" Mrs Anderson darted after Mr Walker, but her husband stayed where he was, his face red.

"I've a good mind to report you to the captain for disobeying rules."

Nell studied the floor as her cheeks burned. "I'm sorry, sir. I didn't realise it would cause so much trouble. I promise not to do it again."

Mr Anderson rolled his shoulders as he straightened his jacket. "Make sure you don't."

Nell lifted her head. "Thank you, sir. Will that be all?"

"No, it won't." Mr Walker emerged from the stateroom, rubbing a fist he'd made with his right hand. "You know that my wife is being kept in here for her own good and is being perfectly well catered for?"

"Nonsense." Mrs Anderson huffed as she rejoined them. "She's done nothing wrong and the only reason you're keeping her locked up is because you're jealous."

"We've been through this, and she encouraged that man."

"She did nothing of the sort."

Mr Walker stepped towards Mrs Anderson. "I caught them in an embrace, the day after I saw her smiling at him."

"An embrace? He had her pinned against the wall."

Nell gasped, causing Mr Walker to round on her. "Are you still here, Mrs Riley? It's rather unfortunate you didn't leave when you had the chance. Were you aware of this?"

Nell's mind went blank. *What had she been told? Officially. Nothing.* "No, sir."

"And you weren't curious."

"I-I … erm … I was told she was ill; but if that's what happened…" She gulped. "…do you know it was your wife's fault? She may be a perfectly innocent victim."

"That's exactly what I've been saying." Mrs Anderson strode back into the room, but stopped and poked her head back out. "Why don't you ask Sarah, instead of assuming she's the one in the wrong?"

"Will you come out of there?"

Mrs Anderson's voice screeched as her husband pulled her arm and led her away, leaving Nell on her own with Mr Walker.

"I'm sorry for the trouble, sir. If you'll excuse me, I need to get on."

"Not quite so quick, Mrs Riley. Why were you helping Mrs Anderson?"

Nell stopped. "She said she wanted to talk to her friend. All I did was open the door."

"But you think she could be innocent?"

"I can't say for certain, sir, not having been there, but ... well, often women don't have a lot of choice if men choose to ... you know ... become familiar. She may have been horrified by the whole experience."

"But she'd encouraged him."

"Forgive me, sir, but it's considered polite to smile at an acquaintance or passer-by. It doesn't mean we're encouraging anyone."

He huffed and turned to pace the corridor. "Very well, I'll speak to her, but I still need to report this to the captain. I can't let someone in your position behave like this and get away with it." He locked the door. "You can come with me."

"Now! But sir... Please..."

"Stop." He held up a hand. "I'm responsible for my wife, and you, by your acquaintance with Mrs Anderson, have deliberately undermined my authority."

"No, it wasn't like that." Nell winced as Mr Walker took hold of her arm. "Please, let me collect my cleaning equipment. I can't leave it in the corridor." She pulled away from his grasp, but he followed her.

"I've heard this isn't the first time you've been in trouble."

Nell gasped. "How do you know that? Who've you been talking to?"

"It doesn't matter who told me, the thing is, I know. The captain won't be happy if you have two charges on your record."

Nell shuddered as footsteps came up behind her.

"Is everything all right?"

Nell spun around. "I ... yes..."

The older Mrs Foster took a step closer. "Is he causing you trouble?"

"No, I'm not." He retook Nell's arm. "If you'll excuse us, we need to see the captain."

"Is this who you were telling us about, dear?" The younger Mrs Foster stared at Mr Walker.

"What have you said?" He glared at Nell, causing her to cower into the wall.

"Nothing ... honestly."

"Didn't you say someone tried to embrace you, but you were the one who got into trouble? Is this the man?" The older woman didn't take her eyes from Mr Walker, but Nell noticed the glint in them and shook her arm free.

"He grabbed hold of me. Twice."

"I did no such thing."

"We saw you." The older Mrs Foster peered at him. "It looked rather aggressive, too. Captain Robertson won't take kindly to passengers manhandling the staff."

Nell stepped towards the Fosters, rubbing her arm

where he'd held it. "We were on our way to see the captain. Do you think I should report it?"

"No, you shouldn't." Mr Walker's voice thundered down the corridor. "I don't want a word of this breathed to anyone. Is that clear?"

Nell's heart pounded. "Perhaps Mrs Walker could join her friends for luncheon, then. Along with Mrs Anderson. I'm sure it will make her feel better."

Mr Walker glared at her. "You ... you..."

"Yes, Mr Walker?" The older sister raised her stick at him. "I hope you're not threatening Mrs Riley. We happen to be dining with the captain this evening. He'll be interested to know what his staff have to put up with."

"I'm doing no such thing." He hesitated as he glanced over his shoulder. "I need to check on my wife. I've not seen much of her today."

The sisters watched him leave as Nell turned back to them. "Thank you for that. I really thought he was going to report me."

"Was he the man who got you into trouble the other day?"

"No, he wasn't, but he's been keeping his wife locked in her stateroom for the last few days. Ever since a steward took a liking to her. Mrs Anderson's been angry about it and wanted to speak to her, so I unlocked the door for her. That was where Mr Anderson and Mr Walker caught us."

The older Mrs Foster sighed. "I thought you handled him very well, although I've still a mind to report him to the captain, anyway."

"There won't be much he can do about how he treats his wife. It's his prerogative."

"Which is why we never married … and why you should stay single, too. Why would you choose to go back to that?"

Nell smiled. "My husband was one of the best, but as for looking for anyone else, you're right. I won't be bothering."

CHAPTER TWENTY-FIVE

Mrs Swift nudged Nell's side as she stood beside the wall, watching the guests arrive for luncheon.

"Come along. You can't stand there waiting. We've plates to serve."

"I'm coming but I'm so nervous. What if Mr Walker punished his wife?"

"The captain will hear about it tonight. I imagine the Fosters will be delighted to speak to him about it."

Nell grinned. "Who'd have thought it."

"Not you, for sure. Now, get a move on."

Nell followed her into the galley and collected a couple of plates before returning to the dining room. She was approaching the Curtises' table when Mrs Anderson waved to her.

"I'll be with you shortly." She put the plates down in front of Mr and Mrs Curtis. "There we are. I must admit, those lamb chops look lovely."

"All the food's been excellent. I'll have to give Cook more instructions when I get home." Mrs Curtis picked up her knife and fork. "I wonder if any of the chefs on board would consider a domestic role. Even if they came to teach my cook."

"You never know. Shall I ask for you?"

Mr Curtis laughed. "There's no need, thank you, Mrs Riley. Our cook is perfectly acceptable."

"Very good, sir. If that's all, I'll leave you to enjoy your meal." She stepped back and studied the room. *Where've they gone?*

"Over here."

A smile split Nell's face as she stepped towards the group of five.

"Good afternoon, ladies. How lovely to see you back together again. And in my half of the room too."

Mrs Anderson threw back her head and laughed. "I wish you'd tell me what you said to my husband. He didn't want to face you again today."

Nell pursed her lips. "I didn't mean to upset him."

"Oh, don't worry about him. He fully deserved it, if you did."

"I'd like to know what you said to my husband as well." Mrs Walker's left cheek was redder than the other, but her hazel eyes sparkled as she smiled.

"I couldn't possibly comment, but I'm delighted to see you."

"Aren't we all?" Mrs Anderson brought her hands together. "May we have Manhattan cocktails all round? This calls for a celebration. Could you could join us, Mrs Riley?"

"Sadly not, madam."

"Hmm. They really should give you some time off.

Never mind, we'll have one for you then. Oh, don't let me forget..." Mrs Anderson rummaged in her handbag and produced a piece of paper. "I've a signed letter from my husband. You've no need to ask his permission."

Nell grinned. "I won't keep you waiting then." She took the piece of paper and handed it to Mr Brennan at the bar. "This should cheer you up."

"What's this? And what are you looking so pleased about?"

"The ladies would like five Manhattans and the letter is proof they'll be paid for."

He studied the note. "What's brought this on?"

"They've had a rather successful morning."

Mr Brennan nodded towards them. "That's that woman, isn't it?"

Nell turned to study the room. "Which woman?"

"The one who got Mr Driver into trouble." He picked up the whisky and poured it into the shaker.

"That's rich. I'd say it was the other way round."

"Nonsense. You can't blame him when she dresses herself like that."

"She's someone's wife. She should be able to dress how she likes. She looks very smart to me."

He reached for the vermouth. "Not if she knows what's good for her." He looked Nell up and down. "Why do you think they put you in uniforms like that? I imagine you're quite a looker in your regular clothes, but they don't want you attracting attention."

"It doesn't seem to be working."

Mr Brennan poured out the drinks. "I don't know why

you're complaining; you should be pleased men look at you at your age."

Nell's mouth opened and closed, but she shook her head and picked up the tray. *Ignore him.*

Nell's stomach rumbled an hour later as she went to clear the ladies' table. They were the only ones still in the dining room and looked ready to stay for the afternoon.

"You look as if you've enjoyed your luncheon."

"Oh, we've had a lovely time. So much better than the last few days." Mrs Anderson swayed in her chair, bumping into Nell as she reached for the glasses.

"That's good. Unfortunately, I'm going to have to ask you to move upstairs while we get the room ready for tonight."

"What a shame. We'd rather stay here, if we could." She peered into the men's section. "They'll be upstairs, and the saloon is smaller than down here. They listen to every word, you know."

"I expect you've already said everything you wanted to say. Why not go upstairs and talk about the weather? That will confuse them."

Mrs Walker laughed. "You're a breath of fresh air after everything I've had to put up with lately. You will be our server tonight as well, won't you?"

"As long as you're on this side of the room. I'm avoiding the mixed area as much as I can."

Mrs Walker squinted at her. "I'd say there's more to you than meets the eye. Maybe we'll find out one day."

Nell stood back as they got up to leave and collected the glasses to take to the galley, where Mrs Swift was waiting.

"Is there anything to eat yet? I'm famished."

"It's coming, but Mr Ross seems to have fallen in with everyone else who blames us for what's happened, so we're not his favourite people at the moment. Have you spoken to Mr Ramsbottom yet?"

Nell let out an exasperated sigh. "Give me a chance. I've been rather busy this morning. Besides, I've not seen him, which is unusual."

They wandered over to their table.

"Mr Ross will still bring the food, won't he?"

"Who knows? He will if he wants something. Oh, watch what you say. He's coming."

"Good afternoon, Mr Ross." Nell flashed him a smile, but he didn't return the gesture.

"I can't stop. They're keeping an eye on me." With no further explanation, he disappeared.

Nell waited for him to leave. "What's all that about?"

"He's probably under threat of being ostracised if he stops to talk to us. Don't worry about it. He'll talk to us when he's ready."

Nell eyed the beef stew and mashed potatoes. "The food's gone downhill, too. What happened to the lobster?"

"You'll need to go back to America for that. There'll be none left by now. Do you realise we'll be home by this time next week?"

"You're right. I was thinking about that last night. I hope the girls have missed me."

"I'm sure they will have."

"I hope you're right. They love my niece, Alice, so I may be nothing more than a distraction when I get home."

"I hope not." Mrs Swift smiled across the table at her. "Take them out and buy those dresses. That will make them happy."

Nell nodded. "That's the one thing I'm determined to do, although I won't get so many tips on this trip, so I may have to do without myself."

"You'd better do another trip then."

Nell rolled her eyes and set about finishing her food. "I wonder if we'll get dessert."

"Do you want me to go and ask?"

"Let's wait. Mr Ross will probably be watching us."

A minute later, he arrived and put two bowls of trifle on the table. "Here you are, ladies. Will you bring the dishes back when you're finished?" He turned to leave, but Nell called him back.

"Do you know what's happened to Mr Ramsbottom?"

"Oh, you want him now, do you?"

"I'd like to speak to him, but I've not seen him lately."

"Thanks to you, he's been moved to steerage. There'll be more stewards down there than up here at this rate."

"Why, who else is there?"

"Mr Price and Mr Driver."

Nell raised an eyebrow. "I thought Mr Price was covering upstairs."

"That's what he thought too until you had your little run-in with him. You've not made yourself very popular, I can tell you."

"I was only standing up for myself."

Mrs Swift cocked her head to one side. "Who's head steward, then?"

"Mr Cooper."

"Mr Cooper!" The ladies spoke at once.

"I'm surprised he hasn't told you. He's been busy telling anyone who'll listen this morning."

"I'll bet he has. I imagine he'll take full advantage of his authority." Mrs Swift paused. "Is he the reason you can't stay to talk?"

"Right first time." He picked up their empty plates. "I need to go; I've probably said too much already."

"At least we've been warned." Nell dug her spoon into the trifle.

"We should have been told, though. What he's playing at?"

"He may not have seen us. I've been rather preoccupied."

"But I've not." Mrs Swift carried on eating, but groaned a moment later. "Talk of the devil."

"Good afternoon, ladies." There was no smile on Mr Cooper's lips as Nell responded.

"Good afternoon. It's unusual to see you up here."

He straightened his back and pulled on the lapels of his jacket. "You'll be seeing a lot more of me from now on; I've been promoted to head steward."

Nell forced a smile. "Congratulations."

"There'll be changes, though. Mr Driver was far too lax with his discipline."

"What like?" Mrs Swift's back straightened.

"For starters, I don't want to see either of you near the men's or married couples' segments of the room. You'll deal with ladies only, which I believe was stipulated when you were hired."

Nell curled her lip. *It wasn't, but I can live with that.*

"The same will apply to the saloon. You serve the ladies only."

Mrs Swift's brow creased. "What about those ladies who choose not to sit with their husbands? We need to confirm the payment with the gentlemen."

"You'll pass the request to me for confirmation. Which brings me to my next point. I don't want to see either of you speaking to, or in any way interacting with, any of the other stewards. You've both done more than enough damage to the morale of the men, and it has to stop."

"What about ladies who require assistance in their staterooms? Is it prohibited if they have husbands?"

"Don't be ridiculous." Mr Cooper's face reddened. "That's what you're here for, to work as a ladies' maid, but you must always wait until the men leave the room. Is that clear?"

"Perfectly. Thank you."

Mrs Swift snarled at him. "I'd say you've done us a favour. Despite what you may think, it's us who are hounded by the men, not the other way around. I hope the passengers don't mind."

"Why would they?" Mr Cooper's voice growled, but Mrs Swift only shrugged.

"They may not. We'll see."

CHAPTER TWENTY-SIX

Nell slumped into her seat with a groan as Matron looked up from her kedgeree.

"What's the matter with you?"

"The thought of going back over there."

"It's not the place that's the problem." Mrs Swift took a seat beside her. "It's the bully who's running it."

"Is he no better?" Matron poured the tea, but Nell left it where it was.

"I'd say he's worse. For the last two days he's guarded the entrance to the galley like a soldier, only letting us in once the stewards have finished."

"How's that been for the passengers?"

"Not good, I'm afraid. He won't even let us order drinks from Mr Brennan. We have to give the orders to him, but he doesn't rush to pass them on. I'm sure he'd be happier if there were no ladies on board."

Mrs Swift nodded. "He admitted as much to me last night when I reminded him I was waiting for some drinks."

"The Foster sisters aren't happy either." Nell reached

for her tea and stirred in two lumps of sugar. "They know the trouble we're having and complained to him, but they were given short shrift."

Matron cleared her plate. "I believe they were on the captain's table the other evening."

Nell dropped her teaspoon into the saucer. "How do you know that?"

"The captain mentioned it. They complained about the way you'd been treated and asked what he was going to do about it."

Nell's cheeks coloured. "They told me they'd spoken to him, but not what they'd said. Why did the captain mention it to you?"

Matron hesitated. "I probably shouldn't tell you this, but he wanted my opinion."

"What did you say?"

"I told him what you'd told me. That your encounter with Mr Ramsbottom was accidental, and that you were considering leaving the ship when we reach Liverpool."

Nell's eyes widened. "You said that? What did he say?"

Matron reached for a piece of toast. "The captain's a good man. I don't think he'll punish you unnecessarily. He knows Mr Ramsbottom was in the wrong, which is why he's ordered him to work in steerage."

"Is he the reason Mr Price and Mr Driver are down there too, because of what happened with Mrs Walker?"

"He's trying to run a tight ship because Mr Guion is adamant that ladies are treated properly. He can't advertise the Guion Shipping Company as being the friendly way to travel if women are put off sailing with us."

Mrs Swift looked up. "Is that what this is all about? Making money from female passengers?"

"Isn't that what all shipping companies are for? The thing is, you have to admire Mr Guion wanting to do it properly. That's why a big part of your job is to keep the ladies and gents segregated unless they're married."

"And we do, but only the passengers. It's the stewards who are the problem, yet we have no authority over them."

Nell's forehead creased as she stared at Matron. "Keeping them separate shouldn't be the only thing to consider. If our ladies are getting a second-class service because Mr Cooper won't give them any priority, surely we should do something about that too."

"I wasn't aware of these latest developments, and I suspect the captain won't be, either. Mr Cooper will be reporting on how the new arrangements are working, and I imagine he'll be rather pleased with himself."

"Oh, he is. It makes me realise how reasonable Mr Driver and Mr Price were." Nell set down her knife. "Will you tell Captain Robertson what's happening?"

Matron huffed. "I most certainly will. We need to sort this out; it's taking up way too much time. I'll have a word with him as soon as I reach the bridge."

Nell and Mrs Swift followed Matron across the promenade as the Fosters walked in.

"Good morning, ladies." Nell paused by the table. "You're up early."

"We're hoping to get served in a more timely manner." The older Mrs Foster's tone was frosty.

"I'm sorry about yesterday. Let me take your order and I'll get it in straight away."

Mr Cooper was nowhere to be seen when Nell arrived at the galley, and she hurried in, delighted to see Mr Ross at the counter.

"May I have two kedgeree, tea and toast for the Fosters, please? Before Mr Cooper arrives."

"You'd better get out of here. I'll call you when it's ready."

Nell had no sooner returned to the room when Mr Cooper marched towards her. "Have you been in the galley?"

"I have two passengers who'd like to be served before the tables fill up."

"I've given you instructions not to go in there without my express permission."

"And I've been recruited to take care of the ladies on this ship. There seems to be some conflict between the two."

"I'll have less of your insolence..."

Nell noticed Mr Ross signal to her. "Will you excuse me? My tray's ready." She headed for the galley, but Mr Cooper chased after her.

"Come back here. I need to check who's in there."

"I've been keeping an eye on the door and there's no one except the chefs."

"I'll be the judge of that." He barged through the door, colliding with Mr Ross and the Fosters' breakfast tray, as he did. Nell shuddered as the plates crashed to the floor.

"You fool. What were you doing standing there?"

"Don't blame me." Mr Ross shook the food from his legs and feet. "You're the one who won't let the ladies in, so I was going to pass the tray to Mrs Riley so she didn't have to break your rules."

"I'm doing it for everyone's benefit. Now tidy this up and get back to work."

Nell waited by the door, watching as a junior chef arrived with a brush and shovel, but flinched as Mr Cooper pushed past her.

"Don't just stand there, woman. Haven't you got tables to see to?"

Nell gritted her teeth as she scowled at him. *Thanks to you, not as many as I used to have.* "No, we're strangely quiet this morning." She walked from the door scanning the men's side of the room, where the stewards darted between their full tables. *Has Mrs Anderson taken to sitting with her husband again so she can get decent service?*

She smiled as Mrs Anderson waved.

"Over here, Mrs Riley."

Nell waved back and walked to the wall of flowers partitioning the room, but hesitated as she reached the divide. *Where's Mr Cooper gone?* She did a full turn. *He's not here. How much trouble will it cause if I'm caught?*

Mrs Swift came up behind her. "What are you doing?"

"Mrs Anderson wants me to go to their table."

Mrs Swift shuddered. "I wouldn't if I were you. You've seen the mood Mr Cooper's in this morning."

"Shouldn't the passengers come first? It can't hurt approaching men who are with their wives."

"Maybe not in your mind."

Nell's brow creased. "Do you know what? I don't care. I'm not planning on coming back for the next voyage anyway, so what harm can it do?" Without waiting for a reply, she stepped forward into the mixed section with a smile on her face.

"Good morning. You're bright and early today."

Mrs Anderson put her hands together. "Apparently, we're close to land, so we wanted to take breakfast now so we can go out on deck and see it."

"At least the weather's fine for you."

Mr Anderson looked up at her. "Have you been out already?"

"We have to walk along the promenade every morning and evening. Our quarters are at the back of the ship and that's the only way over there."

"But the weather's been appalling some days."

Nell grimaced. "I'm afraid it comes with the job. Now, what may I get you...?" Her sentence was cut short as Mr Cooper strode to the table.

"I'll take over here, Mrs Riley. Get back to your station."

Nell lowered her eyes. "I'll see you later, Mrs Anderson."

"Wait a moment." Mrs Anderson placed a hand on her arm as she glared up at Mr Cooper. "We were in the middle of giving our order to Mrs Riley and I'd prefer it if she continued to serve us."

"We have a strict policy, madam. The stewardesses are only allowed in the ladies' area."

"What nonsense." Mrs Anderson's chin wobbled as she caught her breath. "She served us all last week. Most satisfactorily I might add. Who's responsible for these rules?"

Mr Cooper stood up straight and clicked his heels

together. "I am, madam. They've been introduced to keep the stewards and stewardesses apart."

"Well, send the stewards away then." Mrs Anderson extended her arm around the room. "Look at the place. The majority of the people in this room are in the men's area. It's nonsense to expect them to serve here as well when the ladies' area is so quiet."

"We'd rather not have the stewardesses coming into contact with the male passengers."

"And I would rather deal with a stewardess than a steward. Do you seriously think there will be any inappropriate behaviour between her and my husband while I'm sitting here?"

Nell's heart pounded as she glanced at Mr Cooper, his ruddy cheeks giving the impression he was about to burst. After what felt like an age, he released his pursed lips.

"Very well, madam. Mrs Riley, carry on." He marched towards the galley as the surrounding passengers muttered amongst themselves.

"Trumped-up little man. Is he the reason you've not been serving us? I thought it was because of Mr Anderson's behaviour."

"No, not at all. Mr Cooper wants us to stay in our own area."

"Well, tonight I'll be with my friends and we'll all join you."

"I'll look forward to it." With the order taken, Nell hurried back to the galley and handed it to Mr Ross.

"Is this for the Fosters?" She picked up the tray.

"It is..."

"Not so fast, Mrs Riley."

Nell froze as Mr Cooper came up behind her. "If you'll excuse me, I'm delivering this breakfast to my passengers before it goes cold. They've already been waiting for over a quarter of an hour. Thanks to you." She stormed through the door into the dining room and strode to the Fosters' table. "Here we are, ladies, I'm sorry for the delay. Our head steward, Mr Cooper, dropped the last one."

"He's going to get a piece of my mind. I've been watching him while you spoke with the Andersons. Is he causing you trouble?"

Nell sighed. "Nothing I can't deal with, I hope."

"Nonsense. I don't like the look of him." The older Mrs Foster picked up her knife and fork. "You must tell us what he's up to when you come to collect the plates."

Mr Cooper followed Nell to the galley.

"I don't know what you're playing at, but you can wait there. I'll bring out the breakfasts."

"You heard Mrs Anderson; she wants me to serve her."

"Mrs Anderson will get what she's given and like it. If she wants you to serve her, she can sit away from her husband."

Nell turned on her heel and stormed to the nearest table to collect the empty plates. *Matron's going to hear of this.*

"Good morning, Mrs Riley."

She looked up to see the captain smiling down at her. "Good morning, Captain."

"That's a weary smile."

"I'm sorry. I'm feeling a little off colour. I try to be cheerful with the passengers. Not that we have many this morning." She extended an arm to the Fosters and another couple, who were the only ones in their section.

"I'm sure the stewards would welcome some help in the mixed area. They seem to have their work cut out."

"I don't doubt it, but..." Nell paused as the captain raised an eyebrow to her. "Actually, Mr Cooper would prefer Mrs Swift and I stay in this part of the room. He doesn't want us being near any of the stewards or male passengers."

The captain's brow creased, but Nell interrupted his thoughts.

"Excuse me, but Mrs Foster would like to speak to you." She led him to their table. "I'll leave you to it."

"Thank you, Mrs Riley." He nodded as she left, and Nell wandered back to her place by the wall.

"Cheer up." Mrs Swift joined her.

"I'm trying, but I've had enough. We've only a couple of days to go and I'm ready to go home. Will you come onto the deck with me later to see the land? Once we're past Mizen Head."

"As long as the rain stays off. It will be nice to get some air." Mrs Swift stepped to the wall. "You're not coming back, are you?"

"No." Nell shook her head. "I'm not cut out to be in service. I don't take orders very well."

"You've enjoyed some of it. You got along well with the Scotts on the outward journey, and Mrs Anderson and the Fosters have appreciated you."

"Perhaps, but the way I feel right now, it's not enough. I'm going to ask the captain if I can speak to him later."

Mrs Swift nodded towards him. "Why not do it now? He's coming over."

"Good morning, Mrs Swift."

"Captain."

"What time do you finish in here?"

She shrugged. "About half past nine, but it will be earlier today. We usually go straight up to the staterooms."

"And then it's luncheon?"

"Morning coffee first, then luncheon."

He paused as he studied them. "Could you come to my office at three o'clock ... and don't worry, you're not in trouble."

Nell smiled after him as he left. "He tries his best to make us feel welcome."

"He does, but who's he looking for now?" Mrs Swift pointed to the men's section.

"I'm sure we'll find out if we wait. It's as well we've not much to do."

The wind swirled across the first-class promenade as Nell pushed herself away from the rails and pulled her cloak more tightly around her.

"We'd better go. The land will still be here when we come back. It somehow doesn't seem as exciting as the approach to New York."

"You're right. The clouds are thicker and greyer for one thing." Mrs Swift followed Nell to the door. "I wonder what the captain wants."

"He's probably going to tell us we've been disciplined and that if there's one more incident, we'll be out. Well, he needn't bother. I'll beat him to it."

"Don't be hasty. Let's hear what he has to say first."

Nell sighed. "I will."

The door to the captain's office was open when they arrived, and he stood up as they approached. "Ladies, please come in."

His smile was pleasant as he offered them a seat. "I ordered a pot of tea. Would you care for a cup?"

Nell's hands were cold from being outside, and she exchanged a glance with Mrs Swift as she rubbed them together. "Yes, please. That would be lovely."

He stood up and poured the tea himself, pushing the sugar bowl towards them as they took their cups.

"You're probably wondering why I asked you here."

They both nodded, but neither said anything.

"Since Mrs Riley and I spoke earlier in the week, I've talked to many people and have been doing a lot of thinking."

"We didn't set out to cause any trouble..."

The captain held up his hand to silence Nell. "I'm well aware of that; indeed, I would say you've had a lot to deal with."

Mrs Swift set down her cup and saucer. "It's not been easy."

He sat back, his fingers together under his chin. "Matron told me of the issues you've been having with Mr Cooper."

Nell grimaced. "She said she would."

The captain's eyes didn't leave her. "In fairness to Mr Cooper, he's only trying to put an end to the incidents we've had on this trip, but I agree he could have gone about it differently." He paused and studied them both. "I talked to him this morning, in case you were wondering why I was in the dining room. I spoke to some of our passengers, too. They speak very highly of you."

Nell nodded. "The ladies do."

"Not just the ladies, although I won't deny you've upset a few of the husbands."

A scowl settled on Nell's face. "If you're talking about Mr Walker, I'm afraid he deserved it."

"Whether he did or not, I must remind you that a man may treat his wife as he wishes and it's not for us to interfere."

"I was only helping Mrs Anderson."

The captain's frown lifted. "I can see you're beginning to speak up for yourself."

"I'm afraid I've had to." Nell took a sip of her tea. "It doesn't mean I like it, though."

"No, and you shouldn't have to. In fact, that's why I've asked you here."

"Do you want us to leave?" Nell's heart was racing. *This is it.*

"Gracious, no. What would I tell Mr Guion if we lost both of you at a time we're advertising your services?"

"So what then?" Mrs Swift's tone was harsh.

"I've been speaking to my wife, and she's explained how difficult it must be for the two of you. If I'm honest, it had never occurred to me, but it means I need to sort out the situation with the stewards. I've needed to send three of them to steerage and the man currently in charge hasn't the experience for such a position."

"Isn't there anyone else?"

He shook his head. "Not for the role of head steward. Which brings me to my question. You've worked with Mr

Driver and Mr Price. How comfortable were you working with each of them?"

Nell looked to Mrs Swift. "It's difficult to say. Mr Driver doesn't seem to like us."

"No, he doesn't. He's accused us of things we haven't done, twice, and he's turned most of the crew against us."

"So you've not missed him?"

Nell shook her head. "I've not."

"Me neither. And we know he doesn't keep his hands to himself."

The captain raised an eyebrow. "You do?"

"We caught him with a passenger the night before we arrived in New York."

"Which is why we think he blames us for reporting him over the incident with Mrs Walker."

He continued to study them. "And what about Mr Price?"

Nell shrugged. "He was nice enough until we found out he was the one who reported Mr Driver but deliberately said nothing when we were blamed."

"Which is why you argued outside my office?"

"Yes, Captain." Nell's cheeks coloured.

"Very well." He took a gulp of his tea. "I've made a decision. I'll speak to the gentlemen involved later and tell you what's happening tomorrow."

CHAPTER TWENTY-SEVEN

The following morning Nell stepped onto the deck and, despite the rain in the air, stopped to admire the cathedral of Queenstown.

"I can't believe we're nearly home."

Mrs Swift leaned on the rail beside her. "It's always a nice feeling, no matter how many times you make the journey. We'll be in Liverpool tomorrow."

"I assume there'll be a changed rota today, with everyone packing their bags."

"We will. I need to help some of my ladies with their trunks. I'm surprised the Fosters haven't asked you to do theirs."

Nell tutted. "They're too independent to do that. Mrs Anderson or Walker may ask, but probably not if their husbands are around."

"You can do the tables for luncheon then. Come on, let's see what's waiting for us."

Captain Robertson stood outside the dining room with Mr Price when they arrived downstairs.

"Good morning, ladies. Are you looking forward to our last full day?"

"Good morning, Captain." They spoke in unison, but Nell broke off. *When do I tell him I'm not coming back?*

"A few days ashore will do you both the world of good."

"I hope so." Mrs Swift linked Nell's arm to usher her into the dining room, but the captain stopped them.

"Actually, before you go, I want to tell you that with immediate effect, Mr Price here will resume the role of head steward."

Nell hesitated for a second. "Congratulations."

"Thank you." Mr Price gave a coy smile. "I'm sorry about our little misunderstanding the other day but I hope things will now return to normal after Mr Cooper's *experiment*."

"I should hope so too." There was no joy in Mrs Swift's voice.

"Quite." He paused to clear his throat. "Mr Driver and Mr Cooper will remain in steerage until we get to Liverpool and the captain and I will talk to all the stewards later about their conduct. We want the SS *Wisconsin* to be an example of how a ship should run, and we all need to understand our roles and duty to the passengers. There shouldn't be any more distrust between you and the men."

"That would be nice, but may I ask about Mr Ramsbottom?" Nell's stomach churned at the thought of seeing him again.

The smile disappeared from the captain's face. "He's been spoken to. Whether he'll be with us on the next voyage remains to be seen, but he shouldn't cause you any more trouble."

"Thank you." Nell managed a smile. "We'd better be getting on."

Mr Ross was at the counter in the galley when they arrived.

"Good morning, ladies. It's nice to have you back without supervision."

"Isn't it just?" Mrs Swift picked up the tray rota. "Aren't we delivering trays this morning?"

"We are, but there haven't been any requests."

"That's unusual."

"It means we'll be busy in the dining room." Nell peered out at the tables. "They're filling up already."

"We'd better go and see what they want then."

Nell headed straight to the Fosters' table. "Good morning, ladies. You're bright and early."

The older sister nodded. "It's many years since we last saw Queenstown, so we're going to spend time outside before we start our packing."

"The cathedral looked almost regal when we walked over here."

"I imagine it did; there's little else around it." She handed Nell her menu. "I'll have the kippers this morning, please."

The younger sister pulled up her nose. "There are too many bones for my liking; the poached eggs for me, please."

"Very good, ladies. Is there anything else I can do for you?"

The older Mrs Foster pursed her lips as she placed her napkin on her lap. "Not for the moment, thank you."

Nell turned to go back to the galley, but Mrs Anderson caught her eye and she headed over to her.

"Good morning, are you dining alone?"

Mrs Anderson gazed at the empty seats around her. "Not at all; we're having our final breakfast together, but I wanted a quick word before the others arrived. Would you mind helping me with my packing later? The dresses mainly; I'm terrible at folding them neatly."

"Not at all. It will probably be about ten o'clock by the time I get to you. Would you like to order now, or shall I come back?"

Mrs Anderson glanced at the door and waved as Mrs Walker walked in on her husband's arm. "They're here now. They seem to be getting along better than they were. I hope she still plans to join me."

"You've no need to worry, she's coming this way. I'll give you a few minutes."

Nell strode to the galley, a smile on her face, but froze as Mr Ramsbottom turned to look at her.

"Mrs Riley."

"Good morning, Mr Ramsbottom. May I hand in this order?"

Mr Ramsbottom moved out of the way as she stepped forward, her palms sweating.

"Thank you. How've you been?"

"I'm happier for being up here."

"I'm sure you are." She fidgeted with her fingers as she stared at the door. "I've a table waiting..."

"Why did you report me?"

Nell did a double take. "Me? I had nothing to do with it."

"Well, who did?"

The furrows on Nell's brow deepened. "You really don't know?"

"You don't find out anything in steerage; not once Mr Cooper left us, anyway."

"I suppose not." Nell peered to the far end of the galley. "I shouldn't speak in here. Come and ask me again when the guests have left the dining room."

"If I must." He spoke through gritted teeth as he stepped aside to let her pass.

Mrs Swift looked up as Nell joined her. "Is everything all right?"

"Mr Ramsbottom's back."

"Ah."

"He thinks I was the one who reported him."

Mrs Swift's eyebrows lowered. "Why would you do that, given the trouble it got you into?"

"I doubt he's any idea of what's been going on. He's been stuck in steerage with Mr Driver and Mr Price. They weren't likely to tell him the truth."

"I hadn't thought of that. Did you set him straight?"

"Not yet. I've said I'll tell him later. Will you stay with me while I do? I'd rather not face him on my own."

Mrs Swift placed a hand on Nell's arm. "Of course I will."

The tablecloths had been replaced and Nell was setting out the cutlery for luncheon when Mr Ramsbottom strolled across the room.

"Can we talk now?"

"Erm ... yes." She glanced over to Mrs Swift, who was

on the other side of the room. "Let me finish here. I'll only be a minute."

Her hands shook as she laid the last knife and fork. "There we are." She smiled as Mrs Swift joined them.

"Don't mind me." Mrs Swift ignored the consternation on Mr Ramsbottom's face. "It's better if the three of us talk together."

"If you insist. What can you tell me?"

Nell sighed. "I'm afraid you were part of a plot to get me into trouble."

"What do you mean?" Mr Ramsbottom's brow furrowed.

"The stewards had obviously seen you were being overly friendly to me, and when we bumped into each other in the foyer, the one person who knew he could use the situation to his advantage saw us."

"Who?"

"Mr Driver."

Mr Ramsbottom's eyes widened. "I don't believe you."

"That's why we're both here, to tell you it's the truth," Mrs Swift snarled at him. "Someone had reported him for being with a female passenger, and when he thought it was us, he wanted his revenge."

"How do you know?" His eyes narrowed, but Nell held his gaze.

"Despite everything that's happened, we still have friends who are keeping an eye out for us."

"And ask yourself why nobody said anything about it while you were in steerage. He wasn't likely to tell you, was he?" Mrs Swift raised an eyebrow.

"But Mr Price could have..."

Mrs Swift held up a hand. "Don't even go down that path. There've been a lot of things going on this week, but some are best left unsaid."

Mr Ramsbottom's shoulders sagged. "I've a right to know after everything I've had to put up with."

"Well, you won't hear it from us. Now, if you'll excuse us, we need to go out on deck."

The Queenstown cathedral was fading into the distance as Nell stepped onto the first-class promenade. The wind whipped her face, but she stood and inhaled deeply.

"My heart's thumping."

"You can calm down now." Mrs Swift gazed over the side of the ship, but Nell shook her head.

"I need to speak to the captain."

"You're still determined not to come back? Even after the efforts the captain's made?"

She shrugged as she leaned forward onto the railings. "I've been determined to leave for days now, but if things really do get better... Perhaps I should speak to him either way."

"Well, before then, we'd better get a move on with the ladies' packing. We need to be in the dining room in a couple of hours."

By the time Nell reached the staterooms, Mrs Anderson was standing over her trunk, her hands on her head.

"Ah, you're here. I was beginning to think I'd have to leave everything in the wardrobe and buy new when I got home."

Nell bustled to the trunk. "I'm sure there's no need for that. Now, let me see what you've got."

Mr Anderson hovered by the door. "I'll see you in the saloon, shall I?"

"Yes, yes, off you go. I'll join you shortly." Mrs Anderson didn't turn round as she waved an arm at her husband. "Where do we start?"

"You take a seat and leave it to me." Nell lifted several dresses from the wardrobe and lay them on the bed. "Have you decided what you'll travel home in tomorrow?"

"Oh, yes." She darted to the stack of clothes. "Don't pack that one."

Nell picked up one of the remaining dresses and began folding it. "Where are you travelling on to?"

"Southport. Do you know it?"

"I've heard of it, but never been."

"You really ought to visit. We moved up there several years ago, and it's so much nicer than Liverpool, and cleaner."

"More expensive too, I shouldn't wonder."

"I must admit, I am rather spoiled." Mrs Anderson put a hand to her chest. "Did you say you're a widow?"

"I am. It's nearly a year to the day…"

"Oh, I'm sorry. I'd no idea it was so recent. Shouldn't you still be in mourning?"

Nell grimaced. "I would if I was in your position, but when you need to work, these things have to be set aside."

"I'd never thought of that. I was about to suggest you find yourself a wealthy husband. It worked wonders for me, even though we argue. Is it too early for that?"

Nell sighed. "I'm not ready yet."

Mrs Anderson sat up straight. "Is that why you resisted the advances of that steward?"

"You noticed?"

"Only in passing. I thought nothing of it at the time, but it suddenly makes sense."

"The truth is, I wouldn't want to settle down with another man who goes to sea for a living." Nell walked to the wardrobe to take out more dresses. "How's Mrs Walker? She seemed on good terms with her husband earlier."

Mrs Anderson groaned. "They've made up, for now, but then she had little choice. Did you hear that we're neighbours in Southport, but we didn't realise they were travelling until we bumped into them on the ship?"

"You mentioned that you knew them…"

"Now *they* have a delightful house. An array of servants, too. Not just a cook and domestic, like I have to manage with."

"Is that why she lets him treat her as he does?"

"She has no choice; she just has to get on with it. At least I can keep an eye on her once we're home, so that's something."

"I'm sure she'll appreciate it." Nell reached for the last dress. "We're about done here. I'll get this folded and we can put the trunk outside for collection."

Nell closed the lid and glanced around the room. "Are you sure you've got everything you need for the morning?"

Mrs Anderson stood up and checked the drawers. "Yes, I'm fine. There is one thing though." She reached into the bedside drawer and took out an envelope. "A thank you for being so helpful. I don't know what we'd have done without you."

Nell smiled as she accepted the envelope. "That's very kind, thank you." She felt several coins through the paper. "I should be able to take my daughters shopping for their dresses now."

"Well, enjoy it. You deserve it."

The door to the Fosters' stateroom was open as Nell walked past, and she stopped and called inside. "Is there anything I can do to help?"

"Oh, Mrs Riley, it's you." The younger sister appeared at the door. "We're struggling to lift our trunks. Could you arrange for someone to move them for us?"

"Yes, of course. I'm on my way to collect a steward for the Andersons' room, anyway."

The older sister pushed herself up from her temporary seat on the trunk. "I've had to sit on it to shut the lid. The maid in New York must have been more efficient at packing than us."

Nell sighed. "You should have asked. I'd have done it for you."

"You've already been far more helpful than you needed to be." The elder Mrs Foster reached over to the console table. "We were going to give this to you later, but while you're here, we'd like to thank you for all you've done." She handed her an envelope.

"Thank you." Nell beamed at them.

"We told the captain how good you've been and he was full of praise for you."

"Was he? That's nice."

"We hope you get over the little indiscretions from this trip. We don't think they'll happen again."

"You don't?" Nell's forehead creased.

"We had a word with him and this new head steward. If you have any more trouble, you can always write to us. Our address is in the envelope."

"That's very generous, but…"

"But how can we help?" Mrs Foster's eyes twinkled. "Don't worry yourself about that. Suffice to say, we have some rather useful acquaintances."

Nell left the stateroom with a skip in her step and ran straight into Mrs Swift as she reached the stairs.

"You're looking cheerful."

"I've had some tips."

"I said you would. How much?"

"I've not counted it yet, but Mrs Anderson and the Fosters both gave me envelopes."

Mrs Swift grinned. "I'd open them now then. If they make you change your mind about leaving, it will save you having to see the captain this afternoon."

"But I've already decided. Or at least I thought I had."

CHAPTER TWENTY-EIGHT

N ell placed the final flower arrangement in the centre of the table and stood back to inspect the settings. *Yes, the room looks worthy of the final dinner.* She'd stood up to search for Mrs Swift when she saw the captain approaching.

"That looks splendid, Mrs Riley."

Nell smiled. "Thank you, Captain. We wanted to make an effort for the last night."

He glanced around at the other tables. "There's not far to go now. Have you enjoyed your voyage?"

Enjoyed? How do I answer that? "It's been interesting."

"Matron told me you were considering leaving us. Is that true?"

Nell's heart skipped a beat. "I ... erm, I did consider it ... when things were difficult, you understand."

"And what did you decide?"

"Well..." She struggled for the right words.

"We'd be disappointed to see you leave, especially now we're over the problems."

"I appreciate that." *This is it.* She took a deep breath. "I had planned on leaving, but ... well, because of everything you've done, I've decided to stay."

A smile crossed the captain's lips. "I'm very glad to hear it. Matron and Mrs Swift will be too."

"I hope so."

The captain followed her gaze as she looked across the room to Mrs Swift.

"Does she know?"

"Not yet."

"Then I suggest you tell her. She looks rather concerned. I'll speak to you again in the morning when we disembark."

Mrs Swift wandered towards her as the captain left. "What was that about?"

"Matron had told him I might be leaving, so he wanted to ask what I was doing."

"W-what did you say?"

Nell grinned. "That I'm staying."

"Really!" Mrs Swift's face lit up. "You've had me so worried."

"I know, and I'm sorry. I didn't mean to."

"What made you change your mind?"

"This morning, I suppose. Things have been so much better with Mr Driver and Mr Cooper out of the way. And then there are the tips."

"Have you had some more?"

Nell nodded. "The Curtises and the Walkers both sought me out at afternoon tea. Both were very generous so I've over four pounds from this trip."

Mrs Swift gasped. "That makes it worthwhile."

"Exactly. All I've got to worry about now is telling my sister."

The sky was still dark, and a light drizzle falling, when Nell stepped onto the deck the following morning, but she didn't care. The ship was within an hour of docking and she wanted a glimpse of the city she hadn't seen for a month.

She pulled the hood up on her cloak and wrapped the rest of the material around her. *It's almost as exciting as arriving in New York.*

Mrs Swift followed her. "I thought you'd be here."

"It's so early. I didn't want to wake you. You'll have seen this view often enough."

"It's still special, though. Are you looking forward to getting home?"

Nell gazed out at the shore. "I've dreamt of nothing else for the last week, but now it's here I'm wondering why. I'd clearly forgotten the reason I left."

"I'm sure they'll be pleased to see you. That should make up for it."

"I hope so. Come on, we'd better get some breakfast before the guests are up and about."

As the clock approached ten, Nell stood in the foyer, watching the last of the first-class passengers disembark. She glanced through the door at the Customs House on the dock road. *Not long now.*

The captain opened his arms. "Thank you all. I know

some of you are staying on board to prepare for the next voyage. For those who are disembarking, may I remind you to be back by half past seven on Monday morning, ready for us to sail on Tuesday."

Nell led Mrs Swift back to their cabin. "I might treat myself to a carriage, with all the tips I was given. Although maybe not. It will only give Maria something to moan about before I even go into the house."

"Well, enjoy yourself. I look forward to seeing you again on Monday morning."

Disembarking from the ship was easier than boarding, but Nell still clung to the handrails as she tentatively made her way to the safety of dry land. She waited for Mrs Swift but stopped as she heard her name being called.

"Aunty Nell."

"Vernon! I wasn't expecting anyone to be here on a Friday." She hurried over to him.

"It wasn't planned, but I've not picked up any work today, and so I decided it was safer to take you home with me."

Nell rolled her eyes. "I'm glad I can help."

Mrs Swift laughed. "I told you they'd be pleased to see you. Enjoy being back."

Nell waved her off as Vernon picked up her bag and offered her his arm.

"Come along, let's get you home. How was the voyage?"

"It had its moments, but I met some nice passengers."

"It sounds like you didn't enjoy it."

Nell hesitated. "I did, but it took some getting used to."

"Well, I'm glad you're home. Mam will be too. She's not

known what to do with herself while you've been away, but she was so excited this morning."

Nell's heart pounded as they set off towards the Customs House.

"How have things been? Have I missed anything?"

"Not much. For the last few weeks I've been getting day work three or four days a week, but nothing permanent. At least it's better than Uncle Tom; he's one of those the major companies have blacklisted."

"Oh no!" The blood drained from her face. "How are they managing?"

"They went to the guardians last week for a handout. Not that they got anything without a fight. They said it's Uncle Tom's own fault he's out of work, and that they'd only help once. Thankfully, Sam's had some day work, too."

Nell's heart skipped at the thought of the money in her bag and her plans to go shopping. "What about your dad? Is his leg mending?"

"He's not in as much pain as he was, so it must be. Not that he's walking yet."

"It's a start if he's feeling better." Nell stared at the office buildings on her left and remembered how James had encouraged her to take the job.

"When's James due home?"

"Not for another week yet."

"Oh." Her face dropped.

"He didn't leave Liverpool until a week after you, so it was to be expected."

"I'd forgotten about that. It could be months before I see him again."

"You'll see him next week."

Nell's cheeks coloured as Vernon stopped and stared at her.

"Don't tell me you're going back. Oh, for goodness' sake, Aunty Nell. Mam will be furious."

"We need the money. I can't come home and rely on everyone else when Billy's the only one with a permanent job."

"But you won't earn enough to warrant going away again."

Nell bit her lip. "Please don't say anything; let me tell your mam myself. The time needs to be right."

Vernon shuddered. "I won't say a word, but promise me you'll wait until I'm out."

As they walked along Windsor Street, Nell gasped for breath, struggling to fight the tightening spreading across her chest. "We seem to have got here very quickly."

"Calm down." Vernon prised her fingers from his arm. "Mam won't be mad until you tell her your news."

"You're right." Nell forced a smile as she took another deep breath. "I should be pleased to see her."

They turned into Merlin Street, and as they approached the house, Maria flew out of the front door and hurried down the pavement.

"You're here." She threw her arms around her sister. "And in one piece."

"Of course I am." Nell pulled herself away. "Have you missed me?"

"Missed you! I've been worried sick."

"What about the girls? Where are they?"

Maria grabbed her arm and pulled her indoors. "They're waiting. Come on in."

"Mama!" Elenor jumped from her place by the fire and wrapped her arms around Nell's legs. "Where've you been?"

Nell crouched down and reached out an arm for each daughter. "I told you, I went on a ship so I could get some money to buy us some dresses."

"But you didn't come back."

Maria stared down at her, but Nell refused to look up.

"I'm here now." Nell sat down and pulled them both onto her knee. "Are you going to tell me what you've been doing?"

Alice grinned as she stood up. "They've been as good as gold. Would you like a cup of tea?"

"Ooh, yes, please. The tea on the ship is wet and warm, but not like we have here."

"At least you've got it behind you." Maria finally sat down. "Did you visit New York?"

"No, we weren't allowed off, but my colleague, Mrs Swift, said it wouldn't be very pleasant in January. The weather wasn't much better than it is here."

"That's a shame." Alice placed her cup of tea on the nearby occasional table. "I'm glad you had a friend, though. James told us about her. Was she nice?"

"Yes, we got along very well. She's from West Derby and lives with her mam and sister. The sister looks after the mam while Mrs Swift goes out to work."

"What about her husband?"

"She's not married. She uses 'Mrs' to make herself sound more respectable."

Maria tutted. "Another one of them."

"Don't be like that. We can't all be married." Nell paused. "Where's George?"

"He's in the yard; he'll be in shortly."

Nell's mood brightened. "Can he get around by himself?"

"He's managing ... with his crutches, obviously. He's been talking about going to the alehouse ... although he'll have nothing to spend when he gets there."

"He must feel better, then, which is good."

"I suppose..."

"Did you meet any eligible men, Aunty Nell?" Vernon looked up from his place at the table.

"I wasn't interested. Do you know, they segregate all the passengers except for the married couples in first class?"

"I'm pleased to hear it." Maria folded her arms. "Did they separate you from the stewards?"

"Of course they did."

"Were there many women travelling on their own?" Alice was a little too enthusiastic, and Maria scowled.

"Don't even think you're going. Aunty Nell may have some money for you, but we'll need every penny of it."

"I did rather well out of the trip, as it happens, but I'll sort it all out later." She stood the girls up and pushed herself to her feet. "In the meantime, I need to get this washing done. It won't do itself."

"Now!" Maria's forehead creased. "Can't it wait until Monday? I wanted some help cleaning the windows."

Nell hesitated. "I'd rather get it out of the way." She smiled down at the girls. "Who's coming to help me?"

George was making his way to the house as Nell led the girls to the washhouse.

"Good morning, Nell. I didn't know you were here."

"I've not long since arrived, but I want this washing done."

"You're going back, are you?"

Nell took a step backwards. "How did you know?"

He shrugged. "Why else would you be in such a hurry to get it done. You can't have had time for a cup of tea yet."

"I have, just." Nell ran a hand over the top of Elenor's head. "You won't say anything, will you? Not yet."

"When do you leave?"

"Monday morning."

George nodded. "You've got time, then, just don't leave it too long."

"I won't." Nell gave a weak smile. "Thank you."

"Are you leaving again, Mama?" Elenor's pale blue eyes held hers.

"Not for a few days." She crouched down and put an arm around each daughter. "Were you happy with Alice while I wasn't here?"

They both nodded. "She plays games with us."

"And the park." Leah struggled to get away.

"That's nice. Does Aunty Ria make her do the cleaning, too?"

Elenor again nodded. "She's bossy, but we help Alice. She likes that."

Nell leaned forward and kissed her daughter's forehead. "You're a good girl. We're going into town tomorrow to buy you and Leah a new dress."

Elenor jumped on the spot, clapping her hands. "I'd like a blue one. Isobel's got one, and it's pretty."

"We'll see if we can find one then."

"I'll tell Alice." Elenor ran towards the kitchen.

"No, not yet."

She'd disappeared before Nell could grab her arm, and she dropped to the floor, her heart racing.

"Up, Mama." Leah pulled on her hand as Nell scrambled to her feet.

I'm for it now. She gave Leah several sticks. "There we are. Let's get this fire going."

Leah placed the wood under the washing tub, and Nell was about to light it when the kitchen door slammed. *Oh goodness.*

"What's going on?"

"What do you mean?"

"Don't come over all innocent. Elenor said you're going back to sea."

Nell's cheeks burned, and she turned back to the fire. "We need the money."

"You promised you'd only do one trip..."

Nell picked up Leah, who'd started crying. "Keep your voice down."

"How can I when you lied to me?"

"I didn't lie, but you hardly kept your side of the bargain before I went."

"What's that supposed to mean?"

"We agreed that I'd only go away for a month, if you stopped moaning at me. Which you didn't."

"I've been worried sick..."

"For no reason. Look, I'm here in one piece and, in case

you're wondering, I earned over ten pounds for those four weeks."

Maria stopped, her mouth open. "Ten pounds!"

"Yes, exactly. So stop and think about that before you carry on." She placed Leah back on the floor and picked up the washing paddle. "And don't stand there watching me. If you're staying, you can get that mangle going."

CHAPTER TWENTY-NINE

George and Vernon had disappeared by the time Nell went back into the house, but Maria and Alice were sitting at the table with the girls. Maria looked up as she joined them, but said nothing.

"Is there tea in that pot?" Nell tried to keep her voice light, but when there was no response she lifted Leah from her seat and reached for Elenor's hand. "I'm going to see Rebecca. At least I'll be welcome over there." She walked to the door.

"You were welcome here..." Maria's voice echoed down the hallway, but Nell didn't stop. *She can go and earn her own money if mine's not good enough for her.*

Rebecca was scrubbing the living room floor when Nell arrived.

"You're here!" She jumped to her feet, a smile splitting her face. "How was it?"

Nell grimaced. "Considerably better than being home."

"You've not fallen out already."

Nell tiptoed across the clean floor and sat Leah by her

cousin Florrie. "She was pleased to see me, but then Elenor let it slip that I'm going back to the ship on Monday."

"Aunty Ria shouted at me." Elenor clung to Nell's skirt as she sat down.

"She didn't shout at you." Nell hugged her. "She's cross with me."

"You're going away again?" Rebecca's smile faded.

"I wasn't going to, but by the time I got my tips, I came home with over ten pounds."

"Ten pounds!" Her sister's eyes widened as she perched on the chair opposite. "That's a fortune."

"I know. You'd think she'd be pleased."

Rebecca ran a finger across her left eye. "It's only because she misses you. We all do."

"I've missed you, too, but well ... the captain wanted me to stay, and I decided we could do with the money."

"I'm sure you do. Is Vernon working today?"

"No. He met me off the ship and we walked home together."

"So he told you about Sarah, then."

The colour drained from Nell's face. "No. What's happened?"

"She's fallen out with Maria, again."

Nell glanced at the table. "Is there any tea in that pot? I'll need one before you tell me any more."

"Let me freshen up the pot." Rebecca stood up. "The kettle's boiled."

Nell perched on the edge of her seat as her young niece Florrie handed her several blocks.

"She'll want you to build her a tower with them."

Rebecca nodded to the pile on the hearth. "I had to move them to wash the floor."

"I can do that." Nell knelt down on the rug and gave each of the girls a block as she laid one herself. "What did they argue about?"

Rebecca tutted. "Money. Did you hear that Tom's still out of work?"

"Vernon mentioned it."

"Well, with Vernon getting a few days' work, Sarah asked Maria for help. Needless to say, Maria was having none of it, blaming Tom for the whole situation."

"Is that why Sarah had to go to the guardians?"

"Ah, you heard about that." Rebecca carried two cups of tea to the fireplace. "Sarah was mortified and blamed Maria for shaming her."

"That's not fair; Maria's struggling as it is."

"But not as much as them. They're getting everything on tick at the moment and they've run up quite a tab."

Nell returned to her seat. "They will have done, but Vernon said Sam's working a few days a week, too."

"This all happened before then, but the money he earns doesn't touch the food; it all goes on the rent. It doesn't help that Sam's walking out with a young lady from Windsor Street, now, which is costing him money he hasn't got."

Nell rolled her eyes. "I bet Sarah's not happy about that, either."

"You've no idea. I ended up giving her the bit I'd been saving to buy the girls some new shoes."

Nell bit her lip. "I'd better pay them a visit. I can't keep everything to myself if there's a danger they'll be evicted. I'll pay you some money back, too."

"I'm sure they'll be pleased, but you don't owe me anything. I feel guilty enough as it is with Hugh still working and there only being the four of us. It would be nice if you could stretch to lending Jane a bit, though. She's almost through her inheritance from Mr Read. I don't know what she'll do when it runs out."

"I do feel sorry for her. You'd think Maria would be happy I'm working."

Rebecca took a sip of tea. "I wouldn't tell Maria about helping them. She wants Tom to suffer."

"It's all right Tom suffering, but what about everyone else? Especially the kiddies. It's not their fault."

"I tried to tell her that, but you know what she's like. And George was no help. He's still mad with Tom, too."

"Thank you for the warning. I'd better pay her and Alice first, then see how much I've got left."

Alice was setting the table when Nell returned, and she peered into the kitchen before she spoke.

"Where's she gone?"

"Only to the yard. She's very upset."

Nell sighed as she carried the cups and saucers to the table. "I know, but it's for the best. You understand, don't you?"

"Of course I do. I think it's amazing. I've loved looking after the girls rather than sewing."

"And I must pay you for that." She reached for her bag and dug out three crown coins. "There you are, fifteen shillings."

Alice's face lit up. "Thank you. I've never had so much."

"Well, put it away before your mam sees it. She'll want it all from you. I'll give her three pounds. Hopefully that should keep her quiet." Nell took out an assortment of coins and put them on the edge of the dresser as the door opened.

"Oh, you're back."

Nell took a breath. "Here. Some housekeeping for you."

A smile crossed Maria's face as she picked up the coins, but it disappeared just as quickly. "You said you got ten pounds."

"I did, but if it's all the same to you, I'd like to keep some for myself. I've already given Alice her money and I've promised to take the girls to the shops tomorrow for some new dresses."

Maria's cheeks reddened. "This family is on the brink of ruin, and you're going shopping for dresses? And why on earth are you wasting money on a dress for Leah? Since when did the younger children get anything new?"

Nell planted her hands on her hips. "I don't believe you. I've been away for a month and earned more than any of us could have imagined, and all you can do is moan you've not got enough. With the money me and Alice give you, you'll have three pounds, ten shillings. On top of that, Billy's still working, Vernon's getting back on his feet and James will be home next week. How much do you need?"

"I'll be having a word with James, that's for sure. He must earn more than you, but he's never very generous with it."

"You don't know that. I happened to get a lot of tips from ladies I helped, more than I got from my wages, actually. There are a lot more stewards, so he may not get so much."

"That would be nonsense. When have women ever earned more than men?"

"Maybe we haven't, but stop complaining about it and be thankful. You should also be glad that I'll be bringing a similar amount home every month."

"You're going for the year?"

"I am, and so if I want to buy my daughters a dress each, then I will." She paused as the front door opened and the sound of Vernon helping George up the step filtered into the room. "I'll serve the dinner while you put a smile on your face."

The rain fell in a fine drizzle, and Nell pulled her hood over her forehead as she closed the door behind her. The footpaths were wet, and she shrieked as she stepped in a puddle. *It's worse than being on deck.*

She increased her pace and without knocking on Sarah and Tom's front door let herself in and threw off her hood. She was still shaking the rain from her cloak as Tom stepped from the living room.

"I'm home."

"So I see. You'd better come in."

Jane was at the table with Sarah, and Nell took the chair beside her. "Good afternoon."

"When did you get back?" There was no smile on Sarah's lips.

"This morning. I heard..."

"Come around to gloat, have you?"

Nell's mouth fell open. "No, why would I? I've come to help, if I can."

Sarah snorted. "A likely tale. Did Maria send you?"

"No. She doesn't know I'm here. I just wanted to see how you're doing."

Jane put a hand on Nell's. "You've not come at a good time. Why don't you call again in a few days?"

"I'm ... erm ... I won't..." She stuttered as she glanced around to see all eyes staring at her. "Yes. I'll do that. I'll let myself out."

Nell pulled the front door closed behind her, but stopped and stared down the street. *I'm not surprised they've fallen out with Maria. Where do I go now?*

She strolled to Merlin Street in a daze as the rain ran down her face. *Rebecca will tell me what to do.*

Her sister looked up from her knitting as she walked in. "Gracious, twice in one day. You said you were going to visit Sarah this afternoon."

"I did, but they wouldn't speak to me."

Rebecca's brow creased. "What do you mean?"

Nell shrugged. "Sarah thought I'd gone to gloat and asked if Maria had sent me. The argument must have been serious."

"She must have changed her tune when you offered her the money."

"I didn't get around to it. Jane said I'd called at a bad time and suggested I go again in a few days."

"But you won't be here."

"I couldn't bring myself to tell them. Even Tom wasn't his usual self. He didn't want me to go in the first place, and he'd only have been a bigger, angrier version of Maria."

"Oh dear. Come in and I'll put the kettle on."

Nell followed her to the kitchen. "I'm beginning to wish I didn't have the money."

"Now you're being silly."

"Am I? I earned over ten pounds in four weeks. Probably twice as much as any of the men in the family. What will they think of me?"

Rebecca sighed. "You know your trouble? You're too honest. In future, don't tell anyone. The amount you earn shouldn't be of any concern to them."

"But I thought they'd be pleased; I wanted to help."

Rebecca poured the boiling water into the teapot. "Why don't you put the money somewhere safe for a rainy day?"

Nell wandered back to a chair by the fire. "I don't have anywhere..."

Rebecca cocked her head to one side and studied her. "Didn't Billy open an account for you after Jack died?"

"He did, at the Friendly Society in Liverpool. I'd forgotten about that. If I remember rightly, we took all the money out, so he may have closed it."

"You could ask him. While James is away, he's your best bet."

Nell nodded. "You're right, although I've no idea when I'll get to speak to him on his own. The house has been busy since I got back."

"Could you wait up for him tonight?"

Nell sighed. "I had hoped to get an early night. I've missed sleeping in my own bed."

"I don't know what else to suggest then."

"No, me neither. I'll have to think about it."

CHAPTER THIRTY

Nell was late down for breakfast the following morning, and Billy and Vernon had already left for work. George looked her up and down as she took the seat next to Maria.

"Are you going out?"

"Yes. I promised the girls I'd take them into Liverpool to buy them each a new dress. Alice is coming with us. She's just seeing to Leah."

He nudged Maria. "Aren't you going with them?"

"I've not been invited." She stared at the table as Nell poured herself a cup of tea.

"I didn't think you'd want to come, but you're more than welcome."

Maria clenched her fists. "The cleaning won't do itself. I had hoped to get some help…"

Nell took a breath. "I'll help later; we'll be home for luncheon … I mean dinner, so there's plenty of time."

"Luncheon. Listen to you…"

"Oh, for goodness' sake, will you give it a rest? The way you're carrying on, I'll stay on the ship next time I'm back."

"And not see the girls at all..."

"Don't be so melodramatic." George winked at Nell. "Of course she'll be back once you've calmed down."

Nell pursed her lips at Maria's expression. "You need to get used to this, because this is how it's going to be for the rest of the year, and at least you'll be able to pay the rent."

Elenor ran down the stairs and into the living room, where she gave a full turn for Maria.

"Look, Aunty Ria. It's pretty."

"Yes, it's lovely."

Nell pushed Leah into the centre of the room, her lemon dress a contrast to the pale blue of her sister's.

"And me." She gave her own twirl.

Maria scowled. "They must have set you back a bob or two."

"It was worth it to see the looks on their faces. They don't get many new things." She pulled Elenor towards her and tightened the bow at the back. "They'll grow into them and Leah will get some wear out of Elenor's."

"May we wear them for church tomorrow?" Elenor bounced on the spot. "I want to show Isobel."

"Only if we go upstairs and take them off. I don't want you spoiling it."

"But I like it."

"And I want it to stay clean."

Alice reached out a hand. "You're both very pretty, but you need to do what Mam says. Come on, we'll go together."

Nell stood up and wandered to the kitchen. "I'll put the kettle on. The boys will be home soon. I hope Vernon's had some work and not been holed up in the alehouse."

"He'd better not have been, or he'll be for it. It's bad enough that George insisted on getting himself down there."

Nell's shoulders dropped as she let out a breath. "Listen, stop seeing the worst in everything. You should be pleased George is up to walking around the corner. He couldn't get himself off the settee a month ago."

Maria shook her head. "I am, but the more he's there, the more he'll want to spend money we haven't got."

"I told you yesterday, by the time Billy and Vernon give you their keep, you'll have over five pounds. How much more do you need?"

"It depends on how much George spends on beer."

"Stop it, now. You should be thankful you're not in Sarah's position. Or Jane's."

"Don't talk to me about them." Maria stepped into the living room. "Did you know they had the cheek to ask me for some money, when we only had Billy working?"

"I had heard."

"And then they had the nerve to be upset when I said no. Well, they can go to the guardians as far as I'm concerned."

"Rebecca said that the guardians weren't happy about giving them anything because Tom had caused the problem himself."

"Exactly! And then they come around here making me feel guilty for not helping. That brother of ours has been up to no good for years, and now it's caught up with him. He should have thought of that."

Nell's mouth was dry as she took a seat. "I called to see them yesterday…"

"You didn't offer them any money, did you?" Maria's eyes were wild, but Nell shook her head.

"I didn't have a chance. They didn't exactly throw me out, but they may as well have done."

"Thank goodness. You didn't tell them how much you'd earned, did you? You won't get rid of them if you do. Especially not Jane."

"No, I didn't, but I can't help feeling sorry for them, and it's not Jane's fault she lost her husband and had to leave her home. Imagine what it would be like for you if you didn't have the boys."

"You're right." Maria sat beside her at the table. "Perhaps I'm being too harsh on her."

Nell coughed to stop herself from choking. "You have to feel for Sarah, too. She never could control Tom."

"Nobody can." Maria paused as the front door opened and Billy appeared. "Are you on your own?"

"Vernon's helping Dad up the step. He looks much brighter than he has been. Being in the alehouse has done him the world of good."

"I hope he doesn't get too used to it."

Nell pushed herself up to pour the tea, but leaned into Maria with a whisper. "Smile."

George grinned as he joined them "That was well timed. I'm ready for one of those." He flopped into the chair by the fire. "That was the best afternoon I've had for a long time."

"It's cheered you up, I'll say that much." Nell handed him a cup of tea. "Did it feel strange to be back?"

"Did it ever. Do you realise, it's been nearly a year since I was last in there? Not that anything had changed."

"The price of ale's gone up." Vernon took the seat opposite his dad.

"Aye. A penny a pint. I won't be in there as often as I'd like at that rate."

"I'm sure Maria will be pleased about that." Nell glanced at her sister, who'd stayed unusually quiet. "Will you look for another job once your leg's mended?"

"Are you trying to get rid of me?"

"Not at all, but you're not one for sitting around doing nothing."

Maria walked to the back door. "He might not have a choice."

"What's up with her?" George's voice was harsh as he nodded after her.

"I've no idea, although when you came in, I was telling her to be a bit more sympathetic to Jane."

George groaned. "That won't have gone down well."

Vernon reached for some bread. "We don't talk about things like that when you're not here. That's probably why she's always so grumpy."

Nell's cheeks coloured. "I'm sorry, but she needs to talk to someone."

"As long as it's not me." George straightened himself up in his seat. "When will tea be ready? I'm famished here."

Billy stood in front of the mirror over the fire, fixing his tie as Nell joined him with the girls.

"Look at us, Billy."

He watched as Elenor and Leah twirled around in their dresses.

"Aren't you pretty?" He moved back to the mirror. "You'll have to put your cloaks on to go outside. It's not very nice weather."

"You're right." Nell went to the hall to retrieve them. "Where is everyone?"

Billy shrugged. "No idea. They were here a minute ago."

"I'm sure they won't be long." She strolled to the door and pushed it closed. "May I ask a quick favour? Would you walk to church with me this morning? I'd like to talk to you without anyone overhearing."

Billy shrugged. "I don't see why not, but why can't you talk to me now?"

"I..."

Nell stopped as George joined them. "What's going on? You look very serious."

"Not at all." Nell reached for Leah's cloak and swung it around her daughter's shoulders. "I shut the door to stop the draught. Are you coming to church with us?"

George groaned. "Apparently, if I'm well enough to go to the alehouse, I'm well enough to go to church. I suppose it will do me good."

"I'm sure it will." Nell checked the clock on the mantelpiece. "You'd better set off soon though, with those crutches."

"I will. I've already told Vernon he can walk with me. Where on earth is he?"

"He went outside." Billy peered through the window as Maria hurried into the kitchen.

"Blimey, it's cold out there today. Vernon won't be a minute."

"I'll start walking then." George headed to the front door. "Are you coming, Billy?"

Billy shrugged at Nell. "I'll see you later."

"We may as well all go. Vernon will catch us up."

They hadn't reached the end of Merlin Street when Vernon ran up behind them, and George stopped and ushered them all past. "You all go on ahead. I want a word with Vernon, anyway."

Nell held back as Maria and Alice walked in front with the girls.

"Are you all right, Aunty Nell?"

"Yes, I was letting everyone through. Shall we go next?"

Billy fell into step with her. "This is all very mysterious. What's the matter?"

Nell glanced over her shoulder to see George in conversation with Vernon.

"Do you remember last year, when we found out about your Uncle Jack, you opened an account for me at the Friendly Society. Do we still have it?"

"We do, as it happens, although there's not much in it. Maybe a shilling to keep it open."

"Oh, that's a relief. It's just that I got rather a lot of tips when I was on the ship, and I don't know what to do with them. I've given your mam and Alice some, but there's too much left for it to be lying around the house. Would you put it in the society for me?"

"If you like. How much do you have?"

"That depends on how things go this morning, but four pounds at the moment. I was going to offer some to your Aunty Sarah and Aunty Jane, but they didn't want to know me when I called on Friday, so I didn't bother. The thing is, I feel guilty about it when they're struggling, so if I get a chance at church, I'll offer them something."

Billy patted her hand. "You're too good to them, the way they treat you."

"What else can I do? They're family. Not a word to your mam, though. She won't be too happy if she knows."

At the end of the service, Nell headed towards Jane as she hovered at the back of the church with the children.

"Good morning." She smiled, but when the scowl remained on her sister's face, Nell pulled her to one side. "What's got into you? I don't remember doing anything to upset you."

Jane gazed into the distance. "I can't be seen with you."

"Why not? Is this all to do with Sarah? What have I done to her?"

Nell paused as Rebecca joined them.

"What's going on?"

"I'm trying to find out the same thing." Nell glared at Jane, but she averted her eyes.

"Don't ask me. I only do as I'm told."

Rebecca raised an eyebrow. "A likely tale. Has this got anything to do with Tom? Or is it Sarah?"

Jane sighed. "If you must know, Tom gives the impression he's furious with Nell for getting a job, but at the same time, he thinks Sarah should find something to earn a bit of money. They can't manage on what Sam and Ada are making, but Sarah doesn't want to work. She blames Nell for giving Tom the idea in the first place."

"Tom wants Sarah to go to work?" Rebecca's forehead creased. "That doesn't sound like him."

"Not go out. Just find something she can do at home. Maybe even help Ada so they can take on more sewing."

"That won't earn her much." Nell's voice was sharper than she expected. "She'd be better getting some domestic work."

"Don't talk nonsense." Jane took a step backwards. "Who'd have the children?"

Nell shrugged. "You could. Then if she split her wage with you, it would solve both your problems."

"I can't take care of five children plus my own."

"Why not? It's only the youngest two who need watching. The others will be happy as long as they're fed."

"It's not that simple. Can you imagine Tom being happy for the women of the house to go out and earn a living?"

"He's no one but himself to blame. Perhaps he should bury his pride and help her find something."

"What's all this about?"

The sharpness of Tom's tone caused a shiver to run down Nell's spine, and she stepped to one side.

"Nothing." Jane glared at her. "We were just leaving."

"No, we weren't." Nell spun around to stare at her brother. "I wanted to know why I'm being treated like a pariah."

"Don't be ridiculous." He started towards the door, but as Nell made to follow him, Sarah grabbed her arm.

"Leave him. You've done enough damage."

Nell gasped. "Why? Because I chose to earn my own living?"

"It's not just a job, is it? Going away and leaving those girls."

"Is it really that, or is it the thought of having to work yourself? It wouldn't kill you, and it might help keep a roof over your heads."

"What have you been saying?" Sarah's nostrils flared as she glared at Jane, but Nell interrupted, "She's been telling me the truth, and why wouldn't she? It's not unusual for women to work. None of the big houses in Liverpool would function if we didn't."

"In case you've forgotten, I've eight children to look after."

Nell snorted. "That's why you need the money. Besides, the eldest don't need looking after and Jane could have the youngest. She needs an income, too."

"Well, it's not happening. Tom needs to find some work."

Rebecca hesitated as Sarah stormed away, pulling Jane behind her. "I'd better be going too. Hugh's waiting outside and he has the girls."

Billy sidled up to Nell as Rebecca followed the others to the door.

"I take it that didn't go as you'd hoped."

Nell sighed. "No, it didn't. I'm afraid there are some people you can't help." She reached into her bag and handed him an envelope. "Will you put this in the account for me? I may as well save it for a rainy day."

He creased the side of his lip. "I hope it doesn't rain much more than it is at the moment."

"I hope so too, but you never know."

George and Vernon were halfway home by the time they caught up with them, and Nell walked beside George.

"Has Maria gone on ahead?"

"Yes, she and Alice wanted to get the dinner ready. I'd hoped to slip into the alehouse on the way past, but apparently there's no time."

"I'm sure there'll be time in the week." Nell leaned forward to check Billy had distracted Vernon before she stopped and rummaged through her bag.

"What are you doing?" George rested on his crutches to study her.

"I've got something for you. A little beer money." The coins clinked as she dropped them in his pocket.

"I can't take that off you."

"You can and you will, as long as you don't tell Maria. You've looked after me for long enough. The least I can do is give you ten shillings. Hopefully, it'll last the month."

He grinned at her. "Come on, let's get you home. And if I hear Maria having one more go at you, I'll give her what for."

CHAPTER THIRTY-ONE

Nell paused on the corner of Merlin Street and Windsor Street and turned to wave one last time. Elenor bounced on the spot, her arm swaying frantically in the air, while Alice held Leah close to her. She wiped her eyes as she retook Billy's arm.

"Come on, Aunty Nell, cheer up."

"I will." She wiped a finger across her eyes. "Saying goodbye is the hardest part. I'll be fine by the time we reach the dock road."

"The way things are, you should be glad you're going." Vernon walked beside his brother, his hands thrust in his pockets. "I wish I was coming with you."

"I'm sure you don't mean that."

Vernon said nothing until they arrived in Upper Parliament Street and he gazed down at the river.

"I wonder if I could get a job on the ships."

Billy gave him a sideways glance. "Doing what? Not a steward, I hope."

Vernon shrugged. "Anything that pays a decent wage."

"You know what Dad thinks of James' job. Don't go mentioning it to him while I'm around."

Vernon stared into the distance. "He's mellowed."

Billy guffawed. "I don't think so!"

"Neither do I." Nell grimaced. "You could be a carpenter like he was. He wouldn't complain at that, and it was paid well from what I gather."

"I could, I suppose. Mam wouldn't be pleased, but if I earn some money..."

Nell shuddered. "No, she wouldn't. You're getting day work now, so it shouldn't be long before you get back to permanent work."

Vernon sighed. "You're right. I don't really want to go to sea, but it makes me angry to see what they've done to us all."

Billy stared at him. "You've no one to blame but yourself. Keep your head down next time."

The large clock at the landing stage showed twenty past seven as they walked towards the ship, and Billy placed Nell's bag by her feet.

"Will someone come and collect that for you?"

"I hope so. I need both hands to get up there. I can't be carrying a bag as well." She chuckled as she stood on her tiptoes to kiss them both on the cheek. "I'll see you in four weeks. Good luck with finding some work."

She'd no sooner set foot on the gangplank than she noticed a steward at the top she hadn't seen before. His eyes bored into her and she lowered her head, using her hat as a shield from his gaze.

As soon as she reached the landing, he stepped to one side. "Mrs Riley?"

"Yes. Good morning." She forced a smile as she showed him her pass, but shuddered under his steely gaze.

"I'm Mr Marsh. I've been asked to take you to your quarters."

"Pleased to meet you. I wonder, could someone bring my case on board for me? I always need two hands when I'm boarding."

"Perhaps one of your gentlemen could have brought it up for you."

Nell recoiled at the sneer in his voice as he hurried down the ramp to collect her bag. He returned a moment later, not stopping as he bolted straight into the ship.

"Follow me. I presume you've been on the ship before."

"Yes, I did the January voyage. Will I be in the same quarters?" Nell had to trot behind him to keep up.

"As I wasn't here, I couldn't say, but I've been told you're at the back of the ship on deck two. Another stewardess by the name of Swift is already here."

Thank goodness. "She was with me on the last trip."

"So, you'll know your routine, then. Mr Price has asked us all to meet in the dining room at eight o'clock."

Once they arrived outside the cabin, Mr Marsh put her bag down beside the door and disappeared, leaving Nell to open the door herself.

"What a strange man."

Mrs Swift looked up from her case as Nell walked in. "Who?"

"That Mr Marsh. Where've they found him from?"

"I've no idea, but he seemed pleasant enough to me. Did you have a good few days?"

"It was all right, once Maria got over the fact I was coming away again." Nell lifted her bag onto the settee.

"The money must have helped."

"Not that you'd notice. I reckon I could have given her a hundred pounds and she wouldn't have been happy."

Mrs Swift chuckled. "She missed you then."

"She's a funny way of showing it. I'm sure she only wanted me back so I could help her with the cleaning."

"I bet the girls were glad to see you."

"Oh, they were. We had a nice day out in Liverpool on Saturday, and I got them their dresses. They looked lovely in them."

Mrs Swift nudged her as she gazed into space. "Come along, there's no time for daydreaming. We need to be over the other side in quarter of an hour and it will take us five minutes to get there."

"All right, I'm coming. I wonder what it's about. We didn't have a meeting last month."

"I expect Mr Price wants to show us who's boss. He'll probably introduce any newcomers too."

"I hope they're more cheerful than Mr Marsh. With any luck, he'll be down in steerage."

Most of the tables in the men's section of the dining room were already taken when they arrived, and Mr Price pointed them to a small round table in the corner.

"Good morning, ladies. I've pulled a table across for you."

"Good morning, Mr Price." Nell smiled as they headed for the corner and took a seat.

"Welcome back." Mr Ross appeared on Nell's left with a pot of tea. "Mr Price thought you'd like this."

"That's very kind." Nell raised her eyebrows at Mrs Swift before glancing around the rest of the tables. "What have we done to deserve this? The stewards don't have any."

He winked at her. "Don't worry, it's ladies first; theirs is coming."

Mr Ross was still delivering teapots when Mr Price rang the bell at the front of the room.

"May I have everyone's attention?"

Everyone fell silent as Captain Robertson joined them.

"Thank you, Mr Price." He surveyed the room. "I'd like to welcome you all back. I hope you had a pleasant break and you're ready to go again. We've made a few staff changes, which Mr Price will take you through, but before then, I want to inform you that Officer Hughes has moved to join another ship. He's been replaced by a new third mate, Officer Young. He's currently on the bridge, but I wanted to let you know, in case you see him wandering around." He glanced around the room. "Now, I'd like to wish you all a safe and incident-free journey and hand you over to Mr Price." He nodded to Nell and Mrs Swift. "And please, treat the ladies with respect. They're here to do a job, the same as the rest of us."

Mrs Swift leaned into Nell as the captain turned away. "Things are looking up."

"Let's hope they stay that way." Nell nodded towards Mr Marsh. "Not that he looks very impressed."

"He's probably wondering what the captain's talking about. He won't have had time to hear all the gossip yet."

"I reckon he's been sent here from another ship for causing trouble..." Nell paused as Mr Price clapped his hands.

"Gentlemen, please. I won't keep you much longer. I'd like to mention a few changes since you were last on board. As you know, Mr Driver left the ship when we docked in Liverpool and I've taken over the position of head steward. My role as deputy will be filled by Mr Cooper."

Nell's mouth dropped open as she stared at Mrs Swift. "I thought he'd have been kicked off, too."

"That's wishful thinking."

"Taking over from Mr Cooper, we have Mr Marsh." Mr Price gestured to the tall, thin steward standing near the door. "He's joined us from the SS *Wyoming*, which is the sister ship to the *Wisconsin* and so he'll be familiar with his way around. He'll start by working in steerage with Mr Cooper, but will also serve up here as and when the need arises."

Mr Marsh nodded to the stewards, but Nell grimaced.

"It better not arise very often."

Mrs Swift rolled her eyes. "I don't know what's up with you; he was perfectly fine with me."

Nell had serviced half her staterooms by the time she sat down to luncheon with Mrs Swift, and her stomach rumbled as Mr Ross placed a beef stew in front of her.

"It feels like a long time since breakfast. You must have had this in the oven early."

"I didn't get off the ship, so I had it in by six this morning. I need to spend all my time taking on the new deliveries."

"That must be quite a job."

He planted his hands on his hips. "We're not finished yet. The meat and fish will only arrive tomorrow morning. It has to be as fresh as possible when we leave."

"You do very well keeping it fresh for so long. I couldn't cope if we didn't go to the shop every day."

"Ah, we have ways." He tapped the side of his nose. "Right, I'd better be going. I'll be back with your dessert."

Nell picked up her knife and fork. "How've you got on with your staterooms this morning?"

"I'm about halfway through. If we get a decent afternoon, I'll be done in time for afternoon tea. What about you?"

"Yes, the same. I'm glad we're not full."

"We've probably only got one more trip before we are, but it's worth it. We get more tips when there are more passengers."

Nell groaned. "I couldn't give my money away when I was at home. I left it with Billy to put into a Friendly Society."

"Didn't you say your brother was out of work?"

"He is, but there was something going on and I didn't get chance to speak to him. I was left in no doubt that my sister and sister-in-law don't like me working, though."

Mrs Swift's brow creased. "Why not?"

"Because my brother wants them to get jobs and they don't want to."

Mrs Swift stopped with her fork in mid-air. "I know

what I'd rather do, if it was a choice of working and eating, or being thrown out of the house."

"They've no idea how serious it is. One of my nephews has started to pick up some day work and his eldest sister has a drapery business, so they're hoping they'll provide for them."

"They'll find out soon enough. What did they say about you coming back to the ship?"

Nell grimaced. "They were all in such a bad mood, I didn't tell them. I'll probably be in trouble when I get home. Something to look forward to."

She continued to eat in silence, and once her plate was clean, she pushed it away. "That was lovely. I've missed being waited on."

"You and me both. My sister thinks that because she does all the work with Mother while I'm away, she should have some time off when I'm home."

"All finished, ladies?" Mr Ross arrived at the end of the table with two bowls.

"Yes, thank you. What's next?"

"Peaches and cream."

"Oh, lovely." Mrs Swift leaned forward as Mr Ross put down the bowls. "What do you know about this new steward?"

"Not a lot, I've been too busy."

"So you've not heard why he was moved from the *Wyoming*?"

"Not yet, but give me time." He winked as he turned to leave. "I'll keep you posted."

CHAPTER THIRTY-TWO

Matron was in the sitting room when they arrived for breakfast the following morning.

"Good morning." Nell took the seat opposite her. "We didn't see much of you yesterday."

"I was with the doctor and the captain's wife. She wasn't very well, so I had to sit with her."

"Again! This is getting serious."

Matron sighed. "The truth is, we don't know. I suggested to her that she could be in the family way, but she was adamant she's not. Dr Clarke doesn't think she is either; not that he has much experience, having worked on ships for the last twenty years."

Mrs Swift grimaced as she poured the tea. "It will be a shock to the system if she is. She won't be travelling to New York every month, for one thing."

"I'm sure she'd be pleased though." Nell cocked her head to one side. "I reckon she's a couple of years older than me, so it's about time she settled down. Once the baby's born, she won't mind."

Mrs Swift raised an eyebrow. "Says you, who's left two children at home."

"That's different. If Jack was captain of one of these ships, I wouldn't need the money for myself. I'd travel with him occasionally, but not every trip. We'd already spoken about it..." She paused as she struggled for words.

"Come on, don't get all maudlin." Matron patted her hand.

"I'm sorry, it's just..." she bit on her lip as she took a breath "...it's a year to the day since I lost him. Not that I found out until the following day. I've known the date was coming, and I tried to ignore it, but, well, I suppose talk of babies..." She played with the spoon in her bowl of porridge. "Once we get past Mizen Head, I'll be fine."

"I'll mention it to Mr Price." Matron pushed herself up from the table. "You know where I am if you need me."

Mrs Swift waited until Matron left them. "Why didn't you say anything?"

Nell wiped her eyes. "Like I said, I was trying to ignore it. Don't worry, I won't let it show. I hope we get some nice passengers who'll distract me."

As they made their way to the first-class section, Nell paused on the deck and gazed at the view. She hadn't had a chance yesterday, and with the mornings getting lighter, there was more to see. The Customs House still dominated the skyline, along with the tall chimney of the Pump House, but the fields behind the buildings were suddenly visible. She stared, trying to imprint the image in her mind.

"I wish I could capture that somehow."

Mrs Swift laughed as she pulled at her arm. "You'll need to bring your paintbrushes."

"If only. Wouldn't it be nice if one of the passengers was an artist?"

"I doubt they'd be travelling in first class if they were."

"You're right, although maybe if they painted a picture they could use it as part payment."

Mrs Swift rolled her eyes as she opened the door on the far side. "I doubt Mr Guion would be very keen on that idea."

"Probably not..." Nell stepped into the foyer but flinched as Mr Marsh appeared in front of them.

"Good morning, ladies."

She put a hand to her chest. "Mr Marsh. You gave me quite a start."

"My apologies." He inclined his head. "I was on my way downstairs. Good day."

He hurried on ahead and disappeared.

"What was he even doing up here?"

Mrs Swift shrugged as she followed him. "He must have had his reasons. Now, come along. Those tables won't set themselves and the passengers will be boarding shortly."

The tables in the dining room were bare other than the starched white tablecloths covering them, and Nell walked to the drawers near the galley to collect the cutlery.

"Mrs Riley!"

Nell took a step backwards as Mr Ramsbottom approached. "Good morning. I'd forgotten you'd be back upstairs."

A broad smile lit up his face. "They couldn't keep me in steerage for long. Did you miss me?"

"I, erm … I did wonder where you were."

"I believe you know it was Mr Driver who nearly did for the two of us. Good riddance to him, I say."

"He certainly didn't make life easy. Anyway … it's nice to see you again. I'd better get a move on." She grabbed for the cutlery and hurried to Mrs Swift, who looked up as she approached.

"What's the matter?"

"I need company; Mr Ramsbottom's working with us, again."

Mrs Swift tensed her jaw. "What did he say?"

"Nothing of importance, only that he was glad to see the back of Mr Driver. He was rather pleased I was here, though."

"You need to nip that in the bud. Don't give him any encouragement."

"I don't, but I can't be rude."

"You need to take after me and keep a scowl on your face."

Nell laughed. "The Mrs Fosters told me to do that. I'd better practise." She pulled her face straight, but broke into a grin. "Perhaps it's easier with a steward."

"Good morning, ladies. You seem to be in high spirits."

"Mr Price." Mrs Swift continued to lay out the dessert spoons. "What can we do for you?"

"I wanted to make sure you'll be ready to greet the guests. They'll be boarding in half an hour."

She checked the room. "We should be."

"Splendid." He turned to Nell. "Matron told me about the date. I'm sorry."

Nell's lips twisted. "Thank you, but I'm fine. Keeping busy helps."

"I'm glad to hear it. Right, well, I'll leave you to it. Please be upstairs for five to ten."

By the time they reached the deck, the wind had picked up and Nell held her cloak tightly to stop it blowing as they hurried to the far side.

"It's going to be choppy on the sea if it stays like this." Nell held open the door.

"Matron will be busy if it is. Let's hope it drops before we leave."

Once their cloaks were hung up, they joined the captain, and first mate, Officer Jones, in the foyer.

"Are we all here?" He scanned the line of stewards on the opposite side. "Splendid. Our guests should be arriving imminently."

A number of gentlemen arrived up the gangplank and after a brief word with the captain, the stewards took them to their staterooms. Nell glanced to her left and stood up straight as a nervous-looking woman, wearing a heavy navy cloak with a velvet collar and matching hat, joined them. She appeared to be alone, but a tall, thin gentleman with a dark pencil moustache followed, walking two steps behind. He stayed with her as she greeted the captain.

"Miss Ellis. Welcome on board. Your father wrote to tell me you'd be travelling with us. I hope you have a pleasant journey."

"Thank you, I hope so, too. May I introduce my

chaperone, Mr Rodney?" She extended an arm to her companion. "We should have separate staterooms."

Mr Rodney removed his hat and accepted the captain's handshake. "I did make a request for them to be next door to each other. I need to liaise with Miss Ellis regularly, and we won't always want to sit with the other passengers."

Miss Ellis's eyes darted to Mr Rodney. "It really doesn't matter if we have to walk."

"Nonsense, I'm always happy to help a friend." The captain summoned Mr Price. "Let's see what we can do."

After a great deal of gesturing, Mr Price beckoned Nell over.

"Would you direct Miss Ellis to stateroom nineteen?"

"Yes, sir." Nell smiled at her new passenger. "If you'll follow me."

The woman walked behind Nell as they headed towards the front of the ship.

"Will you be on your own, miss?"

"I should say so. My chaperone will be in the stateroom next door. That's close enough for me."

"You're very fortunate..."

The woman studied Nell as they reached the door. "Fortunate? I've worked hard for what I have."

"Oh, I didn't presume..."

"No. Nobody ever does. Everyone thinks Mr Rodney supports me ... or my father. They couldn't be further from the truth."

She stepped into the room as Nell pushed open the door.

"Your trunk will be delivered presently, miss. Would you like any help unpacking when it arrives?"

"Actually, I would. I'd also like the bag Mr Rodney was carrying. Has he arrived next door yet?"

Nell peered down the corridor. "He's on his way. Shall I ask him to bring it?"

Miss Ellis gave a deep sigh. "No, it's quicker if I fetch it myself."

She stepped out into the corridor, holding onto the wall as she approached Mr Rodney. "I'll take that." She reached out for a square black case. "The maid's going to help me unpack later, so I'll sit with my writing for an hour and see you in the dining room for luncheon."

"Yes, miss."

She carried the bag back to her stateroom, placing it on the table. "My typewriter."

"Typewriter!" Nell stared at the case. "Why would you bring one of those onto the ship?"

"To write." The woman's green eyes sparkled. "It's quicker than writing by hand, and so much easier to read."

Nell peered into the case as Miss Ellis opened it. "What do you write?"

"Books." She picked up a wad of paper and flicked through it. "Story books, to be precise. This is my latest creation, or a first draft at any rate. I'm hoping to have some time to myself so I can work on it before I hand it to the publisher."

"Gosh. You must be very clever."

"I have a good imagination, that's all. You'll know when I'm stuck, because I'll take to sitting in the saloon. It's amazing how much inspiration you get from watching fellow passengers. Or crew." She grinned. "If anyone upsets or delights me, they may end up in the book."

"Oh!" Nell stepped backwards, but Miss Ellis laughed.

"Don't worry, I'll be kind to people who help me. Now–" she glanced around the room and sat down at the writing desk "–this won't do. It's too small. Would it be possible to get a table in here for me to work on?"

Nell studied the desk. "You want something bigger than that, but not so big that it takes up all the space? I don't know if we have such a thing, but I'll ask. If not, perhaps you could use a quiet corner of the dining room."

Miss Ellis's face clouded. "Gracious, no. It would never do for people to see me. Will you try to get something for in here?"

"Leave it with me."

The guests were still arriving when Nell returned to the deck and took her place next to Mrs Swift.

"Where've you been?"

"Settling in a passenger."

"You took your time. I had to show another of your ladies to her room. A Mrs Barrington. She's married to a colonel. She asked if you'd help her unpack."

"I thought people like that had maids."

Mrs Swift gave her a sideways glance. "There'll be a story as to why she hasn't. I have no doubt she'll tell you."

Nell watched as four young men in smart suits congregated around the captain. "How can they afford to travel in first class?"

"I imagine they'll all have rich fathers who've paid for them. A word of warning, though. I've come across their type before, and they think the rules that apply to us are there to be broken. They could be trouble; I'd stay out of their way."

Nell eyed the tallest of the group. He had dark brown hair that wasn't greased down in the way the others wore theirs, and when he smiled he had a look of Jack about him. *If only.* She let out a deep sigh, but jumped as Mrs Swift nudged her.

"Enough of that, today of all days, too. I'll have to keep an eye on you."

"You won't need to do anything of the sort." Nell struggled to keep her voice steady. "For a second he reminded me of Jack, that's all. It's passed now."

"I should hope so."

The young men disappeared with Mr Ramsbottom, as Nell noticed another married couple arrive.

"These will be for me. I've one couple not arrived yet. Mr and Mrs Stewart, if the guest list's right." Mrs Swift watched as they joined the captain, but suddenly groaned. "Typical. They're the ones with a maid. I won't get many tips from this voyage at this rate."

"I'm sure you'll get some. The maid will only help her to dress and with her luggage."

"Whatever she does, I could do with them being generous." Mrs Swift sighed. "Never mind, I need to get on. I'll see you in the saloon later."

CHAPTER THIRTY-THREE

N ell stood by the door to the galley, watching the stewards usher the guests to their tables. *What sort of voyage can we expect with these passengers? Uneventful, I hope.*

"We could be in for a quiet crossing." Mrs Swift joined her. "There are no ladies travelling on their own; they're all with their husbands."

"That'll be why the room's been rearranged. There is one unmarried woman, though. Miss Ellis."

Mrs Swift studied their section. "I've not seen her; is she with you?"

"She's the one who took up my time when they were all arriving. She's with a chaperone."

"Someone's well-to-do if they can afford two staterooms."

"I get the impression she's in charge and he's here to escort her. Here they come now." Nell watched as Mr Rodney helped Miss Ellis to her seat. "Look at her dress; it's rather elaborate for luncheon."

"She must be another one with a father who has more money than sense."

"I don't doubt it, but she writes books, too."

"Really?" Mrs Swift raised her eyebrows. "That's exciting, not that she'll make anything from them."

"I've a feeling she does. Once I get to know her better, I'll ask what she's written."

Nell strolled to the table with a smile. "Good afternoon, Miss Ellis. Have you settled into your room?"

"Not yet." Her manner was stiff, not at all like the person she'd spoken to in the stateroom. "A table arrived as we left to come here, but it's rather large. I'm assured it's the smallest available."

"Oh, I'm sorry. I'll take a look after luncheon. Perhaps we can move some of the furniture around to accommodate it."

"You'll need to do better than the stewards who brought it. They didn't have any idea what they were doing."

"I'm sure we'll sort something out. May I get you a drink?"

"Some China tea and several slices of lemon, please. My companion will take his with milk."

Mr Rodney nodded, but said nothing.

"Very good, miss." Nell headed towards the bar, but was distracted by a large man with a handlebar moustache waving an arm at her.

"You'll be Mrs Riley, I presume."

"Yes, sir. May I help?"

"We were told you'd be taking care of my wife, Mrs Barrington, but this is the first time we've seen you."

"I'm sorry, sir. It's always hectic on the first morning. May I get you anything?"

"An elderflower cordial for my wife, and I'll have a large brandy."

"Yes, sir. I won't keep you waiting."

Mr Brennan was shaking a cocktail as Nell approached. "I may have a good customer for you." She pointed to the Barringtons' table.

"You mean the colonel? I wondered if he liked a tipple. What's it to be?"

"A large brandy."

Mr Brennan's lip curled up. "Splendid. We've plenty of that on board although I'd better keep a bottle back. The more they drink on the last night, the more they're likely to give us tips."

Nell sighed. "It's all right for you; he only ordered an elderflower cordial for his wife."

"Don't worry, she'll have a sherry before dinner, you wait and see. That lot usually do."

Nell hesitated and stepped away from the bar as Mr Ramsbottom approached, a tray of empty glasses held over his shoulder.

"Those young men can drink. They want another already."

Nell glanced across to the men's section, where the four friends were laughing with each other. "It makes a change to see people enjoying themselves."

"It does, but if they're like this at luncheon, I'll be carrying them to their staterooms by this evening. They've had a Manhattan each, and one of them's ordered a whisky."

"Maybe it's because it's their first meal on the ship. They may calm down once they settle in."

"I hope not." Mr Brennan studied them. "I reckon they've got a bob or two. We could be quids in by the end of this trip."

Nell rolled her eyes. "Is that all you think of?"

"What else is there? The better service I give them, and the more Mr Ramsbottom has to help them to their staterooms, the more they'll tip us. That's the way it works."

"It most certainly is." Mr Ramsbottom handed Nell the brandy, waiting for her. "So the quicker you take these drinks, the faster Mr Brennan and I get the gentlemen served."

Miss Ellis barely acknowledged Nell over luncheon, and desserts hadn't been served when she stood up and left the dining room. Nell saw her leave and strode to the table, smiling at Mr Rodney as she arrived.

"Will Miss Ellis be back?"

"No."

"Dessert for one then? It's apple pie with custard."

"Fine."

Nell hesitated as he rested his arms on the table and glared through the partition to the men's tables.

"Very good, sir. I won't be a moment."

Mrs Swift followed her to the galley. "What's going on over there?"

"I've no idea, but I'm helping Miss Ellis unpack as soon as we're finished here, so I'll find out."

"You've not forgotten Mrs Barrington, have you?"

"Hardly. Colonel Barrington must have told me three times that he'll be in the saloon all afternoon, while I do the unpacking."

"I'd see to her first, if I were you. I suspect he's more important."

Nell carried the apple pie to Mr Rodney and put it down without a word before moving to the Barringtons' table.

"Is there anything else I can get you?"

"No, that was lovely, thank you." Mrs Barrington dabbed her lips with a napkin. "I'll wait for you in my stateroom, shall I?"

"There's no need if you'd prefer to join Colonel Barrington in the saloon."

The colonel spluttered. "Good grief, woman. Can't a man have a bit of peace and quiet?"

"Of course, forgive me." Nell's cheeks coloured. "I'm happy to work while Mrs Barrington's there. I'll be as quick as I can."

She collected the empty bowls, but stepped nearer the flower partition as a chorus of laughter erupted on the other side. *The four men, again.* She paused with a smile on her face as they jostled over a piece of paper. The apparent leader snatched it from his friend and pushed it into his pocket.

"Enough." He ran a hand through his hair, causing Nell's pulse to race.

If it wasn't for the fancy clothes...

"Mrs Riley."

Nell jumped as Mr Marsh strode towards her. "Oh ... Mr Marsh ... I ... I didn't think you were working up here."

"I'm not, and neither are you by the look of things."

Nell glanced down at the dishes in her hands. "I'm tidying up, but got distracted..."

"It would appear you have a fondness for young men."

"Excuse me!" She stepped backwards. "What's that supposed to mean?"

"I'm sure you're well aware." He glared at her as he stormed off.

He can't report me for watching the passengers have fun.

"Are you all right, dear?" Mrs Barrington stopped on her way to the door. "You've gone rather pale."

"Yes, thank you." She took a deep breath. "Give me half an hour, and I'll be with you."

By the time Nell was ready for luncheon, Mrs Swift was waiting at the dining table.

"You took your time."

"I'm sorry, it's that Mr Marsh. I don't know what I've done to upset him, but he makes me shudder whenever I see him."

"I don't know why, he's always perfectly civil to me. What's he done?"

"Oh, nothing..." Nell paused as Mr Ross brought their food. "Do you know why Mr Marsh was up here?"

"Mr Marsh? No, I didn't see him."

Mrs Swift picked up her knife and fork. "He is allowed up here."

"He may be, but Mr Cooper was never up here that often when he was in steerage."

Her friend shrugged. "Or maybe we just didn't notice him. You'll get used to Mr Marsh soon enough."

. . .

Mrs Barrington was on the settee reading when Nell arrived at her stateroom.

"I'm sorry to keep you waiting."

"Not to worry; I'm quite enjoying myself. I picked up this magazine yesterday, and it's got a marvellous new story."

"I am glad. Shall I start with the trunk?"

"Yes, please. I'm not used to dealing with all the material in the bustles. My maid packed it for me, but she wasn't able to travel with us."

"That's a shame. Will you be away for long?"

"No, only a couple of weeks. We're visiting friends from India."

Nell's forehead creased as she hung up a dress. "In America?"

Mrs Barrington laughed. "They're not *from* India, but we met them while my husband was stationed out there in the sixties. The men went off to the war in Bhutan, and so we ladies spent a lot of time together."

"So it's a reunion?"

"Exactly. Our friends are British, of course, but they decided to join the hordes moving west. It's all very exciting."

"It sounds like it. Are you planning to move yourselves?"

"Good gracious, no, Colonel Barrington wouldn't hear of it. He's too set in his ways, even now he's left the army. Thankfully, he's happy to visit."

"I'd love to visit too, but I doubt I ever will. We only stop for a day in New York, and so there isn't time for everyone to disembark."

"That's a pity. I'll make a note of things to tell you about it if I see you on the return voyage, but you must answer me something first. Are there any guests of importance on the crossing? You know, any dukes or earls, and their ladies?"

"Not that I'm aware of. We had Lord and Lady Faulkner on board in January."

"Really?" Her eyes widened. "Do you know when they're due back? I'm sure we could change our dates."

"I'm afraid I can't help. They're travelling home with *Cunard*."

"What a shame." Mrs Barrington's shoulders slumped. "I should be a lady, you know. When my husband was made up to colonel, you'd imagine I'd have received a title too, but no. The wives of baronets, or even mere sirs, are made ladies, but not the wives of men who've fought so gallantly for our country. It's quite a travesty."

"That's unfortunate. Is it because the men are the ones who do the fighting?"

"That's what they say, but they can't do it without the support of their women. I feel quite forgotten." She ran the back of her hand across her forehead.

"You must be proud walking into a room on the arm of the colonel, though. Especially with all his medals."

"Oh, I am." She recovered her poise. "Still, it's not the same."

"I'm sure it's not." Nell stopped to survey the room. "That's all the dresses hung. Will you be able to manage with everything else?"

"Yes, thank you, dear. I think I'll wander up to the saloon. It must be time for afternoon tea."

Nell grimaced. "I hope not. I've another trunk to

unpack first. Will you excuse me?"

She hurried along the corridor and turned the corner to find a group of stewards outside Miss Ellis's stateroom.

"What's going on here?"

Mr Price walked towards her. "She wanted a table in her room, but there are none small enough up here. I've asked Mr Marsh to bring one from steerage to see if it fits better. They tend to be smaller down there."

"Where's Miss Ellis?"

"She's gone to the saloon; she said she couldn't rest with so much going on."

"I'm sure she couldn't." *Why does it need four stewards to sort this out?* "Would you mind if I went in to unpack her trunk? I'll be late for afternoon tea, otherwise."

"Of course not." Mr Price cleared a path as he ushered her into the room. "Take your time. I'll ask Mr Marsh to leave the table outside the door and we'll sort it out once afternoon tea's over."

"Thank you." Nell stepped into the stateroom and immediately locked the door behind her. *I'm not risking Mr Marsh walking in. Right, what have we got here?*

She stood with her hands on her hips and surveyed the room. Most of the furniture had been moved to the bed area, blocking access to the wardrobe. *For goodness' sake. What were they trying to do?*

She pulled on the arm of the settee to move it out of the way, but it refused to budge. *Now what do I do? Is there anyone left outside?* She unlocked the door, but stopped as Mr Marsh approached, carrying a fold-down table. *Now what?*

"Mrs Riley." He gave her a curt nod.

"Mr Marsh. Have the other stewards already left?"

"It would appear so. Were you expecting anyone in particular?"

"No ... it's ... well. Never mind."

His eyes bored into her. "I believe you require a table."

"Not me exactly, but the stewards have cleared a space if you'd like to bring it in." She stepped out of the room to let him past, but peered inside when he didn't return. "Will it fit once the furniture is reorganised?"

"I imagine so, but I can't stay to rearrange it. Mr Cooper's expecting me downstairs."

Nell blocked the doorway. "Before you go, could you move the settee back to this end of the room? Please. I'll do the rest myself."

He tutted as he walked back into the room. "Will you assist me?"

"Me!" Her mouth was dry as she tried to swallow. "I can't be seen in a stateroom with you; we'd both get into trouble." She glanced up and down the corridor. "I'm sure a strong man like you can move it yourself. Please. I need to unpack the trunk before afternoon tea."

A trace of a smile flickered on his lips. "If I must." He pulled the settee, causing it to slide along the floor. "Will that do?"

"A little further if you wouldn't mind, to where the marks are on the carpet. Yes, that's it. Thank you."

Mr Marsh straightened up and stepped into the corridor. "I need to go. Good afternoon."

Nell stood against the far wall, but didn't wait for him to disappear before she darted into the room and locked the door. *What a strange man, but at least the table fits.*

CHAPTER THIRTY-FOUR

The following morning, Miss Ellis opened the door of her stateroom as Nell fumbled with her key.

"Good morning, miss. I hadn't realised you'd still be here. I'd like to service the room, if you don't mind."

Miss Ellis gazed at the bed. "I suppose I should take a break. Am I too late for breakfast?"

"I'm afraid so, although coffee will be served in the saloon at ten o'clock."

She sighed. "That's another hour. I really should pay more attention to the time."

"If you prefer to work once you get up, I could bring a tray for you. We deliver them around half past seven, when the main service starts in the dining room."

"That would work, although…" her forehead creased "… I don't usually get out of bed until eight."

Nell smiled. "And you needn't, if you'd rather not. I'll be the one doing the delivery, so I could bring it in."

Her face lit up. "Breakfast in bed. How splendid. Would you do that?"

"Yes, of course. I'll save your tray until last so I needn't wake you any earlier than necessary."

"Thank you, Mrs Riley." She glanced around the room again. "I'd better let you get on. How long will you be?"

"Only twenty minutes or so. Might I suggest you go onto the deck. We're docked in Queenstown at the moment, and it has a rather impressive cathedral. It's worth a look."

"We're not moving?"

"No, we'll be in port until about four o'clock this afternoon."

Miss Ellis put a hand to her chest. "That's a relief. To tell you the truth, I'm not the best passenger. I'd rather people didn't know." She paused. "Was Mr Rodney at breakfast?"

"I didn't see him, but he would have been on the men's side of the room, so that doesn't mean he wasn't there."

"Of course." She reached for her cloak. "Perhaps I'll sneak upstairs without him. He'll come looking for me if he wants me."

Nell was finishing sweeping the floor when Miss Ellis returned.

"That was well timed. I'm about finished here."

"Oh, I don't mind. It's nice to have some female company for a change." She draped her cloak over the settee. "I imagine you feel the same; are you the only stewardess on board?"

"I have a colleague, Mrs Swift, who looks after the ladies on the starboard side. And there's Matron."

"That's nice for you. I'm never allowed to bring a companion; it always has to be Mr Rodney."

"Don't you care for him?"

Miss Ellis sank onto the settee beside her cloak, causing Nell to pick it up. "He's so dull. Don't you sometimes wish you could laugh and be jolly?" She didn't wait for an answer. "I do, although I never manage it."

Nell studied the coat hanger in her hand. "I've never thought about it. I've not much to laugh about."

"Really? Even with friends?" Her brow creased. "I hadn't considered that. I always assumed I was missing out on something."

"Surely you have things to be glad about. Especially travelling like this." Nell gestured around the room with her arm.

"I should, but it's not the same as home, is it?"

Nell raised an eyebrow. *It's certainly not like my home.* "Doesn't the fact you're going to America excite you?"

"Not really, because I won't get to see the place." Her eyes suddenly fixed on Nell. "If it's anything like last time, there'll be a carriage waiting for us at the port, which will take us straight to the hotel. The next morning, I'll be ushered to my publisher in New York, where Mr Rodney will act on my behalf to fix a price for the publication rights."

"But they're your books; won't you have any say?"

Miss Ellis forced a laugh. "Gracious, no. If everyone had their way, I wouldn't be there at all. It's not considered womanly."

Nell studied her. "That surprises me. I thought it was only the likes of me who had to mind my place."

"Not at all. We've probably got more in common than you realise."

I doubt it. Nell plumped up the cushions on the settee. "What happens after you've been to the publisher? Won't you have some free time then?"

"Unfortunately not. If they want the book, I'll be in my hotel suite making any necessary changes to it; but if they don't like it, or can't see any money in it, I'll be paraded around New York until we find someone who will."

"What a shame." Nell straightened up and collected her cloths.

"I'm used to it. My father sends Mr Rodney to talk about the money and make sure I do what the publisher wants."

"I hope you don't think me impudent, but if you'd like a companion while you're on board, I'll be here each day."

A smile returned to Miss Ellis's lips. "That's very kind, thank you."

The ship pulled out of Queenstown at precisely four o'clock, but the saloon was empty as Nell and Mrs Swift arrived from the dining room.

"The passengers must still be on deck." Mrs Swift neatened some of the high-back leather chairs around the tables. "I doubt many of them will stay outside for long; it must be chilly."

"You're right, once the cathedral disappears, they'll be in." Nell's voice faltered and Mrs Swift placed a hand on Nell's shoulder.

"Will you be all right?"

She nodded. "I'll be fine."

"Shall we go on the deck once afternoon tea's over?"

"No ... thank you." Nell shuddered. "I said my farewells to Jack on the last voyage, so I'd rather stay busy. The date doesn't help, either. There are too many memories."

"I'm sure." Mrs Swift removed her hand and wandered to a table where she rearranged the cups and saucers. "I just wanted to check."

"Good afternoon, ladies. What are you doing in here?" Mr Ramsbottom strode across the room. "The sun's come out, so we're serving drinks on the first-class promenade. Aren't you joining us?"

"Since when?" Mrs Swift's brow furrowed.

"It was Mr Price's idea. I'm here for some cups and saucers. Would you help me carry them up?"

They each loaded a tray with crockery and carried them outside to a long table Mr Price had arranged at the front of the first-class promenade. Mr Ross followed them with a large pot of tea.

"I'll pop down for the coffee. The cake should be here shortly."

"What a splendid idea." Colonel and Mrs Barrington strolled towards them. "Are you ready to serve? We'd like to sit and watch the world go by."

Nell's stomach flipped as she glanced at the shoreline. "Almost. Would you prefer tea or coffee?"

"It has to be tea at this time of day. It's no time for coffee. And a couple of scones with jam."

Nell bit back a grin. "We're waiting for the cake, so if you take a seat I'll bring everything to you."

"Jolly good." The colonel raised his hand in a wave as he guided his wife to a pair of chairs overlooking the shoreline.

"It must be nice for Mrs Barrington to have her husband back after him going to war." Nell watched as she lay a blanket over her husband's knee.

"What did you say?" Mr Ramsbottom stared at Nell, but she shook her head.

"I'm sorry, nothing. Will you excuse me, I'll see where those cakes have got to."

She hurried along the promenade, but slowed as she approached and peered over the side of the ship. *I can't run away every time we're close to Mizen Head. I need to get used to it.*

"Is everything all right, Mrs Riley?" Mr Price appeared behind her, carrying a tray of cakes.

"Yes, I'm fine, thank you." She wiped her eyes with a finger. "I'll be with you in a moment."

She waited for him to leave and retrieved her handkerchief. *Come on, don't be silly.*

She was about to follow him, but stopped when the man resembling Jack burst through the door, almost knocking her over.

"I do apologise." He caught her arm to steady her as his friends joined him. "Now then, what do we have here?" He looked her up and down. "I've not seen you before."

Nell's cheeks burned as he studied her. "I'm here to help the ladies, that would be why."

"I'd rather you help with us, instead of having us put up with these chaps." He gestured to a nearby steward as he laughed to his friends.

"Come on, Olly, leave her alone." A tall, thin friend

with fair hair pulled him away. "Not everyone knows when you're joking."

"She does. Look."

Nell took a step backwards as he grinned at her.

"Oh, perhaps not." His face straightened as he offered her his hand. "Forgive me. I'm Oliver Hewitt, and these are my friends, Mr Cavendish, Mr Derbyshire and Mr Bracknell." The gentlemen gave her a bow, but Nell hesitated as she accepted his hand.

"Pleased to meet you. I'm Mrs Riley. If you'll excuse me..."

"Mrs Riley! What's going on?"

Nell snatched her hand away as Mr Marsh arrived on the promenade with a second tray of cakes.

"Nothing. W-we were..."

Mr Hewitt stepped forward. "We were introducing ourselves. What's wrong with that?"

Mr Marsh stared between the two of them. "Men and women should not be mixing. Mrs Riley, please excuse yourself."

"Don't be such a stick in the mud." Mr Hewitt waved his arm around the deck. "What harm can it do with so many people here?" He stepped back to open a space for Nell to walk through. "Good day, Mrs Riley. It was nice to meet you."

"And you..." *Olly*. Her heart pounded as she walked to the other end of the promenade. *Those beautiful brown eyes looked so familiar. And his jawline...*

"Are you all right?" Mrs Swift ushered her to a quiet corner. "You've gone very pale."

Nell clung to the railings. "I feel such a fool. What's Mr

Marsh even doing here? Doesn't he know he's been assigned to steerage?"

"I didn't mean him, I meant that group of men. What were they saying?"

Nell's knuckles were white as she struggled to stop herself from swaying. "They were only introducing themselves because they hadn't seen us before, but Mr Marsh interrupted. I don't know what his problem is."

"Don't you?" Mrs Swift gave her a stern look. "The captain's trying his best to keep the men and women separate. Shaking hands with a male passenger is hardly going to help."

Nell groaned. "It wasn't my fault. I only wanted a minute to myself. Will I be in trouble again?"

Mrs Swift straightened her dress. "You shouldn't be, not this time, because so many people saw what happened, but you need to be careful."

Nell took a deep breath. "I will. I'm sorry." She glanced over her shoulder. "Has Mr Marsh gone?"

"He has, but we've a full selection of cakes, so we'd better start serving."

The wind was picking up as the staff collected the crockery from the assorted vantage points on the deck but Nell paused as the rugged coastline of Ireland disappeared into the sea. *Keep going; it's no different to any other part of the voyage.*

"Mrs Riley."

Nell's heart sank as Mr Price joined her. "Yes, sir."

"I heard about the situation with Mr Hewitt and his friends."

"I'm sorry, sir, I didn't mean..."

He held up a hand. "Please, Mrs Riley. I'm not here to reprimand you. I believe they were the ones surrounding you, and I wanted to ask if you were all right."

"I am now. It's just that it was here..." She waved a hand over the ocean as the last of the rocks slid past.

He took the plates from her. "If you'd like to go downstairs and start in the dining room, I quite understand."

Nell wiped her face with the back of a hand. "Thank you. I will."

CHAPTER THIRTY-FIVE

By the time Nell called to collect Miss Ellis's tray the following morning, she was out of bed and dressed.

"Did you enjoy your breakfast?"

"I did. It was such a treat. Father never allows it at home. He always says breakfast is a time to be together."

"Well, you make the most of it. Do you mind if I start tidying the room?"

"Not at all." She perched on the settee as Nell straightened the sheets on the bed. "You do an unusual job for a woman. You must have an understanding husband."

"I ... erm." Nell bit on her lip. "Actually, I'm a widow."

"Oh, I'm sorry. That's thoughtless of me. Does that mean the ship's your home?"

"No, I still live in Liverpool. My family's there."

"You have family?" Her brow creased. "Why do you need to work then?"

"We need the money..."

"I'm not being very tactful, am I?"

Nell shrugged. "You're not to know. I imagine you live in a big house."

"Not especially. Not compared to the neighbours, at least. We only have a handful of servants, too."

Poor you. "Do you live in Liverpool?"

"Toxteth. Near Princes Park. Do you know it?"

"I do. I'm not far from there myself. I often walk in the parks when I can. We may have passed each other."

Miss Ellis shook her head. "I doubt it. I rarely go out, except to church."

Nell's brow creased. "You don't go out? Don't you like walking?"

"It's not a matter of liking it, there's never anyone to chaperone me, and I can't go alone."

"Don't you have any friends who could walk with you?"

"I have acquaintances, but they've no desire to visit the park. We sit and take tea with Mother. It's usually the highlight of the day."

"That's a shame." The words were out of her mouth before Nell could stop herself. "Oh, I'm sorry, I didn't mean to sound rude."

Miss Ellis cocked her head to one side. "Why do you think that?"

"Only because I enjoy walking and the parks are so pleasant."

"We can see Princes Park from the window, so we've no need to walk around it."

"It can't be the same." Nell reached for the brush to sweep the floor. "And what about Sefton Park? It's a lot bigger, and there are different things to see."

Miss Ellis smiled. "I read about that in a magazine. It did sound splendid."

"Oh, it is, especially when the sun's shining. Perhaps you could visit one day."

"Maybe." Miss Ellis stood up and gazed through the porthole. "Mother's always badgering Father about finding me a husband, but he and my brother don't want me to marry. My brother says he's perfectly capable of taking care of me, and I don't object because I've no desire to marry, either."

"You don't want a husband?" Nell gasped as she struggled for words. "But ... that's not right."

Miss Ellis's forehead creased. "I'm a woman of means. My writing earns me enough to keep myself. Why would I marry and lose it all?"

"To have your own family. And children."

Miss Ellis returned to the settee. "My books are my children. That's all I need, along with the support of my brother."

"I hadn't thought of that." Nell shuddered as she continued her sweeping. "In my world, we've nothing to start with and need to marry to survive."

"Unless you work."

Nell paused as she collected up the dust from the floor. "You're right, but it's a last resort for many of us. I've often wondered if I'm strange because I choose to work rather than stay at home with my daughters."

"If you are, then I am, too. Do you like what you do?"

Nell stared at the snippet of sky she could see through the porthole. "It's not what I expected."

"That sounds like you're not sure."

"I keep telling myself it will get better, but it's harder than I expected. There was something about the job I couldn't resist." She shrugged. "Perhaps I thought it would make me feel closer to Jack. I don't know." She carried on with her sweeping.

"Was Jack your husband?"

She sighed. "He'd qualified as a master mariner, and was about to take control of his own ship. I should be travelling with him, like Mrs Robertson is with the captain, but instead I've got the cleaning to do and the stewards to deal with."

"Well, for what it's worth, I'd say you do a splendid job." Miss Ellis studied her. "Do you know, you'd make an excellent character in my next book. You wouldn't mind, would you?"

"Me!" Her heart skipped a beat. "I-I don't know. I'm sure I should be flattered, but what if anyone found out?"

Miss Ellis laughed. "I wouldn't tell anyone it was you. You could help me choose the name of your character, if you like."

Nell's cheeks flushed. "Oh, no, I'd rather leave that to you."

As the dining room filled up for luncheon, Nell nudged Mrs Swift as Mr Rodney led Miss Ellis to their table.

"I feel sorry for Miss Ellis."

"Sorry for her?" Mrs Swift raised her eyebrows. "She's travelling first class with a man who's waiting on her hand and foot."

"But she's trapped. Between her father and brother she's

not allowed any sort of life other than occasional friends who visit."

"You mean travelling first class to America is being trapped?"

Nell grimaced. "I know it sounds strange, but yes. The man with her, Mr Rodney, he's employed by her father to chaperone her and make sure she does what she's supposed to."

"Aren't we all like that? The only difference for us is we're told what to do by Mr Price or Captain Robertson."

"But when we're at home, it's different. We can walk out by ourselves whenever we choose; she can't even do that. Her brother doesn't want her to get married."

Mrs Swift's forehead creased. "Why not? Don't they usually want to arrange the right marriage to someone with a fortune?"

"They do if the woman has no personal property of her own, but she's an author. She earns her own money, so I guess her brother wants to keep control of it."

"If she makes so much that he wants it for himself, she's no one but herself to blame. If she stops writing, he'll soon find a husband for her."

Nell studied Miss Ellis's rigid frame. "She doesn't look happy with Mr Rodney, does she? She was talking to me quite happily earlier."

Mrs Swift suppressed a grin. "You've a way of getting passengers to confide in you."

"You don't do so badly yourself. I'm just fortunate to have interesting people to talk to. You'll get them on the way back."

. . .

As luncheon ended and Nell set about clearing the tables, Colonel Barrington indicated to her by waving an empty glass in the air. She put the pile of plates she was carrying onto a spare table and hurried over.

"Would you like another one, sir?"

"Yes, indeed. The stewards seem to have disappeared."

"They look rather busy in the men's section at the moment. Would you care for anything, Mrs Barrington?"

"Another coffee would be lovely, thank you."

Mr Brennan was shaking a cocktail when Nell reached the bar.

"You've been busy today."

"All thanks to those gentlemen." He nodded to Mr Hewitt's table. "Did you hear that the taller one with dark hair is the nephew of an earl?"

"Who? Mr Hewitt?"

"That's him. It explains all the behaviour, don't you think?" Mr Brennan poured four cocktails from his shaker.

"What do you mean?"

"All the drinking and practical joking. This is their third cocktail already, and it's not yet two o'clock."

"Gracious." Nell peered through the flowers. "They are rather boisterous."

"It never stops. They'd have cocktails with breakfast if they could."

"I thought you were happy with them drinking a lot."

"I was, but at this rate, we're going to run out of whisky. Exactly around the time they'll be giving out their tips."

"You need to warn them, then."

He grimaced. "It's all right for you... Wait a moment, what's going on here?"

Nell turned to see Mr Hewitt walking towards them, with Mr Cavendish in tow.

"I say, barman, are those drinks ready? The stewards have all disappeared."

"Yes, sir, they're coming. I'll bring them myself, if you'd care to take your seat."

Mr Hewitt rested a hand on the bar as he smirked at Nell. "I'd rather stay here. It's a much nicer view."

"Now sir, don't embarrass Mrs Riley."

His eyes sparkled as he winked at Nell. "I wouldn't dream of it."

"That's enough, sir. This way, please." Mr Brennan tried to usher him away, and Nell's cheeks burned as Mr Hewitt resisted.

"Forgive me, Mr Hewitt, I'd love to stand and talk but I need to carry on." She scurried to the Barringtons' table, which was as far from the bar as she could get. They looked up at her as she arrived, but the colonel's smile immediately faded.

"You've brought back an empty glass."

Nell stared down at it. "I'm sorry, so I have. The bartender was busy and..." She sighed and glanced over her shoulder as Mr Hewitt was being ushered to his table. "I had to get away."

"Is that chap bothering you?"

"Not exactly, but we're not allowed to deal with the single male passengers. I wanted to stay out of trouble."

"Quite right, too. I've met his type before. He needs a spell in the army; they all do. That would sort them out."

"I'm sure it would." At the sight of Mr Brennan

returning, Nell straightened herself up. "If you'll excuse me, I'll fetch your drinks."

Once the dining room was empty, Mrs Swift wandered over to Nell. "Are you nearly finished? I've told Mr Ross we're ready for luncheon."

Nell's face brightened. "I am. Shall we sit down?" She followed her friend to the table in the far corner and took a seat as Mr Ross arrived at the table.

"Here you are, ladies. Fillet of plaice with caper sauce."

"That looks nice, thank you."

There was a twinkle in his eye. "Do you have any gossip for me? It's far too quiet at the moment."

Nell shook her head. "Nothing of much interest, except, I presume you've heard about Mr Hewitt."

"What? That he's been called to see the captain?" Mr Ross grinned, but Nell put a hand to her mouth.

"He's not!"

"No, but I wish someone would have a word with him." Mr Ross's smile faded. "That's what happens when you've got an earl for an uncle."

"Ah, that was my news."

Mr Ross tutted. "That's not news. The whole ship knows."

"I didn't." Mrs Swift pursed her lips. "When were you going to tell me?"

"I was about to." Nell looked back to Mr Ross. "What about his companions, do they belong to anyone important?"

"Not that I've heard, and I'm sure we would have if they did. I'll check with Mr Marsh."

"Mr Marsh?" Nell's forehead creased. "Why would he know? He's hardly made them welcome."

"Exactly. Apparently, if he's ever offhand with anyone, which happens more than it should, they've a habit of asking if he knows who they are and then promptly telling him." Mr Ross sniggered. "That's why he was moved from the *Wyoming*."

"Because he was rude to a passenger?"

"Not any old passenger." Mr Ross gave an exaggerated glance over both shoulders. "Mr Guion's personal assistant, no less."

"No!" Nell's eyes widened. "What did he do?"

"The man was being overfamiliar with one of the female passengers, and Mr Marsh decided to put an end to it. What he didn't realise was that the lady in question was an acquaintance of Mr Guion, and they were permitted to be together."

"And they moved him for that?" Mrs Swift glanced up from her plate.

"The incident happened on the outbound journey, and the man in question was so furious with Mr Marsh that they transferred him out of the way before the pair made their return journey. He said it was a precaution."

"I bet he did." Nell laid down her knife. "Is he likely to go back to the *Wyoming* once these passengers return to Liverpool?"

Mr Ross shrugged. "I don't think he knows. It may depend on how many people he upsets on here."

Nell sighed. "He's doing a good job with Mr Hewitt and

his friends. Perhaps I should ask them to make a complaint to the captain."

Mr Ross gave her a blank stare. "Don't you like him?"

"Not especially. He manages to find fault with everything I do and loves embarrassing me when I'm talking to passengers."

"That's unfortunate." Mr Ross's face twisted.

"Yes, it is..."

"No, I didn't mean that ... oh, never mind. I shouldn't have said anything."

"What are you talking about?" She gaped at him, her mouth open.

"Don't look at me like that. We've obviously got the wrong end of the stick."

"What stick?" Nell looked over to Mrs Swift before staring at Mr Ross. "Who's *we*?"

"Look, forget we had this conversation. I'll go and get your dessert."

CHAPTER THIRTY-SIX

The weather had deteriorated since they'd left the coast of Ireland, and Nell pulled the hood of her cloak tightly around her as she raced across the deck to the first-class area.

"Oh goodness, what a horrible day. It's a good job they've taken the sails down."

"It's a dreadful storm for sure. We're likely to have a lot of seasickness, too. Poor Matron."

"Poor us, as well." Nell took off her cloak, but grabbed hold of the wall to save herself from falling. As the ship righted itself, she shook it out and hung it up. "If it stays like this, we should go past the boiler rooms to our cabin tonight."

Mrs Swift shuddered as she hung up her own cloak. "Let's wait and see. I'd rather not go that way if we don't have to."

Nell gripped the handrail as she set off down the stairs. "I don't know why; we were fine last time." When she got no reply, she continued to the dining room. "Let's see how many trays we need to deliver."

"Good morning." Mr Ross greeted them as they went into the galley, but scrambled for the counter as a wave hit the ship, sending him crashing into the wall. "Mr Price has said we're not doing deliveries while the weather's like this. We'll have more food on the floor than make it to the staterooms."

"He's probably right."

"He also said that those who insist on staying in their rooms are unlikely to be in any fit state to eat, so it would be a waste."

"What about the ladies? Have they been told?"

"All those with husbands have."

Nell braced herself against the wall as the ship continued to roll. "I need to see Miss Ellis. She may not have heard, and she's a nervous passenger at the best of times. I'm guessing she won't like this storm. Such a shame; she enjoys breakfast in her room, too."

Mr Ross grinned. "Tell her I'll make her whatever she wants if she graces us with her presence."

Nell laughed. "Anything to get a mention in her book."

There was no reply when Nell knocked on Miss Ellis's door, and she tried again, harder.

"Miss Ellis, are you there?" When there was no answer, she reached for her key and let herself in. "Miss Ellis."

She stared into the gloom at the crumpled sheets over the shape on the left-hand bed. It was several seconds before she heard muttering. "Miss Ellis?" She approached the bed, crouching down beside the curled-up figure.

"What's the matter?"

"I can't move." Miss Ellis's breathing was rapid. "The ship's going to go down."

Nell's heart rate quickened. "I'm sure it's not. The storm will pass."

"No, it won't. We're going to drown. Can't you see?"

Nell ran a hand over Miss Ellis's head. "We'll be fine. Let me fetch the doctor and he'll give you something for the seasickness."

"I'm not sick." Her eyes widened, emphasising the white around the iris. "We're going to die."

"No, we're not." Nell stood up and took a deep breath as Miss Ellis curled into a ball. "I'll get the doctor, anyway. Stay where you are." She darted to the corridor, locking the door behind her, and raced to the bridge.

"Good gracious, what's going on here?" Captain Robertson caught hold of Nell's shoulders as she rounded the corner, almost running into him.

"Oh, Captain, I'm so worried. It's Miss Ellis, she's convinced herself that the boat's about to sink. I need the doctor."

"All right, calm down. I saw Dr Clarke not five minutes ago." Captain Robertson nodded to the officer he was talking to. "Let me take you to him."

Dr Clarke was about to leave his office when they arrived.

"Ah, Doctor." The captain's voice rang out down the corridor. "Mrs Riley has a passenger who requires your services. Could you assist her, please?"

The doctor checked his watch. "I was due to see someone in steerage. Do we know what the problem is with Mrs Riley's lady?"

The captain looked to Nell for an answer.

"I-I'm not sure. It's Miss Ellis. She thinks the boat's about to sink and is curled up in bed muttering to herself."

"It sounds like she's hysterical. I always said women shouldn't work or travel, let alone both at the same time. It takes too much out of them. Come with me, Mrs Riley."

The doctor strode off down the corridor, and with a brief smile at the captain, Nell trailed after him.

"It's stateroom nineteen." She paused for breath as she caught up. "I'll have to open the door for you."

Miss Ellis was in the same position Nell had left her, and once the wall lamps were lit, the doctor leaned over to check his patient.

"As I thought. Now, miss, I need you to sit up for me. Can you do that?"

Dr Clarke helped her up, but Miss Ellis clung to the bed sheets. "We're going to sink."

"We'll do nothing of the sort." The doctor sat on the bed beside her as a wave rocked the ship. "The storm will pass by this afternoon."

"That's too late ... don't you see?" Her eyes were wide as she grabbed his hands, but he pulled them away and reached into his bag.

"Captain Robertson has it all under control, but I'd like you to take this until the storm passes."

"What is it?" She pushed herself back into the pillow.

"A tonic to calm your nerves. We need you to do as you 're told. Mrs Riley, will you come and help?"

Nell clasped Miss Ellis's hands as the doctor forced the liquid into her mouth and held it closed until she'd swallowed it.

"No. Get off me. I need to be able to swim…"

Dr Clarke grabbed her shoulders and shook her. "You'll do no such thing. Now stop. The tonic will help you sleep."

Miss Ellis stiffened. "You're trying to kill me."

"No, really, we're not." Nell retook her hands. "We want to help. Please don't be frightened."

"How can I not be? This is God's punishment… It's all my fault, I should never have come."

Dr Clarke slapped Miss Ellis across the face, causing her to fall silent. "That's enough. You're going to be fine. Now rest back into the pillows and relax."

It felt like an age that Nell sat on the opposite side of the bed to the doctor, but gradually Miss Ellis's breathing slowed and her eyelids closed.

"That should do it." Dr Clarke stood up. "I suggest we lie her down and make her comfortable."

Nell tucked the sheets under the mattress as the doctor packed up his bag. "Will she be all right?"

"I hope so, but I need your help. Who's her guardian?"

"She's travelling with Mr Rodney, her chaperone. He's in the next stateroom."

"Splendid. Come with me. And lock the door behind us."

Mr Rodney appeared ready for breakfast when they arrived, but he invited them into his still unserviced room and offered Dr Clarke a seat. The doctor studied the middle-aged man with his greased-back black hair. "I need to tell you that the storm has caused Miss Ellis to have a bout of hysteria."

"Hysteria? Will she be all right?"

"In due course, but I've given her some laudanum and she needs to rest."

Mr Rodney snarled. "Damn fool of a woman. Her father told her not to travel, but she wouldn't listen."

Dr Clarke tutted. "He shouldn't have taken no for an answer. I understand she earns her own living."

Mr Rodney nodded. "She writes."

"That will have to stop for the rest of the voyage, along with any other excitement. It's all obviously too much for her. Mrs Riley..."

Nell had stayed by the door, but she jumped at mention of her name. "Yes, sir."

"I want Miss Ellis to remain in her room. She needs a complete break. No one is to go into her room except for you and Mr Rodney until she's feeling better. Is that clear?"

"Yes, sir. I often bring her meals on a tray, anyway."

"But she's a book to prepare..." Mr Rodney towered over the doctor, who got to his feet and stared him in the eye.

"And I'm afraid it will have to wait. Mrs Riley, I saw a typewriter in her stateroom, and several magazines. I'd like them removed along with anything else that may cause any intellectual stimulation. She needs complete rest."

"I'll take the typewriter..." Mr Rodney glared at Nell.

"Mr Rodney." The doctor's voice was stern. "I'm sure we both want what's best for Miss Ellis. The hysteria is caused by her working. Women are not capable of such strenuous activities, especially not when travelling, and her body needs time to recover. It will be better for you all in the long run if we put the typewriter out of harm's way. As my patient, I demand she has the time and space she requires."

Mr Rodney cracked his knuckles, but the doctor ignored him.

"I've given her a dose of laudanum, which should keep her calm for several hours. Once she's recovered, she can receive her meals from Mrs Riley, and you, Mr Rodney, may visit her for no more than ten minutes in the morning and ten minutes in the afternoon. Mrs Riley will accompany you. I'll call again this afternoon and then each day until we reach New York. Is that clear?"

"Yes, sir." Nell and Mr Rodney spoke in unison as the doctor opened the door and beckoned Nell to follow him.

"We need to keep an eye on him." Dr Clarke spoke in a whisper as Nell locked the stateroom door. "Does he have a key?"

"Not that I'm aware, but it may be worth checking with Mr Price."

"Very well, I'll do that. I fear he wants to keep her working."

"It would seem so." Nell hesitated. "What about the typewriter? I can remove it from the room, but where do I store it?"

The doctor stroked his greying beard. "Why don't you fetch it now and I'll take it to my office, along with any reading material?"

"Yes, sir." Nell reached for her keys again.

"I'll be relying on you to keep her safe, Mrs Riley. If there are any problems, you must let me know."

· · ·

Mrs Swift was hurrying from the galley when Nell returned to the dining room. "Where on earth have you been? I've been rushed off my feet with everyone forced to come down here."

"I'm sorry, there was an emergency..."

Mrs Swift huffed. "Why does it always happen to you...?"

"I've no idea, but I'll tell you about it later. What do you want me to do?"

"Take Colonel and Mrs Barrington's order, for one. They've been waiting over five minutes."

"Very well." Nell hurried to the table. "I'm sorry to keep you; I'm afraid the storm's wreaking havoc at the moment."

"It isn't doing much for Mrs Barrington's insides either; she needs something bland to settle her."

"Yes, sir. Might I suggest the porridge?"

"An excellent choice." He answered without consulting his wife. "I'll take a couple of boiled eggs with toast. Boiled water for Mrs Barrington and a cup of Grey's tea for me."

Nell glanced at Mrs Barrington to get her consent, but when her face remained fixed on the table, she left them.

"Ah, there's a sight for sore eyes." Mr Ramsbottom stepped back to make room in the galley, where they both held onto the counter to stay upright.

"Why, what's the matter?"

"The storm, that's what. I wish we weren't serving breakfast. Half of it's going to go to waste."

"At least the dining room's full. If the passengers were ill, they'd still be in bed."

He gazed at her. "That's where I'd like to be."

"Mr Ramsbottom!" Her cheeks flushed, and she turned away as Mr Price joined them.

"Might I have a word, Mrs Riley?"

"Oh ... yes." She put her head down and followed him through the dining room to the foyer. "Are you all right?"

"I'm fine, just struggling to stay upright." She moved closer to the wall.

"Aren't we all?" He gave a brief smile. "Dr Clarke came to see me about Miss Ellis and told me you'll be taking all her meals. He also mentioned Mr Rodney."

"Did you find out if he has a key to her stateroom?"

"Not exactly. He should never have had one, but we fear he might somehow have acquired the spare key, because it's missing. He denies all knowledge of it, of course, and so unless we catch him with it, we'll have to trust him."

"Oh dear. Perhaps I could ask Miss Ellis when she's well enough. I know she'd tell me if he's letting himself into her room."

"You would hope so." He sighed. "I'll use that corridor as often as I can, but I need you to be vigilant. Keep an eye on the comings and goings when you're servicing the other rooms. I need to know what's going on."

"Yes, sir. I'll try my best."

CHAPTER THIRTY-SEVEN

Nell held onto a chair back as she peered through the skylight in the saloon. The rain still lashed against the sides and streaks of lightning lit the sky. She looked over to Mrs Swift as she collected up some glasses.

"We can't go out in that."

Mrs Swift sighed as she joined her. "I know. We'd be washed overboard with the waves as high as they are." She studied the tables in the ladies' section. "I'd say we're about finished here. Are you done?"

Nell nodded. "I am. I checked in on Miss Ellis earlier. The doctor had given her more laudanum, so she was sleeping. The rest of the passengers are settled for the evening."

"It's a strange old trip, isn't it? But we may as well make the most of it. Let me get rid of these." She held up the glasses as she hurried to the galley.

Nell wandered to the door of the saloon, arriving as Mr Ramsbottom and several stewards were leaving. He paused to look her up and down.

"How's that passenger of yours?"

"Still asleep from the laudanum. Hopefully, the weather will be better tomorrow and she'll improve."

He nodded to the outside door. "It's a wild night for you to be crossing the deck."

"I suppose..." Nell bit her lip and glanced at the stairs leading to the boiler room. "We ... erm..." She stopped as Mrs Swift rejoined them.

"We'll be fine. Come on. We need to get our cloaks."

"Yes. We'd better be going. Goodnight, Mr Ramsbottom."

"If you must." He gave her a wink. "Goodnight."

They waited for him to leave before heading for the cloakroom.

"Take your time." Mrs Swift fastened the clasp on her cloak and poked her head into the foyer. "The stewards have gone. We should be in the clear."

They hurried down the stairs, past the dining room that was now in darkness, and onto the steerage level.

"I don't know how Mr Cooper manages down here all day."

"Shh. Keep your voice down. We don't want to attract any attention."

Nell said no more as she clung to the handrail, eventually reaching the bottom. "Are you ready?"

Mrs Swift nodded, but suddenly put a hand to her head. "Mr Price gave me a letter to pass to Matron, and I've left it in the dining room."

"You can't go back up there; it was all in darkness."

Mrs Swift hesitated. "I have to. He said it was urgent. I left it near the door. You wait here; I won't be long."

As Mrs Swift's footsteps faded, Nell cowered in a dimly lit area of the corridor, pulling her cloak tight. She listened to the rhythmical sound of the coal being loaded into the furnaces, but the sudden voices of the men shouting to each other sent a shiver down her spine. *What's keeping her?*

After what felt like an age, footsteps sounded on the stairs and her shoulders relaxed as a shape rounded the corner.

"Here you are. What kept you?"

"That's a nice welcome."

Nell froze at the deep growl of a man's voice.

"Mr Ramsbottom!" She pressed herself into the wall as he approached.

"I wondered if that look was an invitation, and I'd say it was." He put his hands on the wall above her shoulders, his face only inches from hers.

"No, please. I thought you were Mrs Swift." Even in the dull light, she saw the twinkle in his eyes.

"A likely tale, but there's no need to be frightened."

He leaned towards her, but as their lips touched, a hand grabbed his shoulder and pulled him backwards.

"What do you think you're doing?" Mr Marsh stared down at her.

"Me? I-I ... nothing." Nell shuddered, thankful for the dark.

"You seem to make rather a habit of this. That's at least four men I've seen you with, and we only met a week ago. Is it any wonder Captain Robertson has trouble with you?"

Tears welled in her eyes. "But it wasn't me ... I've done nothing wrong. Please, Mr Ramsbottom, tell him."

Mrs Swift stepped forward. "That's right, she was

waiting for me. If someone hadn't moved the letter I was looking for, none of this would have happened."

Mr Ramsbottom rounded on her. "Don't lie. She encouraged me down here."

"I didn't." Nell sobbed into her handkerchief. "We only came this way so we didn't have to go out in the storm."

"Then why did you give me that look? And why did Mrs Swift conveniently leave you on your own?"

"What look?" Nell shrank back to the wall as they all stared at her.

"You eyed the stairs when we met outside the saloon."

"I don't know... I was nervous about coming this way, that's all. I didn't mean for you to follow me."

Mr Marsh stepped forward and pushed Mr Ramsbottom out of the way. "I suggest you go to your quarters; I'll speak to you later."

"Who are you to give me orders?" Mr Ramsbottom squared up to him.

"The man who'll save your job if you do as you're told. Now go."

After a moment's hesitation, Mr Ramsbottom ran up the stairs as Mrs Swift put an arm around Nell's shoulder.

"Did he do anything?"

"No." Nell sobbed. "Thanks to you."

"It should be thanks to Mr Marsh. I met him upstairs, and he offered to escort us to our rooms."

Nell gulped in a mouthful of air as she struggled to breathe. "I don't ask for any attention. I just want to do my job."

"There, there." Mrs Swift stroked her head. "Let's get you back to the cabin."

"And let that be a lesson to you." Mr Marsh glowered at her. "You should know better than to be down here on your own. What were you thinking?"

"I don't know. I wanted to save my legs..."

"At the cost of your reputation? You should be ashamed of yourself. Now, be quiet, I don't want to attract attention down here."

Mr Marsh opened the door to the boiler room and ushered them through as a blast of heat engulfed them.

They waited while he closed the door and led the way down the corridor, peering into each room as he did. As they reached the third opening, a deep voice boomed out.

"Who's there?"

"Mr Marsh, one of the stewards."

"What are you doing down here?"

"I'm escorting the ladies to their quarters."

"Ladies?" A giant of a man poked his head around the door, the whites of his eyes widening as he gazed out from his soot-covered face. "This is no place for ladies."

"Which is why I'm escorting them. The storm's too severe for them to go across the deck."

The man's brow creased. "I thought it was choppy; I've not been out of here since six this morning."

"You're in the best place. Now, if you'll excuse us."

Mr Marsh continued walking, but the man stepped out in front of Mrs Swift.

"If you need chaperoning again, I'm your man. Ted's the name. Ted O'Connell."

Nell shivered as his gaze lingered a little too long. "Thank you, sir."

The man threw back his head with a laugh. "Sir. There's no need for that."

"Well…"

"Excuse me, Mr O'Connell." Mr Marsh had retraced his steps. "Would you mind if the ladies came with me?"

"Don't be like that; we were only talking."

"I can see that, but they must get back. Matron will be wondering where they are."

"Matron." A smile flicked across Ted's lips. "A lovely lady, she is. But it was nice meeting you, too. Don't forget, walk this way any time you like. I won't bite."

Nell moved closer to the far wall as she hurried past him. *I'm not risking that.*

Mr Marsh reached the door ahead of them and held it open. "After you."

Nell didn't need to be told twice, and she raced up the stairs and into their sitting room.

Mrs Swift arrived with Mr Marsh moments later. "Thank you, Mr Marsh. I shudder to think what would have happened if you hadn't been with us."

"You're welcome. I hope the weather doesn't force you down there again." He turned his attention to Nell. "I seem to be turning a blind eye to your indiscretions rather too often, Mrs Riley."

Nell gasped. "What indiscretions?"

"Mrs Riley. No more than twenty minutes ago I pulled a man from you who claimed you encouraged him, and it was only a few days ago that I saw you being overfamiliar with one of the passengers."

Nell's brow creased. "You mean Mr Hewitt? That wasn't my fault; he was introducing himself."

"There was no need for him to have anything to do with you; you seem to attract this sort of behaviour. I saw you on the landing stage, too. Kissing two young men."

Nell squealed. "They're my nephews. They'd walked me to the ship..."

Nell hadn't finished when the door to the cabin opposite opened and Matron strode across the corridor. "What on earth's going on here?"

"He's trying to ruin my reputation, that's what." Nell glared at Mr Marsh, but he stood up straight.

"I can assure you, I'm doing nothing of the sort. I'm trying to save you from yourself."

Nell's pulse was racing. "Then how many of the stewards know I was with two men before I boarded? Is that why I'm getting so much attention? And why Mr Price is constantly watching me?"

Mr Marsh ignored her and turned to Matron. "I walked them past the boiler rooms so they didn't need to go outside. Good evening." Without a second glance, he headed back the way they'd come and disappeared.

"Is that why he's been so horrible to me? Because he saw me give Billy and Vernon a farewell kiss and assumed I was up to no good." She took a seat in the sitting room and put her head in her hands. "The Mrs Fosters were right. I should walk round with a scowl on my face and not talk to anyone."

Matron took the seat beside her. "Do you want to tell me what happened?"

"No. I want to forget about it." Nell reached for a handkerchief.

"But if he's causing trouble..."

358

"It's not like that. Please, leave me be."

Matron rolled her shoulders. "If you insist, but if anyone's been behaving inappropriately, the captain needs to know."

And turn all the stewards against me again. No, thank you. Nell's hands shook and she clutched her handkerchief to steady them. "I'm sorry I woke you."

"I wasn't asleep, I was reading the Good Book to give me strength for tomorrow. The captain says the wind should lessen overnight."

"That's a relief. It's been a bad day all round." Nell smiled as Mrs Swift appeared with a bottle of brandy in one hand and two glasses in the other.

"I nipped up to see Mr Potter. He'll be down with the food shortly, but he told me to give you a spot of this first."

Nell sat up straight. "You didn't tell him."

"Of course not; I said you'd had a busy day with Miss Ellis being ill."

Nell took a sip of the amber liquid. "Can you believe I'd quite forgotten about her?"

CHAPTER THIRTY-EIGHT

M r Marsh was waiting outside the dining room the following morning, and he stepped in front of Nell, stopping her and Mrs Swift from going inside.

"Good morning, ladies."

"Mr Marsh." Nell's tone was harsher than she liked, and she took a breath. "Good morning. What brings you up here?"

"Mr Ramsbottom and I have agreed to swap roles for a few days."

Mrs Swift raised an eyebrow. "That was devious. Is that why you didn't report him?"

Mr Marsh stood up tall. "I don't know what you mean. He told me he felt uncomfortable working up here after what had happened, and so I offered to change positions."

"I should think so, too. Poor Mrs Riley had a sleepless night worrying about seeing him again."

"Oh, I'm sorry to hear that." His eyebrows drew together. "Are you well enough to carry out your duties?"

"Yes, I'll be fine, thank you." She coughed to remove the

squeak from her throat. "I'd rather be working, and I need to take Miss Ellis her tray. At least the storm's passed, so hopefully she'll be feeling better." She began to follow Mrs Swift into the dining room, but he reached out a hand to stop her.

"Before you go, I'd like to apologise for assuming the worst of you. If it's any consolation, you don't look old enough to be an aunty to those boys."

"My sister's quite a lot older than me."

"Ah. That would explain it."

Nell shrugged to remove her arm from his hold, but as she did, Mr Hewitt and his friends joined them.

"What's going on here?" There was no smile on Mr Hewitt's face. "I hope you're not harassing Mrs Riley."

Mr Marsh's cheeks reddened. "I most certainly am not."

"Then why were you holding her? I seem to recall you assumed the worst when we were only shaking hands."

"I wanted to talk to her."

"So did I, but that didn't stop you coming over all high and mighty."

"Please, gentlemen." Nell's heart rate quickened. "I'm perfectly fine, but I need to go. I have breakfasts to serve." She scurried away, leaving the men where they were.

"What did he want?" Mrs Swift kept her voice low as Nell joined her in the galley.

"He wanted to apologise for assuming I have no morals."

"That's something. Let's hope we can put this behind us and get on."

"I won't argue with that. Now, I need to see how Miss Ellis is this morning."

. . .

Dr Clarke was with Miss Ellis when Nell arrived, and he stood up from his seat on the side of the bed.

"I'm sorry for interrupting." She put the tray on the table. "Would you like me to come back?"

"Not at all, I was about to leave."

Nell smiled. "How is she?"

"A little better, although she was agitated when I got here. She's dozed off again, but needs to eat. Wake her once I'm gone."

He picked up his bag and Nell closed and locked the door after him before crouching by the side of the bed.

"Miss Ellis, are you awake? I've brought you some breakfast."

Her head turned towards her. "What time is it?"

"Half past seven."

"I feel like I've been asleep forever. What happened?"

"The storm frightened you, but it's over now. Would you care to sit up?"

Nell arranged the pillows as Miss Ellis slid up the bed. "There you are. There's a couple of boiled eggs and some bread and butter. Can you manage that?"

"I think so." Tearful eyes stared up at Nell as she placed the tray on Miss Ellis's lap. "You won't leave me, will you?"

"I have to go and help with breakfast, but I'll come back as soon as I can." She studied Miss Ellis as her hands shook. "What's the matter?"

"I don't want Mr Rodney visiting me."

"I should think not. It wouldn't be right for him to be

here unchaperoned. I'll lock the door after me when I leave, and you'll be fine. He hasn't got a key."

Miss Ellis twisted the napkin from the tray.

"What's the matter?"

"He does have one. He insisted."

Nell's stomach clenched. "Our head steward, Mr Price, asked him if he had one, but he said he didn't."

"Then he's lying. Please, Mrs Riley, don't leave me. You've no idea what he's like."

"Has he been in here since yesterday?"

Miss Ellis nodded. "He was so angry... I've never seen him so bad before."

Nell held up a hand as a door slammed. "That may be him going for breakfast." She hurried to the door and peeped into the corridor. "Yes, he's going towards the dining room." She walked back to the bed. "You'll be safe while he's away, and if I go now, I can tell Mr Price he has a key. That way we can get it off him."

"Thank you, Mrs Riley." She clutched Nell's hands. "I'm frightened. You can't let him in."

"Don't worry, we won't." As soon as the door was locked, Nell hurried down the corridor but slowed her pace as she entered the dining room, giving herself time to scan the men's tables. *There he is.*

A wave of relief washed over her. *How do I keep him there?* Her head furrowed as she moved on, but she paused as Mr Hewitt stood up and signalled to her.

"Mrs Riley."

"I'm sorry, I really can't talk." She kept on walking.

"We need to." His voice left no room for argument and she stopped at the end of the flower partition.

"Were you searching for Mr Rodney?"

"I-I wanted to check he was in here. How did you know?"

"I saw you looking at him ... and heard him talking to my pal, Derbyshire."

Nell raised an eyebrow. "What did he say?"

"That his fiancée is ill."

"His fiancée?" Nell's mouth dropped open. "But he's her chaperone; he works for her father. There's been no mention..."

Mr Hewitt ran a hand through his hair. "I thought something didn't sound right. He certainly doesn't seem to hold any affection for her. He's more angry than anything."

"She's frightened of him, too. Oh my goodness." Nell puffed out her cheeks. "Can you keep him at the table for as long as possible? I need to speak to Mr Price. Have you seen him?"

"No. I can't say I have."

"I'll check the galley. Thank you, Mr Hewitt."

Nell strode across the room, but as she passed the Barringtons, the colonel summoned her.

"Mrs Riley. I wonder if we might have more tea."

She forced a smile. "Yes, of course, I'll bring it straight away." She set off again, but Mrs Barrington spoke up. "You look rather flustered, my dear. Is everything all right?"

"I'm sure it will be. If you'll excuse me..."

"Is it Miss Ellis?"

Nell stopped. "Miss Ellis? What makes you ask?"

"Nothing really, but we heard she was ill. *Hysteria.*" She mouthed the last word.

"I ... erm ... I can't comment on the doctor's diagnosis."

She glanced round the room. "I'm sorry, I need to find Mr Price and I've just seen him." She didn't wait for any further questions as she hurried to the ladies' section, looking for Mrs Swift.

"Have you seen Mr Price?"

"Not for half an hour or so. Why?"

"There's a problem with Mr Rodney and I really need to speak to him."

"If it's urgent, you could talk to Mr Marsh. He seems to have assumed second in command."

Nell looked towards the men's tables. "I'll have to wait for him to come to the galley. Oh no!"

"What's the matter?"

"He's going back to the staterooms."

Mrs Swift stared at her blankly. "Who?"

"Mr Rodney. I'm sorry, I need to go. If you see Mr Price, will you send him to Miss Ellis's stateroom?"

Nell ignored the gesture from Colonel Barrington as she hurried past the table and into the foyer. *I'm sorry, Colonel, the tea will have to wait.*

Mr Rodney was near the far end of the corridor when she saw him again, and as he approached Miss Ellis's room, he slowed and checked over his shoulder before carrying on.

He was going to go in. Why did I let him see me?

Nell scrambled to get her key in the lock, and Miss Ellis looked up as she went in.

"I wasn't expecting you yet." She pushed her breakfast tray to one side.

"We weren't busy in the dining room so I thought I'd keep you company instead."

Miss Ellis let out a sigh. "It's such a relief having you here. Did you speak to Mr Price?"

"I didn't see him, but Mrs Swift will ask him to call here as soon as he reappears. Don't worry, we'll get the key off him."

Miss Ellis twisted the napkin on her lap as Nell sat beside her.

"You're still not happy. Is there something else troubling you?"

"Not that you can help with, unless I can take you with me into New York. Would that be an option?"

Nell's brow furrowed. "You're serious, aren't you?"

"Deadly. You can keep Mr Rodney from me all you like while we're on the ship, but once we get off, I'm under his guardianship."

The hairs on the back of Nell's neck rose. "I hadn't thought of that. What will he do?"

Tears welled in Miss Ellis's eyes. "I don't know."

"Will he hurt you?"

She shook her head. "I don't think so, not so people can see, anyway. He'll break my spirit though."

"How?" Nell sat on the bed and held Miss Ellis's hands.

"He wants to marry me."

"But I thought you said…"

"I know, that my father and brother don't want me to be married, but it appears he's been planning this for months and I was too foolish to see it. He wants us to be married in New York and then he'll force me to write to my father and explain."

"Why would he want to marry someone who doesn't want to be with him?"

"For money." She gulped in air through her sobs. "It's all he cares about. It's all everyone cares about."

"Is that why your father doesn't want you to marry, so he can keep control of the money?"

"Exactly." She buried her face in her hands. "I told Mr Rodney yesterday that I wouldn't marry him, and he threatened me."

"What did he say?"

Miss Ellis shook her head. "That if I knew what was good for me, I had no choice."

Nell stood up and passed Miss Ellis a handkerchief.

"I wish I'd never written anything and had a simple life like everyone else."

A lump formed in Nell's throat. "Have you spoken to anyone about this?"

"No. I wanted to speak to Father before we left Liverpool because I wasn't comfortable being on my own with Mr Rodney, but he was angry about something or other and the time was never right."

"Then why did you come? Couldn't Mr Rodney speak to the publisher on your behalf?"

"No, that's the problem. He negotiates with the publisher, and I've suspected for a while that he's been taking a large cut of my advances, so I wanted to keep an eye on him. Much against my father's wishes, I might add. It was only after we left Queenstown that he told me we were getting married."

"How awful." Nell shook her head, but got to her feet, wiping her hands on her apron as a key turned in the lock. It partially opened but immediately closed again. "That was Mr Rodney."

She raced to the door, pulling it open in time to see him disappear into his stateroom. She stopped and stared at Miss Ellis. *What now?*

"Was it him?"

Nell nodded and closed the door. "He's back in his room, but at least we have proof that he has a key."

Miss Ellis shuddered and pulled the sheets to her neck. "What am I going to do? I don't want to see him ever again."

Nell wandered to the bed. "I could speak to Mr Price about escorting you to New York, but we're only there for one full day, so I won't have much time. How long are you due to stay?"

"Two weeks."

Nell sighed. "I really need to go home. My daughters..."

"There's no need to explain, Mrs Riley. I fully understand..."

They both stopped at the sound of a knock on the door.

"Mr Price?" Nell raised an eyebrow and walked to open it. "Oh, Mr Price, it is you. Come in."

Mr Price glanced from one to the other. "Is there a problem?"

"Not five minutes ago, Mr Rodney let himself into the room."

Mr Price's nostrils flared. "I knew we couldn't trust him. What happened?"

"Nothing. As soon as he saw me, he rushed into his stateroom."

"I'll go and speak to him. You stay here."

The door slammed after Mr Price, causing Miss Ellis to slide further down the bed.

"I hope there's no trouble. He'll only take it out on me

when he sees me." Tears once again fell onto Miss Ellis's cheeks, and Nell sat on the edge of the bed to stroke her hair.

"Try not to worry, Mr Price will sort him out."

It was no more than five minutes later that Mr Price returned and Nell let him in. He held up the spare key as he approached Miss Ellis.

"He claimed to have forgotten about it."

"Was he angry?" She cowered under the bedcovers.

"I would say he was irritated, but he put up no fight. He even seemed a little sheepish to have been caught out."

"That doesn't sound like him. You're sure he can't get in?"

Mr Price smiled and walked to the door. "I'm sure. Now, if you don't mind, I'd like to escort Mrs Riley to the dining room. We have been rather busy this morning."

"But Mrs Riley said..."

"Never mind what I said." Nell straightened the covers over her. "I'll be back to tidy the room when breakfast is over, and the doctor will call this afternoon. If you hear anyone at the door, it's likely to be one of us."

"How will I know?"

"I'll let myself in, but if there's a knock, ask who it is through the door."

Miss Ellis nodded. "Nobody will let Mr Rodney in, will they?"

Nell looked at Mr Price. "I won't, but Dr Clarke doesn't know not to. We need to speak to him."

"Very well; I'll try to find him, but at least Mr Rodney can't get in here without one of us letting him in."

CHAPTER THIRTY-NINE

Once luncheon was over, Nell and Mrs Swift took their usual seats in the dining room, and Nell sighed as Mr Ross put a roast beef dinner in front of her.

"That looks nice. I'm starving."

"I've not seen much of you this morning. Where've you been?"

"With Miss Ellis. She's not been feeling herself and needed attention."

Mr Ross tutted. "It's all right for these first-class passengers. I had Mr Ramsbottom up here this morning moaning about how many they had in steerage who were ill, and how there was no one to care for them."

Mrs Swift shrugged. "That's what you pay for."

"But what was Mr Ramsbottom doing up here?" Nell studied Mrs Swift as she looked up from her plate.

"He wanted to talk to Mr Marsh."

"Oh." Nell's pulse raced as Mr Ross stared down at her.

"You seem very touchy about him."

"He ... he makes me feel uncomfortable, that's all."

Mr Ross smirked. "It's only a bit of fun."

"Maybe for him." Nell shuddered and picked up her knife and fork.

"Come on, cheer up. It's Queen of Puddings for dessert."

Nell didn't speak until Mr Ross returned to the galley. "Mr Ramsbottom's not going to swap jobs again, is he?"

"It wouldn't surprise me if that's what he wants, but I can't see Mr Marsh agreeing to it. I'd say he rather enjoys being up here."

"I'm not surprised. He certainly likes to be involved in everyone's business. Why don't the other stewards say anything?"

"You're being unfair." Mrs Swift sliced through a roast potato. "He's actually got quite a nice manner about him."

"Well, I've managed to miss it. He's always very formal with me."

"I doubt he knows how to take you."

Nell shook her head. "Why wouldn't he?"

"Because you've got all these men after you, that's why."

"Don't you start. It's only Mr Ramsbottom, and hopefully I've seen the last of him, for now at any rate."

"I wouldn't bank on it." Mrs Swift nodded towards the galley. "He's coming over here."

Nell dropped her knife and fork as Mr Ramsbottom approached. "Sorry to disturb you, Mrs Riley, but Mr Price wants you in stateroom nineteen, immediately."

"Oh goodness, what now?" She jumped to her feet and raced to the foyer, thankful there were no passengers to see her. She ran along the corridor, but when she arrived, Mr Price was waiting outside for her.

"Mrs Riley, thank goodness. I didn't like to go in without you."

She reached for her key. "What's happened?"

"I couldn't find Dr Clarke when I left you earlier and I'm sorry to say I gave up looking."

"And?" Nell's eyes were wide.

"Mr Rodney persuaded him to let him into the room."

"How do you know?"

Mr Price sighed. "When the doctor finished his visit, Mr Rodney wouldn't leave, so Dr Clarke asked me to deal with it."

"You mean he's still in there?" Without waiting for a reply, Nell knocked on the door and let herself in. "What's going on?"

Mr Rodney was standing over the bed, but at the sound of Nell's voice, his head jerked up.

"Who gave you permission to come in?"

Mr Price stepped in front of Nell as Mr Rodney strode across the room.

"Mrs Riley is Miss Ellis's companion for the rest of this voyage, and I must ask you to leave."

"I'll do nothing of the sort. Miss Ellis is my responsibility."

"I'm afraid the captain won't allow unmarried men and women to be alone together. I'd rather not send for him, but I will if I have to."

Mr Rodney took another step forward, but Nell dashed past him and crouched beside Miss Ellis.

"Miss Ellis, it's me. I'm so sorry..."

A single sob came from beneath the bed sheets that covered her head.

"Don't cry, it's over now."

"No, it isn't," Mr Rodney bellowed across the room. "She'll do as she's told."

Mr Price opened the stateroom door. "Mr Rodney, I insist you come out of here. You've wasted enough of Mrs Riley's time today. We need her to prepare for afternoon tea."

"I'm not keeping her here."

"Yes, you are." Nell stood up and held his gaze. "I'm not leaving Miss Ellis alone with you, even if it means I'm here all afternoon." Nell stepped closer to Mr Price. "Perhaps we can stop the restaurant from providing tray service for Mr Rodney."

"You can't do that."

"Actually, we can, if you choose to be uncooperative." Mr Price glared at Mr Rodney as he kicked the bed.

"Confound you and your hysteria. You'll regret this."

"That's enough, sir." Mr Price took Mr Rodney's arm and led him from the room. As the door closed, Nell uncovered Miss Ellis's head.

"It's over. He's gone and won't come in again."

"I didn't mean to let him in; he pushed past Dr Clarke."

"Don't blame yourself, you weren't to know. Now Mr Price understands what he's like, he'll speak to the captain and we'll make some arrangements to keep him away from you. At least you're not married to him."

"Not yet, but how will I get out of it once we're in New York?"

"I've been thinking about it and suspect you'll need to be in there for longer than two weeks before the church will allow you to marry. That's how it works at home, anyway."

Miss Ellis finally lifted her head. "You're right. I hadn't thought of that. What if he changes the return voyage, though?"

"Then you'll have a chance to write to your father. If I were you, I'd do it as soon as you arrive in New York."

Miss Ellis sat up. "He won't leave my side once we're off the ship. How will I post a letter?"

Nell banged her head with a hand. "We're on a mail ship and we'll be taking letters back with us. If you write while you're still on board and leave it with me, I'll make sure it reaches Liverpool."

Miss Ellis sank into the pillows. "What would I do without you?"

Once Miss Ellis's dinner tray had been delivered later that evening, Nell returned to the dining room to see Colonel Barrington beckoning her. She sighed and hurried to their table.

"Good evening, Colonel, Mrs Barrington. May I get you anything?"

Mrs Barrington's brow was furrowed. "We wanted to know how you are. You've been quite distracted today."

Nell's cheeks flushed. "I'm sorry, I'd hoped you hadn't noticed."

Mrs Barrington leaned across the table. "Is it Miss Ellis you're concerned about?"

"I'm afraid she's been feeling off colour and ... well, I can't go into details, but she's on the mend."

"I am glad." Mrs Barrington lowered her voice so Nell had to bend forward. "Is it correct that she's an author?"

Nell jerked up. "May I ask where you heard that?"

"Ooh, that's a question. I don't remember." Mrs Barrington put a finger to her chin. "It came up in conversation in the saloon this afternoon."

"I see. Yes, it's true, but she's been overdoing it a little."

Mrs Barrington clapped her hands. "How exciting. I hope she gets better soon. It would be most enlightening to talk to her."

"Nonsense, it shouldn't be allowed." Colonel Barrington emptied his brandy glass and offered it to Nell. "Whoever heard of ladies working?"

Nell glanced down at her uniform.

"Oh, I didn't mean you, my dear." Colonel Barrington's already ruddy cheeks darkened. "I meant, well, you know what I meant. Another brandy here, and an elderflower cordial for my wife. Before the food arrives, if you don't mind." He waved his hand to dismiss her.

Nell scurried across to the bar.

"You're here, are you?" Mr Brennan scowled at her. "Poor Mrs Swift's been run off her feet today."

"I know and I've already apologised, but there was a crisis I needed to attend to."

"There's always something going on with you, isn't there?"

"It's not my fault…"

"Good evening, Mrs Riley."

Nell looked up to see Mr Marsh standing beside her. "Good evening. I shouldn't be long. I only need a brandy and a cordial." She took a step backwards as Mr Marsh smiled.

"Don't worry about me. I have an order for that group of

young men, and the more we can slow them down, the better."

"No, it's not." Mr Brennan glared at him. "Don't you realise that if we treat them well, the more tips we'll get? Mr Ramsbottom always gave them preferential service ... I suggest you do, too." He splashed the brandy into a glass and handed it to Nell. "There, I'm ready. What are they drinking?"

Nell left the bar without listening to the order and hurried to the Barringtons' table. Mrs Barrington looked up as Nell put down the cordial.

"I've remembered where I heard about Miss Ellis."

"Oh." Nell cocked her head to one side.

"It was from Mr Hewitt and his friends. They were discussing her earlier."

"Really. I didn't think they'd pay any attention to someone like Miss Ellis. They seem to spend most days drinking cocktails or playing practical jokes on each other."

"Take no notice of that," the colonel interrupted. "I was talking to them earlier, and they took me by surprise. Sharper than he looks, that Hewitt. They all are, but him especially; his uncle's an earl, too. The army would make splendid officers of them."

Nell's brow creased. "I'd no idea. I'd better watch what I say."

"I wouldn't worry." The colonel took another gulp of brandy. "He's already got the measure of you."

Nell's eyes widened. "He has?"

"He likes you."

"Oh ... that's good to know." *I like him, too.*

CHAPTER FORTY

Nell groaned and rolled over in bed as the morning bell rang outside their door.

"I could swear these nights are getting shorter. Or they're ringing that bell earlier." She rubbed her eyes as they struggled to open.

Mrs Swift looked up at her. "I thought you'd have been up early today so you can go on deck."

Nell swung her legs over the edge of the bed. "It's funny how the excitement wears off, when you've seen land once. And when you're tired. I'll see it soon enough as we walk over to the other side."

"That's why I wasn't so excited last month, although it's interesting to see how it changes with the seasons. For one thing, the snow disappears more quickly with each trip."

"That's a shame. It always looks so exciting. Hopefully, we'll find half an hour this afternoon to go on deck and there'll still be some left."

"You could take Miss Ellis with you. It would probably do her the world of good."

Nell smiled. "I think I will. It will be the perfect excuse to stay outside for longer, too."

As soon as they were dressed, they walked across to the sitting room, where Matron was eating a bowl of porridge.

"Good morning, Matron." Nell flopped into the seat beside her, causing the older woman to stare at her.

"You're not very sprightly this morning."

"Spending so much time with Miss Ellis must be catching up with me."

"I'd heard she was feeling better."

"She is, but she still needs company, which means I'm rushing to do everything else."

"It shouldn't be your job to sit with her. We have another fifty or more women on board."

Nell accepted the cup of tea Mrs Swift pushed towards her. "But we don't deal with steerage."

"Perhaps not, but if they're a member of staff short in first class, one of the stewards from down there needs to be upstairs. Haven't you've noticed how much Mr Marsh is in first class?"

"I'm sorry, I hadn't thought of that. Mr Price was happy for me to sit with her."

"Because he's not downstairs." Matron's voice rose. "If I sat with every passenger who was ill, half of them would die waiting for me."

Nell's cheeks burned, and she focussed on her boiled egg. "I'll try to encourage her into the saloon, although with Mr Rodney around, it won't be easy."

"The saloon's segregated well enough."

"The problem is, he doesn't seem to recognise

boundaries, and she'd be frightened he'd want to talk to her."

Matron shook her head and stood up. "Shocking state of affairs. She should never have travelled in the first place."

Nell sighed. "She knows that now."

Miss Ellis was sitting up in bed when Nell arrived, a scowl firmly settled on her face.

"Good morning, miss. Did you sleep well?"

"No, I didn't. Do you know what's happened to my typewriter?"

Nell placed the tray across her lap. "Dr Clarke has it."

"Dr Clarke? Why?"

"When you were ill, he said it was because you write and that you needed a full rest for the remainder of the journey."

"But I need to work on the manuscript."

Nell stood by the side of the bed, her hands clasped in front of her. "I'm afraid he won't allow it. He insisted on taking your magazines, too, so you had no mental stimulation."

"But that won't do." Miss Ellis's voice rose. "I'll have more mental stress by worrying about what I'm not doing. I lay awake for half the night thinking Mr Rodney had taken it."

Nell sighed. "I'm sorry, but it's for your own good."

"How can it be? I'm much better and I'm bored to tears."

"I'll tell you what. Would you like to come out on the deck with me later? I'm sure Dr Clarke wouldn't mind you socialising now you're feeling better, and we've reached Newfoundland. It's rather special seeing the snow on the hills. You could take afternoon tea in the saloon, too."

Miss Ellis stared up at her. "I can't leave this room. *He'll* be there."

"We can keep you apart…"

"That's not good enough. I don't want to see him ever again. Did you speak to the captain about finding me another chaperone?"

Nell bit her lip. "I haven't had chance yet, but I will. I thought it would help with the boredom."

"So it would, if we could lock him in his room, but nobody's likely to do that."

"No." Nell's face suddenly brightened. "I know, rather than you going out, perhaps I could arrange a visitor for you. Mrs Barrington's very keen to meet you."

Her eyes narrowed. "Why would anyone want to do that?"

"Because you're a famous author." Nell grinned.

"I may be an author, but I'm not famous. I don't even publish books under my own name."

"Why not?" A frown settled on Nell's face.

"Because no one would take me seriously. I use a man's name."

"But you said you write books for women."

"I do, but that doesn't matter. My publisher says that nobody would buy anything written by a woman."

"I hadn't thought about that." Nell paused as Miss Ellis focussed on her tray. "I'm sure Mrs Barrington wouldn't mind. She'd love to know how you write a book. I even fancy she'd like a mention in your next one."

A smile flitted across Miss Ellis's lips. "That might be fun. Nobody ever pays much attention to what I write, only the money the publisher gives me." She nodded. "Yes, why not? I don't have nearly enough company. Why don't you invite her this afternoon?"

Nell leaned on the rails of the first-class promenade and took in a deep breath. The ice had disappeared, but she coughed as the cold air hit her lungs. Not that she minded. Mrs Barrington had been safely escorted to Miss Ellis's stateroom, which meant she had half an hour to herself.

Mrs Swift gave her a sideways glance. "You're happy."

"I am, even if it is just to be outside and see land again. Look at that." She pointed at the white-topped rocky outcrops that passed in front of them. "You don't get that in Liverpool."

"It never feels this cold either." Mrs Swift rubbed her hands together.

"I'm sure it does, but it's different. There's more rain at home, for one."

Mrs Swift nodded. "You're not wrong there."

"Wouldn't it be fabulous to get off the ship and visit everything close up? We're too far away here."

"That's not likely to happen. I didn't get off once last year."

Nell groaned. "That's all the more reason for you to be given a chance this time. I'll ask for you; I might even suggest I escort Miss Ellis while she's ashore. She asked me if I'd stay with her for two weeks so she can keep Mr Rodney away, but I told her I couldn't."

"I should think not. I need you on the way back. It's been bad enough you pandering to her for the last week."

"Perhaps I could ask to go for the day. To make sure she reaches the hotel safely."

"And then what? You'll still have to leave her with him."

Nell sighed. "I know, but it's worth a try, wouldn't you say?"

"Only if I can come to chaperone you back to the ship."

Nell laughed, but stopped as the door burst open behind them and Mr Hewitt appeared with his friends.

"Good afternoon, ladies. Enjoying the view?"

"Yes, thank you, but we're about to leave." Nell's pulse quickened as he stepped closer. "It will be time for afternoon tea shortly."

Mr Hewitt's friends had continued along the promenade, but after a quick glance around, he grinned. "How lovely to speak to you without having Mr Marsh poking his nose in."

Nell put a hand to her chest as the heat rose in her cheeks. "I'm sure he means no harm; he just wants us to stick to the rules."

"Maybe he does, but what harm is there in me talking to one of the staff? We do it at home all the time."

Nell winced. *Staff.*

"Will you get to see anything of New York when we arrive?" He gazed out at the coast. "It shouldn't be long now."

"I'm afraid not. We only have a day to clean the ship before the next passengers arrive."

"Ah. It's a hard life." He glanced over his shoulder to his companions. "I'd better leave you to it then."

Nell hesitated. "Actually, before you go, may I ask you about Mr Rodney? I couldn't help noticing you've spent a lot of time with him this week."

Mr Hewitt threw back his head as he laughed. "Hardly. He attached himself to us, something like a limpet, and we're too nice to say anything to him."

"Oh." Nell's cheeks coloured. "I'm sorry."

"No need to be. Why are you interested in him?"

Nell looked out over the sea. "As you know, he's the companion of one of my ladies, Miss Ellis, but they've had a bit of a falling-out."

"Ah. That would explain why he sits with us making strange comments. I'm sure he'd mellow if she apologises."

"You're probably right, but I worry about what will happen to her if they don't. She can't go to the city by herself. Or visit her publisher."

"She's the author, isn't she?" His eyes twinkled. "Perhaps I could spend some time with her."

Nell gasped. "Mr Hewitt…"

"I'm only teasing." He winked at her, but a second later, his arm flailed behind him as Mr Marsh pushed him on the shoulder.

"What's going on here?"

"I might say the same to you." Mr Hewitt straightened his jacket. "If you must know, we're talking. Do you have a problem with that?"

"You've been told to stay away from the ladies. Just because…"

"Because what?" Mr Hewitt squared up to him. "If I

want to talk to any of the staff, I jolly well will." He gave Nell a wink. "Good day, ladies. I'll see you later." Without a second look at Mr Marsh, he strode down the promenade towards his friends.

Nell glanced at Mrs Swift as Mr Marsh rubbed his neck.

"These posh types." He tutted and gazed out over the side. "It's lovely here, isn't it?"

Nell pulled up the hood of her cloak. "We need to go in soon; it's gone rather chilly out here."

Once they'd laid out the cups and saucers for afternoon tea, Nell collected up a small tray she'd put to one side and carried it to Miss Ellis's stateroom. Mrs Barrington's face dropped as the door opened.

"Is it that time already?"

"It is. I didn't bring any sandwiches, given you'd already had some, but I thought you'd like another cup of tea."

"I would, thank you."

Mrs Barrington clapped her hands in front of her chest. "We've had a lovely afternoon, but what a shame I have to leave already. I've so much more to tell you."

"Perhaps another time." Nell guessed she'd said the wrong thing as Miss Ellis's face dropped. "If the colonel doesn't mind, that is. I suspect he's missed you this afternoon."

"Oh, I doubt it." Mrs Barrington gave a coy smile as she stood up. "I should be getting back, though; he'll be wondering where I am. It's been lovely talking to you, Miss Ellis. I hope we can do this again."

"We'll see. I do have rather a lot to do."

"Of course. You've been so kind, breaking off for me. I hope I've given you some ideas."

Miss Ellis didn't stand up as Nell ushered Mrs Barrington to the door. "Thank you, Mrs Riley. I'll see you later."

Nell hadn't turned the key in the lock before Mrs Barrington began recounting the afternoon.

"Such a lovely lady; what a shame about Mr Rodney."

Nell raised an eyebrow. "She told you about him?"

"She said she has a meeting with her publisher and how Mr Rodney's forcing her to work on her manuscript, despite the fact she's been ill. That's why she's not been to the saloon. She's too busy."

Nell pursed her lips together. "He certainly has a way with him."

"It's about time somebody did something about it. He's supposed to be here to look after her, not make her worse. I'll be speaking to the colonel about this. You see if I don't."

CHAPTER FORTY-ONE

Mrs Barrington waved at Nell as she and the colonel walked into the foyer outside the dining room.

"My, you both look very smart." Nell smiled as they stopped beside her.

"I thought I'd make the effort. It's not every night you dine with the captain." Mrs Barrington ran a hand down the front of her royal blue dress.

"No, it's not. That's quite a collection of medals, Colonel."

He patted the left breast of his jacket. "Only the best for the captain."

"Enjoy your evening. I'll see you both later."

Mrs Swift watched them enter the dining room. "She's had a busy day. She won't know which story to tell first, when she's in the saloon tomorrow."

"I'm sure that won't stop her talking about everything. Come on, we'd better go inside ourselves." Nell glanced around the tables as they headed to the galley.

"I'll take Miss Ellis's tray before anyone else arrives. It doesn't look like we'll be busy tonight."

"It's been a strange trip with so many passengers keeping to themselves. Still, I shouldn't grumble." Mrs Swift nodded towards the door. "Mr and Mrs Stewart are here. I'll see to them while you're gone."

Miss Ellis was pacing the floor when Nell let herself in.

"Oh, Mrs Riley, thank goodness you're here."

Nell put the tray on the table. "Is anything the matter?"

"Yes. I can't even write a letter; they've taken everything from the room." She held up the lid to the writing desk. "After spending an afternoon with Mrs Barrington, I decided it was time to write to my father, but I can't."

"I'm sorry, I'd forgotten about that. When Dr Clarke said you needed complete rest, I did as I was told."

"Might you be able to bring me some paper and a pen? I did have my own, but it's with my typewriter."

"I can, but not now. I open up the storage cupboard when I'm servicing the rooms, so I'll slip some in tomorrow morning. Just make sure you hide it from Dr Clarke."

"Don't worry, I will." She slumped onto the settee and stared at the tray. "What is it tonight? Not too much, I hope. I feel as if I've been eating all afternoon."

"It's a nice piece of cod in a butter sauce. Nothing heavy." Nell lifted the silver cloche from the plate.

"Thank you, but you can replace the cover, I'll eat it later."

Nell cocked her head to one side as she studied her. "Didn't you enjoy Mrs Barrington's visit?"

Miss Ellis sighed. "Is it obvious? I must be so used to my own company that her constant talking was too much.

Especially when she was telling me how to write my next book, with *her* as the leading lady."

Nell grimaced. "I'm sorry. I thought it was a good idea. At least you told her you were busy. I doubt she'll bother you again."

"I must sound so ungrateful, but I don't mean to be. Perhaps I'm not as well as I thought."

"I'm sure you're improving, but why not sit and relax? I need to get back to the dining room, but I'll call in later for the tray."

Several ladies were waiting to be served when Nell returned, and with their orders taken, she headed to the bar.

Mr Brennan looked up as she approached. "Good evening."

"You're quiet tonight."

"My best customers are on the captain's table, so they're drinking wine. All I have to do is open the bottles."

Nell studied him. "You mean Mr Hewitt and his friends are there?"

He nodded. "And the Barringtons."

"I knew about them. I hope Mrs Barrington doesn't feel isolated with all those men. The colonel on his own is too much for her at times."

"She'll manage. The captain's wife's is with them and Dr Clarke. He knows how to look after ladies."

"Oh good, but she must be feeling better. I hope they've sat her with Mrs Barrington. If they've spaced them out, it won't be so pleasant."

"Well, there's nothing we can do about it, so I wouldn't worry... What the heck...?"

They both grabbed for the bar as the ship rocked and a blast sounded around the ship.

"W-what was that?" Nell's heart raced as screeches filled the air.

"Wait here." Mr Brennan ran to the galley as Nell searched for Mrs Swift amongst the melee.

There she is. She watched as her companion tried to reseat Mr and Mrs Stewart, but seconds later her head jerked to the left as the captain ran between the tables, immediately followed by Dr Clarke. They stopped to talk to Mr Price before heading to the foyer.

"What's going on?" Mrs Swift arrived seconds after Mr Brennan returned to the bar.

"Search me. I've checked the galley, but it's nothing in there."

"It must have been something..."

Mr Brennan held up a hand. "Wait a minute. Listen."

Nell paused, but shook her head as the passengers continued to scream. "How can we hear anything with all that noise? What are we listening for?"

"The engines. They've stopped."

Nell focussed, listening for the deep rumble she'd grown accustomed to. *Nothing.* Her eyes widened. "Are we going to sink?"

Mr Brennan's face was white as he ushered them to an empty table. "Sit here until the captain tells us what's happened."

"But he's gone." Nell's voice squeaked.

"Gone?"

"Yes. When you were in the galley, he and Dr Clarke raced out."

Mr Brennan took a seat beside them. "It's serious then."

Mrs Swift stood up again. "We must see to the passengers. Should we get them to the lifeboats?" She ran to the door, but returned seconds later with Mr Price.

"Please, may we have calm?" He held up his hands. "If everyone could see to the passengers while we wait for a report from the captain. Mr Brennan, a tot of brandy for everyone might be in order."

"But the engines..." Nell struggled to breathe. "And Miss Ellis. I have to go to her." She tried to stand up, but Mr Price put a hand on her shoulder.

"Stay there and take a breath. I'll go and bring her here."

"She won't leave the stateroom..."

"Which is why I need to tell her she has no choice. I won't have the two of you locked in there. Now, collect yourself and help Mr Brennan hand out those brandies."

Mr Brennan darted back behind the bar and lifted out a selection of glasses. "Mr Marsh, over here." He beckoned him over. "You make a start with these while the ladies recover. Tell some of the other lads, too."

"In a moment." Mr Marsh hurried past the bar to the table. "Are you all right, Mrs Riley, Mrs Swift?"

Nell's hands shook. "I don't know."

Mr Marsh perched on the edge of the chair beside Nell. "We need to wait for the captain's orders, but at least we're near the coast."

"But it's all rocks! And snow!" Nell's voice was an octave higher than it should have been. "We won't survive there. My husband died on rocks..."

Mr Marsh stood up and took two glasses of brandy from

the bar. "Mrs Riley, please, drink this. And you too, Mrs Swift. You both look as if you've seen a ghost."

"You're rather peaky yourself." Mrs Swift grabbed the glass from him.

"I'll be fine. Will you be all right if I go and see to the passengers?"

Nell took a gulp of the brandy. "I hope so." The heat of the liquor burned as it ran into her stomach. "I can't leave the girls. They need me..."

"You'll see them again." Mrs Swift put a hand on hers.

"You don't know that." Nell finished her drink.

"I trust Captain Robertson, and you must, too. The ship isn't listing, which is a good sign."

Nell shuddered as the image of Jack clinging to the rocks flashed through her mind. "I should never have come..."

"Mrs Riley."

Nell looked up as Miss Ellis hurried towards her. "I was so frightened. I couldn't get out of the cabin."

"Please, miss, take a seat." Mr Price held out a chair and indicated for Mr Brennan to bring her a drink. "You'll be safe here. We've not had word from the captain, which suggests everything is fine. If there was an immediate problem, he'd have called for the lifeboats to be lowered, which he hasn't. I'll let you know as soon as I find out myself."

Nell gulped. *I hope he's not just saying that.* She watched as Mr Brennan put a glass of brandy in front of Miss Ellis. "Drink that, it will help."

"I can't take alcohol... My father..."

Mrs Swift stared across the table. "Pretend it's medicine. It will do you good."

Miss Ellis lifted it to her lips but screwed up her face. "It smells horrible."

"Hold your nose while you drink it. Or give it to me." Mrs Swift grinned, but Miss Ellis was uncertain as she pinched the end of her nose and took a sip.

"Urgh. It's horrible."

Mrs Swift rolled her eyes. "Since when was medicine nice?"

The passengers had long since forgotten about their meals by the time the captain returned. He strode to the centre of the room and indicated for Mr Price to ring the large bell in the corner.

"Ladies and gentlemen. May I have your attention?"

Nell's stomach churned as she waited for the chatter to subside.

"Thank you all for your patience. I'm sure you heard the noise earlier, but I'm delighted to say that there's no lasting damage."

There was a collective sigh, and Nell turned to see Colonel Barrington and the others from the captain's table standing behind her. She immediately stood up to offer Mrs Robertson a seat.

"You look like you need to sit down."

"Thank you, dear. I have come over rather faint."

"Let me get you a brandy, then. I suspect you should have stayed in bed."

Mrs Robertson grimaced. "Please don't say that. I had

enough earlier with my husband saying I shouldn't come. I'd have been fine if it hadn't been for the noise..."

Colonel Barrington's voice cut short their conversation. "What's the problem, Captain?"

Captain Robertson's face dropped. "Unfortunately, there was a malfunction in the boiler room, which caused the engines to stop. The noise was a valve shooting off and colliding with the outer wall of the ship. Thankfully, because the hull's made of metal, there was no serious damage done. It does mean, however, that for the rest of the journey, we'll be travelling with the sails only, which will delay our arrival into New York by approximately a day."

"But I have a meeting."

Nell peered into the men's section as Mr Rodney got to his feet.

"Trust him." Miss Ellis spoke through gritted teeth.

"I'm sorry, sir. We'll do our best to reach New York as soon as possible, but unfortunately there's nothing we can do to mend the problem until we get to port."

Nell sighed. If we're going to be a day late, there'll be no chance of getting off the ship.

"In the meantime, may I offer you all another drink and encourage you to relax? We're in no danger, but we'll have a more leisurely journey into New York."

Conversations started up again as the captain marched to his wife and took her hand.

"Come along, my dear. It's time you were in bed."

Nell watched them leave. "I get the impression he wasn't very pleased she was here."

"I'm not surprised. She's been ill on and off all week and

was deathly white all evening. The noise won't have helped."

"I'm sure it didn't." Nell groaned as she got to her feet. "We'd better start clearing the tables if we want to get ourselves to bed."

Mrs Swift didn't argue and headed straight for the Stewarts' table, but as Nell picked up a tray, Mr Hewitt stepped in front of her and ushered her to the bar.

"Are you all right?"

"I am now, thank you. Are you?"

"Never better." A broad smile crossed his face. "I need to talk to you."

"Me." She put a hand to her chest.

"Not here." He glanced over both shoulders and stepped closer. "Not when Mr Marsh is around, either. Can you meet me later?"

Nell's heart fluttered. "I-I don't know. It would be most improper. If anyone saw us..."

"You needn't worry, I'm not about to take advantage of you; I want to talk about Miss Ellis."

"Oh." Nell's shoulders sagged. "I'll bring Mrs Swift with me then. It will look more acceptable."

He smirked. "If you like. Shall we make it ten o'clock on the top deck?"

"T-tonight? Well, yes..."

"Splendid. I'll wait for you outside." He was about to leave when he held out an arm to keep Nell where she was as Mr Rodney approached. After giving a slight nod to those around the table, he addressed the colonel.

"Excuse me, sir. Might I interrupt and take Miss Ellis to one side? I'd like to talk to her."

The colonel nodded. "I suppose..."

"No!" Mr Hewitt stepped forward. "Not without a chaperone."

Mr Rodney looked him up and down. "And who are you to stop me from speaking to my charge?"

"You know perfectly well who I am."

"Not in the context of Miss Ellis. I'm responsible for her while she's away from her father, and I must speak to her."

"And I said you're not taking her anywhere without a chaperone."

"Now steady on." Colonel Barrington banged a hand on the table, but Miss Ellis fled to Nell's side.

"I'm not going anywhere with you. I never want to see you again."

"You'll do as you're told." His voice was calm, but his steely eyes sent a shiver down Nell's spine.

"Not without Mrs Riley." Miss Ellis clung to Nell's arm.

"And Mrs Riley isn't going anywhere without me accompanying her." Mr Hewitt moved to Nell's other side. "I'll bring my companions, too."

The two men glared at each other, but Nell flinched as Mr Marsh interrupted.

"What's going on here?"

Nell's mouth opened, but words failed to materialise.

"It's nothing." Mr Rodney was about to leave but changed his mind and took a step towards Miss Ellis, lowering his voice as he bent forward. "Don't think you've got away with this. You'll have to speak to me sooner or later."

CHAPTER FORTY-TWO

The clock in the foyer showed one minute to ten as Nell and Mrs Swift fastened their cloaks.

"I'd pull your hood up if I were you." Mrs Swift flicked her own over her head. "It should keep anyone from seeing us."

"We don't want to be any longer than we need to be, either." Nell took a deep breath as she stepped outside and scanned the deck. "He's here already, with Mr Cavendish, by the look of it. Come on, let's hurry."

Their footsteps clanged on the metal decking, and as they approached, the gentlemen turned to lean on the rails.

"Good evening, again." Mr Hewitt's eyes twinkled in the moonlight. "At least the rain's stayed off."

"We have to walk this way, anyway." Mrs Swift's tone was curt.

"Really?" He raised an eyebrow at them.

"The ladies' quarters are at the back of this ship."

"Ah, we'll escort you while we talk, then." Mr Hewitt indicated for Nell to walk with him, while Mr Cavendish followed with Mrs Swift. "I've been mulling over what you said about Miss Ellis, and my companions and I have become rather concerned for her safety. Even more so after what happened in the dining room."

"Many of us are worried." Nell stared at the far end of the ship. "Why should she concern you, though?"

"As you know, Mr Rodney's been following us around this week, and I don't trust him."

Nell glanced up at him. "What's he been saying?"

"There's been a lot of muttering under his breath that she won't be able to avoid him forever."

Nell puffed out her cheeks. "That's my biggest concern once they're off the ship…"

Mr Hewitt sucked air through his teeth. "It's not only that. When I asked him what he meant, he said they were getting married while they were in America. I didn't think anything of it at first, but then I began to wonder why she'd be marrying him if she was doing her best to avoid him."

"I think it was obvious earlier that she doesn't want to marry him. I've told her that he can't force her to make her vows."

Mr Hewitt shook his head. "Men like him don't take no for an answer; he'll find a way. He's not said anything specifically, but I'd guess he wants her money."

"He does. She told me he's always the one who deals with the publisher, but what can we do about it?"

"That's what I wanted to talk to you about. I sat with Colonel Barrington this evening and he's worried, too."

"I presume Mrs Barrington's been talking to him."

He nodded. "She has. We all agreed that she shouldn't

be in Mr Rodney's care; the problem is, she can't leave the ship without a chaperone."

Nell studied him. "Was the captain aware of the conversation?"

"Not initially, but once Mrs Barrington had given his wife a full rundown of her visit, Mrs Robertson had no option but to tell her husband."

"So, why are you speaking to me, rather than leaving it to the captain?" Nell's heart fluttered as he grinned at her.

"I like talking to you." He winked at her. "Besides, he was otherwise engaged tonight, so I offered. What better way to do it, than with the captain's blessing? I love how much it annoys Mr Marsh, too."

Nell's shoulders sagged, but his laugh became infectious. "You're going to get me into trouble."

"Not at all. We need to talk." His face straightened. "Miss Ellis strikes me as being very naïve. Rodney will run rings around her."

"You're right, but she's aware of that. She asked me if I'd accompany her into New York. As much as I might want to, I'll only have a day in port, and she's not due to sail home for at least two weeks."

"Even if you were here for two weeks, we couldn't let the pair of you travel alone. She needs a man with her. As would you."

Nell sighed. "That's easily said, but who would you ask? She has nobody else."

"We realised that, which is why the captain suggested she stay on the ship."

Nell's brow creased. "How could she do that when we're due to leave again so soon?"

"She'd travel straight back to Liverpool with you, and Mr Rodney would stay over here."

"She won't do that." Nell glanced back to Mrs Swift as she stood in silence with Mr Cavendish. "The whole reason for her travelling was so that Mr Rodney doesn't visit the publisher alone. She doesn't trust him."

"Ah. We didn't appreciate that." He lowered his voice. "I knew it was worth talking to you; the colonel tried to stop me. I reckon he sees me as a bad influence."

"Come on, Olly. It's freezing out here." Mr Cavendish pulled up the collar of his coat and thrust his hands into his pockets.

"I'm coming." He looked down at Nell. "Leave it with me. I may be free for a meeting with the publisher while we're there. If Miss Ellis can't be present, one of us should keep an eye on him."

Nell grimaced. "He won't be happy about that. I'm not sure she will either."

"I'm afraid Miss Ellis won't be happy with any of her options, but this way we can keep her safe ... and single. As for him, he doesn't have to like it, and I happen to have a few contacts who may be able to help."

Nell shuddered as a gust of wind swirled beneath the hem of her cloak. "Someone needs to tell her, but it shouldn't be me."

"You're right." Mr Hewitt shivered as he wrapped his arms around his torso. "I'll speak to the captain tomorrow and see what he suggests. I'll find you in the dining room to tell you what's happening. And don't look so worried. I'll deal with Mr Marsh if he causes any trouble."

Nell caught her breath. "If you wouldn't mind, could

you please try to find me when he's not around? It will make life easier."

"As you like, but it may not be until the evening. The chaps and I tend not to surface too early, and the captain can sometimes be hard to get hold of. He may want to talk to you first, as well."

"So, it's likely to be the day after tomorrow before you talk to Miss Ellis? Isn't that leaving it rather late?"

"Not at all. As long as she knows not to pack her luggage, she'll be fine. It might be helpful if you could suggest the idea of staying on the ship ... to keep her away from Mr Rodney. You've no need to mention the rest."

Nell nodded. "Very well. She needs to know we're doing it for her own good."

Matron was finishing her dinner when they arrived in the sitting room.

"Good evening, Matron. You're up late." Nell took the seat beside her.

"It's been a difficult evening."

Mrs Swift joined them at the table. "It has. Where were you when the noise rang out?"

"I was on my way over here, thinking I'd have an early night, but as soon as I heard it, I hurried back to the bridge."

"I imagine you were relieved it was only a valve."

"Is that what the captain said?"

Nell looked at Mrs Swift. "Yes, why? Isn't that what happened?"

"Captain Robertson wouldn't lie..."

Mrs Swift leaned on the table. "But I've a feeling there's something you're not telling us?"

Matron emptied her plate and laid down her knife and fork. "There was an injury."

Nell's brow furrowed. "An injury. How?"

"When the valve exploded it shot across the boiler room and struck one of the firemen."

Nell put her hands to her mouth. "Oh no! Was he badly injured?"

Matron reached for the small bowl of trifle on her tray. "It wasn't as bad as it might have been. It caught the side of his leg but thankfully missed the bone. Had it hit him any higher, it could have killed him."

Bile rose from Nell's stomach. "That's awful. Will he be all right?"

"He should be, but it's difficult to see how deep the gash is in this light. He's in a hospital bed for now, and Dr Clarke will take another look in the morning."

"He's probably happier in there than in the bunks downstairs." Mrs Swift smiled as Mr Potter placed their tray on the table.

"I'm afraid it's only leftover stew tonight, with all the excitement."

"It's still welcome, thank you." Nell pulled her plate towards her as he raised a hand in a wave.

"Sleep well then. It's a lot quieter down here without the sound of the engines."

Nell cocked an ear to the air. "So it is. It's amazing how quickly you get used to it."

"You'll have to get used to cold water, too. We usually

rely on the boilers to heat it." Matron didn't look up from her food, but Nell groaned.

"I hadn't thought of that. I was hoping to have another bath before we reached New York. That will have to wait."

"Weren't we all."

They ate in silence until Matron finished her dessert and stood up. "Right, I need to get some sleep if I'm to be up early. I'll need to attend to Mr O'Connell ahead of my usual rounds."

"Ted?" Nell's head jerked up, but her cheeks coloured as Matron looked between her and Mrs Swift.

"How do you know his name?"

"We ... erm..."

Mrs Swift emptied her mouth. "We met him on the night of the storm when Mr Marsh escorted us through the boiler room."

Matron gasped. "Was he the one who caused Mrs Riley so much anxiety? Wait until I see him."

"No, it wasn't." Nell's voice rose. "He was really very nice."

"You were fortunate, then. You've still not told me what went on, but you should know it's not safe down there. I'd rather you didn't go that way."

Mrs Swift picked up her fork, but stopped to study Matron. "How did you get back that night?"

Matron stared at her feet. "The same way as you, but it's not the same. The men treat me differently."

Mrs Swift huffed. "We had a chaperone. It was perfectly safe. Why can you stay indoors when we're expected to brave the elements?"

"You know very well..." Matron paused as Mrs Swift's

cheeks coloured. "All right. We'll say no more about it. I'm off to bed."

Nell waited to hear the click of the key in Matron's door before she spoke. "Why's she so bothered about us going past the boilers?"

Mrs Swift said nothing as she continued with her food.

"Is it because of the men? Doesn't she trust them?"

Once her plate was empty, Mrs Swift pushed it away. "No, she doesn't. There was an incident last year, similar to your experience with Mr Ramsbottom ... but it all got out of hand."

Nell's eyes widened. "You? With a fireman?"

Mrs Swift's hands shook. "You saw how big Ted is. Well, they're all the same. It's not easy to fight them off."

"And one of them forced himself on you?"

"Not exactly, but it was a close thing." Mrs Swift ran a hand over her forehead. "Thankfully, another firemen was sick and Matron was visiting him. She heard me scream."

"Why didn't you tell me? I thought you just wanted to stick to the rules."

Mrs Swift shrugged. "I didn't want to admit to being stupid. It was my own fault."

Nell placed a hand on her colleague's. "But you should have said something before going that way again."

"Well, you know now." Mrs Swift reached for her dessert. "Hopefully, we won't need to go down there for another six months."

CHAPTER FORTY-THREE

Once breakfast was over, Nell knocked on Miss Ellis's stateroom and let herself in.

"Are you ready to go?"

Miss Ellis raised her arms and let them drop by her sides. "As ready as I'll ever be, but what's this all about?"

"I told you. The captain's worried about you getting off the ship with Mr Rodney and has a suggestion for you."

"Why couldn't he have come here? I can't risk seeing Mr Rodney."

"We're going to the dining room. All the passengers have finished breakfast, and the tables are set for luncheon. Once we're in, we'll lock the door."

Miss Ellis didn't look convinced. "Very well, after you."

Nell stayed one step ahead as they walked down the corridor towards the foyer.

"Keep taking deep breaths and you'll be fine."

Miss Ellis's voice was low. "I'm struggling to breathe at all, never mind deeply. You're sure the captain will be there."

"I'm positive, now stop worrying." Nell took her arm and led her down the stairs. "We're going to sit in the married couples section, because there are a few gentlemen who've agreed to join us."

"Gentlemen! Why?" Miss Ellis froze and Nell took hold of her arm to coax her forward.

"The captain will explain everything. Come and sit down while I lock the door."

Miss Ellis hesitated as she stepped into the room. "What's going on?"

Captain Robertson stood up and escorted her to the table he occupied with Dr Clarke.

"Please, take a seat." He pulled out a chair and held it for her.

"Thank you." Miss Ellis glanced at the adjacent table.

"Let me introduce you. This is Mr Hewitt and Mr Cavendish." The captain gestured to each. "Fellow passengers."

"Why are they here?"

Dr Clarke smiled at her. "There's nothing to worry about, my dear, but you may be surprised to hear that a number of us are extremely concerned about you."

"But I'm fine. If only you'd give me my typewriter back..."

"Not yet, I'm afraid. You're still overly anxious and I don't want you having another attack."

"That's only because I'm here..." She spun in her chair, searching for Nell, who stood behind her. "Tell them, Mrs Riley."

"There's no need." Captain Robertson held up a hand to Nell. "Your recent illness isn't the only reason we want to speak to you. It's your relationship with Mr Rodney. I understand it's deteriorated since your confinement."

"Who told you that?"

"I'm the captain of this ship, Miss Ellis. It's my duty to be aware of the well-being of all my passengers."

"He was angry with me for being ill." She flicked a speck from her skirt.

"Are you sure that's all? I heard that you never want to see him again."

Miss Ellis spun to stare at Nell. "Did you tell them that?"

"No, she didn't." Mr Hewitt winked at Nell as Miss Ellis turned back to face him. "You told the whole restaurant the other evening, after the incident in the boiler room."

"Oh, yes." Her cheeks were scarlet. "Why should it matter to you, though? I've never met you before."

"All in good time." Captain Robertson took the seat beside her. "The thing is, when you joined us on the ship, Mr Rodney was acting as your guardian. If it's true you no longer wish to travel with him, then it leaves me with a predicament. I can't allow you to travel into New York alone."

Miss Ellis's eyes widened. "But I must. I've a meeting with my publisher. It's the sole reason I travelled."

"And yet you don't want to see him again?"

"But once I'm at the office, my publisher will take care of me."

"And afterwards?" The captain raised an eyebrow. "Your return journey isn't for another two weeks, and I can't allow you to stay alone in New York for all that time. Your father would quite rightly have some very stern words for me if I did."

"But I need to go. This is my business. My money. If I don't go, Mr Rodney will take it for himself." Her eyes were wild as she stared between the tables. "You can't let him go on his own."

The captain stood up and paced the room. "You put me in a rather difficult position." He paused to study her. "When is your meeting?"

Her shoulders slumped. "It was due to be on Wednesday, but if the ship's late arriving, we'll need to rearrange it."

Mr Hewitt spoke up. "May I ask who the publisher is?"

"Putnam's. Why?"

"Years ago, my father mixed in publishing circles. He wanted to publish a book on the family seat in Cornwall. In the end, it didn't get very far, but he did make some useful contacts. George Putnam. That's a name I remember. I believe he lived in London for a while. Is he still around?"

Miss Ellis shrugged. "I couldn't say, although the Mr Putnams I deal with are a similar age to me, so maybe you're thinking of their father."

"Quite possibly. Still, if I mention Sir Basil Hewitt to them, it's bound to ring some bells." He grinned at Miss Ellis. "The Americans love our aristocracy."

The captain stopped pacing and studied Mr Hewitt. "What are you suggesting?"

"That as soon as we reach port, we should telegraph ahead and rearrange the meeting for Friday. I'd be happy to escort Miss Ellis, and Mr Rodney needn't know."

The colour drained from Miss Ellis's cheeks. "We can't

do that. He works for my father ... I'd be in so much trouble when I got home."

Mr Hewitt held her gaze. "And does your father know that Mr Rodney is trying to take a large part of your advance? Or that he wants to marry you so he can control all of it?"

"No." Her cheeks flushed.

"I'm sure that if you told him..."

"No." Her hands flew up to her face. "He'd never believe me. Mr Rodney's been with him for years. He trusts him."

Mr Hewitt shrugged and sat back. "It's up to you, of course, but as I see it, you either leave the ship with Mr Rodney, and trust yourself to his care, possibly becoming his wife within the month, or you let us help you."

She buried her face in her hands, gentle sobs shaking her shoulders as Nell pulled up a chair beside her.

"Don't cry. The captain and Mr Hewitt will sort something out."

"But my father. He'll be so angry."

Nell glanced at the captain as he retook the seat on the other side of Miss Ellis.

"I fear your father won't be happy whatever you do, and so you need to do what's best for you. I'd like to propose that you stay on the ship while we're in New York, rather than go to your hotel. We have to repair the engines, and so we'll be there for longer than expected. If Mr Hewitt can arrange a meeting for Friday, I suggest you allow him to escort you and I'll give Mrs Riley permission to travel with you, as your chaperone."

Nell's heart leapt. *He's going to let me visit New York!*

"You have my word you can trust Mr Hewitt, and once your business is finished, you return to the ship, ready to sail to Liverpool."

"And you've written to your father explaining what's happened." Nell looked to the captain. "Could you get Miss Ellis's letter onto an earlier mail ship so it arrives home before we do?"

The captain nodded. "Certainly, but I'll do better than that. I'll telegraph your father to inform him of what's happening. I'll also ask him to collect you from the ship in Liverpool, so we can talk."

Her sobs started again. "You're all being so kind, but ... I-I don't know."

Nell squeezed her hand. *Please say yes!* "We'll look after you."

Miss Ellis wiped her eyes. "I know you will. You already have, but may I think about it? For an hour or so?"

A smile split Nell's face as she hummed the tune to *Amazing Grace*, her favourite hymn. The Lord had blessed her indeed.

"What are you looking so cheerful about?" Mrs Swift joined her. "You disappeared for ages this morning, and since you came back, you've not lost that huge grin."

"Give me a minute." Nell carried the last of the dirty dishes to the galley and led the way to the dining table. "Can you keep a secret?"

"Of course I can. What is it?"

"You know the trouble between Miss Ellis and Mr

Rodney? Well, the captain heard about it and he wanted to speak to her this morning."

A frown crossed Mrs Swift's brow. "Why's the captain so bothered about her?"

"He knows her father. Anyway, he invited me to sit in on the meeting with her." Nell pursed her lips to suppress her grin.

"Come along. Don't stop there."

"The captain and Mr Hewitt have worked out a plan to get her to her publisher's without Mr Rodney."

"Mr Hewitt?"

"He's rather well connected. Or at least his father is."

Nell leaned back as Mr Ross delivered their luncheon. "Here you are, ladies. Lamb's liver today."

"Lovely. It looks a lot nicer than what we buy at home."

He laughed. "I should hope so. I'll bring dessert shortly; I've something to tell you."

"That sounds exciting." Mrs Swift grinned at Nell as he disappeared into the galley. "You'd better get a move on with your news before he gets back."

"Well, the captain has said Miss Ellis can stay on the ship while we're in port."

"It doesn't surprise me. I imagine we'll be in and out pretty quickly given the delay and Mr Rodney will be able to visit the publisher for her."

"No! That's the thing." Nell's face broke into a grin again. "According to the captain, we'll be in port for several days while they mend the engines. There'll be enough time for Miss Ellis's visit to the publisher's to be rearranged and for her to be back on board ready to sail home with us."

"Is that why you're so pleased, because she isn't getting off?"

Nell shook her head. "It's because she is getting off. The captain asked me to go with her as a chaperone! I'm going to New York!"

Her joy faded as Mrs Swift concentrated on her liver. "That's nice. You'll have to tell me all about it."

Nell sank back in her chair. "I'm sorry, I'm being selfish. I've been on the ship for six weeks and suddenly I'm allowed off. It should be your turn first."

"It's not your fault. You're the one who's been with Miss Ellis, so it makes sense. My time will come. Eventually."

Nell paused and stared towards the galley. "I'll ask the captain if you can come with us. While Miss Ellis is with her publisher, I'll be outside on my own. I'll need my own chaperone."

"He'll arrange for one of the stewards to do it. Two women together isn't much better than one."

"But that's not fair..." She gritted her teeth. "Oh, Mr Ross is coming."

"Here you are." He put down two bowls of rice pudding and took the seat beside Nell. "You're very slow today."

"We're too busy talking." Mrs Swift scraped up the last of her mashed potato.

"Well, have I got some news. Mr Price says we're going to be stuck in New York for longer than planned while they mend the engines."

"It's nice of him to tell us." Mrs Swift reached for her bowl.

"He only mentioned it an hour ago, but..." Mr Ross

checked over his shoulder. "Word has it that we'll all be allowed off the ship."

Mrs Swift's face brightened. "Really?"

He nodded. "It's not definite, but that's what Mr Price thinks. Not all at once, mind."

"Will that mean us?"

Mr Ross shrugged. "I don't see why not. Anyway, you might want to freshen up your outside clothes. We won't want to be walking around New York in our uniforms."

Nell gasped. "I hadn't thought of that. I'll get the iron out later. We'll be there the day after tomorrow."

CHAPTER FORTY-FOUR

Nell and Mrs Swift stood in the foyer as the passengers bid farewell to the captain and filed past them onto the gangplank. As the last of them left, Mr Hewitt approached the captain.

"Have you had a response to the telegraph yet?"

The captain nodded. "Shortly before I came up here. You're to be at Putnam's offices on Fifth Avenue at ten o'clock tomorrow morning."

"Splendid. Did they say anything about Rodney?"

"Only that they wouldn't see him without her."

Mr Hewitt rubbed his hands together. "Excellent. I'll fill them in more when we meet, but in the meantime, I trust you'll make the arrangements for Miss Ellis and Mrs Riley."

"Leave it to me." The captain offered Mr Hewitt his hand. "I'll have someone arrange the carriages as soon as all the passengers are off the ship."

Mr Hewitt winked at Nell. "I'll see you tomorrow, then."

"You will." Her grin grew as she watched him leave, but it immediately faltered as Mr Rodney appeared.

"Captain." He didn't extend his hand. "You've not heard the last of this. I'll be filing a complaint once I get ashore."

"I'm sorry, sir, but I had to put Miss Ellis's best interests first."

"Her interests are best served by me, as her father can attest to. He'll be hearing of this."

"I'm sorry it's come to that, Mr Rodney, but I've sent Mr Ellis a telegraph informing him of events. I expect he'll want to talk to you when you return to Liverpool."

"A telegraph? You had no right..."

"Actually, I had every right." The captain's chest bulged as he held back his shoulders. "Mr Ellis and I have known each other for several years, and so following your falling-out with Miss Ellis, I took it upon myself to become her guardian. As a result, it was my duty to let him know what had happened ... and to cancel your appointment with Putnam's."

Mr Rodney's cheeks reddened as he thrust his hat on his head. "That's it. I'll be changing my booking for the return journey and shan't be travelling with the Guion company again, and Mr Guion will hear the reason why. Good day to you."

Thank goodness for that. Nell took a step back as he glared at her, but refused to lower her eyes. *I've done nothing wrong.*

As the last of the passengers disappeared, the captain extended his arms to them and the stewards, who stood on the other side of the foyer.

"Thank you, ladies and gentlemen. It's time to get this ship ready for her next voyage. If you could all return to your duties, Mr Price will join us for dinner tonight to discuss the arrangements for your shore visits."

Nell gazed out over the railings. "I can't believe we're actually getting off the ship. It looks like I'm going tomorrow, I hope you can come with me."

"So do I." Mrs Swift sighed. "I'd rather not spend the day with a group of stewards."

"Well, let's get a move on, then. We've work to do."

Mrs Robertson and Matron were seated at the ladies' table in the dining room when Nell and Mrs Swift joined them for dinner.

"Good evening." Mrs Robertson was still pale and her smile weak. "Have you only just finished?"

Nell took the seat opposite. "I needed to take a tray to Miss Ellis. Captain Robertson invited her to join us, but she said she preferred to stay in her room. It's probably explained by Dr Clarke returning her typewriter."

"I presume she's feeling better, then."

"Thankfully. She's much better today, knowing that Mr Rodney's no longer on the ship."

"I'm sure she is." Mrs Robertson shuddered. "It sounds like she's had a terrible time."

Nell looked up as Mr Brennan arrived at the table. "Cocktails, ladies?"

"Manhattans, I think." Mrs Swift waited for everyone to nod. "Four, please." She nudged Nell as Mr Price and several stewards huddled around a table in the men's section. "What's going on there? Would you say they're arranging the shore visits? Captain Robertson said we'd find out about them tonight."

Mrs Swift nodded. "They keep looking over here."

"Of course they do." Matron tutted. "They won't let you go ashore on your own."

"Will you get off, Matron?"

"Dr Clarke and I are going to take a carriage ride." She rolled her shoulders. "I'm quite looking forward to it."

"And I presume you and Captain Robertson have plans." Nell paused as Mr Brennan put down four drinks.

"We have friends here and so we're hoping to pay them a visit." Mrs Robertson reached for her glass. "I'd like to make a toast. To safe excursions abroad."

The others raised their glasses as Mr Price joined them.

"Good evening, ladies. Are you looking forward to seeing New York?"

"Oh, yes." Nell cast her mind back to their small house in Newton Street. "I've wanted to visit since I was a young girl. It feels like a dream come true."

"You've not long to wait now." He placed a sheet of paper on the table. "Mrs Riley, as you know, you'll be travelling into New York with Miss Ellis tomorrow."

Nell nodded.

"Assuming you won't be going into the publisher's, I've arranged to come with you along with Mrs Swift..."

"That's splendid." Nell bounced on her chair.

"...and Mr Marsh."

"Oh." Her grin froze.

"Is there a problem?" Mr Price studied her.

"No. Not at all. I'm thrilled Mrs Swift will be with us. But ... erm ... will five of us fit in one carriage?"

"Oh, yes. That's not a problem in America."

"Well ... good. I'll look forward to it." *As long as you keep Mr Marsh away from me.*

Nell was out of bed before the bell rang the following morning, and after washing in cold water, she picked up her emerald green dress and stepped into it. *Thank goodness I didn't bring my old grey one.*

She stood on her tiptoes to see her reflection in the small bathroom mirror. The colour still suited her dark hair, even though there were flecks of grey running through it. *I can't go out looking like that.* She removed all her hairgrips and ran a hairbrush through it, untangling the knots, before she tied it back and fastened it into a bun at the nape of her neck. *That will have to do.*

Mrs Swift and Matron were already taking breakfast when she arrived in their sitting room.

"I was beginning to think you'd fallen asleep in there." Mrs Swift poured her a cup of tea.

"Gracious, no. I'm much too excited. I brushed my hair out and it's so long, it takes an age." She helped herself to some bread. "I barely slept last night, either."

"That won't do you any good." Matron glanced at the clock on the wall. "At least you've time for breakfast. I'd eat as much as you can, because you probably won't eat again until you're back on the ship."

Nell beamed at Mrs Swift. "I'm sure we'll be too busy to worry about that."

"All the more reason to eat now." Matron stood up. "I'm going to get myself changed. Dr Clarke and I won't be leaving until ten o'clock, so I've plenty of time."

"If we don't see you before we go, have a nice day."

Mrs Swift reached for a boiled egg. "Will you collect Miss Ellis from her stateroom?"

"No, she's meeting us in the foyer. Since Mr Rodney left, she's found her confidence again. I'm so pleased for her."

"It's only because she got such preferential treatment."

"That's not her fault, although it's as well she did. Can you imagine what would have happened if Captain Robertson hadn't known her father? It doesn't bear thinking about."

Mrs Swift's scowl remained. "It would be nice to think he'd do the same for anyone else."

"I suspect he would, if he knew about it. He's a decent sort if you ask me."

"Maybe." Mrs Swift emptied her teacup. "Come on, let's finish up here and we can go to the foyer."

CHAPTER FORTY-FIVE

The sun threatened to break through the clouds as Nell followed Mrs Swift across the deck towards the first-class accommodation.

"It looks as if God's smiling on us. I don't think it will rain."

"It's still chilly." Mrs Swift held her cloak close. "At least we'll be in a carriage. That's exciting in itself."

Nell grinned. "And we get to visit New York without wearing out our shoe leather."

They bustled through the door to the foyer, where Mr Marsh was waiting. He ran his eyes over Nell. "You look nice, Mrs Riley. And you too, Mrs Swift."

Nell's cheeks coloured as she studied him and Mr Price. "We could say the same about you. It's strange how we only see each other in uniform."

"Unfortunate, too." A wistful expression crossed Mr Marsh's face.

"Has the carriage arrived?" Mrs Swift peered through a porthole.

"It should be here any minute, but we need to wait for Miss Ellis. The reason for our special treatment." Mr Price peered down the corridor. "She's coming now."

Miss Ellis appeared, wearing a dress of similar colour to Nell's that highlighted the green of her eyes. Her blond hair was arranged on top of her head and was complemented by a matching hat.

Nell forced a smile. *I feel positively dowdy now. Why did she have to choose that shade of dress, out of all the ones she has with her?*

"Are we ready?" She surveyed the group. "You all look very different. It hadn't occurred to me you'd wear your own clothes."

Nell flicked out her skirt. "I brought this on the off-chance I may need it. I've not worn it since Christmas."

"We can pretend we're sisters, wearing the same colour." She linked Nell's arm. "Shall we go?"

Mr Marsh stood by the carriage door and held out his hand to help the ladies climb the steps before speaking to the coachman.

"The Putman offices on Fifth Avenue, please."

"How many avenues are there?" Nell asked, as she took her place between Mrs Swift and Miss Ellis.

Mr Price settled himself opposite Miss Ellis. "I've no idea. This is the second time I've been to New York, but I must admit I didn't take much notice. They've a grid system and count up the number of streets and avenues. It's very clever."

"So much easier, too, I imagine." Nell followed the gaze of Miss Ellis as she looked through the window at the lines of steerage passengers. "Why are they queuing?" Miss Ellis looked over to Mr Price.

"They need to present their papers and have a medical examination before they're allowed into the country. Thankfully for those in first class, the captain and ship's doctor can sign the relevant documents and you get waved through."

"And a jolly good thing, too." Miss Ellis shuddered. "Remind me never to give up my money."

They left the port and travelled a distance along the edge of the river.

"I didn't realise there'd be so much water." Mrs Swift stared out of the window.

"We're on an island, not that you'd know when you're in the middle of it." Mr Price gazed out of his side of the carriage. "Some of the immigrant houses are on this side and there are a lot more than last time I was here."

Miss Ellis pressed her nose to the glass. "They're tiny ... and so crammed in."

"The newcomers don't have much money when they arrive, and so they have to make do with what they can get. You'll notice the difference with the American houses when we get closer to Fifth Avenue. Only the rich live there."

Mrs Swift's brow creased. "How do you know all this?"

"I talk to passengers and remember what they tell me. The Putnam offices are in one of the most expensive parts of the city, I believe."

Miss Ellis nodded. "I've only been once before, and it is splendid. I don't know where they get their money from, though. Judging by the amount they give me, it can't come from selling books."

"Perhaps it comes from better-known authors." Mr Marsh tried to sound diplomatic, but his cheeks coloured as Miss Ellis sighed.

"You're probably right. I don't have a nom de plume anyone would recognise. Not that I'm aware of, anyway."

They continued along the side of the river until finally they turned right and a large park appeared on their left.

Mr Price pointed to the window opposite. "There's Central Park. Once we've dropped Miss Ellis off, I'm hoping we can take a walk around."

Nell leaned across Mrs Swift to get a closer view. "One thing I miss about being at sea is the parks we have at home. Not that I spend much time there in the winter."

"Do you enjoy walking, Mrs Riley?" Mr Marsh studied her as she sat back in her seat.

"I do when the weather's nice."

"I must admit, I do myself. We've been fortunate with the weather today." Mr Marsh's leg rubbed against Nell's, and she moved it immediately.

"How long will you be with your publisher?"

Miss Ellis sighed. "Most of the morning, I should imagine. It took that long with Mr Rodney, but he always liked to make a fuss. I'm hoping Mr Hewitt will be more amenable."

"I expect he will be." Mr Price swivelled in his seat as they rounded the corner of the park. "He should be along here somewhere. Can you see him, Mr Marsh?"

"Not yet."

The sound of the horses' hooves filled the carriage as they travelled between the park on their left and the magnificent buildings on the other side.

Nell leaned across Miss Ellis. "Are these houses or hotels? They're incredible."

Mr Price peered through the opposite window. "These are houses, or apartments. I can't recall where the main hotel is, but if we drive past it later, you'll be able to tell the difference."

"My nephew James told me about the big houses, and how they made those in Liverpool seem small, but I could never have imagined this." She stared up at the Roman columns and turreted roofs adorning the oversized buildings. "He didn't tell me about these lovely wide roads, either." She peered through the window as the horses slowed to a walk before coming to a halt.

"Are we here?" A smile broadened on her lips as Mr Hewitt waved to them and waited for the coachman to open the door.

"Good morning." He stood by the steps while the coachman helped Miss Ellis down. "You look happier than the last time we met."

"I am, thanks to you." She stepped to one side as Nell followed her.

"Mrs Riley, look at you." Mr Hewitt studied her. "Very nice."

"Be off with you." Nell's cheeks burned, and she moved towards Miss Ellis, gazing at the sight in front of her. "Is that all one park?" She turned her head in both directions. "Princes Park really is small by comparison."

"It is, indeed. I'm glad I'll be with my publisher. I wouldn't have the stamina to walk around it."

"I'm not sure I do either." Mrs Swift joined them. "A nice bench will do me."

Miss Ellis laughed. "Perhaps we should both start with Princes Park when we get home."

"Nonsense, you'll be fine. Both of you. I can't wait to see what's beyond the boundaries." Nell's heart fluttered as she studied the trees, but was distracted when Mr Hewitt offered Miss Ellis his arm.

"Shall we go, miss? We need to be there in ten minutes." He took out his pocket watch and walked over to Mr Price. "Might I suggest we meet here again in three hours."

Miss Ellis put a hand to her chest. "As long as that?"

"We may not need all that time, but we can take our own walk if we're out early."

Mr Price checked the time. "So, by my reckoning, we'll reconvene at ten to one. That will allow us to ride around the rest of the city before we head back to the ship."

"Splendid! We'll see you all later."

Nell stood with Mrs Swift as Mr Hewitt led Miss Ellis across the road.

"I hope it goes well for her."

"I'm sure it will now she has Mr Hewitt with her. He'll have her best interests at heart." Mrs Swift studied them. "Do you think they could have a future together?"

"Mr Hewitt ... and ..." Nell spluttered. "No, not at all. He's just being a gentleman."

"You know he's not for the likes of us."

Nell took a breath. "I'm well aware of that."

Mrs Swift raised an eyebrow. "Do you? You seem rather fond of him."

Nell's cheeks coloured. "There's nothing wrong with liking him, but I know my place. Come along, the gentlemen are waiting for us."

Mr Price and Mr Marsh were discussing the surroundings when they arrived.

"Are we ready?" Mr Price checked the time once more. "I presume we're all happy to walk through the park? There's a magnificent lake in the centre by all accounts."

"It sounds lovely." Nell linked Mrs Swift's arm, while the gentlemen walked to either side of them.

"This way, I reckon." Mr Price indicated to a walkway.

"Have you seen that?" Nell pointed to the stone building with the appearance of a Roman temple. "It's like the libraries in Liverpool, only bigger. In fact, everything's bigger."

"Don't they say that about everything American?" Mr Marsh held his hands behind his back as they walked along a tree-lined path that opened out into a large grassed area. "Take that, for example."

Nell took a deep breath as the sun appeared from behind a cloud. "This puts Sefton Park to shame, never mind Princes Park. It's days like this that make you glad to be alive."

An image of Maria and the girls sitting around the dining table with rain beating on the window flashed into her mind, but with a shake of her head, she dismissed it and turned in a full circle, smiling up at the trees and the smattering of blue in the sky. *I'm not going to feel guilty today.*

"Shall we turn to the left?" Mr Price ushered them to a wide footpath. "I think the lake is this way."

Mrs Swift tutted. "As if we haven't seen enough water."

"I don't care where we walk; I want to see everything." Nell inched closer to Mrs Swift as Mr Marsh walked beside her. "I remember Lady Annabel, a passenger on last month's voyage, mentioning Central Park to me. It sounded wonderful, but it never occurred to me I'd be able to visit myself. Not so soon, anyway."

"It was worth losing the engines to be here with such good company." Mr Marsh smiled down at her before turning his gaze to the expanse of lawn. "I've not seen so much greenery since I was last at home."

"I presume you're not from Liverpool, then."

"No. My family live in Carlisle, up near the Scottish border. I caught the train to Liverpool in 1872 and haven't been home for more than a couple of days at a time. My last visit was for Mother's funeral."

"I'm sorry." Nell studied the trees to her left. "Do you have any other family up there?"

"Three brothers and two sisters, but we're not close. It's probably as well. As soon as I arrived in Liverpool, I got a job as a steward, and haven't had more than four or five days off at once ever since."

"That must be awful." Nell's face dropped. "What do you do when you have shore leave?"

He shrugged. "Sometimes I stay on the ship, but if I'm not able to, I rent a bed in a boarding house."

Like Jack did on Windsor Street. Nell sighed. "I suppose there are a lot who do that."

"I don't mind, and you get used to it. I'll tell you what would be nice, though." He searched her face. "I'd be delighted if you'd accompany me around one of the Liverpool parks when we can. To see how it compares to this."

Nell's heart skipped a beat. "Well, I-I don't know." She

focussed on the footpath ahead. "I like to spend time with my daughters when I'm home."

"You have children?" His eyes bored into her.

"Yes. Elenor and Leah. My niece looks after them while I'm away. She's very good with them."

"I see." He pushed his hands into his pockets, but Nell pursed her lips as the silence grew.

"I don't like leaving them, but, well ... we need the money."

"It's none of my business."

"No." Nell glanced to Mrs Swift, who was in conversation with Mr Price. *Would it be rude to interrupt?*

"How long have you been a stewardess?" Mr Marsh's voice was flat.

"Only since the beginning of the year. This is my second voyage."

"You've been fortunate to visit New York so soon."

"Yes. So I believe..."

"What's going on here? You're both looking far too serious."

Nell's shoulders relaxed as Mrs Swift linked her arm.

"We're only talking. Oh! What's that over there?" She pointed to a series of bushes. "Is that the lake glistening through the gaps?"

"I'd say so." Mr Price quickened his pace. "Shall we go and investigate?"

CHAPTER FORTY-SIX

I t took over two hours for them to walk around the lake, and as they returned to the start, Nell flopped onto a bench overlooking the water, indicating for Mrs Swift to join her.

"That took longer than I expected."

"Me too. The lake alone is bigger than the parks at home."

"My feet are throbbing." Mrs Swift stretched out her legs to reveal her ankle boots. "I'll need to give my feet a soak when we get back to the ship."

Nell chuckled. "Thank goodness we don't have passengers tomorrow."

Mr Price had remained standing, and he pulled out his pocket watch. "We can't stay here for long. We need to be at the entrance in quarter of an hour."

"I could always walk on ahead to tell them you're coming." Mr Marsh gazed at Nell. "If you need more of a rest, that is."

"We can manage another fifteen minutes." She stood up. "Thank you, anyway."

"We don't have to; we have visitors." Mr Price pointed to the footpath behind them and waved as Mr Hewitt and Miss Ellis came into view.

"What a stroke of luck." Mr Hewitt grinned at Nell. "You look worn out."

Her cheeks reddened. "We've walked around the lake. It's further than it looks."

Miss Ellis shuddered. "I'm glad I wasn't with you, but I'm delighted Mrs Riley talked me into taking Mr Hewitt to the publisher."

"Did you have a good meeting?"

Miss Ellis gazed at Mr Hewitt as he spoke.

"I'll say. The publisher offered her a deal, but assumed I'd take a fifty pounds per hundred cut, because that's what that scoundrel Rodney always took."

"Fifty?" Nell's brow furrowed. "Half of everything Miss Ellis earns!"

"Exactly. Mr Hewitt, on the other hand, agreed to represent me for nothing." Miss Ellis clung to his arm. "Isn't that wonderful?"

He pulled away and gave a modest bow. "I was glad to be of service. It was also a pleasure to help out my friend Mrs Riley."

"Me!"

"Yes." He grinned at her. "You were the one most concerned about Miss Ellis. And with good reason. If it hadn't been for you, we may not have realised what was going on."

Nell lowered her eyes. "I didn't do anything special, but

I'm glad it worked out for the best ... and that Miss Ellis is travelling home with us."

"Oh, so am I." Miss Ellis beamed. "I'm not worried about seeing Father when we get home, either, because we've proof of what Mr Rodney was up to. It will be so nice to leave my stateroom whenever I choose, too, even if I do end up sitting by myself."

Nell's face brightened. "You needn't be on your own. I met a lovely couple on my first outward journey, Mr and Mrs Scott. They're due to rejoin us when we leave, so I'll introduce you."

"They won't want me with them for the whole journey."

"That's where you're wrong. Mrs Scott will be delighted to have a companion."

The smile returned to Miss Ellis's face, but Mr Price held up a hand. "Could we start walking while we talk? If you'd like a tour of Manhattan, we'd better hurry up."

Mr Hewitt checked his pocket watch. "I need to be going, too. I told the chaps I'd join them for a late luncheon. I'll walk with you to the carriage before I go."

Nell beamed as they set off. "Where are you staying?"

"At the Fifth Avenue hotel. I must admit, it's rather splendid."

"If it's anything like the buildings around here, it must be." Nell gazed through the trees to the houses on her right. "Everything's incredible."

"Isn't it?" Mr Price breathed in the air. "How long are you here for, Mr Hewitt? Will we have the pleasure of your company on the return journey?"

His forehead creased. "Now, that's a question. We've

not decided yet. Maybe three, possibly four weeks."

"If you stayed for four, then you'd be on our next voyage home." Nell's heart fluttered as his face lit up.

"That's settled it then. Four weeks it is. I doubt the chaps will complain."

"I wouldn't if it were me." Nell sighed. "Maybe one day I'll come for longer. Do you live in Liverpool, Mr Hewitt?"

"No, London, but it was easier to catch a ship from Liverpool. I'll probably stay in Liverpool for a few days when we arrive back. I need to spend more time there over the next few months, so I want to test out the best of your hotels."

"If you don't mind me making a recommendation, I'd suggest you try the Adelphi. It's the fanciest hotel I know, although compared to New York, it may not be grand enough for you."

Mr Hewitt laughed. "If you say it's fancy, then I'm sure it will be perfectly fine. Perhaps you could show us around."

Nell giggled. "I'd love to, but I'd better bring a friend if I'm to walk around with four men. What would people say?"

Mr Marsh glared at her. "I doubt you'd notice. If you'll excuse me, I'll go and find the carriage."

The smile fell from Nell's lips as Mr Marsh strode to the exit. "What's up with him?"

"He's been rather sullen since we reached the lake." Mrs Swift studied her. "What were you talking about earlier? You both looked terribly serious."

"Me? Nothing. He just..."

"He just what?" Mr Hewitt raised an eyebrow.

Nell shrugged. "He was surprised when I told him I had

two daughters. I get the impression he doesn't approve of me being here."

Mr Hewitt puffed out his cheeks. "That's one explanation."

"What do you mean?"

Mr Hewitt glanced at her. "I may be wrong, but ever since we met, when he caught us shaking hands that first afternoon, he's been determined to stop me talking to you."

Nell sighed. "It's not only you, it's whenever he sees me with a man. I don't know why it bothers him so much; he never says anything to Mrs Swift."

"Have you noticed that, Mrs Swift?" Mr Hewitt leaned forward to talk to her.

"I suppose so. He does seem to pick on Mrs Riley more than me."

"Then I reckon my second explanation is more likely to be correct."

"Are you thinking what I'm thinking?" Miss Ellis's eyes sparkled as she caught hold of Mr Hewitt's arm. "That Mr Marsh has fallen in love with her?"

Nell nearly stumbled as she turned to glare at her. "Love!"

Mr Hewitt laughed. "That sounds like a line from one of your novels. I wasn't going to say quite the same thing, but that's the general gist. I reckon he's got a soft spot for you and he's jealous whenever he sees you with another man."

Mrs Swift nodded. "That would explain a lot. You started off on the wrong foot with him because he saw you with your nephews. And then, Mr Hewitt... Well, you know."

Nell's stomach fluttered. "When we were talking, earlier, he asked if I'd walk out with him when we're in Liverpool. To the park..."

"I knew it!" Miss Ellis laughed. "I'll have to keep an eye out for you when I'm at home sitting by the window."

"I'm not going with him!" Nell gasped. "I told him I needed to spend time with the children."

"Ah. That explains it then." Mr Hewitt gave her a knowing look. "You didn't say that to me when I suggested you show us around Liverpool."

"Oh goodness." She put a hand to her mouth. "What do I do? It's going to make things terrible on the ship."

"Don't you like him?" Miss Ellis was a picture of innocence.

"Not the way he treats me. He's always talking down to me."

"He may be trying to look after you." Mr Price guided them towards the exit. "The last few voyages haven't been without incident."

Nell's heart pounded, and she stopped to sit on a nearby bench. "I can't go back. Not if he's on the ship."

"But you must." Mrs Swift turned to Mr Price. "Can't you do something? She can't stay in New York."

"But I can't face him. I feel so terrible..."

She buried her head in her hands. "Why can't he leave me alone?"

"Give me two minutes." Mr Price's voice barely pricked Nell's conscience, but she glanced up as Miss Ellis sat beside her.

"If this was a storyline in my book, I'd have Mr Marsh and Mr Hewitt duelling over you."

Mr Hewitt threw his head back with a laugh. "You probably would, too, but poor Mr Marsh wouldn't stand a chance. I doubt he's even held a sword."

"It would be so romantic, though. The wealthy…"

"No." Nell stood up. "I'm afraid this isn't a story. Oh goodness. Why did I think taking a job was a good idea…?" She paused as Mr Price rejoined them.

"Mr Marsh will take a separate carriage to the ship. He's sorry for any upset he may have caused."

"Thank goodness for that." Mrs Swift stared at Nell. "At least we can get you back to the ship."

"And then what?" Nell's eyes widened.

"Then you can go home." Mrs Swift's voice pleaded with her. "You have to see sense. You wouldn't last two days in New York on your own."

Miss Ellis pulled her from the bench. "You might grow to love him on the way home and take that walk…"

Nell shook her head, but couldn't keep the smirk from her face. "I'll be taking that typewriter off you again if you carry on like that."

"Ladies, please, if we could stop all this chatter." Mr Price urged them forward. "We have an hour to drive around Manhattan Island. I suggest we don't waste it."

"In that case, I'll say my farewells here." Mr Hewitt surveyed the group. "I won't forget this journey in a hurry. You've all made it special in your own ways."

"Goodbye, Mr Hewitt." Miss Ellis beamed at him. "When you reach Liverpool, please call at the house. My father will be delighted to meet you."

"I most certainly will. He needs to hear about that

434

scoundrel Rodney. I hope you don't come across him again when you get home."

Miss Ellis shuddered. "I hadn't thought about that, but I'm sure Father will send him packing once I tell him how much money he's stolen from us."

"I imagine he will." He turned to Nell. "Goodbye, Mrs Riley."

Nell flushed as he offered her his hand. "Thank you for everything. At least we can say farewell without Mr Marsh scowling at us."

"I hope you'll be able to do your job without him distracting you, too."

Nell grimaced. "That would make a change, but I'm not hopeful."

"Don't let him put you off. I'll be disappointed if you're not on the ship in four weeks. There might be a tip for you, if you are."

Nell grinned. "Are you trying to bribe me?"

"Perish the thought."

He shook hands with Mr Price and, with a final wave, he set off along the footpath through the park.

"Such a nice man." Miss Ellis watched him until he disappeared. "You've both given me so many ideas for my new book, too."

Nell shot her a glance. "Well, don't put my name in it! And don't have me marrying Mr Marsh either. I don't want anything to do with him."

Mr Price walked behind them and once again tried to usher them to the exit. "Please, Mrs Riley. I'll speak to Mr Marsh later, but if we could make our way to the carriage. Let's see the rest of New York first."

The Captain's Order

Working on a ship is tough ... but it's about to become a whole lot worse...

October 1882

How can a smile be so misunderstood?

For Nell, it's a sign of friendship.

To her male colleagues, it's so much more...

With two men intent on securing her affections, and little chance of escape, life for Nell is challenging. Until she finds an unexpected guardian.

Her saviour is charming and chivalrous, but when he unwittingly causes more problems than he solves, she finally snaps.

Determined to be left alone, she sees an opportunity to be rid of her most troublesome admirer. But not everything goes to plan.

When an emergency threatens both passengers and crew, the captain announces a new way of working, and Nell has no choice but to obey his orders...

To get your copy visit my website at:
https://valmcbeath.com/windsor-street/

If you're enjoying the series, why not sign up to my newsletter?
Visit: https://www.subscribepage.com/fsorganic

You'll receive details of new releases, special offers and information relating to *The Windsor Street Family Saga,* and my other series, The *Ambition & Destiny* Series. Occasionally, you'll also receive details of other offers relating to historical fiction.

AUTHOR'S NOTE AND ACKNOWLEDGEMENTS

The Stewardess's Journey is the third book in *The Windsor Street Family Saga*.

As I've mentioned before, the series was inspired by research into my family history, and this is the book I initially set out to write.

Who knew that in the early 1880s, women could work on transatlantic liners? I certainly didn't, which is why I knew I had to write about it.

At first, I didn't know how I was going to approach it, but as I looked into archive records, historical reports of life on board transatlantic ships, and studied the crew lists of Nell's ship, I got the sense that being one of only three women in an eighty strong crew would probably be one of the most challenging aspects of life at sea.

In the late Victorian years, men essentially saw women as wives, mothers and housekeepers. Those of the lower social classes would also be expected to work in menial jobs, such as domestic service, or as labour in the workshops that dominated towns across the UK.

To have this new breed of women doing more professional work in a world that had been the preserve of men for centuries must have been challenging for them all.

The role of the stewardess was varied, and included things such as:

- Dealing with women and young children
- Enforcing the segregation of passengers
- Linen mending
- Bedmaking
- Producing clean sheets and tablecloths
- Serving meals, especially breakfast to cabins
- Helping women get ready for dinner
- Caring for the seasick
- Attending to ladies' bathrooms and lavatories

They also had to work alongside the male stewards, who did heavier jobs, such as making up the upper bunks.

Stewardesses generally had a few hours off in the afternoon but had to be on call in case they were needed.

If a female passenger had a complaint, they would report it to the stewardess or matron. They would pass it to a male steward, who in turn would pass it to an officer or the captain.

The idea that sexism and inequality were probably rife among the crew gave me a backbone to the story.

In terms of passengers, I found a website that gave me some fabulous insights into life on board for first-class guests.

One of the main topics of conversation on arrival on the ship was the passenger list. Often titles and levels of importance were not included, and so passengers had to resort to their own devices to 'announce' their importance.

Including the names of maids or valets on the guest list became a popular way of doing this and indicated a certain status.

Travelling with a maid or valet could have its drawbacks, though. They were prone to talk about their employers, which meant it could be very lucrative for a stewardess to be on good terms with a maid to find out snippets and impart them before the maid herself had a chance.

Secrets of the daily lives of the snobby aristocrats were always welcome, and bored passengers would also make up stories about other interesting looking passengers. Scandal was always enjoyed as it added excitement to the crossing.

Honeymooners, for example, could have exotic tales made up about them, such as who they were and where they were from. Musings as to what the husband saw in his new wife ... and much more besides.

Lady authors were revered for what they did and became very popular by promising to make passengers a character in their next book. Similarly, the playwright was popular and young girls were known to follow them around the ship.

There were a number of other notable groups of passengers, but I'll save their descriptions until the end of the next book!

If you'd like to join Nell on her subsequent voyages, you can preorder your copy of *The Captain's Order* at:

https://books2read.com/TCO

As ever, thanks must go to my husband Stuart and friend Rachel for providing feedback on my early drafts. I'd also like to thank my editor Susan Cunningham for her excellent work, as well as members of my Advanced Review Team for providing additional comments.

Finally, I'd like to thank you to you for reading.

Best wishes

Val

ABOUT THE AUTHOR

Val started researching her family tree back in 2008. At that time, she had no idea what she would find or where it would lead. By 2010, she had discovered a story so compelling she was inspired to turn it into a novel.

This first foray into writing turned into The *Ambition & Destiny* Series. A story of the trials, tragedies, and triumphs of some of her ancestors as they sought their fortune in Victorian-era England.

By the time the series was complete, Val had developed a taste for writing and turned her hand to writing Agatha Christie style mysteries. These novels form part of the *Eliza Thomson Investigates* series and currently consists of five standalone books and two novella's.

Although writing the mysteries was great fun, the pull of researching other branches of the family was strong and Val continued to look for other stories worth telling.

Back in 2018, she discovered a previously unknown fact about one of her great, great grandmothers, Nell. *The Windsor Street Family Saga* is a fictitious account of that discovery. Further details of all series can be found on Val's website at: www.vlmcbeath.com.

Prior to writing, Val trained as a scientist and has worked in the pharmaceutical industry for many years. In 2012, she set up her own consultancy business, and currently splits her time between business and writing.

Born and raised in Liverpool (UK), Val now lives in Cheshire with her husband, Stuart. She has two daughters, the younger of which, Sarah, now helps with the publishing side of the business.

In addition to family history, her interests include rock music and Liverpool Football Club.

ALSO BY VL MCBEATH

The *Windsor Street Family Saga*

The full series:

Part 1: *The Sailor's Promise*

(*an introductory novella*)

Part 2: *The Wife's Dilemma*

Part 3: *The Stewardess's Journey*

Part 4: *The Captain's Order*

Part 5: *The Companion's Secret*

Part 6: *The Mother's Confession*

Part 7: *The Daughter's Defiance*

The *Ambition & Destiny* Series

The full series:

Short Story Prequel: *Condemned by Fate*

Part 1: *Hooks & Eyes*

Part 2: *Less Than Equals*

Part 3: *When Time Runs Out*

Part 4: *Only One Winner*

Part 5: *Different World*

A standalone novel: *The Young Widow*

Eliza Thomson Investigates

A Deadly Tonic (A Novella)

Murder in Moreton

Death of an Honourable Gent

Dying for a Garden Party

A Scottish Fling

The Palace Murder

Death by the Sea

A Christmas Murder

To find out more about visit VL McBeath's website at:

https://www.valmcbeath.com/

FOLLOW ME

at:

Website:
https://valmcbeath.com

Facebook:
https://www.facebook.com/VLMcBeath

BookBub:
https://www.bookbub.com/authors/vl-mcbeath

S·T·C

Printed in Great Britain
by Amazon